PENGUIN BOOKS

THE BRIMSTONE WEDDING

Barbara Vine is Ruth Rendell. Viking have published her seven previous novels: *A Dark-Adapted Eye*, *A Fatal Inversion*, which won the Crime Writer's Association Gold Dagger Award, *The House of Stairs*, *Gallowglass*, *King Solomon's Carpet*, *Asta's Book* and *No Night is Too Long*.

The
BRIMSTONE
WEDDING

Barbara Vine

Penguin Books

PENGUIN BOOKS

Published by the Penguin Group

Penguin Books Canada Ltd, 10 Alcorn Avenue, Toronto, Ontario,
Canada M4V 3B2

Penguin Books Ltd, 27 Wrights Lane, London W8 5TZ, England

Penguin Putnam Inc., 375 Hudson Street, New York, New York
10014, U.S.A.

Penguin Books Australia Ltd, Ringwood, Victoria, Australia

Penguin Books (NZ) Ltd, cnr Rosedale and Airborne Roads, Albany,
Auckland 1310, New Zealand

Penguin Books Ltd, Registered Offices: Harmondsworth, Middlesex,
England

First published in Viking by Penguin Books Canada Limited, 1996
Published in Penguin Books, 1997

10 9 8 7 6 5 4 3 2

*Publisher's note: This book is a work of fiction. Names, characters, places
and incidents either are the product of the author's imagination or are
used fictitiously, and any resemblance to actual persons living or dead,
events, or locales is entirely coincidental.*

Manufactured in Canada

Canadian Cataloguing in Publication Data

Vine, Barbara, 1930–
    The brimstone wedding

ISBN 0-14-026597-X

I. Title.

PR6068.E63B8 1997   823'.914   C96-931792-1

Visit Penguin Canada's web site at **www.penguin.ca**

Many of the superstitions in this novel come from A Dictionary of Superstitions *by Iona Opie and Moira Tatem, for whose knowledge and expertise I am very grateful.*

Part One

1

The clothes of the dead won't wear long. They fret for the person who owned them. Stella laughed when I said that. She threw back her head and laughed in the surprisingly girlish way she had. I was telling her Edith Webster had died in the night and left cupboards full of clothes behind her, and she laughed and said she'd never known anyone as superstitious as me.

'Her granddaughter's here now,' I said, 'handing her things out to everyone who'll take them. You know what they say, as the body rots the clothes rot.'

'Is that what they say, Genevieve? Who are they?'

I didn't reply. She was teasing me and didn't expect an answer. But I like it when Stella calls me Genevieve, because though I'm Jenny to everyone else, always have been since I was born, I was christened Genevieve. My dad called me after a vintage car in a film, if you can credit it, and to most people it's a bit embarrassing, but the way Stella says it it's got a pretty sound. Of course Stella has got a nice voice, what you'd call a beautiful voice, even though she's old and past having a nice anything really.

I told her some more about Edith, how Sharon found her at seven o'clock when she went in with her tea and how the granddaughter was there within the hour, though she hadn't been so conscientious about coming when her nan was alive, I'm not a specially tactless person or insensitive and I'd have stopped if I thought it upset Stella hearing about another old lady dying. But I could tell she was interested. The truth, I suspect, is that Stella thinks of herself as quite young compared with Edith, who was ninety-four, she thinks she's got a long time left yet, and that she's one of those cancer patients who'll live for years.

She's been at Middleton Hall for six months. We all look after all the residents but we each have three in our special care, and Stella is mine along with Arthur Harrison and Edith. Now Edith's gone I suppose I shall get someone new but not someone who needs a lot of care, I hope. That's not because I'm not a hard worker, I'm on my feet most of my eight-hour shift—at £3.50 an hour, which is hardly brilliant—and Arthur's always ringing his bell for me, but the fact is I don't want to have to give less time to Stella. I like her, you see. I actually like her, and that's not something I can say about Arthur or Maud Vernon or any of the rest of them. I'm sorry for them, I want to help make their lives as pleasant as can be, but as for liking, they're past all that. It's as if they've gone into a twilight world where they've forgotten everything, don't really know where they are half the time and call you by the names of all their relations until you remind them you're Jenny. But Stella is different. Stella is still a person in the land of the living. The other day she said to me, 'I don't think of you as a nurse, Genevieve. I think of you as my friend.'

I was pleased. I suppose that was because she's what

my nan would call a lady, in a different class from me any-way, but all I said was she was right not to think of me as a nurse, I'm a care assistant, I've the experience but no qualifications. She smiled. She's got a nice smile, her teeth are all her own and quite white still.

'I came here because of you, you know.'

She always says that. It's silly of course, it isn't true, but it amuses her to say it. Her son took her round a good many residential homes in Suffolk and Norfolk for her to choose the one she liked best. I was in the lounge with Edith when they came in, and Stella's regular joke is to say she took a fancy to me and decided on Middleton Hall because I worked there. It wasn't the house or the grounds or the food or the private bathroom that decided her, but me.

'And I was right,' she said. 'It's made all the difference to me to have you here.'

She likes me to talk about the village and my family, and God knows there are enough of them, and I told her about my mum and Len the lover and his mother who inherited a fur coat from her sister which fell into rags the first time she had it on. I was telling her about holes appearing in a dead woman's clothes as if the moth had been at them when, to my surprise, she reached out and took my hand. First she squeezed my hand and then she held it quite lightly. She must have held it for about five minutes before giving it another squeeze and releasing it. Then Lena put her head round the door and made faces at me the way she does, so I got up—I didn't leap up, I wouldn't give her the satisfaction—and when I looked at Stella I saw her wink at me.

She winked at me and she smiled and for a moment

you could see what she'd looked like when she was my age. I hope she'll show me some photos of herself when she was young, I'm quite curious to see them. I said she hadn't got anything nice left any more, but that was a bit sweeping, that wasn't exactly true. Actually, she's wonderful for seventy. Her skin isn't all that wrinkled except round the eyes and her eyes are still a strong bright blue. Of course her hair is white but it's thick and wavy and she'll never wear a wig like some of them do. Sadly, she won't live long enough to have to. She always dresses nicely, in a dress and stockings and proper shoes, and I don't know why it should but that irritates Lena. Behind her back, and not always behind her back, she'll refer to her as 'Lady' Newland, or 'the duchess', and grin to take the sting out of it. I suppose she'd rather Stella got herself into a track suit and cardigan like most of them do. I can't explain why, but I think people ought to take more care of themselves when they get older, do the best they can. Stella likes me to manicure her nails and set her hair and I'm happy to do it.

So you can see she's rather special. If I'm her friend, she's mine, though so far I don't know much about her, while she knows plenty about me: how long I've been married, for instance, that I've lived at Stoke Tharby all my life, that my husband's called Mike and he's a builder, my mum keeps the pub and my dad lives in Diss, and a whole lot of other things. And if there's one thing she doesn't know, the biggest thing in my life really though it shouldn't be, I may even tell her that some day. But all I know about Stella is that she had to sell the house she had in Bury St Edmunds to afford the fees here, and of course I know about her children because they come and visit.

Well, children—one's my age and the daughter has teenage kids of her own.

Bury is about twenty miles south of here, beyond the Breckland and the country we call the plough. She sold up when she got too tired and too ill to be on her own any more and having someone to look after her had its attractions. It's what I've read somewhere is called a social phenomenon, the number of residential homes there are these days, and the hundreds of old people who fill them. And nearly all of them have had to sell their houses to find the fees, thus robbing their descendants—if you like to look at it that way—of what they might have inherited.

It goes into the pockets of people like Lena. Still, Middleton Hall is one of the best of them, a manor house once, with beautiful grounds, gardens with flower beds shaped like hearts and diamonds cut out of the lawn, cypress hedges and yew hedges, a lily pond and great stands of old chestnut trees. I will say for Lena, she loves animals and we've got two labradors here and three cats that are supposed to be so good around geriatrics. Mind you, for what they pay a week they ought to have all mod cons *and* pets *and* gourmet food, to say the least. It was quite a surprise to me to see Sharon serving drinks to the residents before dinner the first day I came, dry martinis no less, that you read about in American books, with Japanese rice crackers and macadamia nuts in little dishes. But why not? I hate to see old folks treated like kids.

Stella has one of the nicer rooms here, and with a view all the way across the meadows to the river and the woods beyond. Her room has french windows and she can step out directly on to the terrace and the lawns if she likes, though she seldom does. Of course she goes into the lounge with the others and she's always there for her pre-dinner drink, it's always gin-and-something that was so fashionable when she was young. She usually has her dinner in the dining room, though at her own table, she won't share, she's rather reserved, but she spends a lot of time in her room, reading books, watching television and every day she does a crossword puzzle, one of those tricky ones that I can't even get started on.

All the rooms have a single bed and a clothes cupboard, a coffee table and a couple of armchairs, and some of the residents bring in pieces of their own furniture. Stella has brought a desk. It's walnut with a complicated grain and very highly polished. She must polish it herself, because I'm sure Mary doesn't. She has her photographs and her books and she's hung some pictures on the walls. There's nothing mysterious about the photos, there's one of Marianne that looks as if it was done for her agent to send to TV producers or whatever they do, and one of Richard in a black cloak thing and those hats they wear at universities, and there's another of Marianne's children when they were little and before they went in for black leather and more rings in their ears than on a curtain pole. Any picture of Stella's late husband is what you might call conspicuous by its absence.

I don't know what his name was or what he did or when he died or anything about him and that's what I mean by mysterious. Stella *is* a mystery. She never talks about her husband, never even mentions that she had one. I could add that she never talks about the past at all and that's quite amazing in a place like this because the past is the only thing most of them talk about. It's their sole topic of conversation. And for some of them, Maud

Vernon for instance, it's the distant past, it's as if the world stood still after 1955. The other day she asked me if chocolate was still rationed.

But Stella lives in the present and that's what we talk about. We talk about what's been on the news and what's on telly, new films that have come out, though neither of us are likely to see them till they're on video, whether skirts are going to be six inches above the knee or a foot below it, what's happening in the village and what's happening at Middleton Hall, and we talk about what I've been doing—or as much as I let her know I've been doing. She says she misses me on my days off and I have to admit that I miss her. The truth is she talks about herself very little, so why is it I'm beginning to get this feeling she wants to talk about herself a lot? Because of the way she sometimes looks at me, summing me up? Because of her abrupt changes of subject, as if she'd meant to make a sudden confession? Perhaps it's more on account of the sentences she starts to speak and then breaks off, smiling or shaking her head.

I get to work at eight, which is fine with me as I'm an early riser and when Mike's away, as he mostly is in the week on this new job, there's not much to do at home. It's only a couple of miles from the village to the nursing home. The first thing I do when I get there is pick up the post. The papers and the post are left in a metal box with a lid that's fastened on to the back of the sign at the gates that says 'Middleton Hall: Residence for the Elderly', with, for some unknown reason, a picture of a badger at one end and a bluebell at the other. In the post box are always a whole bundle of newspapers but not many letters and postcards. Some of the old people never get a letter and to get more than one a week is rare.

On the morning of Edith Webster's funeral, which incidentally was the 13th of the month, there were just three envelopes in the box, two for Mrs Eileen Keep, which is Lena's real name, and one for Mrs S. M. Newland. Of course there was the usual stack of papers as well as Arthur's *Economist* and Lois Freeman's *Woman's Own*. The letter for Stella was in an envelope made of thick brown paper, about five inches wide and maybe a foot long. It was thick, as if something stiff was folded up inside it. I thought I knew what that something was and I didn't much like it.

The dogs came leaping out to meet me the way they always do, jumping up, and Ben, who's a bit forward, tried to lick my face. The care assistants don't wear uniforms the way proper nurses do, just white nylon overalls over our ordinary clothes, but I was dressed for Edith's funeral, so I pushed the dogs down and got quite severe with them. When I'd put my overall on and trainers on my feet and laid out everyone's newspaper marked with their names on the table in the lounge, I went along to Stella's room with her letter.

She was up but not dressed. Sharon or maybe Carolyn had brought her breakfast and she was sitting at the table in her dressing-gown. Stella has a black quilted satin dressing-gown with red satin binding round the collar and the cuffs. It's really what my mum calls a housecoat. She'd obviously had her bath and her hair was combed but she looked a bit washed out, the way you do in the mornings when you're her age. If she hadn't done her make-up yet she'd painted her nails, and they were dark crimson. I wish she wouldn't and I wish she wouldn't ask me to do it as she sometimes does. It looks ugly on old hands with purple veins, but I can't tell her. It's not something even a friend can tell you.

There's no roughness in Stella's voice and it doesn't sound old but like the voice of a clever girl at one of those fancy private schools who's had no experience of life and no hardship. It sounds untouched, if that's possible. She said, 'Good morning, Genevieve,' the way she always does, and smiled at me and asked me how I was, and I said what I always say, asked her if she'd had a good night and how she was feeling. Although I'm supposed to leave it in the lounge along with the other papers, I'd brought up her *Times* and I handed it to her with the thick brown envelope.

It's funny how when people are really anxious to look at something their faces don't light up or their eyes get narrow the way they do on telly. What they do is go blank. Stella's face went absolutely expressionless when I put that envelope into her hands. I had the feeling she wanted to tear it open and because I was there was forcing herself to go about the business of ungluing the flap very slowly and methodically. Indifferently, really. Stella often makes her own bed but she hadn't that morning, so I busied myself with doing it. I turned my back on her to pull up the fitted sheet, but when I went round the other side I saw that she'd taken whatever it was out of the envelope and it was lying in her lap.

I say 'whatever it was' but of course I thought I knew what it was. I'd known from the moment I picked it out of the post box. The only thing that comes in an envelope like that and is on stiff paper like parchment is a will.

Stella had apparently satisfied herself that all was well, that it was what she thought it was, and now she felt able to postpone taking a further look at it. She laid one hand over the top of it and asked me if I was going to Edith's funeral. I said I always did if it was one of my own, but I didn't want to dwell on that. I wished there'd been some more tactful way of saying it. Still, Stella only nodded.

'Why aren't you wearing black, Genevieve? You're quite conservative in some ways, you know, and I was sure you'd be wearing black.'

I could have told her the truth, that I hadn't got any black, but that would only have made her embarrassed, so I took off my overall to show her my denim jacket and skirt and said what was also the truth. 'Blue protects. It's a lucky colour.'

'I might have known there was a superstition there somewhere. So you need protection at a funeral?'

You need protection everywhere all the time, in my opinion, but I didn't say that. I told her about my nan wearing a necklace of blue beads to keep away arthritis.

'And does it keep it away?'

'She's never had an ache or a pain in her life,' I said, knowing that would make her laugh, because maybe my nan wouldn't have even if she'd never worn the beads.

Stella did laugh, but not unkindly. In my family we all respect the powers that guard us, my nan and Mum and my sister Janis and my brother Nick and even my dad, though he denies it. But if refusing to change your sock if you've put it on inside-out and blaming your troubles on a green car aren't superstition, I don't know what is. Still, it's not a word we like. We prefer to talk of supernatural powers or the weird. Stella hadn't noticed the date, I suppose, or wouldn't have thought much about it if she had. It made me feel I needed special protection, I needed luck that day, for I needed the good thing to happen in the evening. And unless I took steps what chance did I have on the 13th?

When I'd finished the bed, I collected up Stella's washing for the laundry. She always folds everything and puts it in the laundry bag so that it's no trouble. Something unusual that morning was that she was watching me, and watching me intently. I sensed it even when I wasn't looking at her. I began to have a really powerful feeling that any minute she was going to break through the barrier and say she wanted to talk seriously to me. I was growing more and more uncomfortable by the minute. I went into the bathroom and replaced the towels with fresh ones, touching wood all the time, the underside of the counter, the roller the toilet roll was on, even Stella's wooden-backed hairbrush. When I came out she'd turned the will over, or turned a page of it over, and she looked up at me and smiled.

I didn't want that to happen, what I *knew* was going to happen. Let's face it, in these places old people are always being—well, manipulated is the word, I think—to remember the nurse or the carer in their will. In the years I've been at Middleton Hall I've seen it time and time again, I've seen Lena herself try it on with at least two of the residents. Maybe she succeeded with Edith, we shall see, but she was always talking to her about disposing of one's money to do the maximum good and remembering those who had been of real service 'in the evening of one's days'. That, and telling her she could have her solicitor come to Middleton Hall if she wanted to, just say the

word. I've seen enough to make me resolve to have nothing to do with it. It made me shiver to think there were
some who'd say I only spent so much time with Stella
because I was after her money. It made me sick to think
I might have to face up to the fact that perhaps I had—if
I was in that will.

So I was going to take care I wasn't in it. I was going
to get fierce and maybe rude, and of course I didn't want
that, I dreaded that. But why else would she have got on
to her solicitors to send her the will? And who else would
be a what-d'you-call-it, a beneficiary, but me that only
the day before she had called her friend? So I didn't smile
back at her. I asked her if she would like the french windows open, it was going to be another hot day, and she
just nodded and said yes please.

Opening those windows, I hung on to wood. I pressed
my fingers into the wood, scared to take them off, and I
thanked my stars, my guardian angel, that I'd put on
blue.

Stella said, 'Genevieve?'

'Yes?' I said, sounding really gruff.

'Do you know how pretty you are?'

What a shock! You see how touching wood works.
Something had deflected Stella from that will and what
she'd intended to say. The powerful wood had turned her
purpose and my blue clothes had protected me. Of
course I didn't answer, I didn't know what to say.

'Not pretty,' she said, 'no, that's the wrong word.
Beautiful. You're a beautiful girl, Genevieve.'

'I'm not a girl,' I said. 'I'm thirty-two.'

She laughed. Her voice was as sweet as honey and
innocent as milk. 'That's very young, though you don't

know it now. It's a pity you don't know it.' She sighed, I don't know why. 'Sit down a minute, Genevieve.'

'I mustn't be long,' I said, which is not what I usually say when she asks me to stay for a bit. But I had my eye on that will. It seemed to be getting larger. I could almost read 'This is the last will and testament of . . .' on it. 'We've got a busy morning,' I said, 'on account of me and Lena and Sharon all going to the funeral at two.'

'Is your husband in London this week?'

'Coming back on Friday,' I said.

'What exactly are the builders doing?'

I told her about the three big houses on the edge of Regent's Park that were being gutted and turned into luxury flats. She wanted to know where the men stayed, if it was a hotel or a hostel, and I told her it was a B. and B. in a place called Kilburn. It's been going on for weeks now and they don't expect to be finished till Christmas.

'You must miss him.'

The funny thing is that I did in a sort of way. You can't understand how I did in my situation, how I could love one man and miss another when he was away, but I was half-glad I missed Mike. On the other hand, I hated to be a hypocrite. I just couldn't sit there and tell Stella I longed for my husband, I couldn't wait till Friday. She was looking at me in a really penetrating way, and I thought, how can I tell her? It was crazy thinking I could tell her, even that she was the one person I could tell. What does she know? Married, widowed, got these two kids, she's so *old*. She'll have forgotten what sex is, even if she ever liked it, and lots of her generation didn't.

Then she gave me a shock.

'You told me once you wanted to have children,' she

said. 'Is there some reason you can't? Perhaps I shouldn't ask. If I've been impertinent you don't have to answer.'

Nobody had ever, not ever, asked if they'd been impertinent to me before. It made me laugh. I couldn't help it. Her eyebrows went up and she made a funny little cautious sort of smile. I had to say something, so I said, 'You know how it is, you leave it so long, I mean, thirteen years with us, you just keep putting it off. Don't want to lose your freedom, I reckon. You think to yourself, OK, one day, there's plenty of time, but there's not really, is there?'

'No.'

Nearly everything I'd said wasn't true. The truth would have taken half an hour to tell and I didn't know what reception it would get. I stood up and as I did so she slipped that will back into the envelope. It was quite a relief, I can tell you. I said, 'I don't suppose you'd want to come this afternoon, would you?'

'To Edith's funeral?' She sounded surprised, as well she might. I'd only asked to get off the subject.

'There's a spare seat in the car. You wouldn't have to go in the crem if you didn't want. It's going to be a lovely day and the crem's got beautiful gardens.'

'The crem?' she said.

It took me a second or two to understand she didn't know what that was. 'The crematorium,' I said, though it's a long word to get one's tongue round.

She shivered. You know how sometimes when you're cold you hunch your shoulders and give yourself a shake, you do it purposely, I suppose it must make you warmer. Stella didn't shiver like that but as if something from outside affected her and made her body first jump, then tremble.

'Why on earth didn't she choose burial?'

'I don't know,' I said. I didn't even know if she had chosen or if Lena had made that decision. 'Cremation's more hygienic.'

Stella said, quite violently for her, 'It's horrible!'

'I expect that's a matter of opinion,' I said. 'We can't all feel the same. So you won't come then? You could sit outside in the shade.'

'I don't think so, Genevieve. The garden here is quite beautiful enough.'

She didn't say it but I knew it was because she doesn't like being in a car. She'll go in one for necessity. I mean, she had to when she came here for instance. The nearest train's at Diss and that's ten miles away, so she didn't have a choice. But she'll never go in a car for pleasure, I don't know why not, perhaps she gets car-sick. I wouldn't ask, it's not my business.

My nan says that blood must always be shed at a funeral. If it isn't the dead person's ghost will walk. Well, I know there's a lot in these things, I know you've got to protect yourself and others in this life, but there are limits. It turned my stomach after my grandad's funeral seeing a big cut on my nan's hand where she'd let her blood to stop him walking.

Still, having said all that, I had my doubts after we'd watched Edith's coffin slide away and the chapel curtains close. It's a small thing really, but not so small if you don't do it and then something bad happens. So while Lena and Sharon were sort of leaning forward in their seats and covering up their faces to say a prayer, I unpinned the brooch from my jacket lapel, took a deep breath and stuck the pin into the ball of my thumb. It only hurt for a second. A big bubble of blood came welling out.

We all got back into the car and it was as hot as an oven on mark seven due to having been locked up in the full sun for three-quarters of an hour. Sharon sat in the front beside Lena and I was in the back, which was no hardship to me, as Lena drives like a madbrain. Mike calls where Sharon was sitting the suicide seat, and my dad calls it riding shotgun. Whatever you call it it's the most dangerous seat in a car, yet car-sick people usually feel ill through sitting in the back. Maybe Stella was once in a car accident and that's where she was sitting, in the suicide seat.

Going to the crematorium we'd taken the by-pass but coming back Lena drove us through the village. Through Stoke Tharby, I mean, my village. She took the road that comes into the High Street by the pub and when I saw where she was going I realized we'd have to pass *the* house. It's called Rowans but for some reason—well, I know the reason—I call it *the* house.

Lena came over the brow of the hill and down the other side at a good sixty. That's crazy, because the road is too narrow for two cars to pass. Her car's too old to have seat-belts in the back, so I held on tight to the seat in front and if Lena didn't like that she'd have to lump it. I was glad I'd pricked my finger at the funeral and I was glad I'd worn blue. There wasn't any wood to touch in the back of Lena's car, only plastic, plastic everywhere. Lena said it was exhilarating driving fast and she couldn't wait to get her new car that would do over a hundred with ease, and I knew she meant when she came into whatever Edith had left her.

We got to the bottom without mishap. By a piece of luck there hadn't been anything coming in the opposite direction. Sharon doesn't come from round here, she commutes from Norwich, so Lena started pointing places out to her. That's where Jenny lives, she said, the council estate, though in fact the council has sold off all the houses including ours and everybody calls it Chandler Gardens. Everybody but Lena, that is.

She showed Sharon the church, St Bartholomew's, and the rectory and our village hall. She'd slowed down to a snail's pace. They were thatching a cottage and she wanted Sharon to see. I used to hear about people—well, lovers—getting a big thing about the place or the house the person they love lives in. Like that song in *My Fair Lady* about the street where you live. I used to think that was crazy, how could you get that way about bricks and mortar? How could it be that a place like that looks bigger and brighter and more important than all the places around it? I didn't believe it, I thought it was rubbish. I know it's true now.

And he doesn't even live there. It's a weekend cottage, but he and his wife don't even come every weekend. Of course he comes mid-week to see me, and once we met here. But why does my heart beat so hard just when I see *the* house? Why does my mouth go dry? I have to hold my hands tight to stop them shaking. If you rescue a bird and it dies in your hands, your hands will shake for ever. Stella wouldn't believe that but it's true. That's how I feel when I look at *the* house, Ned's house, as if I'll shake for ever.

It's not a very nice house, it's not really old and it isn't thatched. Mainly it's made of wood and joined on to the

brick one next door. Lena wouldn't look twice at it and
she didn't. So why does the sight of it stun me more than
any palace would? Why am I turning round and practically kneeling on the back seat to go on seeing it till it
fades from view? Lena would have forty fits and so would
Stella. My thumb has healed where I stuck the pin but the
blood was shed. Tonight, if I'm lucky, oh, I must be lucky,
he'll phone me and say when we can meet.

I was gazing back at the house and nearly fell on to the
floor when Lena took the turn too fast. If she knew we
were coming into the major road she gave no sign of it.
The High Street was lined with parked cars, the way it
usually is, but I think Lena was looking at it with half-
closed eyes.

'Picturesque, isn't it?' she said. 'A wee bit chocolate-
boxy, but that's a detail. It won the best-kept village in
Norfolk contest last year, didn't it, Jenny?'

'The year before last,' I said.

'And there's the quaintly named pub, the Thundering
Legion. Now I wonder where that strange name comes
from?'

I didn't enlighten her. As a matter of fact I don't think
even Mum knows. For years she thought the Roman soldier on the sign was a woman on account of him wearing
a leather skirt. It was Ned told me—who else? Lena
pointed out the Weavers' Houses and Sharon craned her
neck to see, but I shut my eyes and held between my fingers the luck-bringing fern leaves I'd picked as we came
out of the chapel.

2

When you deceive people you make fools of them. You make them act stupidly, act as if things which are aren't and things which aren't are. And that's what fools do or people who are mentally disturbed and we look down on them for it or if we're unkind we laugh at them.

There's a film my friend Philippa's got on video about the sinking of the *Titanic*. It was a long time ago, eighty or ninety years, and in those days men used to treat women as if they were fragile creatures that had to be sheltered from unpleasant or horrible facts. In the film the men never tell the women that the ship will sink in an hour and there aren't enough boats. They keep saying, we'll be a bit late getting to New York, and so the women are ignorant of the true facts and look complete fools. They say it's so bad for the children to wake them up, and should they cancel a hairdresser's appointment.

All deception is like that. The deceived person asks if you're ill or tired when you won't make love to him. You didn't hear the phone when he phoned last night because you weren't there but he's been deceived and he says maybe we should have a bedside extension, you can't always hear it ring when you're upstairs. Unless you're a complete bitch you don't let yourself think he's making a fool of himself, but the thought is there deep down. It's the beginning of contempt. I hate saying these things and I hate doing what I have to do, but I do have to do them. For a while. Until something changes.

Mostly, I don't lie to Mike. That is, I don't make untrue statements. I just don't tell the whole truth. When he comes home and asks what I've been doing, I tell him everything but that one thing. But I'm not such a lost soul that I don't know that's lying too, that's deliberate deception. One thing, I resolved I'd never let Ned come to our house that's half Mike's house. I've been to his once. It was dark and I was careful but next day when I went in the Legion with Mum's shopping she was alone behind the bar, they'd only just opened, and she said,

'Shirley Foster saw you go in Rowans last night.' She gave me a narrow look. 'I said you'd popped over with their eggs.'

Mum keeps a few bantams, so I reckoned that was all right. 'OK, I'll remember,' I said.

'You want to watch your step.' She was very cool. She's had two husbands since my dad and the second one caught her in bed with Len that she lives with now, so she's not likely to lecture me on morals. 'Don't you even think of having Prince Charming to your place. Myra Fletcher'll have it all over Norfolk by next day.'

I didn't know what to say. Mum's all right and she'd never say a word or drop a hint to a soul, but I couldn't confide in her. I couldn't say, I love him, I have to see him, we have to meet, because it's like food and drink, and without him I'd starve to death, because she'd laugh.

She'd give one of her great belly laughs and tell me he'd got it made, hadn't he? A wife and kid in Norwich and a girlfriend in the country who's got to be discreet because she's married too. No expenses but his petrol, can't even take you out for a drink. Oh, I know what she'd say and she wouldn't believe me if I told her it wasn't like that, that he feels just the same as me, that I am all his life and without me he'll die. I can just imagine her comment on that. How old are you, Jenny? Are you thirty-two or are you fifteen?

Since then we still meet down here but not at his house and of course not at mine. He drives down mid-week and because it's summer time and a lovely summer I find places for us to go that most people don't know about, hidden places in the fen and the woods. We never see another soul. Farm workers aren't out in the fields like they used to be when I was a little kid, it's all machines now, and people don't go for walks any more. The countryside is empty and in the summer evenings we lie in the long grass or in a clearing among the trees and make love. Hardly anyone builds haystacks these days, the hay gets rolled up in those swiss roll shapes, but the thatchers do, they grow the old-fashioned long corn for roofs, and last week I found us a haystack with an opening like a room inside. The summer evenings are long and warm and I try not to think about what will happen when winter comes.

I didn't say any of this to Mum, of course. I changed the subject. But as I was leaving she came after me and made me put on her quickthorn charm. Thorn is supposed to be lucky because they say Jesus was born under a thorn tree, though I've lived in the country all my life and I've never seen a hawthorn growing inside a stable.

Mum's charm is a bit of carved wood you hang round your neck on a thong and not very attractive but I kept it on to save me and Ned from the Shirley Fosters and Myra Fletchers of this world. I was still wearing it next day and Stella remarked that it 'looked interesting'.

That started me off again wanting to tell her about Ned and me. It would be a great relief to talk and there's no one to talk to. And when she mentioned Mike and wanted to know if he was going to be away from me for another week, it was on the tip of my tongue to say something. What stops me? I think it's something innocent in her eyes, almost childlike. She's not child*ish*, I don't mean that. I've never heard her say a silly thing or have any sort of tantrum. But her voice is soft with a really youthful intonation, simple and genuine—I mean there's no side to her, and those clear blue eyes look at you as if they don't know what secrets are.

I don't say anything to her because I think she'd be shocked. The world she's lived in hadn't room in it for love affairs, I suppose I'd better say *adulterous* love affairs. Stella is the most *refined* person I've ever come across. 'Dainty' is the word my nan would use to describe her. It's almost as if she's not quite flesh and blood but a porcelain doll, if they ever make dolls that don't look like little girls but like old women. She covers her mouth when she coughs and wipes her lips with a tissue with rosebuds printed on it. And yet none of that seems to go with those long crimson fingernails of hers. When I look at them they give me a shock. It's such an odd picture: the wavy white hair, the touch of face powder and blusher, pearls round her neck, the floral silk dress, and lying in her lap those gnarled old hands with sapphire-and-diamond rings and blood-red nails.

Then there's the gin she drinks and the cigarettes she smokes when she gets the chance. She's often told me about her smoking, how she'd smoked forty a day since forever, she'd started when she was seventeen. Somehow it went with the red nails, though not with the sweet voice and the blue eyes. I've seen enough old Hollywood films on video to know just what she must have looked like in the forties, with her blonde hair in long curls and a cigarette in a holder. But I was a good bit taken aback by what she said.

'That's why I've got lung cancer now, but they didn't know it was bad for you then. Everyone smoked. And the few that didn't—well, they were the greenhorns.'

I had to ask her what that meant.

'Ninnies. Silly people. Not sophisticated.'

I was clearing up her breakfast things and I came round to the bedside table for the cup she'd had her morning tea in, when I saw the long envelope containing the will. It was pushed inside the book she'd been reading. I was wondering where the will was, if maybe she'd had a solicitor come while I was away on my day off, I was hoping it had gone and we'd heard the last of it. The next time she spoke it was so softly I had to ask her to repeat what she'd said.

'I said that I don't regret smoking. I enjoyed it. I don't know how I'd have got through some things without a cigarette.'

There wasn't much I could say, so I just smiled and opened the french windows for her.

'If I had my time all over again I'd smoke again, even knowing what I know.'

'It's just as well you do feel like that, isn't it?' I said.

She gave me one of her very direct looks. 'No, I don't regret it. There are some things in my life I regret, some things I regret very bitterly, but not that.'

'Is Richard coming to see you today?' I said. It was a bit of a stupid remark but I reckon what I was doing was veering away from dangerous ground. And anyway, he often came on a Monday.

'I hope so. Perhaps this afternoon. I've had a postcard from Marianne in Corfu. It's by my bed, have a look at it.' Talk about lulling me into a false sense of security! 'And while you're over there, would you pass me that envelope, please, Genevieve? The one inside the book.'

I passed it. What choice did I have?

'I'd better get on,' I said. 'Arthur wants wheeling outside, it's such a nice day.'

'Someone else can wheel him,' she said and she took the long envelope in her hands. 'Sit down a minute, Genevieve.'

Out came the long folded-up sheets of paper again. I was thinking I probably didn't have the strength to say no, to say, please don't leave me anything, for I thought as I always do of Ned and me and how money surely would somehow help us.

Stella held up the paper and said, 'Do you know what this is?'

I said gruffly, 'Is it your will?'

'My will? Good heavens, no. Have a look. These are the deeds of a house.'

It was a relief. Temptation had come and I had faced it. I'd known I couldn't have resisted, but I was glad not to have to try. I put my hand up to the thorn charm and held it for a moment. She must have thought me stupid because I didn't know what the deeds of a house were and the first one she handed me meant nothing. It was done in sloping handwriting with loops and flourishes, a bit the way my grandad used to write. I started reading it aloud.

"This conveyance is made the twenty-ninth day of July, one thousand nine hundred and forty-nine, between Thomas Archibald Wainwright of Palings, Hemingford Grey in the County of Huntingdon, Royal Navy (here-inafter called 'the Vendor'), of the one part and William John Rogerson, of . . ."

She interrupted me. 'Yes, I've read it. Have a look at this one.'

It was typed and looked a lot more modern, though the date was only fifteen years later. Stella didn't seem to want to hear it so I read it, or part of it, to myself. On the outside it said: W. J. Rogerson Esq. to Mrs S. M. Newland, and under that, 'Conveyance of freehold prop-erty known as Molucca and situate at Thelmarsh in the County of Norfolk.' Inside was much the same stuff as I'd read aloud, only this time 'the Vendor' was this William John Rogerson and 'the Purchaser' was Stella.

'It's a house I bought in 1964,' she said, and her voice had suddenly become serious and quite heavy. She might have been talking about some very important step she had taken, one of the most important of her life. Perhaps she was. She raised her eyes from the other papers she was holding, looked at me and looked away. 'This is just between you and me, Genevieve. It's not . . .' she hesitated and seemed to be looking for the right word '. . . common knowledge.'

What was I supposed to say to that? I handed back the

deeds. She put them into the envelope with the others. 'Would you come upstairs with me?'

'Pardon?' I said.

'I want to show you something.'

Stella can walk quite well. She can't go fast because she gets breathless, but there's nothing wrong with her legs, she's not arthritic like Maud or Gracie. I offered her my arm but she shook her head. The main staircase at Middleton Hall is wide and quite shallow, but difficult to climb because the treads are made of polished wood and there's no carpet. It used to puzzle me why there wasn't a carpet and then I realized it's because Lena doesn't want the old people nipping up and down stairs. It suits her better to have them go slowly, clinging on to the banisters, or, preferably, staying in their rooms or the lounge so she knows where they are. Stella kept to the side and held the banister. Seeing that old hand of hers with the young girl's red nails clutching on to the slippery wood made me feel sorry for her again. And I felt angry with Lena for not having a chair lift. Considering what they all pay, surely she could find a few hundreds for one of those.

Stella had to stand still at the top to get her breath. I hadn't had the faintest idea where she was taking me because I'd forgotten that it wasn't all residents' rooms up here. But at the end of the passage is a room that's called the upstairs lounge. The trouble is that no one in the upstairs rooms ever seems to use it. They're either too decrepit to leave their rooms or else they prefer to risk the danger of the stairs twice a day for the company on the ground floor.

The upstairs lounge is quite small, with a three-piece suite in it and a few odd chairs all facing the telly. But the telly's black-and-white and the picture jumps about. The best thing about the upstairs lounge is the view: you can see for miles. Stella led me over to the window and we stood there looking out across the meadows and the fen, as far as the Little Ouse that becomes the River Waveney at that point and is the county boundary, with Suffolk on the other side. It was a warm day but clear, and you could see the horizon, it wasn't blurred with mist as it often is, or blackened by smoke as it used to be at this time of the year. The sky was a pale blue with a lot of high cloud and the landscape out there was the way it always is in late summer, fields of green where the beet grows and fields the colour of blond hair where the corn has been cut and fields which look full of white sails fluttering that are the goose farms. The hedges are rows of dark tufts separating the meadows but the fen beyond looks blue, a soft cloudy blue.

'D'you remember,' I said, 'how they used to burn the fields at this time of year? Sometimes you could hardly see the sky for the clouds of smoke. And the air was full of black bits.'

She looked at me, a blank look as if she didn't understand.

'The farmers,' I said, 'after the corn was cut, they set the fields on fire. They first started doing it just after World War II, my grandad told me. They were asked to leave a six-foot break between the straw and the hedge, but they didn't have to and lots of them burnt the hedges too. It's stopped now, this is the first year they're not allowed to do it.'

Her head was turned away. I don't think she'd been listening. 'Now look straight ahead,' she said. 'Do you see that church tower, the square tower?'

'That's St John's, Breckenhall,' I said.

'I don't know about that, Genevieve, but I'm sure you're right. Now look to the left of the church tower, Breckenhall Church as you say, and come down a bit and you'll see a white house. It looks just like a plain white square. Do you see it? Go to the left a bit more and you can just make out something brown with a red roof.'

'I can see it,' I said. I was going to say that I could see it clearly, not just make it out, and then I realized the difference was in the age of our eyes. 'A square house with a red roof. That must be on the Curton road.'

'It is. That's my house.'

"A freehold property," I said, "situate at Thelmarsh in the County of Norfolk."

'That's it.'

'Did you come to Middleton Hall because you could see your house from here?'

'Rather the reverse. I mean, if I had known, perhaps I wouldn't have come.' She laughed, a little nervous laugh. 'Even though you were here . . .' The laugh again, embarrassed maybe, or just shy, anyway, not happy, 'I came into this room one day, I don't remember why—oh, yes, someone said there was a bookcase with books in it, only there wasn't—and I looked out of the window and I . . . I thought it was my house, you understand. Then I asked Richard to bring me in a map, the appropriate sheet of the Ordnance Survey.'

She talks like that, very precise and correct. I don't suppose she's made a grammatical error in all her life. Sometimes it's as if she's reading what's already written down.

'Of course, I told him I wanted it just to get my bearings. He has no idea I've ever been here in this part of the country before, and nor has Marianne. They know absolutely nothing about it.'

She was leaning on the windowsill, gazing out at where her house was. Her shoulders lifted and seemed to shiver just a little, though maybe I imagined that. I asked her if she'd like to stay alone there for a while. I had to get on, I really did, and I thought she might like to be alone. With memories. With something. She turned and it seemed to me that her face had aged.

'Perhaps I will. For a little while,' she said, but when I got to the door, as I opened it, she changed her mind. 'No, I'll come. I'm just wasting time, I haven't got much, and I can't say looking at this view gives me a great deal of pleasure.'

This time she took my arm. From her expression, uneasy or perhaps just indecisive, I thought that she was going to say something startling, something that would really astonish me, make some statement about this house with the red roof out on the Curton road. But all she did was ask me why I had mentioned the stubble burning and when I explained seemed dissatisfied with my answer. We made our way along the passage, necessarily walking slowly, Stella clinging to my arm. I felt her nails dig into the muscle, I'd be bruised there later, but I didn't say anything, she didn't know she was doing it. Then she shocked me because what she said was so unexpected, though I should have been used to the way she suddenly changed the subject.

'There was some music I liked on my radio this morning, Genevieve, and I thought what a pity I can't manage to hear that again. Do you think there's some way I could record music that I like?'

I said of course she could, she could get a tape recorder. You could get little ones, it didn't have to take up a lot of space. She nodded. She would ask Richard or Marianne. And another thing she wanted was a reading stand, a frame that would hold a book when she was sitting up in bed. She talked about how her arms got tired and her hands got cold if she had to keep them outside the covers. It was ridiculous, she said, she knew that, to have cold hands in August, and a hot August at that. We came round the corner to the top of the stairs where there's a gallery and you can look into the hall below. Richard was down there, talking to Lena's husband Stanley. It looked as if he had just come in. Their backs were to us and they hadn't seen us. Richard is lanky and six feet tall and Stanley's one of the fattest little men I've ever seen, so together they were quite a sight.

Stella is usually delighted to see her children. She calls them 'darling' and is very welcoming, so I was surprised when she didn't call out to him but clutched my arm even tighter. She whispered to me, 'Genevieve, not a word to Richard about my house.'

I just looked at her.

'He doesn't know, you understand. He doesn't know and Marianne doesn't know I own that house.'

'I won't say anything,' I said, and I felt a bit stunned.

She'd tell me but not them? To tell you the truth, I did wonder for a moment if she'd started wandering in her mind. It's sad when that happens but it does happen to cancer patients if the malignancy gets into the brain as well. On the other hand, I had the evidence of the deeds, and anyone could see she was totally *compos mentis* (as Lena always says) when she went up to Richard and gave him a hug and told him how well he was looking.

Richard isn't a bit like his sister except in being tall and thin. He's very fair, the sort of person whose hair would have been white when he was a child, and he's got blue eyes. Stella told me he's a doctor, a GP in a group practice in Norwich. He wears the kind of glasses that have no rims and they give him a studious look, but his face is quite boyish and when he smiles he looks eighteen. He's lovely with Stella and he makes me think, *if* I ever have a son and *if* I ever get old I hope my boy will be as nice to me.

He'd brought her pink lilies and gypsophila. I found a pink china jug to put them in and when I took them along to her room she and Richard were sitting talking, he was holding her hand, and the deeds in the envelope that she'd left on the desk were nowhere to be seen. Sharon took their coffee in, I had to see to Gracie, my new old lady, so I didn't have a chance to check out where those deeds might be, but I kept thinking about what she'd said. That her children didn't know she owned that house, that it was a secret. And then I remembered the date on the last deed; 1964. She'd owned a house and kept it a secret for *thirty years*?

Gracie's not like Stella. She's an old grey lady, heavy and sad. A stroke has pulled her face down on one side so that her plate doesn't fit properly any more and she's very self-conscious about it, won't talk if she can help it and hardly eats. She's always pointing to her mouth to excuse herself. If she's got any children, or even a niece or nephew, I haven't seen them yet. Nobody thought of making an appointment with a dentist for her to get her plate fixed, so I did that on her own phone in her room and I've arranged to drive her into Diss on Friday. Lena didn't like that, it was taking too much on myself, she said, but she wasn't going to cancel the appointment I'd made, she's too much in awe of doctors and dentists to do that. She calls Richard 'Doctor' every other word.

Off and on throughout the day my mind kept going back to that house of Stella's and once I went up to the upstairs lounge to take a look at it from the window. In front of it was a field full of the white shifting shapes of geese and behind it the darkness of the fen. Ned and I had been there once, to that bit of fen I mean, and walked in deep among the dogwood and the mead-owsweet, I remembered it now, exactly where the house was. I think we'd even remarked on it as we passed, that it looked forlorn, as if no one had lived in it for years.

Richard came out just before Sharon took Stella's lunch in. He asked me how I thought his mother was and I said, fine, as well as she could possibly be in her condition.

'Is there anything I should be getting for her, Jenny, that I've forgotten or she doesn't like to ask for?'

He's a very nice man. He's thoughtful, like a woman. Well, some women.

'She said something about a tape recorder,' I said.

'To record some music? Yes, she does love music. Chamber music, you know, small delicate stuff.' I like the way he understands that I *do* know, that just because I'm a carer in a nursing home I'm not an utter moron. 'I should have thought of that,' he said. 'I've got a little recording device she could have. But no, on second thoughts, it would be best to buy her a combined recorder and player, wouldn't it?'

It would really, I said, and to bring her some tapes of that stuff she liked.

'I'll remember. She's not a great telly addict, is she?'

'She likes a good play,' I said, 'and she's like me, she likes the old movies.'

'All the best people do,' he said. And he thanked me for my suggestion and said goodbye very nicely, so that for a moment I thought never mind what Stella asked me, I ought to tell him. I ought to run after him and tell him. There might be something all wrong there somewhere, and if Stella died, if Stella died tonight, which could easily happen, there'd be those deeds and that house and no one knowing anything . . . But I didn't. I watched his car go, a surprisingly low-slung sporty car for a doctor, but he drove it gently, not with a spurt and a surge and a leap forward like Lena would have.

I was due to go off at four. Ned was coming from Norwich and I was meeting him at seven, and when that's going to happen I can't think about much else. He fills my mind and if I didn't watch it I'd go about in a dream. But I usually try to spend the last half-hour of my stint with Stella, in her room talking to her, or in the lounge if she's in a lounge mood.

Arthur was having his nap and I'd found a quiz show on the telly for Gracie and they'd both had their tea, so I tapped on Stella's door at twenty past three, but she wasn't there. I found her in the lounge all on her own and if you'd seen her there as I saw her without her seeing me, you'd never have thought she was some poor old thing dying of cancer. I'll tell you what she looked like, she looked like a lady waiting for her lady friends to come to tea. She was sitting in an armchair with a magazine on her lap but she wasn't looking at it, she was looking out of the window at the green garden and the butterflies on the buddle bush. Her chin was resting in one of her hands and the other held her wrist so that the blood had run down out of those veins and the hands looked smooth and young. The hairdresser had been round and given her a shampoo and set and she was wearing the dress I liked best, blue silk with cream-coloured coin spots. The very pale stockings she always wears that would turn some women's legs into tree trunks were fine on hers that are smooth and shapely.

The tactful cough I gave made her turn round. It was a lovely smile I got, the smile that Richard gets and I get but I don't think anyone else does. She had blusher on her cheeks that she calls rouge and a little blue shadow on her eyelids but she never makes the mistake poor old Maud does of painting on a slash of crimson lipstick. Stella's lipstick is pale rose pink and I think she puts it on with a brush.

'I was hoping you'd come, Jenny,' she said.

I said I always did if I got the chance and I sat down beside her and we looked at the butterflies, counting ten small tortoiseshells, seven peacocks, a red admiral and another one Stella said was a comma. She's knowledgeable about things like that, nature, wildlife. She said she'd like to see a swallowtail and she's heard you only see them in Norfolk, maybe she'll see one here.

'Before I die,' she said. 'Perhaps I'll see a swallowtail and die happy.'

I'd no answer to that.

'I don't suppose I could have a cigarette, could I, Genevieve? I'd love a cigarette.'

'Better not,' I said. 'You're not supposed to smoke anywhere in this building.' The thought of it made me giggle. 'Certainly not in here.'

'Certainly not when you've got lung cancer. But it's rather silly, isn't it? It's too late now, the harm's done, it wouldn't matter any more. There's another red admiral. It's got such a pretty Latin name, *Vanessa Atalanta . . .*' She turned away from the window and looked at me. 'I want to ask you something. That is, I want you to do something for me, if you will.'

'I will if I can,' I said, but I had the feeling, I don't know why, that this would be no small thing.

'You must say if you don't want to.'

'All right.'

'Genevieve, if I give you the key and tell you exactly where it is, will you go to my house and have a look at it and tell me—tell me what sort of state it's in?'

'You mean that house on the Curton road?'

'Yes, that one. It's called Molucca. I believe Captain Wainwright who owned it before Mr Rogerson was a seafaring man and had been to the East Indies.' She smiled at me and said gently, 'Would you do that for me? Go and look at it and tell me what you think?'

'Yes, I suppose so,' I said and, because that didn't sound very gracious, 'Of course I will, Stella.' I hesitated, I didn't know how to say this, but I had to try. 'Stella, wouldn't it be better for Richard to do this? Couldn't you tell him about the house and ask him to go? He's so nice, he won't mind, will he? He won't be cross or upset or anything.'

She liked me saying her son was nice. She went a little pink. 'I want you to do it, Jenny,' she said. 'It's best for Marianne and Richard not to know. Not yet. If this doesn't sound too melodramatic, not till after I'm dead.' Her eyes turned away from me but not to the window, to look at a blank wall. 'It embarrasses me,' she said very quietly. 'I'm sorry, but—but it's not the sort of thing one would—want one's children to know. Will you go there for me?'

'I'll go this evening,' I said.

'Oh, and Genevieve? You will drive carefully, won't you?'

3

It was about seven miles away by road. Much nearer, of course, as the crow flies. Stella and I had probably looked over no more than a mile or two of countryside from that upstairs window. The road took me out of Tharby and past Thelmarsh Mill, it's absolutely straight and all the hedges have gone, a Roman road, where the thundering legion marched up the eastern side of England. I went through Newall Pomeroy and followed the sign for Breckenhall. I was almost sure I knew the precise spot and I was right. The road was narrow, straight and flat, and the houses stood well back from it, first the white one that Stella had seen dimly and I had seen clearly, then, about a hundred yards further along, her house.

The white house had a garden with a fence that separated it from a strip of field, then the road, but the fen came right up to Stella's house, up to the walls and the front door. The fen had spread itself across the field in gorse and wormwood, nettles and rose and elder, and pushed in over whatever garden there once had been, so that the house now stood in the midst of it. Along the left side had once been a track beside a ditch full of bulrushes and hemp agrimony, but this path was overgrown with thistles. Ned says the seed heads on the willowherb look like wool spun on a distaff. They were everywhere, their white fluff blowing.

It was a dull, warm evening. The sun had quite gone. I drove the car a little way up the thistly path to get it off the road. It's very silent around here when all the birds have gone to roost and even the cackling of geese has stopped. If you know our countryside you'll understand how still it can be in the evenings, how soft and hushed, almost as if it were listening for something. The fen has big trees in it but mostly it's like a forest of bushes, the water not far below the surface, and all the reeds and rushes, the hazel and the dogwood, moving very faintly, whispering and shuffling. When all else is quiet you can still hear the trickle of water.

I was very aware of all this as I approached the house. It was the only one I'd ever seen that was actually in the fen, or that the fen had taken over. A mountain ash had grown from a seedling right up against the front door, its berries the same colour as the red clay tiles on the roof. Four windows looked back at me. They were shaped like windows in a church with pointed tops, but the glass in them was clear, not stained. The front door was inside a little porch with a peaked roof and on the left hand side was a garage made of black weatherboard. It was a flint house, the walls were of uncut flints that look like pebbles from a beach, but these pebbles came from the stony ground. My nan's mother, when she was young, used to get paid a halfpenny a basket for picking the flints out of the fields so that they wouldn't blunt and buckle the plough. The ones on the walls of Stella's house were brown and grey and white and nearly black, all mixed up but closely matched for size and arranged in neat parallel rows.

Up above the front door was a whitish plaster oval, that builders like Mike call a plaque, with 'Molucca' written on it, surrounded by a wreath of leaves, all done in pargeting. I had to trample down the nettles to get to the door, I didn't want to get my legs stung. Cobwebs covered the front door, one with a dead hornet caught in its threads. The key turned quite easily in the lock. I wondered—I'd never thought to ask—how long it was since anyone had been in here. Not thirty years, of course not, but twenty? Inside, the hall was papered in a silvery pattern with faded blue flowers and there was a blue runner of carpet on the dusty wood floor. It was airless but without any smell. The front door closed itself behind me smoothly, not creaking or sticking.

I was in the sort of house you'd expect from the outside, a room on either side of the front door, a passage down the middle, a kitchen and another room at the back, stairs going up along the right-hand wall. You get to know the ages of houses if you live round here and I thought this one must be about a hundred and twenty years old.

The first room I went into was a sort of sitting room. It was on the right and it was quite big and furnished like—well, how am I going to put it? Let's say the way the middle classes and the weekenders furnish their places, the way it's done by the people my nan used to call the gentry, but not by us. By that I mean that they don't have new furniture but what they think are antiques or at least old stuff, and they have their chairs covered with fabric called chintz and rugs from India and old china. Stella's

was like that. It was a pretty room, like a picture in one of
those magazines about houses that you look at when you
have to hang about in the medical centre. I wonder what
my neighbours would say if I furnished my place like
that?

There were china plates up on the walls and paintings
of flowers and fruit, but the largest picture was a portrait
of a woman. You could tell this was a picture someone
had painted in oil paints, it wasn't reproduced or pho-
tographed or made by some other process. It must have
been a yard wide and two yards long. The woman had
dark hair and a pale, pretty face, she was dressed in dark
pink silk, low cut and with a stiff full skirt, and there was
a double strand of pearls round her neck. In her hand she
held a single pink rose. The canvas had just been pinned
round a wooden base and there was no frame around it or
glass to cover it. I don't know what there was about it that
gave me the feeling that the painter had loved the woman
in the picture, had been in love with her, perhaps the tender care with which he'd done her mouth and put the
light into her eyes.

The bits of silver that were standing about were dark
brown with tarnish, a silver bowl had a deep blackened
dent in it, and the brass had turned black. Someone had
left love-in-a-mist and sweet peas in a vase, though the
water had long dried up. The flowers were dead as if
they'd died a score of years ago, so that you felt they'd fall
to dust if you touched them. In the bookcase were a lot
of books. I like books, which surprises some people. I like
handling them as well as reading, so I took one out and
saw that the paper was yellow and smelt sour. Dust was
everywhere, blue on the wood surfaces and fluffy grey on

the upholstery, puffing out of the curtains in a cloud when I tapped them with my finger.

There was just as much in the dining room. You couldn't tell what colour the table was, the dust on the surface was so thick, like a fluffy cloth that had been laid on the wood. I opened the sideboard and found it full of framed pictures. Someone had taken them off the walls and stuffed them in here. Now I knew that fact I could see the pale squares where the pictures had hung.

There were paintings of children and animals, nice enough but I didn't pay them much attention. At the bottom of the stack was a photograph of a man and a woman standing close together. It wasn't that old. I mean, it had been taken in my lifetime, maybe in the sixties. The woman's hair made me think that. It was dark hair back-combed, with two side bits curling on to her cheeks. She was the woman in the oil painting and she was wearing the same pink evening dress. That seemed strange to me, for they were obviously outdoors, the background was a cliff or rock face, but she was in a low-cut silk dress and he was in jeans and a check shirt. He was tall and thin, fair and with the sort of face that looks as if he'd always be laughing. Smiling came naturally to him and you could see the lines his smiles had left behind. The odd thing was that I felt I'd seen him somewhere, even that I knew him. And that was ridiculous because I don't meet many new people, as you can imagine. Besides, it's a sad fact that if he looked like that when I was a baby he wouldn't look like it now.

I went on upstairs where there were three bedrooms. Heat rises, they say, and it was very warm up there. The dust was even worse. Downstairs had been fully furnished but upstairs only the front bedroom had any furniture in it, a double bed, a wardrobe, a dressing table, a couple of chairs, all of it Victorian stuff. The bedcover was of patchwork, hand-stitched, I should think, in various shades of blue and red. I pulled it back in a cloud of dust and saw that the sheets were still on and the pillowcases. The summer had been warm but when I put my hand inside the bed the sheets felt damp, a chill against my palm. I'd been wondering how they heated the place, there were no radiators, only fireplaces, but in here was an oil heater, the really old-fashioned kind like a black funnel on legs.

As I've said, the other two bedrooms had no furniture in them. They had no carpeting on their floors. It was as if the people who'd lived there had said, there'll never be anyone here but us, we'll never have friends to stay, so why furnish those two rooms? The bathroom was old-fashioned and a bit grim the way the kitchen was, very much in need of a re-fit. Another oil heater, the panel kind, was pushed up against the wall. I tried one of the basin taps but of course the water had been turned off years before.

I was thinking I'd explored the whole house, and at the same time wondering what I'd explored it *for*, what I was supposed to find out, when I noticed another door out of the kitchen apart from the one that led out into the garden—into the fen, in fact. That door, the other one, must be to the garage. It was locked.

I opened a couple of drawers to see if I could find the key but they were empty apart from linings. This particular newspaper was *The Times* and the date on it was 1965. Nothing very surprising in that. It was then that I looked at my watch and saw that it was six-thirty. I was meeting Ned two miles away at seven, so I had a long while, but something happens to your sense of time when there's a treat in store for you in half an hour. You have to prepare yourself, you have to be in the right frame of mind. For me that meant being there first, enjoying the waiting, watching for his car to appear on the road. You can see so far along these roads where the legion marched, you can see for miles. It was a marvellous experience for me to sit and watch the cars coming, not many, there's not much traffic, and hope and long, be disappointed, hope again, and then at last see *his* car, see *him*.

I left the house and shut the door behind me. I don't know why I walked round the garage, perhaps because a whole half-hour was too long to get to Thelmarsh Cross and then have not ten but twenty minutes to wait. The fen was trees here as well as weeds and bushes, hazel and rowan and a maze of white willow. I had to push my way through a thicket to get round the back. There was a small window in the rear of the garage and if you see a window you have to look through it, don't you?

A car was inside. Garages are for keeping cars in and what else would you expect to see in one? Not, though, in the garages of empty abandoned houses. This car was red and a Ford Anglia, a few years older than me. I knew that because my dad once had exactly that model, with a grid like a wide downturned mouth and the rear window turning inwards in a Z-shape, only his was dark blue. This one's tyres were flat. It was thickly covered with dust. I wondered if Stella knew it was there.

I went back to my own car and drove by a roundabout route to Thelmarsh Cross, through Breckenhall and

Curton and past the garage my dad used to have a part share in. Curton village street is wide but the back lanes are narrow with high hedge banks and you can't go fast. If you do more than about twenty miles an hour you can go head-on into someone coming the other way, which happened to my brother when he was seventeen. The other person wasn't hurt but he broke two ribs and his left arm. It suited me to go slowly, to while away the time.

Thelmarsh Cross was one of our regular meeting places, but as I sat there in the car I thought that maybe we shouldn't meet there any more. It was too open, the place where the two roads crossed sheltered by woodland on only one quarter, the rest exposed. I suppose we'd chosen it because there were no houses and because no one in a car would choose to pass this way going to or coming from Tharby. But you can never really bank on that sort of thing. It may be true for some people that danger adds spice to a love affair, but I don't need it, ours isn't that kind of love affair, and if danger means the chance of being found out, I'm afraid of it. I'm afraid of the consequence of that, never seeing him again.

So I sat there, watching the cars come down the long white road. There weren't many and mostly it was empty. It was silent too until someone in the distance fired a shotgun and the plovers in the field took to the air in a cloud of rustling wings. I saw a car like his, same make, same colour, come over the hill, and I felt my heart turn over. Of course it's not your heart, it's a nerve pulling at your stomach or your gut. I put my hand up to the wooden charm and held it. The car wasn't Ned's, a woman was driving it, and it was no one I knew.

When he did come, two minutes late, it wasn't from

that direction at all, but along the other road and I wasn't prepared, I didn't see him until the car drew up alongside mine. We looked into each other's faces and we both smiled. In that moment, for me, there's no past and no future, just the present, the absolute here and now. He drove deeper along the track into the wood and I followed. We stopped when we knew the cars would be hidden under the trees.

At those meetings, at first, we never talked much. We put our arms round one another and held each other tight and kissed. It was always like that. Out of doors, in the warm summer air. We kissed as if it was the first time, as if it was that night all over again when I gave him the love charm, and we had our first kiss in the open air, in the dark.

After a while he said, 'Where are you taking me?'

'A place in the wood,' I said. 'A hidden place. I found it when I was a child.'

'No more haystack?'

'They've taken it away to thatch Fletchers' roof.' I took his hand. We walked along hand in hand. 'I love you,' I said.

'I know,' he said. 'I need you to love me. If you'll only say the word, one word, I'll leave Jane and come to be with you.'

We had had this conversation before and we would have it again. 'For ever?'

'For ever, as far as I can tell. Yes, for ever. Why not? I'll burn every one of my boats for you, Jenny. I'll poison the wells and sack the city and come over the river and burn my boats.'

'Then I must be careful not to say that word by

accident,' I said and I was clutching the charm till my hand hurt.

'We'll live in the cottage and make a big scandal.' He's got a lot of imagination. 'Your mum will have to give up the Legion. The *Bury Free Press* will interview me and take pictures. But we'll be in bliss.'

'You know I can't.'

'Because of Hannah?'

'No, *you* can't because of Hannah. You know that, don't you? You know you can't.'

'I know,' he said. 'Well, I think I know. But there has to be a way. There's always a way, isn't there?'

'No,' I said, to avoid saying yes.

So we lifted aside the branches and went into the little sheltered grassy place and made love on the warm dry ground.

When I told Stella I'd been to her house she blushed. I used to think old people couldn't blush but they can, just like anyone else.

She was in her room, having her mid-morning coffee, and I sat with her. It was Maud's day at the hospital for her radiotherapy, Arthur had been taken out by his son, and I hadn't much to do, having settled Gracie in front of a video of *The Inn of the Sixth Happiness*. I expected Stella to ask me all sorts of questions about the house but she was a bit subdued, she seemed more embarrassed than anything. The blush died away and she gave me a long, curious look as if I'd changed from the woman she knew into someone else, as if seeing her house had in some way altered me.

'Don't you want to hear about it?' I said at last.

It was a strange answer she made. 'I suppose I must.'

'Shall I just tell you, then?'

The word isn't one I'd usually have associated with her but she looked a bit sulky. A bit like a child who's had a disappointment. 'I didn't believe you when you said you'd go there so quickly,' she said.

'If you'd rather not talk about it, Stella, it doesn't matter. It was no trouble going there. We can forget it.' I looked round the room for inspiration. 'I see you've had another card from Corfu. Is your daughter having a nice time?'

'Don't humour me, please, Genevieve. I'm not in my second childhood.' She had never spoken to me so sharply before, she had never spoken to me at all sharply before, and I was taken aback. I wouldn't have guessed that voice could have a hard edge to it.

'I'm sorry,' I said.

She was straightaway remorseful. 'Oh, Genevieve, I'm the one that's sorry. I shouldn't speak to you like that. It's just that one of the things I like about you is the way you don't talk down to me the way the others sometimes do. It's a very common attitude to old people, it's as if when you get to seventy, no matter what sort of a person you are or how much intelligence obviously remains to you, you're to be treated like a child. Especially if you're in a home. There's no more speaking to you as if you're a rational being, you have to be cajoled and—and bullied and lied to.' She drew breath, she gasped throatily, her face flushed again, more darkly this time. 'Please don't change and become like that. It would be too much. I couldn't—I really couldn't bear it.'

This outburst shocked me. It was so unexpected, it was

such obvious evidence of how upset she was. I wanted to put my arms round her and hold her until the fast beating of her heart slowed. But that would have been disaster. That would be to do just what she had warned me against. All I could do was apologize and wait for her to make the next move.

'Stella, I'm sorry, I really am. It was clumsy of me but it was because I didn't know what to say.' I dared the next bit. 'I don't—well, I don't understand your attitude to your house, so I'm sort of in the dark, I don't know what to say or do.'

She looked down, shaking her head a little. The cough she gave reminded me she had, after all, got cancer of the lungs, she was dying of it. She put out her hand, covered mine and squeezed it. 'Tell me, then.'

'There really isn't much to tell. It's all OK there. Just dusty.'

'I suppose the fen has grown up right against the walls, has it?'

'Yes, but it looks all right. There's a mountain ash with berries on it by the front door.'

She closed her eyes briefly. 'How strange. How strange it all is.' After a little hesitation, she said, 'Did you look in any of the cupboards or drawers?'

It's a weird thing, but maybe because I have to lie about Ned, or not tell the whole truth, I've become specially careful not to tell lies in other areas of my life. Still, I wanted to lie then. There was no reason for me to have looked in that drawer but nosiness. You don't like to have to admit to being nosy, it puts you on a par with Shirley Foster. I told myself I couldn't afford to be proud and said yes, I did, I'd looked in the sideboard and found some paintings and a photo of a man and a woman.

Old people are always saying they know how much they've changed but they don't really. They don't know that the face they had thirty or forty years ago isn't just a younger version of the face they've got now, it's utterly different, it might be a different person. And that's why Stella looked disbelieving when I talked about 'a woman'. She even smiled, shaking her head.

'Didn't you recognize me, Genevieve? I was that woman. I suppose it's my hair turning white . . .'

A bit of belated tact made me say quickly that I'd *thought* it was her. In fact, it hadn't crossed my mind. For one thing, I don't know why, I'd always supposed she'd been blonde. A change of subject seemed in order and I told her about the car. Having started off truthfully, I kept it up—it's amazing how you can get into good habits if you try!—and I said I'd tried to unlock the garage door but couldn't find the key so I'd done the next best thing and looked through the window.

'Your car's still there, safe and sound. It'll soon be vintage.'

She didn't smile. 'Not mine,' she said. 'Not my car. But it doesn't matter.'

'Here's your key back,' I said.

She seemed to flinch from it. I expect that was my imagination. 'No, you keep it. I want you to hold on to it.' Some explanation for that was called for and she said, after a moment's hesitation, 'If I do decide to sell someone should have a key for the agents . . .' She made it sound like some vague future possibility, but she had no future, she only had months.

'Do you want me to phone an agent for you?' I said.

'Not yet. Perhaps not at all. I don't know. I really don't know why I asked the solicitors to send me those deeds.' She cleared her throat. 'It's not as if I needed deeds.'

'You can send them back. It's easily done.'

She didn't answer. She said, like someone making small talk, 'My husband was a solicitor. Did I ever tell you that?'

She hadn't told me anything about him. 'Was that in Bury?' I said.

'In Bury. It was a family firm. His grandfather started it. They were called Newland, Newland and Bosanquet. Later on they changed it but that's what its name was when I first worked for them. Solicitors always have ridiculous names like that, don't they? My husband's first name was Rex, which I thought sounded like a dog when I first heard it. I was his secretary, that's how we met. He was twenty-two years older than I. That's too much, Genevieve. Is Mike older than you?'

I was afraid to get on to me. Mike was just six months older, I said, and then, 'Was it Newland, Newland and Bosanquet who—' I had to search for the right word— 'who acted for you in the, with the, buying your house?'

It was a very strange look I got then. 'That would hardly have done. Oh dear, no. I used some people in Ipswich. Don't you think we've talked enough about me for one day? I seem to dominate all our conversations.'

She was chatty and bright, her voice clearer, the throatiness gone. Sharon put her head round the door, then came in and took the coffee tray. Stella waited till she'd gone, looked down at her red fingernails. 'How did you meet your husband, Genevieve?'

'I didn't exactly meet him. I'd sort of always known

him. You do in a village. We went to the village school
before they made one big school for all the villages at
Thelmarsh.'

'He was the boy next door?'

'Not exactly next door,' I said. 'Near enough.' I was the
one who was blushing then and I hated it. I could feel my
face go burning red. Stella had her eyes on me and a look
had come into her face of deep sympathy, of deep understanding and kindness, though why she should have
thought I needed those things I don't know. 'We went to
the upper school together and I stayed on into the sixth
form. He left at sixteen. We were going out together by
then. He wanted to do a City and Guilds building course
to get the qualification.' Why on earth was I going on like
this? This wasn't what she'd asked me. I just blundered
ahead. 'But he had to start earning. He's a good earner.
We got married when we were both nineteen.' I looked
up at her, right into her eyes. 'But please don't say it's
romantic, don't say that.'

'I won't,' she said, and her hand which had slackened
held on tightly to mine.

'We're going to have our thirteenth wedding anniversary this year. It was never romantic.' I looked away, out
through the window at the garden and the roses shedding
late summer petals. 'And now I don't know what will happen because I'm in love with someone else.'

4

Village life seems strange to townsfolk and no one really knows about it till they've lived it. It's the only life I've ever lived but I've talked to enough people and read enough books to know it's different. We, the people, in a place like Tharby, are like a big family. There may be four hundred of us but everyone knows everyone else and everyone uses first names. You'll have been at school with all your generation and your parents with their generation and your grandparents with theirs. You'll marry the boy next door, as Stella put it. Take my mum, for instance. It doesn't sound very country village-ey to have had three husbands and a live-in boyfriend, but my dad and the one after him were both Tharby boys and Len the lover's got a smallholding at Tharby Heath. Her third was the only outsider and he came from Eye, which is hardly a foreign land.

Lots more people go away than they used to, they can't find houses to live in for one thing, but fresh people don't come in. Not *our* sort, anyway. Some come here to retire, but they keep themselves to themselves. It's not too far from London for commuters, for the truth is that some will commute from anywhere to anywhere, but there aren't many of them, and there are only two sets of week-enders. Even in these days Mr Thorn up at the hall gets called the squire, and not always with the tongue in the cheek.

I've said we're a family but you have to remember families are where most of the trouble starts in this world. We don't all get on, far from it, but I reckon we'd all stand together against an enemy. Still, I expect they said that in Bosnia and look what happened there. Anyway, for good or ill we all know each other better than we know anyone else, we know whose mother someone is and who's niece to this one or brother-in-law to that one. That's the sort of thing we never make mistakes about. More important, we feel comfortable with each other. Going to a country-music evening in the village hall like the one where I met Ned, you know just who will be there, you needn't feel shy the way you would going to some gathering in Bury or Thetford, it'll be the same old faces and the same people you sat in the classroom with when you were five.

Except that, this time, Ned and Jane were there.

The purpose of it was to raise funds for something, probably the church bells. I don't know how it can cost a hundred thousand pounds to re-cast some old bells and hang them up in the belfry again, but that's what they tell us. So we're always having music evenings and dances and bingo and car-boot sales to raise money for the bells. It was a Saturday and Mike was home. We got there a bit early. Mike gets everywhere early, he's one of those obsessively punctual people. He put on a suit but I refused to dress up. Isn't it crazy to wear a dress for country music? If I'd had them I'd have liked to wear cowboy boots and a jacket with fringes but I hadn't, so I settled for a good pair of Levi's and a checked shirt.

My sister Janis was there and my brother Nick with his girlfriend Tanya. Mum had left Shirley Foster in charge at the Legion and was doing the drinks. She looked a bit like she came from Nashville herself, did my mum, in a miniskirt and leather jacket with a ten-gallon hat. Janis had told her to stop wearing miniskirts, it was the limit at her age, and when Mum said she was only fifty-three and her legs were thirty years younger, Janis said, 'It's not your legs, it's your face,' which was unkind, but Mum didn't seem to mind and she went on wearing short skirts. A lot of Mike's relations were there and Philippa, who's been my best friend since we were given our names together at one of the vicar's mass christenings. Even my dad turned up with his girlfriend Suzanne, who's younger than me. Everyone was there, including the Thorns and one of the retired people called Lady Something and all the commuters and the weekenders who've bought the mill.

They stuck together, of course. They always do. Mr Thorn called Mike over and got him to move two tables side by side and all the chairs so that the nine of them could sit together. He called him over as if he was a servant and when he'd done it he didn't thank him. I ought to be used to that sort of thing, I've seen it all my life, but I still don't care for it, and if it was me he'd asked I like to think I'd have the guts to say do it yourself. But maybe I'd just do it meekly, like Mike did.

When the other weekenders came in I expected them to make straight for those tables. I hadn't seen them before, not many of us had seen them, and we all stared, some of us openly and some with a bit more discretion.

The woman was tall and thin, about thirty-five, with a thin, pointy face, one of those foxy faces, and a mass of ginger hair. I mean ginger, not red or carrots or auburn. She wasn't pretty and she was very plainly dressed in black linen trousers and jacket with a white T-shirt, but she was easily the most elegant woman in the room. The man was Ned.

Mr Thorn got up when he saw them and so did the couple from the mill. I couldn't hear what was said, they were obviously introducing themselves and inviting the new people to their table, but not succeeding. A long time afterwards I asked Ned how he'd got out of sitting with the squire and the rest of them and he said he'd told them the truth, that he'd cause too much disturbance. Their daughter wasn't well, and though they'd left her in bed with a sitter in the house he wouldn't feel easy if he didn't go back and check up on her a few times during the course of the evening. The truth, or half of it.

'I did a programme last year about people like James Thorn,' he told me a lot later. 'The subject was the remains of the squirearchy and we called it *The Rich Man in his Castle*.'

'From the hymn,' I said. I'm proud of myself if I can keep up with Ned. 'From "All Things Bright and Beautiful".'

'I didn't think things would have been too bright and beautiful for me if he'd remembered who I was.'

But that was in May and the country-music evening was February. It would be ridiculous to say that I fell in love with Ned the first moment I saw him. You only do that if you think love is just going to bed with someone. When I saw Ned I did have an immediate reaction. I thought, what must it be like to live with someone like that, to see his face on the pillow when you wake up in the morning, to know that he's yours?

Well, he got to be mine. In a sort of way. If anyone ever is anyone else's. A month later I was fathoms deep in love, but not then. Not then. Like the rest of the village, I turned my head to look at Ned and Jane, to see what they would do. And what they did was come up to us.

Ned said afterwards, a long while afterwards, that he and Jane were used to going up to people at parties and introducing themselves. They were trained to it. In their jobs—she's a casting director—they were always meeting new people. They couldn't afford to wait to be intro-duced, they couldn't stand about in silence (like Mike and I would have) waiting for someone to take pity on them. He said he saw me and 'liked the look of me', those were his words, and the rest of us, that is Philippa and her husband Steve and Janis and her husband Peter, they looked all right, about their own age. It never occurred to him that we weren't his class and if it had I don't think he'd have cared. We were a better bet than the squire and the snobbish couple from the mill and so he came up to us and said,

'Hello. I'm Ned Saraman and this is my wife Jane Beaumont.'

I could see they were all digesting that, thinking fast. It's not exactly the usual thing for married women in Tharby to have different names from their husbands.

'We've taken the house called Rowans,' he said.

I was the first to hold out my hand. I wanted to find out what his hand felt like, the touch of it. He had a firm handshake—has, I suppose, though I've never shaken his hand again. I'm not really a shy person but I found myself shy with him. Women are, I think, with men who attract them. Mike wasn't shy and Steve wasn't. They started giving advice about Rowans, though neither Ned nor Jane had asked them for it, all about how it must need rewiring, and how it was twenty years since that tiling job had been done on the roof, it was Steve's uncle who'd done it, and all the problems there'd be if a proper damp course wasn't put in. Janis wasn't to be outdone and was reeling off the names of people who'd deliver their papers and do their dry-cleaning.

Philippa, on the other hand, was as silent as me. I could tell what was passing through her mind, I often can, she was thinking the same as I was, that this was the first time in her memory, the first time to her knowledge, that people like that (Nan's gentry) had ever associated with people like us at one of these dos. It was the first time we'd ever seen that kind of people act as if we were all the same class.

As soon as there was a break in the conversation Ned looked at our glasses and asked if he could get us another drink. It was only Janis and me that wanted anything and we both said white wine. Jane spoke for practically the first time.

'Right, darling, go and see what the superannuated Dolly Parton can come up with.'

There was a sort of embarrassed hush. I didn't know what 'superannuated' meant then but I knew it wasn't polite and I was angry. Ned began to make his way over to the bar Mum was running and I caught up with him.

I said, 'Excuse me.'

He turned round and smiled. He's very tall and he had

to bend a bit to talk to me. His eyes are a clear very dark grey with black round the irises. 'Jenny?'

'You ought to know that you have to be careful what you say about people in this village to other people. I mean your wife ought to.' I didn't speak loudly or crossly. I tried to keep my voice calm. 'Everyone's related to everyone else. The whatever-she-said Dolly Parton is my mother.'

He stood still, taking it in. Then he said, 'I'm truly sorry. I'll tell her.'

I knew I'd gone bright red in the face. I went back to the others. They were all talking nineteen-to-the-dozen about wine, the merits of French against Australian Chardonnay, that sort of thing, all except Jane. Jane was looking bored. When she found out what she'd said I didn't think she'd care much. Just as Ned came back with our drinks the music started. It was Len the lover on the guitar, Paul Fletcher on the tenor sax and his cousin, another Mike but from Curton, on the drums. Philippa's sister Karen started singing 'Stand by Your Man' in a passable Tammy Wynette imitation, and we all sat down.

A couple of songs later Ned said he'd nip back and see how Hannah was. Hannah's mother didn't show much concern, I thought, but perhaps I was feeling a lot of resentment still. I watched him go. When he got to the door he turned round, saw me looking and put up his eyebrows. I smiled and he smiled back as if he was relieved. Then I went over and talked to Dad because it pleases him so much. He's never got over his guilt at splitting up from Mum and leaving us kids and he is so happy if one of us treats him like a real father.

❧

After I'd fetched Gracie back from the dentist, I went to find Stella. The day before I'd been off and the day before that was when I'd told her about Ned. Confiding in someone, the way I'd confided in her, ought to make you like them and want to be with them. It doesn't. It's as if you've poured stuff out of your heart into some container, you've got rid of it, and all you want is to throw it away and never come near it again.

That was why I had to find her and get rid of that feeling, get the awkwardness over. I knew I'd feel deeply embarrassed in her company. Well, I should have thought of that before I shot my mouth off, not punish her for listening and letting me talk. She'd been so patient and I'd told her so much, all about how I didn't see Ned again for nearly a month after that country-music evening until we met by chance in the village shop. All the details of what had happened next.

That same Saturday I was walking past his house and there he was in the front garden trying to prune roses. I say 'trying' because he didn't have a clue, he was just nipping the tops of the twigs off. So of course I took over and did it for him and he asked me in for a cup of tea. I won't say I'd have refused if I'd thought Jane wasn't there, but she wasn't, she'd taken Hannah to her mother's, and we had the tea and sat talking.

I'd lived thirty-two years in this world and I'd never talked to anyone the way Ned and I talked. There's Philippa, of course, we talk, but not much about the big things of life, more about shopping and what we're going to make for supper and old movies, which are her great passion. Ned and I talked about what we believed in and what we wanted and hoped for and what life should be.

All that had been shut up inside me. I'd thought about it, I thought about it all the time, and I'd put it into words in my own mind, but never uttered it. He fetched my thoughts out of me just by talking and later on he said I had fetched things out of him he'd never told another soul.

Stella listened to me while I told her all this, how at first I thought I'd found a friend, that him being of the opposite sex didn't matter, we could still meet when he came down at the weekends and there needn't be any sex involved, she listened and she said she understood. She understood only too well, she said, that you could fool yourself along those lines and what a shock it was when you found out you were fooling yourself.

So I went looking for her. She wasn't in her room or in the lounge. I thought she might have gone up to take another look at her house across the fields but she wasn't in the upstairs lounge either. Stella didn't much like sitting about in the open air, she had to have a reason for being outdoors and the weather being fine wasn't suffi-cient. I smelt the reason before I found her. She was on a stone seat behind the high cypress hedge and she was smoking a cigarette.

That could have given me an opening line to cover my embarrassment. Lena would have made a big fuss, would have behaved as if Stella was ten and caught smoking in the garden shed. But what was the point? She was dying anyway, poor Stella, and might as well have a bit of plea-sure before the dark.

When she saw me she smiled and held up the cigarette in a film-star gesture, her fingers extended. She reminded me of Bette Davis in one of those old films.

'Are you going to scold me, Genevieve? I have to have

a cigarette sometimes. I may as well tell you I occasionally do when no one's looking.'

'What you do is your own business,' I said, and if it was a bit brusque that was my way of getting over awkwardness.

'Wild horses wouldn't drag out of me who gets my Silk Cut for me.'

Not Richard, I thought. Not the doctor. Marianne. I'd have done the same for my mum. 'Lena wouldn't set any wild horses on you,' I said, 'but somehow she'd see to it you didn't get any more. So be careful.'

She blew smoke out through her nose. I'd never seen anyone do that before except in films. She was very pale and it wasn't only due to the powder she put on. The colour was draining out of her. Even her blue-green eyes were fading. Her lips parted and a thin cloud of blue smoke emerged and hovered. She waved it away with one hand.

'Genevieve?'

I looked at her.

'Would you go to my house and bring me back the photograph you found? Any time will do. If you're ever up in that area, if you could just go in and pick up the photograph.'

'Stella,' I said, 'how long is it since anyone lived in that house?'

She didn't have to think back or calculate. 'Twenty-four years.'

'*Twenty-four years?*'

'It's quite a long time, isn't it?' She considered. 'And not to say *lived*, Genevieve. Twenty-four years since anyone has been there.' The look on my face amused her and she smiled. 'I paid the rates, of course. I mean, it was rates and then it was poll tax and then council tax. But I paid up. Oh, and I had the roof seen to. Those flint walls are very tough and of course they don't need painting.'

'You never had tenants in?' I asked her, and, when she shook her head, 'Why on earth didn't you sell?'

This was a bit strong for her. I'd spoken more directly than I usually do and she retreated a little, withdrawing into her shell.

'I didn't want to.'

It's easy for people like me to resent people like Stella. Money is a daily issue with us. We find it hard enough to pay the council tax on the one property we own—or the building society owns—and when someone like her talks about easily and thoughtlessly paying tax on a house no one lives in, that she can't be bothered to let and just doesn't feel like selling, we don't take kindly to it.

'It was mine, Genevieve. I had the right to keep it empty if I chose. I bought it myself, with what my father left me when he died in 1963. My husband didn't pay for it.'

How to tell her that wasn't the point? Not to tell her, of course. She was so pale and, suddenly, so thin, growing transparent and skeleton leaf-like as she sat there holding up the end of her cigarette between red fingernails.

'You can sell it now,' I said. 'I'll handle it for you, if you like.'

'I know you would.'

She stubbed out her cigarette on the bench, took a tissue from her handbag, wrapped it in the tissue, and put it into the bag. It was all very precisely done, fastidiously done, and when the operation was completed she rubbed at the blackened place with the toe of her navy court shoe.

Once she was standing up, holding on to the back of the seat, and puffing a bit at the effort it had been, she said breathlessly, 'If I were to sell the house, Genevieve, there would be this advantage, that Marianne and Richard would never have to know. There would just be rather more money to inherit than they expected.'

'Would you like to take my arm?' I said.

'Thank you. I think I will. You're too polite to ask me why I don't want them to know, aren't you? I may tell you one of these days. But not now, not today. The thing is, Genevieve, I'm afraid to sell it.'

I looked at her. We were walking along the path, by the herbaceous border. The lawns fall away from there in green terraces and then there's a plantation of old chestnut trees. She clung to my arm, walking slowly. The smell of cigarette smoke clung to her, mingled with the White Linen perfume she always wears.

'Oh, not afraid because there's something there I don't want anyone to find. It's all too long ago for that.' She shook her head. 'At least, I think so. There were never any letters and only that one photograph.' Her need to express herself seemed to have conquered her breathlessness and she was speaking in a steady normal voice, quietly but cheerfully. 'I suppose I say I'm afraid because I feel all that should be left alone and hidden, left in peace instead of brought out into the open—I mean, not have the fen cleared and the lawn mowed, perhaps the house converted in some way or another, builders there. And I can't bear to think of my things, my furniture—well, thrown out or sold for practically nothing. They get those men in, don't they, who clear houses for the price they get from a junk shop? I've seen the signs in shop windows, "Houses cleared at no extra cost". I know it must seem ridiculous to you, but I don't feel I could bear it.'

I said it didn't seem ridiculous and just as I was going to say something about not to sell if she didn't want to and trying to think how to say tactfully that she wouldn't know what Marianne and Richard thought anyway, not after she was dead, a dog came bounding out from among the chestnut trees and raced across the lawn towards us. It was a white dog with black spots, a Dalmatian, and I recognized it as belonging to Lena's sister, who must have called to see her. Stella drew back a bit and held on to me more tightly but this dog is a real softie and wanted more than anything for me to stroke its head and talk to it. Stella wanted to know why I had my fingers crossed.

'It's lucky to see a Dalmatian,' I said. 'Cross your fingers and make a wish. Go on.'

She did what I told her, though she looked doubtful.

'Don't tell me your wish,' I said, 'and I won't tell you mine but we'll tell each other if they come true. How about that?'

I'd wished of course for things to come right for Ned and me, though I didn't see how they could. You can't be like my dad, have a child and then walk out and leave her. The only thing that would make that possible would be Jane dying, and why should she die? She was a normal healthy woman of thirty-seven and likely to live another fifty years. I didn't want her to die and that wasn't what I'd wished for. In fact, I'd made a mental reservation and added on, 'but not at the price of Jane dying'. I could just imagine the remorse I'd feel, the endless guilt, if I'd wished for her death when I stroked the spotted dog and crossed my fingers and it had actually happened.

Stella and I went back into the house, meeting Lena as we crossed the lounge from the french windows. Lena took one look at Stella and said in the way she has when she's trying to be funny, 'And how does "Lady" Newland find herself today?'

Stella said quietly she was quite well, thank you.

'You know, those shoes of yours aren't a brilliant idea, Stella. The heels must be two inches high. It's vanity, isn't it, dear? That's what it all boils down to, vanity.'

'I'm afraid I only have these sort of shoes.'

'And the budget couldn't run to a pair of trainers like the other ladies have? Think about it, dear, it's for your own good.'

Halfway up the stairs Stella said something about how you ought to be allowed to wear what you like if you were paying what she was. Four hundred pounds a week it is, though she didn't say so. She was brought up, she once told me, not to mention money, and though she's got over that she doesn't like naming specific sums. I think you ought to be allowed to wear what you like if you're *not* paying too, if you get it on the NHS, it's something Ned and I talked about, freedom and dignity, but I didn't want to get into politics with Stella.

She was breathless by the time we reached her room. She sat down and said, 'Richard phoned to say he's bought me the tape recorder. He's going to bring it in on Saturday.' The swiftness of her change of subject, and not only that, gave me a shock. 'What did you mean, Genevieve, by not at the price of Jane dying?'

'Did I say that aloud?'

She gave a little nervous laugh. 'I'm afraid you did. It doesn't matter. I don't even know who Jane is.'

'She's Ned's wife.' I turned my face away. 'It was the wish I made— I mean, I don't wish for her death so that I can . . .'

'I know what you mean. And he doesn't either, does he?'

I was mystified and at the same time becoming uncomfortable. 'We've never discussed it. She's young and healthy. Why should she die?'

Stella's answer was another laugh, but the kind that you'd think was a sob if you were only listening and not looking. She said very quickly, too quickly,

'Have you ever heard of Gilda Brent?'

She was staring straight ahead of her.

'I don't think so,' I said carefully. 'Should I have?'

Stella went on. 'You tell me you like old films. You're always making videos of them. She was an actress in films. A British film actress.'

'I'm sorry, Stella. I've never heard of her.'

'Then do you know anyone who might have. A—do they call them movie buffs? A movie buff?'

'There's my friend Philippa,' I said.

She had gone very red. You don't do athletics at her age but that was the impression she gave, of someone who'd just tried to run a race or climb a hill and had failed.

'You could ask her,' she said. 'Ask her about Gilda Brent.'

5

Stella had been writing, using an old-fashioned fountain pen, marbled blue, with a gold nib. The result was like someone who knew nothing of Arabic attempting to inscribe it. Or, as Richard, as a precocious adolescent, had once said, like spiders copulating.

She took a deep breath, or as deep a breath as she was able to take. Once again she turned her attention to the instructions that came with the tape recorder, but this time she persevered. She took the covering off one of the new cassettes, an operation that required the use of her nail file to split the transparent paper. It was something to have discovered how to open the machine. The cassette went in satisfactorily at her third attempt.

Footsteps passed along the passage outside her door. Stella screwed up the piece of paper on which she had been writing. She put the cap back on the fountain pen. Then she went to the door, listening to the silence for a moment before reaching for the only upright chair the room contained. She put the chair against the door, its back under the handle, holding it in place. This activity took away her breath and she had to sit down again.

After a few moments, when she thought she could

summon an adequate voice, she pressed the red button on the recorder and began to speak, tentatively at first.

I am speaking, she said, into a machine that describes itself as a cassette recorder and computer data recorder, whatever that may be. I have never done this before, and I can't yet tell if the device is working or not. I shall stop now and try to play it back.

I am speaking, said the recorder, into a machine that describes itself . . . Stella listened to her own voice and thought how much lighter it sounded than she had expected. It sounded light and precise and old-fashioned and *old*. She was still vain, she thought, even now. Dying, actually dying, she would probably still care how she looked and sounded. She closed her eyes briefly, then pressed the red button and began again.

My purpose, she said, is to set on record something that no one knows but me and which should be known, a question that unless I answer it will be left unanswered for ever.

A more obvious way of doing that would be to write it down. I have made an attempt at that but the results didn't please me, not only because, after all, I'm not a writer, but also because my handwriting is not particularly legible. The alternative would have been to have asked Richard for a typewriter instead. No doubt I can still type perfectly well, but what reason could I possibly have given for wanting a typewriter? A lot of writers, or so I'm told, speak their words into a microphone and have a secretary transcribe them. No one will ever transcribe mine, but one or two may listen.

Writing, though, is a silent activity. You can do it surreptitiously and hide it. I think I've read somewhere that

Jane Austen did that, slid her writing under a book she pretended to be reading when someone came into the room. It's possible that one of the people here, pausing outside my door, in innocence or deliberately to listen, can hear my voice if not what I'm saying. Fortunately, in one way, I'm no longer able to speak very loudly. I don't really mind if they do hear a continuous murmur from inside. They will only think I'm talking to myself and that won't surprise them. Everyone in here except Genevieve takes it for granted the residents have softening of the brain or are dropping into a second childhood. I have put a chair under the door handle to stop anyone coming in. If I can. Needless to say, as if we were children using a bathroom, there are locks on the doors but no keys available to those inside.

There. I've succeeded. And now that's done I'm wondering how to begin. I'm still testing, really, and I'm going to play it back again.

My purpose, she heard, is to set on record something that no one knows but me . . .

The door is secured, the tape recorder is working, and I feel I must waste no more time. For, though I'm going to tell Genevieve a lot about myself and a good deal of the background to this story, there are many many things that, while I can speak them aloud in private, I know I can't actually utter to another person. And perhaps I don't have much time to utter them at all. So I'll begin by explaining why I sent for the deeds of my house or with the obituary in *The Times*. No, I won't. I'll begin with Genevieve.

Richard and I must have visited at least ten of these residential homes. What was I looking for, beyond comfort and attractive surroundings and some sort of proximity to him? Someone who wouldn't patronize me perhaps, someone young and pretty and honest. One person among those who would look after me that I could talk to. If I don't know what I was looking for I know what I found. She would probably say that fate directed me to her. Yet I had never met her, never thought of her since that day, but when I heard her name . . .

Mrs Keepe, Lena, isn't a bad woman at heart. Basically she is kind-hearted, and she runs this place with efficiency and—yes, consideration. But she is insensitive to other people's vulnerability, or perhaps I should say she believes vulnerability shouldn't be allowed. Her sense of humour, which I'm sure she believes she has in abundance, is the banana-skin kind. It's concentrated on making others look foolish or, rather, on finding those areas where they differ from the common run and pointing out the peculiarity. I, for instance, have to be given a mock title because I dress as I've always dressed and wear make-up and don't have the local accent. But this—this propensity of hers, served me well that day Richard and I walked into the lounge on our exploratory visit. She might be in the habit of calling the carer who was sitting there with a resident Jenny the rest of the time, but here was her chance to expose someone's sensitive place to Richard and me.

'This is one of our care assistants, Jenny Warner, or *Genevieve*, if you like a real mouthful.'

The day I can never forget for long came back to me, and the smell of smoke and the tiny glass cuts on my hands. I could almost see the blood on my fingers. But I looked at her, I was intrigued by her. In the beautiful face was something of a face from long ago, a tilt of the eye, a colour in the cheek, a curve of the lip.

I said to Richard as we got back into the car, 'I think that's the place for me, don't you?'

Simply on account of Genevieve? That was only part of it. How did I know what sort of person she would be? That I would even like her? I might be wrong, that christian name might have been a favourite in the Waveney valley thirty years ago. The truth was that I was tired of looking for somewhere to live. To die. Every time we went out I had to suppress my fear of riding in a car. I was tired of these toothy, smiling matrons—heaven knows what they call them these days—their waiting lists, their patronizing ways. Middleton Hall it would be, for good or ill, by destiny, or far more likely, by chance.

She stopped the recorder. I am digressing, she thought. I must keep to the point. Rex used to complain of how I let the association of ideas spoil my train of thought and he called me a mistress of the *non sequitur*. She pressed the red button.

Seeing the obituary was a shock, she said. I don't know why I even looked at the obituaries page, I don't usually, just the front page and an article or two before I turn straight to the back and the crossword puzzle. But that day in early August I happened to open it at the obituaries page and saw his face looking at me from a small photograph, his youthful face as he was when I first saw him. I gasped and it was quite a loud sound I made, like the breath one draws after crying. His name, in upright black type, jumped out at me and seemed to dance on the air in front of my eyes.

It wasn't a long obituary. I have it almost by heart. Oh, yes, it's still possible to learn something by heart when one is seventy, the memory doesn't fail in all ways. But I won't repeat it now. What would be the point? If I keep this tape and anyone ever listens to it, if he or she wants to know more, the obituary exists, it can be found in some archive or other or in a newspaper library. Richard would know, but do I want Richard or Marianne ever to hear any of this?

The writing was impersonal and cold. It described him as a painter and illustrator of children's books, notably the well-known *Figaro and Velvet* series. His portrait of Edwina Mountbatten was named as his best-known work. The writer followed this statement with an under-hand remark about the picture finding no favour with its subject and the artist therefore receiving no more commissions from that quarter. But I won't go on. I am already doing what I said I would not. It is the last sentence which is responsible for my speaking now, and that I must repeat from memory.

'He was married to the film actress Gilda Brent in 1949 and they separated, though were never divorced, in 1970. She survives him.'

That is how I know that no one knows.

The other day I tried out the name on Genevieve but it meant nothing to her. I knew then that I was going to make this tape or series of tapes and it was an effort for me to say 'Gilda' aloud. It is an effort now. Gilda, Gilda, Gilda. Of course it gets easier as I persist . . .

With Genevieve I felt frightened, embarrassed, shy and distressed all at the same time. But I spoke it and the name meant nothing to her, just as his name would mean nothing. I shall play back the tape now.

⌒

It works, she said. I have done it. Like most people of my age I have a deep distrust of these so-called modern conveniences. And that is not because they are modern or we are old-fashioned so much as because we have lived in this world a long while, at some time or other have experimented with the latest gadget and usually found it inadequate. I am glad my tape recorder functions properly, as much as anything because it was Richard's present to me.

The subconscious acts in strange ways. When I played the tape back I saw, I heard rather, that I had never uttered his name. I suppose, I know, that I couldn't bring myself to speak it aloud into an empty room, even though there is no one to hear it and never will be if I erase the tape as I very likely will. Inside my head I can say it over and over softly to myself, but it seems that my lips will not actually form the consonants nor my tongue make the sounds.

Will I ever be able to say it to Genevieve? Am I going to try? And if I am, is it because she is the only possible person to be the recipient of my—what?

My confession.

I'm not doing it for Genevieve, but I am doing it because Genevieve is here and because of a child's face seen twenty-four years ago.

Stella stopped the recorder and into the silence poured an overwhelming tiredness. She held the screwed-up paper in her hand but when she fell asleep her fingers relaxed and it fell to the floor.

6

Mike never proposed to me. I wonder if men do in real life as against in books and films. Does anyone really say, Will you marry me? We were walking up the hill one evening and he pointed over to Chandler Gardens and said,

'We ought to put our names down if we're going to have one of them when we're married.'

I wasn't surprised. I took it for granted too. It wasn't mentioned again for a few months but by the end of that year everyone was talking about us as an engaged couple and Mum was thinking about our wedding reception. We used to make love in the back of Mike's car, an old yellow Triumph Herald, parked in the pine plantations behind the Legion. That's all right when you're eighteen but I wouldn't do it now. You know you're not a girl any more when you can say you're too old for something.

Mike wasn't the first boyfriend I'd had, he was the third, and I hadn't even liked the others much, they were just people to go out with when you're afraid of the other girls seeing you without anyone. The main reason I got married was to get away from home. Mum was married to her second husband, Dennis, then but she'd got a relationship going with a chap called Barry from Breckenhall and the atmosphere was scary, what with Barry sneaking in when Dennis was on nights and Dennis drinking more than he should have and the endless fighting. Mike is placid and calm and even-tempered. He never has a row, he'll just say, 'Let's not get on to that,' go out of the room and shut the door. He's not a talker or a reader, come to that. Most of the time he's at home he's doing something to improve the house.

So am I saying I got bored? I don't know. People in our village don't expect to talk to the people they're married to. The women expect their husbands to spend their free time in the garden or doing some DIY. Mum never talked to my dad or he to her, she never talked much to the rest of them either, they had plenty to do together without talking. I never thought of being bored till I met Ned, or, rather, I thought boredom equals marriage, you can't expect excitement.

Because we never talked much, Mike didn't notice the change in me. That was how it came about that I hardly had to lie. If I was a bit more silent than usual he probably thought it was because I was getting older. In the country people start getting old when they're young. I don't know much about other people's sex lives—does anyone?—but I knew a bit about Philippa's and Janis's and they both said the excitement had gone out of it long ago. After her second child was born Philippa and Steve didn't do it for months and now they hardly ever do. She even talks the way my nan does, as if she'd never enjoyed it and it was something to put up with, and I've had to remind her of what she was like once, crazily in love and not able to stop herself touching Steve and fondling and kissing him all the time.

Mike was away so much that the weekends were the only opportunity, but often weeks went by without him touching me and I sensed that the times I said no he wasn't bothered. Before I met Ned I even used to wonder how Mike and I were going to have a family, the way we went on. I once said to Janis, what was marriage for, what was the point of it if you had no kids and hardly any sex and you never talked except to say tea was ready and ask what was on the telly. Janis being Janis said that was immature and typical of me. Marriage was a partnership, a commitment, and for making a home together.

When we first thought we could be friends I used to meet Ned in the Legion and of course Mike and Jane were there too. It all looked as if it happened by chance but in fact it was the result of some careful planning on my part. Until Jane got bored, that is, and stopped coming. She didn't like Mum having a juke-box and a space-invaders game, not to mention horse brasses and china gnomes on shelves in the alcoves.

'English country pubs used to be marvellous until they got fucked up with Muzak and kitsch,' she said.

Mike got the look on his face I know so well. It creases up his forehead and pulls his mouth down at the corners when he hears that sort of language from a woman.

'I get enough of that on the site,' he said later. 'It's one thing hearing it from brickies. She's supposed to be an educated woman.'

So he stopped going to the pub too, and for a while Ned and I had a couple of drinks there alone together on Saturday nights. He'd go in there at about eight and I'd just turn up with shopping I'd got for Mum or to fetch my eggs. Then one Saturday she said to me, leaning across the bar and whispering, 'You may have the hots for him but you don't have to write it all over your face.'

Apparently I needed my mother to tell me when I was in love. I knew then that I wanted him to be in love with me, to love me back. Well, I had a remedy for that. I don't know why I'm ashamed of it, I shouldn't be, because it worked. It was a charm that's been working for centuries.

Three or four years ago my nan gave me something to bring back Mike's love. It sounds crazy, doesn't it? Preposterous. I didn't know his love had gone, still less if I wanted it back again. But Nan had noticed the way he was, she noticed in the village hall at her eightieth birthday party. I suppose he was off with the boys as usual or at any rate not taking much notice of me. It was a love potion she gave me that she'd made herself, she called it a philtre, or sometimes an elixir, brown liquid the colour of tea in a little bottle that had been a Cointreau miniature.

Mike never got a taste of it. Perhaps by then I was indifferent as to whether he wanted me or not or perhaps I didn't believe it would work. But when you're in love you'll try anything. Knowing no one ever drank miniatures in our house, I'd kept the bottle in the back of our sideboard, so the next Saturday I got it out and went down the Legion at eight.

I don't know to this day if Mum saw me put it in Ned's half of Abbot. I did it while he'd got up to talk to Mrs Thorn who was nagging him for a donation to the bells fund. My heart was thudding when he came back. He drank the Abbot and had another and then, instead of saying as he always did that he'd have to go and leaving me there, he just looked at me and said, 'Coming?'

I followed him out and it was dark as pitch. He took my hand and led me a little way down the narrow lane where the hedges are high. Nan's elixir makes the man who drinks it love the first woman he sees and I'd had twenty minutes of terror lest the first woman had been Myra Fletcher or even Mrs Thorn. But it was all right. It had worked. In the dark that my eyes were getting used to I saw his face transfigured. He put his arms round me and kissed me. He said something but I don't remember what it was and I don't remember what I said. We kissed and we were into love, we were lost.

I never told Mum anything. She just assumed. She took it for granted it was magic too, her own mother's magic. Nan had done the same for her when she met Dennis, though I can't say hearing that pleased me. Magic, she guessed it was, and something else.

'No doubt about it, we're a good-looking family.' She laughed. 'You've got a better figure than I ever had, girl. Easy to tell what he sees in you.'

I wanted to tell her that it wasn't for the way I looked that Ned wanted me, he loved me, that magic only started things off, but that would have meant admitting too much. I wasn't going to admit anything. Going back alone to my empty house I thought about what she'd said, I sat down and thought about it for a long while. She hadn't said any more, hadn't touched on what I could see was in her mind, but she'd been thinking: what else but her figure and her face would a fellow like that see in Jenny? He's educated, he's been to Cambridge University, he's in television, and what's she? A Tharby girl who's got no qualifications in anything and was a home help till she got that care assistant's job at Middleton Hall. It stands to reason it's just one of those physical things, he fancies her like mad, and no wonder.

Mum knows a lot about sex but she doesn't know much about what goes on in people's minds. She only knows about love in terms of bed and only about bed in terms of a bit of fun. But what Ned and I have isn't fun, it's good and sometimes it's grand, and sometimes it's awe-inspiring and then it frightens me. For what will I do when it's past and gone?

That was back in April and luckily for Ned and me it was a warm April. The day I was walking with Stella and we saw the Dalmatian was the 6th of September and you could feel autumn in the air. Ned was coming down on the Thursday and I was praying for a fine evening, not cold and wet as it's been since Saturday. But that Tuesday I walked round to Philippa's about seven with a couple of videos I'd done for her, knowing they'd have finished their tea and the children would soon be off to bed.

Philippa lives in one of the Weavers' Houses. There are a row of them, half-timbered places with no front gardens and steps up to the front doors. Silk weavers lived in them when they were first built in the 1600s. Everyone thinks them very wonderful and when you see a picture postcard of Tharby it's usually of them. But I don't know, I think they're a bit dark and grim with their tiny windows and the plaster you're not allowed to paint. I asked Ned why it was that everything over two hundred years old was supposed to be beautiful and he laughed and he said he didn't know, he'd never thought of that before but I had a point. The way he likes the things I say, the way he agrees with me and sometimes says I make him see things with new eyes, that would convince me if I needed convincing that it's not just for the way I look that he wants me.

The seven-year-old and the five-year-old were both in bed and Steve was out helping his father get the potato crop in. I gave Philippa the videos I'd made, they were *Steel Magnolias* and *Dangerous Liaisons*, and she gave me *The Young Lions* and *The Anderson Tapes*. Not that I'm likely to get around to watching them, I'm not film-mad the way she is, and I only do the videos for her because she can't watch one and record one at the same time. Her house isn't big but it has lots of rooms, all of them tiny, and we had to sit in the one where the television is because she was halfway through watching John Wayne being a captain in the US Cavalry. She couldn't video it, she was already videoing *Hi-de-hi* on BBC I, so we sat there drinking Diet Cokes while the soldiers fought the Indians until twenty to eight and it was over.

'Will you do *On the Waterfront* for me on Thursday if I do *The Paleface* for you? I want to do *The Trials of Rosie O'Neill* myself and I can't do that and the Marlon Brando. And I can't sit up that late to actually watch either of them because the kids get me up at six.'

Philippa's life is as complicated as if she was juggling a marriage, a job and a couple of love affairs but her affairs are with video tapes and her job programming the VCR. I said I'd record anything she liked and nearly added I'd be out on Thursday evening, stopping myself just in time.

'Have you ever heard of someone called Gilda Brent?' I said.

Philippa looked at me as if I'd asked if she'd ever heard of Marilyn Monroe.

'Ealing comedies,' I said. 'Is that right?'

'*Of course* it is. Everyone knows that. Not just Ealing comedies. She was in a lot of war films. *HMS Valiant* and *The Skies Above Us.*'

'Tell me something I'll have seen.'

'I'm just amazed by the films you *haven't* seen, Jenny. Let's see. *The Wife's Story?*'

'I've heard of it.'

'Well, it's on next week, so I'll video it for you. It'll be a change to video something you really want to see.'

'What did she look like?' I said.

'Blonde, but face a bit like Joan Crawford's. Great legs. Why d'you want to know?'

Why did I? Stella had only asked me if I'd ever heard of her. I suppose I thought that if I found something out Stella would tell me more and that would have some connection with herself.

'There's a woman at the home who knew her.'

Did she? 'Did she?' said Philippa, and her whole face lit up. It's her dream to meet a real actor or actress, and if she knew how well I knew Ned she'd want me to ask him to introduce one of them to her. But she doesn't and she won't. 'Did she know her well?'

'I've no idea,' I said. 'When I find out I'll tell you.'

'I've just remembered something,' she said. 'Wait there,' as if I was going to jump up and run away.

She came back with a little book in her hands. In fact it was a cigarette-card album. I don't know if you've ever seen those things—well, you may not ever have heard of cigarette cards. There used to be one in every packet of cigarettes and it would be a picture of a footballer or a bird or fish or wild flower, anything you can think of. You collected the set of thirty-six, say, and stuck them in an album. I'd seen them before because my nan has a whole lot of them that my late grandad collected. The one Philippa showed me was of film stars. It was nearly full, only one missing, the space being for someone else I'd never heard of, a woman called Corinne Luchaire.

They didn't seem quite like photographs, more drawings that had been coloured in. The one of Gilda Brent showed a girl who looked, as Philippa had said, a lot like Joan Crawford but not so—I don't know what the word would be, positive maybe, dynamic. Her hair was rolled up in front and hanging down behind. She had blood-red lips and eyebrows plucked to hairlines. Underneath, where you slotted the card in, was printed on the album page: 'Gilda Brent, born London, 1920. Real name Gwendoline Miranda Brant. Blonde hair, green eyes. Films include: *HMS Valiant*, *The Skies Above Us*, *The Fiancée*, *The Lady in Lace*, *The Wife's Story*, *Seven for a Secret*, *Lora Cartwright*.'

'They were all sort of supporting roles that she had,' Philippa said. 'She was never the star. No, I tell a lie, she was the star of *The Wife's Story*, but I don't reckon it was much of a box-office success. She never made a film after the mid-fifties. Perhaps she should have gone to Hollywood but I suppose no one asked her.'

It was then that it came into my head that Gilda Brent might have been Stella. The age was wrong, Stella hadn't been born till 1923, but she could have been lying about her age. I hadn't seen her birth certificate and I don't suppose Lena had. Her maiden name could have been Brant and as for the name Stella, you can call yourself what you like, I wouldn't wonder at anyone not liking Gilda. Mum's real name is Doris but she hates it and everyone's always called her Diane. Stella's daughter Marianne is an actress and actresses often have children who are actresses. I was thinking of Judy Garland and Liza Minelli, of Maureen O'Sullivan and Mia Farrow.

'What happened to her?' I said.

'I don't know. She just disappeared. The heyday of British films was over. I reckon there wasn't any work for her. Maybe she got married to some rich tycoon.'

For the first time since the first time, Ned and I met that Thursday without making love. It wasn't just cold, it was pouring with rain. I waited for him at Thelmarsh Cross, feeling miserable and worse than that, feeling *guilty* because it was raining—as if I'd made it rain—and wondering how he'd react when I told him it was no good, I wouldn't do that in the backs of cars.

The marvellous thing was that he already knew, he knew it would be impossible, and he didn't mind. He was fastidious about that sort of thing too. I got into the passenger seat of his car and we kissed, a long sweet kiss that only ended because I heard the watersplash sounds of a car approaching from Curton. I broke away from Ned and looked out of the window and saw that it was the same car I'd seen last time and the same woman at the wheel. It was probably my fancy that she slowed down as she passed us.

'I thought you wouldn't come,' I said, 'because there's nowhere we can be alone.'

'We are alone,' he said.

'Not alone the way I want us to be.'

'Jenny, we don't want each other just for the sex. Does it matter so much if we have an evening or two now when we sit and talk?'

We stayed there for a while and then he drove the seven or eight miles to Newall Pomeroy where there's a little pub, not much frequented, by name the White Swan. The licensee let us sit in a room at the back called the snug, but it was more than we dared even to hold hands. People kept coming in or at any rate putting their heads round the door. Ned talked some more about liking just to be with me, enjoying sitting and talking, and how about coming to the filming with him next day? He knew it was my day off. They were doing a profile of an artist who lives in Wells-next-the-Sea.

I won't pretend it didn't make me happy to be asked. I'd be there with him, the producer, and I'd meet the cameramen and all the crew, the director and perhaps even the artist. We'd eat together and drive to the different locations together and everyone would know who I was and why I was there. It was Ned's way of starting to make a public commitment to me, his way of presenting me to the world and saying: this is my girlfriend that I'll be married to one day. Sad really that I couldn't do it.

'Why can't you, Jenny?'

'Because Jane will get to know.'

'She's going to have to know sometime. I'm not planning on being a bigamist.'

'No, she isn't going to have to know, Ned. And you know why not. Hannah is why not.'

He started to argue but I said there was no way round that, and there wasn't. Because Hannah wasn't just a little girl of five who needed both her parents. She was a little girl of five with asthma. She was on corticosteroids and uses a nebulizer. That was why Ned had kept going back to Rowans from the village hall that night, because earlier in the day Hannah had had one of her asthma attacks. And when she had them, for some reason it was her dad that she wanted with her. It was not unusual for him to get up four times in the night to see to her.

Yet he could say, 'Marriage comes with an escape clause these days. When you go into it you know that if the worst comes you can get out of it.'

'Not when the worst is a child with asthma.'

It wrenched the heart out of me to say these things, to stand up and resist him when he looked at me like that and pleaded with me. He had such a beautiful, sensitive face, the mouth so soft when he kissed me and so firm when he spoke, his blue eyes so direct. The hand that held mine was brown and long-fingered and cool. He had long taken off the wedding ring he wore when first we met. It was hard to deny him, it was hard to be always saying no. And when I looked out at the rain streaming down the windows, at the dark already closing in, I thought how likely it was there would be no expression of love between us for many months, and it frightened me. I felt as if I was putting him to a test. Would he go on loving me when I couldn't make love to him and all we could do when we were together was talk?

He was driving me back to where my car was at Thelmarsh Cross and talking about the filming again, trying once more to persuade me to come to it, when we came slap-bang up against a tractor, parked under a dripping hedge. Not quite slap-bang, for we didn't hit it. Ned braked just in time and the car jumped and shook, jolting me forward in the tight band of the seat-belt. I don't know why that reminded me of Stella unless it was because she had warned me to drive carefully along these lanes, but one thought leads to another and that led me to Gilda Brent. And he *had* heard of her, he'd once even tried to get her to take part in a film he was making.

'It must be all of fifteen years ago,' he said. 'I was just starting out. I was twenty-three and working in casting. I came upon a photograph of her and got on to her agent. The photograph was old then, probably twenty years old. But I thought it was the sort of face that would wear well. Good genes or good bones. Your face is one of those, Jenny.'

'What was the part you wanted her for?'

'She was sixty by then. It was someone's mother who had been a famous actress in her day. Gilda Brent's face was the face I held in my mind.'

I asked if she had played the part.

'We couldn't find her. Her agent said she was still technically on his books but he hadn't been in touch with her for nearly ten years. She'd disappeared, was the way he put it, which seemed rather too dramatic. I think that that only meant he'd had no offers for her in that time. But even before that—although he didn't quite say so—jobs had been thin on the ground. She'd never worked in television.'

I told him who I thought she was and where she was. Ned said he'd like to meet her. I didn't commit myself to anything, I was going through feelings I always had just before parting from him. They're a mixture of misery at having to separate, coming loneliness, a great inner emptiness and, yes, unsatisfied desire. Even when we've made love the unsatisfied desire remains. Only being with him night and day, living with him and sleeping beside him night after night would end that. And this could never happen.

Remembering what Stella's reaction had been when I obeyed her too promptly, I took my time telling her what I knew about Gilda Brent. It was Monday before I told her what Philippa had said and what I'd got from Ned.

The weekend had been long and dull. Mike went to Norwich on Saturday afternoon to see the Canaries play at home and in the evening he went on with what he'd been doing that morning, refitting the kitchen and painting it, but in such a way as to cause me the minimum inconvenience in the week to come. He's lived with me all these years but, despite all evidence to the contrary, he still believes I spend most of the time I'm at home in the kitchen. That's what women do. Bless him, he calls it 'my' kitchen, he's doing up 'my' kitchen, and it's his way of showing his love for me, it's the only present he knows how to give me. We had Sunday dinner with Mum and Len, an hour with my nan in her bungalow afterwards, and tea at Janis's. In other words, the usual way of getting through two days with no work to fill them.

Going off back to London was a relief to Mike on Monday morning. Of course he didn't show it, it wasn't blatant, he gave me a kiss and said he'd miss me, but when his mate Phil came to pick him up ten minutes early he was all ready and raring to go. He jumped into the car, he was listening to some tale of Phil's and laughing so much he forgot to look back, still less wave goodbye. The fact is that Mike, like a lot of men, best enjoys the company of men, he's happiest with his own sex, and when we go to those village hall dos he always ends up at the bar end with the men he went to school with. He even did, eventually, the night I first met Ned.

When I got to work Stella was in her room finishing her breakfast. But no sooner was I inside admiring the new tape recorder on her desk than my bleeper started, letting me know I was wanted in Arthur's room. Arthur had got his sciatica back, and by the time I'd given him a massage and made an appointment with the physiotherapist it was mid-morning and time for everyone's coffee and biscuits. Stella, for some reason, was the last to get hers. I found her in the lounge on her own, reading Sunday's newspaper, which seemed to me a bit sad, though it shouldn't have as Monday's had arrived as usual and were waiting on the table in the entrance hall.

It seems strange to me now that I could have been so naïve. I had a silly sort of smile on my face as I said, 'She was you, wasn't she? Gilda Brent was you.'

She didn't laugh. She turned to me a grave troubled face and said, 'What gave you that idea?'

'I don't know, I just thought . . . Well, the age was nearly right and you were so mysterious about it. I just thought she must be you.'

'I'm sorry to disappoint you, Jenny. I can see you've put in some research, but I was not Gilda Brent and she was not me.' She added rather oddly, 'I wish she had been.'

Saying that brought the colour into her face, or something did. She put the paper aside. She picked up her coffee cup and sipped from it in a weary sort of way, as if she didn't much care whether she had coffee or not, as if it was something to do to pass the time.

'I was never anything, my dear. Just a secretary for a

while and then a housewife and mother, as Gilda never tired of reminding me.'

She gave me a bright smile and quickly switched it off. Her eyes went back to the paper, though she didn't pick it up again. I thought she was ending our conversation as she sometimes did by simply being indifferent, by shutting off all interest and retreating inside herself.

I was going to take myself away, I had plenty to keep me busy, when she said, as if I'd asked a question, 'Her father was quite a well-known Shakespearean actor called Everard Brant. Of course she was on the stage from a young child. I believe she was actually in *The Tempest* as a sprite or something, or perhaps that was *A Midsummer Night's Dream*. That's how she got into films, because her father was who he was.'

'Did she have any connection with your house?' I said.

She seemed not to hear me. 'By the time I knew her she'd finished with films. She was forty, you see, and being forty then wasn't what it is now. Forty was middle-aged and no one wanted middle-aged film actresses except to play someone's mother and Gilda wasn't that type at all. Oh, no, she'd finished with films or films had finished with her. But she never forgot. She never let anyone forget what she'd been.'

I'd never have thought Stella could be bitchy and the way she was talking surprised me. It made me feel uncomfortable, so I repeated my question about the house, just to deflect her, not because I really cared. Stella gave me an odd look.

'None at all,' she said, and, seeming to think better of that, 'she had nothing to do with it and yet she had everything to do with it. She only went there once and that was

on the day of her death.' She spoke with so much deter-
mination that I could hardly believe it when she looked
up at me, her voice changed, her tone quite wistful and
nervous, and said, 'The person who told you about
Gilda, did she say anything about what happened to her?'

'It was two people,' I said, 'but I'm not sure I know
what you mean, what happened to her.'

'I mean, did they say she was—did they say she was
dead?'

'We didn't talk about that,' I said. 'I didn't know you
wanted to know. You didn't say.'

She had such a look on her face that it began to fright-
en me. It was as if her face had suddenly got much thinner and the features had sharpened. Her cheeks had
flushed, a different, duller colour than the rouge. She put
out her hand and took hold of mine. It wasn't done affec-
tionately but as if she was in need.

'Does it matter, Stella?' I said. 'Do you want to know
if she's dead?'

'Oh, I know, *I* know. Of course she's dead. She's been
dead for twenty-five years. It's not that I want to know. I
want to know if anyone else knows.'

A fit of coughing seized her. It's a horrible dry cough
she has and there's nothing you can do for it. She recov-
ers by herself eventually and lies back, spent, in her chair.
That was what happened and I was still holding on tight
to her hand when I heard the door open behind me and
someone come in. Stella saw her over my shoulder.

She dropped my hand and whispered, 'Don't say anything about this in front of her.'

It was Marianne, back from Corfu.

She's always polite and nice, calling me by my name

and asking me how I am. That over, she threw her arms round Stella the way she does and launched straightaway into a breathless account of her holiday, how wonderful it was and how awful, how dire—that's a favourite word with her—the friend's house they stayed in and how fantastic the weather, how appalling the journey, the kids' behaviour, the food. She's always like that. She calls everyone darling, even me.

I didn't stay, though I hung about just long enough to take in her appearance. She must be forty-one or -two but I don't think she looks any older than me, she's really beautiful, slim and willowy, with strong, regular features, and long chestnut hair. Her skin was tanned a rich golden colour and she hadn't a line on her face. I thought of what Stella had said about Gilda Brent being middle-aged at forty. Marianne made me realize how times had changed.

She unloaded gifts from Corfu and duty-frees all over her mother's chair. Stella wasn't tired any more but suddenly twenty years younger, opening her presents and laughing with delight.

7

Married people sleeping in a double bed together is a strange business. Any bed-sharing for a couple who've been together a long time is strange. Yet I'm sure that that never occurs to most people. When I first started thinking about it—if I'd been happy doing it I don't suppose I ever would have—it suddenly seemed to me one of the oddest things in life.

It isn't as if those same people sit close to each other and hold hands all their leisure time or sit in seats side by side in a restaurant. In fact, though I don't often go to restaurants, when I do someone else will always take care Mike and I don't sit together. It's not supposed to be correct. And in their own home a couple will face each other across a table, not sit in adjoining chairs. But at night they share a bed. Visitors from another time or another planet wouldn't believe it. To them it would seem like a survival from olden days, from the Middle Ages.

In the old Hollywood movies couples have single beds. That makes me wonder if the custom nearly died out in the thirties and came back again for some reason. But what reason? Not for making love, most of those couples never do that, and not for warmth these days. Besides, in our double bed Mike and I never touch each other. But we go on sleeping side by side in that four-foot-six bed and if I asked him why and why not make a change, I know he'd think I'd gone mad.

Double beds should be for new lovers. I need one to share with Ned, for it's only when love is fresh and urgent that a big warm shared bed is right. But all I'm getting now is a pub snug and promises of his devotion and that he'll never change. We kiss and kiss and he asks me to come to Norwich and spend my day off with him and every time I say no, his home ground is too dangerous. I said no once more last time we met but I did promise to watch television the next evening and see a film he'd made. It's another way of getting close to him, though not the way I want.

Your judgement, what Ned calls your critical faculty, doesn't work very well when you're looking at something that's been made by the person you love. I couldn't tell you whether Ned's film was good or not. Normally I'd be bored watching a programme about an old man's memories of Norfolk railways, but of course it was Ned's production so I kept imagining him being there and arranging this and that, choosing this set and that location. His name on the credit titles, 'Producer, Edward Saraman', made my heart jump as it always does when I read it anywhere.

A film was on next and the film was *The Fiancée*.

I was on the point of turning it off. Black and white is disappointing when you're used to colour and I'd picked up the remote to switch off when I saw the name Gilda Brent come up on the screen, well below the stars, John Mills, Googie Withers, Bernard Miles. Coincidence, I thought, but it wasn't really. I expect all her films come up on TV from time to time, only I never noticed them before Stella told me her name.

The story was set in World War II and it was about a woman turning up at a great mansion in the country, the kind of place only aristocratic people live in, and telling the couple who own it she's their dead son's fiancée that he got engaged to just before he was killed on a bombing raid over Germany. Googie Withers was the fiancée and John Mills the son who turns out not to be dead after all. Gilda Brent was his sister, a suspicious-minded girl who thinks the fiancée is a fraud from the first time she meets her.

She must have been about twenty-five when it was made and she was very good-looking. But I was reminded of what I'd first thought when I saw the drawing on the cigarette card. It wasn't a face to remember, it was a face to be confused about, and it changed a lot as she spoke and moved and the way the light fell on her, so that sometimes she looked like Joan Crawford but sometimes like Veronica Lake or even Valerie Hobson. I don't know about her acting ability. Ned says you didn't have to be able to act if you were in films in those days. Her voice was one of those voices they all had, upper class, clear, ringing, and if you heard a woman speaking like that now you'd cast up your eyes.

It was something to tell Stella about next morning but by the time I'd seen to Gracie and got Arthur into his chair it was past nine and she was on her way to the hospital for her radiotherapy. Stella is dying, there's no hope of saving her life, but her breathing problems can be relieved, and though she keeps saying there's no point any

more and to let it go, she still has Pauline drive her into
Bury once a fortnight.

Unlike Lena, I don't snoop around the residents' rooms
while they're out. Half of them, certainly the ones who
still have their faculties like Sidney and Lois, and yes,
Stella, would get their children to move them elsewhere if
they knew about Lena reading their letters and looking in
their address books. But when I picked up Stella's breakfast tray, the linen napkin with the tiniest trace of lipstick
on it fell off on to the floor. I bent to pick it up and saw
something white under the bed.

It was a screwed-up piece of paper. Maybe it had been
there for days or maybe only hours. Mary's a good cleaner when it comes to surfaces but not too great on sweeping under things. I shouldn't have read what was written
on the paper, should I? I mean I shouldn't have looked,
because I could scarcely read a word of it. And that's really why I looked and went on looking, scrutinizing it,
because at first I didn't think it was English or even written in the kind of letters we make. It was more a pattern
than a piece of writing, a photo of a piece of lace or a
child's squiggles seen in a mirror. The only words I could
make out, and that with difficulty, were 'Gilda' and something that might, or might not, have been 'disappeared'.

I screwed it up again and threw it in the waste basket.
Sharon caught up with me as I was leaving the room and
said to watch out for Lena because she was in one of her
foul moods.

'She's not getting Edith's money like she thought she
was,' Sharon said. 'Not any of it. Edith left it all to Action
Aid and the Lord Whisky Sanctuary.'

Lena fetched Stella back a bit before lunchtime. She

gave me one of her grins that aren't smiles. When she was a child people didn't take their kids to dentists much, which is why she never had a brace and her upper teeth stick out.

'Lady Newland's been moaning all the way back about my driving,' she said. 'Much too fast for her ladyship, apparently.'

She says these things in a comedienne's voice and with a bright smile, as if that makes every offensive remark all right. Stella was tired, but she had some spirit left. She sat down in the lounge, looked up at Lena and said,

'I am not the widow of a knight or a baronet.'

'You what?'

'I'd prefer you to call me Mrs Newland, but since that seems too difficult or too formal, Stella will do.'

It took courage for her to say it and the effort made her breathless. Lena looked at her open-mouthed.

'We're all on first name terms here, I hope. Mrs, indeed. That *would* be too formal these days. Oh, definitely. You have to go with the flow, Stella, remember that, you have to go with the flow.'

Stella didn't cry until Lena had gone and then it wasn't noisy crying, just a tear from each eye running down her cheeks. I sat down beside her, in such a way as to shield her from Maud's view. Maud was by the french window, craning her neck to get a good look and an earful if possible. So I whispered. Stella isn't hard of hearing but Maud is.

'You don't want to let her get you down. She's crabby because she hasn't come into Edith's money.'

Stella tried to smile. 'Did she expect to? Oh, dear. It's not her, Jenny, it's—well, I'm tired and sometimes—

sometimes I feel bad about things.'

'This'll cheer you up,' I said.

On the way in that morning, walking across the grass from the parking place to the back door, I'd found a four-leaved clover. For the first time for days it wasn't raining. I'm like Mum, when I walk over a field or through grass anywhere I always look down at the clover in the hope of spotting a four-leaved one. They're not as uncommon as you might think. I found one back in July and gave it to Ned to bring him luck with the film he was making in France. He wore it in his buttonhole till it was dried up and unrecognizable. But this time I'd done what I often do, pressed the triune leaf between two bits of paper. I'd meant to keep it for myself but Stella's need was greater than mine.

'What is it, Genevieve? A shamrock?'

'It's a four-leaved clover and about the best luck-bringer you can think of.'

'Better than spotted dogs?' she said.

'Much better.' I'm used to being teased about my protection beliefs and I don't mind. I don't suppose you do mind if you're confident your faith can't be shaken. 'You put it inside a book and press it and it'll last for years.'

She was smart today, the way she especially is when she has to go out somewhere. Her generation dressed up to go to the shops, let alone for a hospital appointment in town. She had on a flowered dress and jacket and pearls round her neck, fine pale stockings and cream-coloured court shoes. Lena in her green cardigan over a shocking pink track-suit—why are track-suits and shell-suits always pink or purple or emerald-green?—wouldn't have liked that much.

Stella seemed indifferent to the four-leaved clover but she was tired and she'd been through a lot that morning, so I found the book she was reading and slipped it inside like a bookmark. I thought she'd want a sleep but when I'd put a blanket over her knees and was halfway to the door she put out her hand and said,

'No, Jenny, stay with me a while. Tell me, did you watch the film last night?'

'*The Fiancée*?' I said. 'I wanted to see what Gilda Brent was like. It wasn't very good, was it?'

'I didn't watch. It was so late.' She corrected herself. 'That's not the real reason. I saw it years ago, when it was first made. And then again, at a cinema with her. With Gilda, I mean. She used to like me to go to the pictures with her and see her in her films. I don't think I could face it now. Well, I wouldn't even try.' The little laugh she gave had a tinny sound. 'I couldn't bear to see her.'

I sat down on the edge of the bed. 'You said she was dead. What did she die of?'

I thought she wasn't going to answer, she took so long about it. First she hung her head and put one hand up to her forehead. But she took that hand down with the other hand and forced it into her lap as if putting it up there had been a sign of weakness. Her chin went up and I thought her lips quivered a little before she spoke.

'She died in a car crash.'

'What, soon after she stopped making films?'

'Years and years after that,' Stella said. 'You notice I said she died *in* a car crash, not *of* a car crash. I don't know quite how she died.'

I was bewildered and must have shown it. 'I shouldn't have told you that, Genevieve. You mustn't repeat it to anyone at all. You won't tell anyone, will you?'

'Who can I tell?' I said. My world isn't exactly full of people who are longing to know how some obscure old film actress met her end. 'I don't know anyone to tell.'

'No. I suppose that's why I've told you as much as I have. But that—friend of yours, the television man?'

It's unpleasant the way we have no control over our blushes. My face felt fiery. 'I won't say anything to Ned.'

'Good. That's sweet of you. I know I can trust you, Jenny. I'd like to tell you things about my life, I will tell you one day, but I have to be allowed to choose what I tell. Do you understand?'

It was that 'one day' that struck me. Stella wasn't going to have a 'one day' and part of her mind knew it as well as I did. But I suppose we're so in the habit of talking about what we'll do 'one day' and 'next year' and 'sometime' that when a limit's been put on our lives we forget we haven't a future. She changed the subject quite abruptly.

'You haven't been to an estate agent, have you?'

I said I wouldn't do that unless she asked me.

'No. Of course you wouldn't. It's just that so much is taken out of one's hands in here and so many people treat one as if one is in one's second childhood. I mean, I wouldn't have been surprised to find my house was already on the market and droves of people making offers.' My face must have shown her how unjust she was being. She put out her hand and touched mine. 'No, you're different from the rest of them, Genevieve. You wouldn't do that.'

'And Richard is different,' I said.

She seemed surprised. 'You're right. He is.'

'Stella, I'll go to an estate agent any time you like,' I said, 'but as for droves of people making offers—it's been empty for all those years, it's very dirty, it's quite dilapidated looking. It'll be quite hard to sell the way it is.'

The tired look came back. 'Do you mean it's going to need repairing and redecorating?'

'It's going to need cleaning up first.' I don't know why I said it, I don't know why I made the offer. It's not as if I like that kind of work or am much good at it. The most likely explanation is that I saw it as a way of spending my day off that was not sitting at home wishing I was with Ned in Norwich and reproaching myself for having scruples. 'Would you like me to clean your house, Stella?'

The 13th. Not the best of days to undertake any enterprise. Mum's wedding to Ron was on the 13th and look what happened to that marriage. But I didn't have much choice, my day off fell on that day, and anyway I couldn't think what could go wrong—a fatal attitude when it comes to ignoring signs and portents, as anyone in our family will tell you.

I set off early for Molucca, just after eight, and along with the spray polish and sink cleaner and cloths I had the sense to take the Dustette with me. It works on a battery which was essential in a place where the electricity was turned off. Mike gave it to me last Christmas and I said it was lovely, taking care not to point out that it was him put most of the mud on the carpets and made the crumbs at mealtimes. As it turned out, taking a Dustette and two J-cloths to clean up Stella's house was like trying to climb Everest in a pair of trainers and carrying a can of Coke.

It wasn't a nice day but grey and windy, though maybe it would have been worse to have had the sun pouring in to show up more of that dust. I don't know what dust is, what is it, that fine grey powdery stuff? It's not something you ever see anywhere else. I mean, it's not crumbs or hairs or fluff, it's not lint off your clothes or fur off animals, it's not ash or iron filings or wood shavings. It's dust and it's made of nothing and comes from nowhere to cover everything everywhere. I suppose that if all the people in the world died of some plague and just the buildings were left, in time they'd be hidden under a layer of dust.

I started in the living room. I opened the window, which was no easy task in itself, and I shook the rugs out on to the grass. It was like the desert storm in *Lawrence of Arabia.* The oil painting of Stella when young I dusted carefully with a soft cloth, removing the grey film which had dulled the pink of her dress and the gleam of her pearls. I worked on all the furniture, shaking my cloth out of the window. By the time I'd dusted all the surfaces and brushed the upholstery, got all the dirt on to the carpet, and sucked it all up, the battery had run out on the Dustette.

Something I hadn't noticed the first time was that there was a deep dent in the wall facing the fireplace, as if it had been struck a blow hard enough to tear the wallpaper. And when I got the silver polish out and started cleaning the silver, I saw that there was a dent in one of the bowls. It looked as if someone had once thrown the bowl at the wall, damaging both. I cleaned all the silver until I couldn't bear the smell of the cleaner any longer or the feel of the grainy pink powder on my hands.

The kitchen and the bathroom should have been

easier than the living rooms because they had no carpets. But they had no hot water either, and I hadn't the means of heating it. Still, I managed to get the worst off the sink and the basin and half-shifted the ring round the bath. The windows were easier because the stuff to clean them comes out of a bottle, not a cold trickle from a tap.

At twelve I stopped for a bit and ate the sandwiches I'd brought with me. Though I'd failed before, this time I could clearly see Middleton Hall far away in the distance beyond the brown ploughed fields and the white goose fields. It made me think about Stella and wonder what went on in her head, what was the reason for being so mysterious about Gilda Brent and what she'd meant about telling me everything 'one day'. Gilda had been to this house once, she'd said, and had died in a car crash. Was that why Stella didn't like going out in cars and hated fast driving, because of the way Gilda had died?

All the women in our family see ghosts from time to time. Mum has seen most. She regularly sees the Man in the Grey Suit who walks across the bedroom that's above the saloon bar. The Thundering Legion was once the courthouse and jail and a murderer spent his last night of liberty there, pacing that room, before being sent to the Assizes and hanged. Janis saw her friend's spaniel and *touched* him a week after the dog had been put down, and as for my nan, in the days when she worked for Mr Thorn's father at the Hall, she saw the Brown Lady twice, on three occasions heard the voice that calls out, 'Elizabeth, Elizabeth!', and smelt the gunpowder smell untold times. That was why I wouldn't have been surprised to have turned round from that window and seen Gilda Brent standing there. She'd have been grey like the dust, grey like she was in the black-and-white film, and maybe wearing the long evening dress in which she'd looked so beautiful in *The Fiancée*, an off-the-shoulder gown with a draped bodice and the skirt a sweep of trailing chiffon, her long blonde hair grey and her face, that was like so many different film-stars' faces, carved in marble.

I turned and there was no one there. And I had to admit the house didn't have that feel about it, that unmistakable, haunted feel when you sense all the time that someone is watching you and where the air is full of tiny whisperings and unexplained sounds. All I felt about Stella's house was that it was waiting for something. Perhaps only for someone to live in it. I went into the bedroom and started cleaning in there, with a broom and a dustpan and brush this time. After I'd got the worst of the dust swept up, I took down the curtains. There was nothing to be done with those curtains but take them home with me and see if I could get them clean or if they'd fall to pieces in the wash.

Between the door to the furnished bedroom and the door to one of the empty bedrooms was an airing cupboard. The linen inside felt damp but it wasn't growing mould. I knew I'd have to come back and finish, it was impossible to get it all done that day, so I took out a pair of sheets and four pillowcases and spread them out on chairs in front of the window for the sun to air them—if we got any sun. Then I stripped the bed and put the bedclothes in a pillowcase to take home with me and wash.

Down in the kitchen again, I wondered what Mike would say if he saw it. The thought made me laugh to myself because Mike is a regular fusspot about things like that. He'd probably start on that kitchen straightaway, prising out chipped tiles and screwing on loose handles.

The first time I was there I hadn't looked inside the fridge. Its door was shut. If you go away and leave a fridge with the power turned off you should always leave the door open or the dampness inside will grow mould. When that happens, no matter how much you clean and air it, the mouldy smell never goes away. I opened the door and looked inside, prepared for the worst.

Mould had been there and a fungus like grey velvet but that was long ago. Nothing remained now but dust, more dust that covered shapeless lumps of what had once been food but which now couldn't be identified as more than a branch of something, a wedge of something. Except for one item on which the dust didn't lie: a bottle of champagne. Bollinger, the real stuff, with gold paper round its top and that sort of gold net they decorate the bottles with. It was lying on one of the shelves among the grey ghosts of food as if it had been put there to chill, but the celebration, or whatever it had been bought for, had never taken place.

Opening the broom cupboard I noticed something else I hadn't seen when I'd been there the first time. There was a row of cuphooks on the back wall and on every hook hung a key, six in all. Some must have fitted the locks on interior doors. The biggest fitted the back-door lock and another slightly smaller one the door into the garage. I unlocked that door and went into the garage to have a look at the red car.

There it rested on its flat tyres. It wasn't locked and there was no key in the ignition. I opened the driver's door and got in, leaned across the driving seat and had a look round. The side pockets were bare and the glove compartment was empty. Nothing was on the back seat and nothing on the floor. When Stella told me that Gilda Brent had died in a car crash I'd had an idea it might have been in this car, I'd thought that perhaps she'd crashed this car and after that someone close to her had never wanted to see it again and got Stella to store it. But the only marks on the car weren't the sort a crash makes. They were burn marks. The car was dusty, coated in a layer of dust that had never been disturbed since it was put in there, but when I wiped that away I could see that the bodywork was singed all over the boot and around it and above the rear wheels. Its red paint was blackened and in the worst parts bubbled so that in places it had flaked off to show the grey metal underneath.

I pulled up the boot lid. The tools were inside, and the spare wheel. There was something else too, a square scarf in emerald-green chiffon, rumpled, loose, looking as if someone had dropped it uncaring on the boot floor. I took it out. It may have lain there for twenty-five years but it was quite clean and it still smelt of something, a very stale, musky perfume. Green is a colour Stella never wears, very wise in my opinion as nothing could be more unlucky, so the scarf couldn't be hers unless her tastes had changed. I took it into the kitchen and hung it over the back of a chair.

The sight of it hanging there carried me back sixteen years to something I'd hardly thought of in all that time: Janis and me divining for our true loves in the kitchen at home on St John's Eve. We'd performed the prescribed ritual, laid the table with a supper of bread and cheese, then taken off all our clothes and hung them over the backs of two chairs. I had a green skirt that my dad had given me, to defy Mum I suppose, and that's what I hung over the rest of my things. We left the back door on the jar and went upstairs, waiting and listening for the men to come.

I was frightened when I heard the footsteps, much more frightened than Janis was, though she was younger, and at first I wouldn't go down, I wouldn't even look over the banisters. But she got hold of my hands and dragged me and we found Peter in the kitchen, eating our supper and drinking a Coke he'd got out of the fridge. She swore she hadn't invited him, she hardly knew him then apart from being in the same class at primary school—but seven years later she married him. So was he her true love?

As for me, no one came. Not my boyfriend of the time, not Mike, not Ned of course, casting his shadow before him. I put it down to the green skirt and I've never worn green since. The scarf, the colour and the square shape of it, brought all that back, but I left it hanging on the chair, not knowing what else to do with it.

Then I remembered the photograph I'd promised to fetch. This time I could see the woman was Stella, but the man no longer seemed like anyone I knew. The stony, cliff-like background now plainly appeared as what it was, the flint wall of Molucca. Over the years the happiness in the picture was still radiant, the charge between the man and the woman, the heat of love.

It made me think of Ned. I was walking down the passage to the front door, I'd got my hand on the discoloured brass knob, when a thought came to me. Why shouldn't Ned and I use this house on the cold, dark winter evenings? We had nowhere else to go and it would be months before the spring. I had a key. No one would know. Why shouldn't we come here to Stella's house?

8

A year ago I wouldn't have dreamt of doing something like that without asking permission. I've said that doing one wrong thing has made me more conscientious in other areas of my life, but it isn't true. When it's love in question and being alone with the person you love, considerations of morality and decent behaviour disappear.

Love is all and it justifies everything. That's what I tell myself and I don't listen to the cold, quiet inner voice that says otherwise. Love doesn't listen to it either but puts forward very convincing arguments: Stella had entrusted me with a key, she was happy for me to clean the place, if she decided to sell she would let me handle the selling of it. I was practically the caretaker. To spend a couple of hours there once in a while was taking it one step further, that's all.

Stella made no mention of the house when I saw her in the morning. Perhaps she had forgotten or else she could think of nothing but being taken out somewhere by Richard. This was odd in itself. With her fear of cars, Stella only goes in them for essential journeys: to her radiotherapy, to the dentist. She didn't tell me where she was going but she dressed up for it in the blue spotted dress with her cream linen coat over it and she was wearing all her rings, the engagement ring with the sapphires and the eternity ring that's a hoop of diamonds which she wears on her other hand.

Richard arrived at nine-thirty. He was wearing a suit but a lightweight one, made to look quite casual, and carrying a parcel. I saw him from the window of Maud's room. He walked over from the car park to the front door the way he always does, lively and brisk, looking as if he enjoys life, yet as if he thinks a lot too. He's not one of those happy-go-lucky, easy-going people whose heads are empty. Thinking seems to make us sad as often as not, and it's rare to find a clever, sensitive person who's also carefree. That reminded me of Ned, as so many sights and thoughts do, and made me think of his frequent sadness and the frustrations of his life.

The reading stand Stella had asked for was on the bed when I went into her room after she and Richard had gone. That must have been what was in the parcel. Stella had left her book on it, the place marked with the four-leaved clover I'd given her. I was the one it had brought the luck to, though, and on the 13th. As Mum always says, those four-leaves are a powerful charm.

It was a lovely day at last, the rain all swept away into the North Sea, and I was walking back from settling Sidney in his chair under the mulberry tree, when Richard came down the steps from the front door. He hadn't had Stella out for long.

'Only as far as Diss,' he said, though I hadn't asked.

'Was she all right in the car?'

'She was fine.' He smiled. 'I drive very slowly when she's with me. I'm a menace to everyone else on the road.

They all hoot at me and Mother says how noisy the roads have got, nobody ever used their horn in the old days.'

That made me laugh. He'd said it very kindly and lovingly, not in Lena's way which is to send up the old folks. I asked if Stella had had her morning coffee out, because it was almost midday, but he said they hadn't stopped for that, he had taken just a few hours off and now he had to get back to the medical centre.

'Mother had some business to see to. I took her to the door and came back for her after an hour.'

I said it was a long way for him to come when one of us could have taken her, I could have taken her.

'I know you could,' he said. 'I'll remember that next time.' He hesitated. 'It's very strange, isn't it, this car phobia of hers. It started when I was a child. I can remember when I was a little boy of six or seven I loved tunnels and a big treat was for her to take me and a friend and drive us through the Dartford Tunnel and back. It must have been a bore for her but she didn't complain. She was quite a dashing driver, and very stylish.'

'Her fear of cars started soon after that?' I said.

'I've always connected it with my father's death, though he died when I was six and I'm sure we did that Dartford Tunnel thing after that. Anyway, Dad didn't die in a car crash, he died in a train. Well, he was taken ill in a train. He died in hospital.'

'Did your mother just stop driving?'

'Yes, but a good while later. I can't remember when and it's not the sort of thing I can ask her, though I don't quite know why I say that. A bit of a mystery, isn't it? I must be off. I've got a surgery at one.'

Stella must have brought her children up on her own

then, a boy of six and a girl of—what? Fourteen? Fifteen? It gave me a surprise. I had thought of her as being widowed perhaps five years before. But Richard is the same age as me, which means his father had been dead for twenty-six years, or as they always say in the papers, more than a quarter of a century. I wondered why he couldn't ask her the reason for her car phobia, but he seemed not to know the reason himself, only to know perhaps that he would be approaching an area Stella always kept private.

She stayed in her room for the rest of the day and in the afternoon she had a long sleep. I looked in once and saw her lying on the bed, wrapped in her black satin dressing-gown, her eyes closed and her breathing steady and peaceful. On the dot of four I left, called in at home to pick up the clean curtains, and at the village store in Curton bought up their entire stock of candles. If I'd done that in Tharby it would have made for talk. 'Your Jenny was in here, Diane, and she's cleaned me right out of them decorative candles we got in for Christmas. What's she want them for, then? Her and Mike've never had their electric cut off, have they?' But I doubt if a Tharby woman has ever set foot in the Curton shop, though it's only four miles distant. I never had since I was a child and my dad used to take me across the road and buy me Maltesers.

Having re-charged the Dustette battery overnight, I did a bit more cleaning. I even managed to heat up some water on the oil stove, though it was a slow process. The curtains had faded in the wash and were raggedy round the hems, but they looked a lot better than they had done. I hung them up. A day of sunshine had dried the sheets I'd spread out. I made up the bed and when the kettle boiled at last I put in a hot-water bottle.

It was a fine evening, though autumnal. But autumn is the prettiest time in the fen when the dogwood turns dark red and the elder fades to yellow. The old man's beard was a mass of silky grey hair and the willowherb underneath it white like goose down. Long tree shadows fell in stripes across the grass in front of the house and the setting sun was a glitter behind the darkness of the woods. Everything was still and windless, and there was a fresh greenness in the grass and the wild plants from all the rain, like a false spring. I picked some sprays of mountain ash berries from the tree by the door and put them in a blue china vase. Tomorrow, I thought, I'll strip our garden of dahlias and chrysanths before the first frost gets them and bring them here and fill the place with flowers.

Before leaving I went round the back and had another look at that car through the garage window. I don't know why, but now I liked the house, now I had done so much to the house and made it better, I didn't like that car being there. It was the flaw that spoiled the whole, as Ned once said about something quite different. It was the maggot, plum-coloured and wriggling, you find inside the Victoria plum that looked perfect on the outside. I told myself it was only an old Ford Anglia, it couldn't hurt anyone, it probably wasn't even drivable. It was no more important than the rusty hulks of cars you sometimes come upon in the depths of the fen, dumped long ago and overgrown now with wild hops and brambles.

Springing surprises isn't always a good idea. Janis and Nick and I had planned a surprise for Mum on her fifti-eth birthday. She knew something was going on and she let us blindfold her and walk her to Nick's car, didn't say a word when we drove her round and round to put her off the scent, but she wasn't too pleased when she found herself in the village hall and a hundred of her friends and relations waiting for her, singing Happy Birthday to You. You see, she'd worked it all out and she thought the surprise was going to be a show in London, in the West End, *Miss Saigon* or *Les Misérables,* and a night afterwards for her and Len at the Strand Palace Hotel. All that driving around made it worse because she reckoned we were taking her to the mainline station at Diss.

So I knew it was a risk arranging a surprise for Ned, but I couldn't see what could go wrong, and in the event nothing did. He was all amazement and appreciation. The scent of the flowers I'd brought took away the musty smell and the evening was too mild to bother with the oil heater. I'd put blue candles with gold stars on them on the dressing cabinet and a red sugarstick candle on each bedside cabinet. He once said he liked Australian Chardonnay, so I'd got a bottle of that and kept it cool by running cold water over it in the sink. While I waited for him to come I washed and polished Stella's crystal glasses I had found in the sideboard.

He was a bit early, which was good because it meant I didn't have to wait and worry. And when he came in and put his arms around me I felt that this was how it would be every evening if we lived together. I showed him round. I showed him everything except the two empty rooms and the car. It was as if the house belonged to me and I was offering it to him.

'I hope it takes your friend months to sell,' he said.

'Only months?'

'It isn't going to be many months before you and I are living together, when we're beyond needing borrowed houses and—' he put out his finger to the flame that made a glow by the bed— 'Christmas candles in September.'

That made me smile but it embarrassed me too because when I bought the twisty red candles I hadn't noticed that the pattern on them was holly leaves and mistletoe. Still, I liked him always saying we'd be together one day, we'd have our own home, even though I knew we never would. It's what women say and then complain because men don't. Men say, let's enjoy what we have, or, let's not waste time making plans—at least, according to Mum they do. With us the roles are reversed, he talks of permanency and I try to live in the present.

He wouldn't drink the wine, he said we didn't need wine, and maybe he'd have a glass later. It's love, he says, that turns him on. He needs nothing else. Tell me you love me is what he says, and telling him that is no hardship for me. I loved him more than ever that evening. He held me against his body in Stella's warm, soft bed, all the length of him and all the length of me, folded into each other and fitting each other so closely, and took his mouth from kissing me and said,

'It's been so long, Jenny. Don't let it ever be so long again.'

He is a lean brown man with long bones and flat muscles. I like the silky dark hair on his head, almost black, and the two peaks of hair on the nape of his neck. No, I love it. I love the smell of him, which doesn't come out of a can or a bottle and isn't sweat, but the smell of skin and hair and nails. His teeth taste of minty water and his tongue is clean and smooth like a live fish. When I tell him these things he says I'm like whoever it was wrote the Song of Solomon in the Bible.

'Behold, thou art fair, my love; thou hast doves' eyes within thy locks.'

'I never said that,' I said. 'I don't even know what it means.'

'And you never said my hair was like a flock of goats or my neck a tower of David, but you've got the general idea.'

'Would you mind if I said those things?' I said.

'I don't mind what you say, Jenny. You can write poetry to me if you like. If you love everything about someone you don't mind.'

Did Nan's love philtre do all this? Would he have loved me anyway even if I hadn't slipped that powerful charm into his drink? I'm glad I didn't risk it, I didn't leave it to chance, and I'll bolster it up when I can.

He closed his eyes. I held his head on my shoulder and gently stroked his hair but when he was asleep—I knew he would sleep only briefly—I slipped out of bed and found his clothes and put a fern leaf I'd kept from Edith's funeral into his left shoe. For if a woman does that, Nan says, without fail the man will love her marvellously.

The remission Stella was having, due to the radiotherapy I suppose, went on right into October. She still had secret cigarettes in the grounds of Middleton Hall, sitting on a stone bench and wrapped up in her thick winter coat, and she still claimed to dislike cars, though she went out a couple more times for rides with Richard. According to Pauline, she still ventured into the dining room for her evening meal, asked for her gin and tonic, her glass of wine and sat alone at her own table.

Marianne came from London to see her. She arrived in her boyfriend's car with the boyfriend, a very tall, rather fat man, and the teenagers from Stella's photograph, Jean-Paul and Kelda. Those two don't speak to their nan but sit about sullenly or else explore her room, picking up books or looking inside her desk. They were on their way to stay with a friend of Marianne's who has a big house called Something Grange near Sandringham. Though an actress, Marianne never seems to have any work and she has friends living in mansions and castles all over the place who all want her to come and stay.

Stella hadn't said any more about selling Molucca. It's funny how when we worry about having not confessed something, we try to make up for it by telling the person something else, some other semi-secret thing. Ned says it's what psychologists call displacement. I wasn't going to tell her Ned and I had spent three evenings in her house and had made love in her bed, I wasn't going to say a word about the scarf in the boot of the car, because then she'd think I'd been prying. But I did tell her about the champagne.

It had an effect on her I hadn't anticipated. She spoke like someone who's got a stammer, like someone with a stammer who can control it after muddling up the first few words.

'Genevieve—Genevieve, did we really leave that in the fridge? It—it *can't* be. After so long? Oh, Genevieve.'

Who's 'we', I thought, but of course I didn't ask. 'I don't suppose it's drinkable now.'

'I don't know, I don't know. Isn't wine better for keeping?'

She looked very pale and shocked, so I told her the tale of how when they were doing some restorations at the Legion, Mum found a bottle of port pushed into an old bread oven behind the fireplace. Someone must have put it there to warm and then forgotten it, so it had got warm and cold and warm and cold for about a hundred years. It smelt fine and Mum and the workmen thought they'd have it for their tea but when they drew the cork it tasted like a mixture of vinegar and paint.

Before I'd finished I could tell Stella hadn't been listening. Her eyes glittered. They had a feverish look. 'Genevieve,' she said, 'I must have a cigarette. I'm going to have a cigarette.'

It would have been less against Lena's rules if Stella had taken all her clothes off and gone running down the passage to Arthur's room. I said it was risky, I said that if she'd had a shock I'd gladly fetch her a nip of brandy.

'I hate brandy,' she said and she got a cigarette out of her bag and lit it. She closed her eyes and drew in the smoke. In fact, she'd smoked it all and stubbed it out before Lena smelt it and came in.

Lena pulled a tissue out of Stella's box. She picked the cigarette end out of Stella's saucer, wrapped it in the tissue, and picked up the saucer that was full of ash and streaked with wet brown stain. Of course she couldn't say much to Stella. Stella was paying her £20,000 a year. All she could do was stage a coughing attack and open Stella's window as wide as it would go. I was to bear the brunt of it, as I knew I would.

She got me outside and had a real go at me. I was spending too much time with Stella; if Stella wanted a private nurse she had better make other arrangements.

And as for that cigarette! You'd have thought she'd caught poor Stella putting cocaine up her nose.

'It's so disgusting in one of these old crumblies. Wouldn't you think that a person who has brought herself to the brink of death through a vile habit would at least have the sense to give it up now?'

That was about as illogical as fitting a smoke alarm after your house has burned down, but I didn't say so. I didn't say anything much beyond being sorry. I knew Lena wouldn't sack me. She'd been advertising for more staff for months and had only had one reply and that was from a woman of seventy whose last job had been gutting fish on the beach at Lowestoft. People don't want to work with the elderly, they don't have the patience, they can't cope with deafness and loss of memory, let alone incontinence, and besides, there's no money in it.

But I was discreet about going back to Stella. In fact, I waited till it was going-home time. After that I'd be just one of Stella's visitors, free to stay and talk as long as I liked. Usually when I go in she's reading the paper or doing the crossword or listening to a concert on the radio, or she's got her latest book. This time she was just sitting. She'd closed the window and she was staring at the tree-tops and the white sky. When she heard the door open she turned round and smiled at me and put out her hand.

'I got you into trouble, Genevieve. I'm so sorry. Was it very awful?'

She spoke as if I was a little girl at school, perhaps *her* little girl, who'd had a telling off from the head teacher. It irritated me a bit because sometimes I felt in an odd way older than Stella, older in experience, older in life. I was still thinking of her as having been sheltered from everything, a protected woman who'd never had to earn her own living, and what she said next—what she said quite unexpectedly—just confirmed that.

'I want to tell you something. It's about my house. I bought that house when my father died. He left me *his* house, that was all he left me, it was all he had, and I sold it and bought Molucca. It was something of my own, you see. I had nothing of my own, everything was my husband's, even the house we lived in in Bury was entirely in his name.'

'I didn't know you could do that,' I said.

'You could and can. Plenty of men had the houses they shared with their wives in their own name. Rex wouldn't have considered putting the house in my name as well. Of course he left it to me, it was mine when he died, but I'd had Molucca for five years before he died.'

'I don't suppose he minded you having it, did he?' I said. 'I mean, it was your money if your father left it to you.'

'I don't know if he'd have minded,' Stella said, and she gave a little laugh. Her laughter is very sweet and warm, though growing hoarse these days. 'He didn't know.'

He didn't know, I thought, and your children don't know . . . 'But why?'

'It was private, Genevieve.'

I tried to picture how Mike would react if my dad died and left me his house. Well, my dad doesn't own a house and he wouldn't leave it to me if he did, but one can still imagine.

'Didn't he want to know what you did with the money?'

She didn't answer. 'You don't know what it was like

when I was young, Jenny. My children don't know what it was like. I didn't have a bank account. My husband did, of course, but it wasn't a joint account. He gave me the housekeeping money every month and an allowance for myself but it was very small and most of it got absorbed in the housekeeping anyway.'

But for nine years till Richard came along you only had Marianne, I thought. 'You never worked?'

'People always say that.' Her voice held a weary note. 'That was what Gilda said. People don't realize it's very hard work making a home and looking after a child and entertaining one's husband's friends. I had very little help, just a charwoman once a week. I was expected to give a dinner party single-handed at least once a fortnight. No one but a wife would do that sort of work and not get paid for it. Besides, my husband wouldn't have let me take a job.'

It seemed a good idea to get her off the subject, but I couldn't help thinking of what my nan says. If work was such a good thing, the rich would have kept it for themselves.

'So you bought Molucca?'

For £4,000, she said.

These days it would fetch £60,000, yet she'd held on to it and paid council tax on it, and she was the one talking about getting no wages for being a housewife.

'That was what your dad left you?'

'He left me his house and when it was sold it fetched nearly £5,000. I needed some extra to pay the charges to the estate agent and the legal fees. I had to buy furniture.' She rested her head back against the cushion, tired from so much talking and tired too perhaps from her long day.

'I'll tell you something about myself when I was young,' she said. 'I'll tell you tomorrow.'

When I walked into the house the phone was ringing. I expected it to be Mike and it was Ned. Sometimes it's such happiness to hear his voice unexpectedly but such a shock too that I have to sit down before I can talk to him. And there are times when my voice won't come, or comes hoarsely, because for some reason I'm seized by fear.

He wanted to tell me he had to go to Denmark on Monday. They were filming in Copenhagen, something about how to make a modern city in the European Union without losing the old style of the place or spoiling the skyline with tower blocks. He'd be away four days and he wanted me to go with him.

I'd told him I had holiday owing me and Lena'd said she'd like me to take some of it soon. There was no reason that he could see why I couldn't go, Mike would be away in London as usual, by the sound of her my mother would cover for me, and he thought it likely I'd never been to a foreign country.

Oh yes, I had, I said, I'd been to Mallorca and Tenerife. I didn't say the first was for our honeymoon and the second our tenth wedding anniversary, both fixed up as surprises by Mike.

'Mallorca and Tenerife aren't foreign countries,' he said. 'They're tourist bedrooms with beaches. You'll love Copenhagen, we'll stay at the d'Angleterre, and I'll take you to Tivoli.'

Of course I couldn't go. I couldn't dream of it. There were all the usual reasons, the film crew talking, Jane finding out, Hannah, lying to Mike about where I was, and one other reason. I had never thought of it before and I didn't say anything about it to Ned, but I knew that if I spent whole days with him and slept beside him all night, if I did this for days and nights, it would be worse for me afterwards, it would make our separations more painful and our final parting, whenever that came, like death to me.

'Don't ask me that kind of thing again,' I said.

My voice must have sounded gruff and cross. It was all I could manage because I longed so to laugh and gasp and say, yes, oh yes, *please*. And when he rang off he was cross too, disappointed, and telling me I was unreasonable.

'Till the week after then,' he said. 'I'll phone.'

I went upstairs and lay on the bed and cried. Mike came home about an hour later. I heard Phil's car and then the front door and I was up splashing my face with cold water, but if it was still puffy Mike didn't notice. He'd bought me a new kind of cheese grater from a special shop in Soho and a hundred grams of Parmesan in a lump so that I could make pasta taste more like it does in an Italian restaurant.

'The London work's stopping by the end of the month,' he said. 'It'll be a relief to be done with all this travelling. And I reckon you'll be glad too, won't you, girl?'

'Of course I will,' I said, and I wonder what it does to you, saying these things, not lying about what's happened but denying your innermost feelings. It must eat you like rust corroding metal.

'I thought of building us a conservatory,' Mike said. 'What d'you reckon? On the back of the dining room, maybe fifteen foot long. It'd keep me busy in the evenings.'

I sat down with the dictionary. An encyclopedia and *Chambers Dictionary* are what keep me busy in the evenings as I look up long words and try to learn about unknown things. It's my way of keeping up with Ned, who is cleverer than I am and knows so much more.

Part Two

9

Stella was born in London, or about ten miles outside it rather, in a place called Wanstead. Her father worked for the Customs and Excise and her mother was a minister's daughter. They had a semi-detached house off an arterial road called Eastern Avenue.

'I expect you went to a co-ed school, didn't you, Genevieve?' she said.

I didn't know what she meant and I was still puzzled when she explained. As far as I knew, all schools were mixed-sex but for a few places like Eton, and I think they have girls now too.

'They were quite a rarity when I was a child,' Stella said. 'But I went to one, so I was used to meeting a lot of boys. I wasn't one of those girls who leave school scarcely knowing any boys.'

She was nearly sixteen when World War II started and her parents were so frightened of bombs that they sent her away to stay with an aunt in Bury. The aunt was really her mother's cousin and Stella was fond of her and had spent holidays in her house in Churchgate Street. Before she left London she'd just passed her School Certificate, which was the exam they did not just in the days before

GCSEs, but before O Levels. They transferred her to a school in Bury and she stayed there for two years and passed another exam called a Higher.

'I didn't want to leave London,' she said. 'Well, what I mean by that is I didn't want to leave my—' she hesitated—'my friend, my best friend. Our school was evacuated, I could have gone with our school, they went to the Essex coast somewhere, but my mother wouldn't have that. She thought I wouldn't be properly looked after. Really, she meant I wouldn't be properly supervised—chaperoned, I suppose.'

I'd assumed the best friend was a girl but I was wrong.

'Alan, his name was Alan.' Stella spoke awkwardly, rather as if that speech impediment I'd noticed before had come back. 'Alan Tyzark.' She moistened her lips as if the effort of saying it had made them dry. 'He wasn't the boy next door either.' The little light laugh she gave sounded forced. 'His parents lived in Snaresbrook, not very far away. We were, Alan and I, I mean, we were—inseparable. Only we had to be separated.'

She told me all this while I sat with her the week Ned was away. I broke in sometimes to ask her questions, like to explain about the School Certificate for instance, but mostly I just let her talk. After she'd repeated it a few times she got to be able to say Alan's name as easily as she said mine.

They thought it was homesickness that troubled her, but it was Alan she missed more than her home. She only wanted to go back to London if he was there, but he was in Maldon. They were neither of them much good at writing letters. She was allowed to have Christmas at home and so was he and they managed to meet. But it was the last time.

'The last time for ever?' I said.

'The last time for years and years. Twenty years, Genevieve.'

The following summer the bombings began. Nearly a year had gone by and she was used to Bury, she was happy enough and she'd made new friends, her memories of Alan were starting to fade. By the time she'd done that next exam, there was no question of her going back to London. It was coming up to the most dangerous time and no one went *back* to the cities unless they had to. Besides, if she was still a bit Alan-sick she was over feeling homesick, she even sometimes felt she liked the aunt and the aunt's husband better than her own parents, who had never shown her much affection. They'd often written to her at first but now letters came further and further apart and when she heard that her mother had been killed in an air raid she didn't feel much. Her father came to see her and talked as if Bury was her permanent home and she'd want to think about getting a job there.

The aunt persuaded him to pay for a secretarial course. There was a place just off St Mary's Square where you could learn shorthand and typing and office management and Stella went there for a year. At the end of it she got a diploma and a job with a firm of solicitors.

They were Newland, Newland and Bosanquet, and the younger Newland was the man she was to marry one day. He was the younger but he wasn't that young. The old man was over seventy, apparently you can go on being a solicitor for as long as you like, and his son was forty when Stella first went to work there. She wasn't working for him though, but for the partner called Bosanquet,

Anthony Bosanquet. And she was going out with a boy.

His name was David, and, can you believe it, Stella had to stop and think and rack her brains to remember his surname. She didn't remember it, not then, but had to go on with the story without it.

'How did you meet him?' I said.

'Not at school. Mine was an all-girls' school. His mother was Auntie Sylvia's best friend. She had a draper's shop and she was the manageress and David's sister served behind the counter. Oh, what *was* their name? I'll think of it in a minute. We were on clothing coupons, of course, and you had to use them for material as well. The only things that weren't rationed were blankets and that sort of thing. I used to make all my own clothes and I made myself a blue coat out of a baby's cot blanket and lined it with an old sheet of Auntie Sylvia's. I got my first pair of nylons from David's mother's shop. I think that was when I developed a clothes sense, Genevieve. When there's hardly anything to buy, and no choice like there is today, you either give up or learn to be discriminating. You learn good taste. And you learn to look after your things.

'He wasn't Alan. I compared him with Alan all the time in my mind. I know you shouldn't do that sort of thing, it's not fair, but I couldn't help it. Beside Alan, or what I remembered of Alan, David was dull. But David admired me and that always goes for a lot with a girl, don't you think? He liked being seen about with me. He was the first person who ever told me I was pretty. It wouldn't have crossed Alan's mind. I wish I'd a photograph to show you, Genevieve, but Marianne has them all, and it's useless asking her to bring them here, she'll only forget. Anyway, the next thing was David was called up, he went into the RAF and I only saw him when he came home on leave.'

Some people would say my life has been dull but it's been a rave compared to Stella's. To the early part, that is. At least I had boyfriends before Mike, I used to go out somewhere every night, and home might have been uncomfortable at times but it was never boring. And if you had a boyfriend in my teenage years, that was before AIDS, you went all the way with him as a matter of course. Not so for Stella. She and Alan had never even held hands. She'd been going to the cinema with David and for walks and round to his house for six months before she'd let him kiss her. If there'd been anything more he'd have lost respect for her, he wouldn't have wanted her afterwards. She seemed sure of that, men really were like that, and perhaps they were, but can there have been such a big change in less than fifty years?

With David gone nothing happened to her at all. She lived at home with Auntie Sylvia and listened to what she calls the wireless and read books from the public library and made her clothes and unpicked old sweaters and used the wool to knit up new ones. Auntie Sylvia did home perms on her hair and she wore it in sausage curls all over her head. It took her fifteen minutes every morning to put her make-up on, foundation and rouge and lipstick, loose powder from a box and then more lipstick, and her eyebrows that were plucked drawn in with a pencil. That was the only eye make-up they used. No shadow, no mascara, no liner. It's funny because that's the only make-up my sister Janis ever does use, she always does her eyes no matter what the rest of her face looks like. Stella said she would never have set foot outside the door without her make-up on, not even to go down to the shop on the corner. The girl who worked in the chemist was a friend of hers and used to save her a lipstick or a bottle of nail varnish when they got their quota in, she'd keep it under the counter for her till next she came in. She actually queued up once for something called Crème Simon and they sold the last jar to the woman in the queue ahead of her.

And all of it was for Auntie Sylvia and Uncle Whatshisname and David's sister and Mr Bosanquet. You could be as beautiful as—Stella had to think about this—as beautiful as Margaret Lockwood, she said, but what was the use if you never met any young men? They were all away at the war. David came home on leave and asked her to get engaged but for some reason she wouldn't.

'Didn't you fancy him then?' I said.

She surprised me by giggling, the sound a young girl makes. 'I never thought about that, Genevieve. I don't know if I did or not. It was the draper's shop, I think, that put me off. He was going to go into the shop and I—well, you'll call me a snob and perhaps I was. I knew these shop people but I wasn't one of them. My mother's father had been a minister, a Methodist, you know, and my father was a civil servant, if not a very important one. Marrying David would have been a retrograde step.'

It made me wonder what she must think of me. My mother's father was a cowman and my dad is a motor mechanic when he's anything. But the truth is she doesn't think about me like that, she doesn't see me in that light.

'You said no?'

'I said no, and next time he came home he brought this WAAF with him that he'd met and they got married on his next leave. Oh, Jenny, I've remembered his name! It was Conroy. He was David Conroy and his sister was Mavis. Of course I always called his mother Mrs Conroy and you'll think this very funny, but when we first met David called me Miss Robertson. It was the same in the office. I was Miss Robertson and of course the partners were Mr Newland and Mr Bosanquet and even we girls, the secretaries, we called each other Miss This and Miss That. It was the custom then. You can see why I'm not always happy about the way it's all christian names here. I mean, I know times have changed, but it's still a shock when the boy who mows the lawns calls me Stella.'

She told me all this in four sessions over two days. Of all the residents at Middleton Hall she had been the one who never talked about the past, but now she'd begun there was no stopping her. It obviously pleased her to have the chance to talk but she got tired as well and sometimes she started coughing. And I had to keep a lookout for Lena. Whenever she caught me she took the opportunity to send me off to wheel Arthur in or out or massage Lois's leg or find a video for Gracie. It must have been malice, or maybe jealousy, that made her determined to keep me away from Stella, I can't think of any other reason. You'd think she'd have been pleased that one of her residents had found a way to be happy, but Lena doesn't want people to be happy, she wants them to be dependent on her. That's why Maud is her favourite now Edith's gone. Maud is always telling her how good she is. She calls her a 'latter-day saint', God knows where she got the expression, and says that if there were more like her the world would be a better place. Lena laps it up and I expect Maud is being lined up as the next maker of wills in Lena's favour.

It was Wednesday afternoon and time for me to go home when I got Stella's next instalment. I was a bit pre-occupied, thinking of a surprise for Ned who was coming home from Denmark next day—fool that I was!—and though I was sitting there and apparently listening I missed a whole lot of the beginning. I suppose it was about those Conroys and the office because she suddenly said something that got me listening again.

'Mr Bosanquet died. He committed suicide.'

You don't know what to say when someone tells you that.

'He hanged himself. His housekeeper found him hanging from a beam in the garage roof. Old Mr Newland said he had a rifle, why hadn't he used that, and Rex, my husband that was to be, he said it was because of all these shortages and he couldn't get the ammunition. I heard them laughing about it.'

She was quite calm but it shocked me. Where her generation are shocked by sex, it's things like that, a thick-skinned way of being uncaring, that gets to mine. It had me wanting to make the sort of face you make when you take the lid off my nan's wheelie-bin before the dustmen come.

'Didn't they like him?' I said.

'Oh, it wasn't so much that. It was that they found out he was a—how shall I put it? Rex called him a queer. That was his word. A lot better than saying pouf like my future father-in-law. Homosexual, I suppose you'd say. Remember that was years before the Sexual Offences Act was passed, the one that made sex legal between consenting adults in private. Oh, Genevieve, don't look so surprised! I worked in a solicitor's office for six years, you know, and one is bound to pick up a little law in that time, not to mention developing an *interest* in the law. I suppose that if I'd been born twenty-five years later I'd have been a solicitor myself.

'Anyway, poor Mr Bosanquet had been caught with a boy in a caravan the boy lived in. The police phoned him and told him they were coming to see him and why—they knew him well, of course, he was always appearing in court, and I think they were gentle with him—but that was one court appearance he was resolved never to make and he was dead before they got there. I don't suppose you can understand what a terrible scandal it was. I think it would be comparable today to hearing that someone you knew had killed a child. People were outraged. They pointed me out in the street because I had been his secretary. I suppose it was silly of me but I thought I'd lose my job over it. I thought I'd get the sack just because I'd been associated with Mr Bosanquet.

'I didn't get the sack. They made me Rex's secretary. It was quite a promotion for me because old Mr Newland was going to retire at last and Rex would be the senior partner. He had a nephew who'd come into the business and someone else was made a partner and they gave the firm a new name: Newland, Clarke and Newland. Of course the main motive was to get rid of the hated name Bosanquet.'

'Just because he was gay?' I said.

'What a ridiculous term that is,' Stella said sleepily. She'd leaned back her head and closed her eyes. 'The

Victorians used to call prostitutes "gay" ladies. In my day that word meant light-hearted and happy.'

I was afraid I'd overtired her. It's at times like this that I can see how thin she is, when she's relaxed and her face slackens. Where her cheeks were full a few months ago there are folds of skin now and her eyes are sunk in deep powdery hollows. The hand lying in her lap was like a bundle of ropes, the nails still bravely painted the colour of the top coat Len's just put on the Legion's front door.

A pity it's not Richard but Marianne who's got those photographs. We all know a Marianne. They mean well, they promise to do something, they're really enthusiastic, but they don't do it. They forget. And then they apologize, they're full of remorse, and they promise again, and the same thing happens. Marianne would never bring those pictures and I'd never see the young Stella in the dresses she wore when she was engaged to Rex Newland, the 'New Look' with long skirts and peplums, or the full-skirted cotton frocks with nipped-in waists and tight belts. I'd never see Stella in high-heeled shoes with thongs criss-crossed up her legs like Roman sandals or wearing 'costumes' and felt hats and twin sets. I'd just have to imagine.

Driving home I went the way that took me past Rowans. Since we'd been using Stella's house I'd got over my feeling about Ned's weekend cottage, it had stopped being *the* house, I hardly associated it with him any more. For one thing, he and Jane and Hannah hadn't been there for weeks, it was always raining at the weekends, which makes Ned say that God was a Tory. He even talked of giving up the cottage, they only rent it and the lease is up in December. There seemed some point in it, he said, when staying there meant a chance of seeing me, but now our meetings depend on that no longer.

I expected to see Rowans as it usually was, all the windows shut and the front grass in need of a mowing, but there was a car on the drive, Jane's car, and Hannah's wellies standing on the step to dry. Half-term, I thought, or perhaps she only went to a nursery as yet. I'd been intending to go round the Legion in the evening, see Mum and have a drink with some of the regulars, but I changed my mind. Jane might be in there and I didn't want to have to talk to Jane.

The next day was my day off and I was going to drive to Stansted and meet Ned. He'd sent me two postcards while he was away, one with a picture of the Little Mermaid on it and the other of a statue of two people blowing long tubular musical instruments. The writing on them was disguised, meant to look as if they'd come from a girlfriend in case anyone but me saw them. One said he'd been to a bar called the Song of Songs which was heated entirely by oil stoves, the fire risk was horrendous, and the other was about buying red Christmas candles with holly and mistletoe patterns. He'd signed both 'Edwina'. I thought they were silly but they made me long for him. The Christmas-candle card said he'd be at Stansted on this flight that got in at five and as soon as he had the chance he'd phone me. I looked up the Little Mermaid in my encyclopedia and learned a bit about Hans Andersen.

Stansted isn't that far from here. I drove down to Bury, then Bury to Long Melford, Long Melford to Haverhill and down the M11. I'd got Stella's house all prepared for us, with more flowers in the vases and more wine and I'd bought the sort of food he liked and I was getting used to, Italian focaccia bread and pâté and a mad-sounding French cheese called Terroir, peaches and bananas and Greek yoghurt. I got to the airport half an hour early, that's the way it is when you're in love, you're always early for meetings, always laying up half-hours of excitement and longing and fear and disappointment for yourself.

I'm not used to airports and I didn't really know what to do but I caught on to the telly screen thing that tells you when flights are expected and when they've landed, so I went to the gate where there were lots of men, hire-car drivers I suppose, standing around holding up cards with people's names on them and the names of companies and I waited behind the barrier. I'd been there ten minutes and the sign was saying the baggage from the flight from Copenhagen was in the hall when I saw Jane crossing the arrivals area, holding Hannah by the hand. All in a flash I understood. She'd stayed the night in Tharby because it was that much nearer Stansted than Norwich was. She'd arranged to meet Ned. Probably she always did when he went abroad.

I didn't stay. For a split second I weighed it up, whether it was better to see him and have him see me and pass me by, or better not to see him at all. I think that what decided me was my feeling for him. I didn't want to embarrass him, have him be forced to decide whether to acknowledge me or pretend to ignore me. So I went back to my car before the first people started coming out of customs. It was my own fault, wasn't it? It was me that had been the fool. He wasn't to blame and nor was Jane. If I'd said yes to all the times he'd begged me to leave Mike and let him leave Jane, I'd have been the one with the right to meet him off the plane, I could have held up one of those cards and written 'Ned, I Love You', on it.

Well, not quite. But you know what I mean.

Maybe they stayed the night in Tharby. I don't know. I didn't go down to see. I went round to Philippa's and we watched a video of *Brief Encounter*, her choice. Of course I'd seen it before but a long time ago and when it started I thought I'd identify with the characters and see it as 'my own story', if that doesn't sound too mushy and daft, but it was too old, it was made too long ago for that. The people just seemed silly with a lot of pointless moral scruples. I couldn't really understand why she wouldn't sleep with him in his friend's flat and I didn't believe in her being put off because she thought it was sordid. All right for Stella, I thought, but it's too old-fashioned for me.

Rex Newland asked Stella to marry him when she'd been working for him for six months. He'd taken her out to dinner three times and then he got his mother to invite her to their house. They had a big Georgian place on Angel Hill. Stella said she thought he was being kind to her because her uncle had died, Auntie Sylvia's husband that is. It surprised her very much when he proposed. He'd never kissed her, he'd never even said anything very personal to her.

She didn't know what to say, so she asked him why. He said she was very beautiful and she knew how to dress and she had the manners of a lady. And then, while she was staring at him, he said, I'm using the words Stella used, 'I want to go to bed with you so much it's killing me, and I know you won't unless I marry you first.'

Times have changed. People must have changed too. If

anyone had said that to me I'd have given him a clout round the face. Stella said it decided her. Can you credit it? *It decided her.* She said it showed real emotion, it showed he had real feelings. And, besides, the words excited her, they made her shiver, they made her wonder what it would be like, going to bed with such a passionate man.

Also, though she wouldn't have married for money, she liked the idea of marrying someone who had it. She didn't know Rex Newland was mean. All she could see was the big house he lived in and the Lagonda car he drove, and she knew the business was flourishing. Marrying him wouldn't be a come-down but a leg-up. On the debit side was his age. He was twenty-two years older than her. And then there was the question of why he'd never been married before.

People didn't get divorced much then and Stella said that, in any case, she wouldn't have wanted to marry a divorced man. She had genuinely thought he was a widower, she seemed to remember from before she worked for the firm, while she was still at school, seeing him in Bury arm in arm with a woman, and was rather surprised to learn that he'd never been married.

'Did you ask him why?' I said.

'I couldn't do that, not then. We weren't on those sort of terms.'

'*He* wasn't gay, was he?'

There's no doubt she doesn't like that word. 'Of course he wasn't, Genevieve. There was another reason but I didn't find out what it was for a long time.'

It was incredible what she did. She asked him to let her have the weekend before giving him her answer. It's like

something out of a Victorian book, isn't it? A far cry from
Janis saying to Peter in front of Mum and Nick and me,
I've fallen pregnant so we'd best get married three weeks
on Saturday. Stella said she thought of nothing else that
weekend. She consulted nobody. On the Monday she told
Rex Newland she'd marry him and he said she'd made
him the happiest man in the world. They weren't engaged
for years the way a lot of people seem to be now but got
married a month later. The wedding was in the cathedral
which wasn't a cathedral then but just a church and Stella
made her own wedding dress.

'Not that anyone would have known,' she said.

'What did he look like?'

'Who, Rex?' She seemed surprised by the question.
'Marianne looks like him,' she said, and then began
describing a man not a bit like Marianne. 'He was tall and
rather heavy, you know. Not stout, that came later. He
was handsome, very handsome, with a mane of dark hair
going grey and rather large features, big nose, full lips,
dark eyes, a very sensual face.'

I wanted to ask if she was in love with him—really, if
she fell in love with him after they were married, but I
didn't quite like to. She seemed to read my mind and
answered the question I hadn't asked.

'I was never in love with him. Sometimes I thought I
nearly was and then he'd do something that put me off
him.'

'What sort of thing?'

'Oh, something brutal. I don't mean he was ever cruel
or violent to me, he never was, but—oh, something in the
way he'd talk to lower-class people, as if they weren't people, you know, and the way he was with animals. He

hunted, of course, and I didn't like it, but hunting was one of the most important things in his life. I mean, he'd be kindness itself to his dogs, we had two spaniels trained to the gun, but he was capable of picking up a wounded hare and throwing it to the hounds and laughing about it. I hated that.'

I knew the type. We get them in the Legion if the meet's been on Tharby Green. I've seen young kids come in, girls of fifteen, with fox's blood plastered on them and proud of it, the huntsmen laughing about how they dug the poor creature out.

'He hadn't any time for sensitivity or imagination, if you know what I mean, Genevieve. I don't think he ever read a book. The only music he liked was Gilbert and Sullivan. He was very witty and charming, of course, there was that. He'd tell me about all the cases he had, divorces and so on, and things that came up in court. Things like—well, indecent assaults, and what they called carnal knowledge then, he'd describe all the details to me, I think it excited him. Strange, really, because I never heard a word of that before we were married, but as soon as we were he acted with me as if I were—well, Auntie Sylvia's name for it was a bad woman.'

There's a lot of complaining about the way the world is today and a lot of talk among the elderly about the good old days, but I have my doubts, I reckon things are better than they used to be. I couldn't be doing with the way Stella had had to live. I'd rather go on the streets in Norwich's red-light district.

'But I was happy enough,' she said. 'I really didn't have anything to complain of.'

Stella smiled and paused. I had the impression there

was something she was hesitating about telling me and that that was probably to do with her sex life. She hadn't touched on it and I realized that she wasn't going to. Not at this stage, at any rate. Another feeling I had was that I wasn't the first person she'd told this story to, for all her earlier reticence and apparent unwillingness to talk about the past. She got tired, of course, and sometimes her voice grew hoarse, but—how can I describe what I mean?—it was as if she'd rehearsed for this performance. She'd rehearsed once long ago and now she was nearer being word-perfect.

Pauline came in with Stella's tea and put up her eyebrows when she saw me there, long after my going-home time. Stella ate a sandwich and nibbled at a macaroon. She's been eating a bit better, though it's made no difference to her weight and she's beginning to get that transparent look.

I thought she'd finished talking for the day and I really hoped she had because I didn't want her overdoing it. But suddenly she began telling me of her and Rex's hopes for a child and how she'd had a miscarriage and then another. Of course, she said, it wasn't just a child Rex hoped for, it was a son. They'd been married five years when Marianne was born, on the Queen's Coronation Day, June 2nd 1953. Stella had spent most of the pregnancy in bed she was so afraid of losing the baby, and after Marianne was born she was rather ill for a long time. She didn't say ill in what way but I gathered it was mainly post-natal depression.

Rex had no patience with illness. He was disappointed in getting a daughter. The combination of the two and a housebound wife sent him back where he'd been all those years when she'd wondered why he hadn't married: to the woman she'd seen him with in the town when she, Stella, was still at school, the woman she described, as if Rex had been a king or a dictator, as his mistress.

She meant his girlfriend, his lover. Our history teacher at Newall Upper told us King Charles II had had a lot of mistresses, and that was the last time I'd heard anyone use the word. A dog or cat can have a mistress and Mrs Thorn used to say to Nan that she was the mistress of the Hall but an ordinary man having one made him sound far from ordinary. It made me see Rex Newland as very grand, with a cloak and a sword, and the mistress hanging on his arm, wearing a crinoline.

But of course it couldn't have been like that. I made what I thought was an intelligent guess at the mistress's identity.

10

Ned and Jane and Hannah spent that weekend in Tharby. He managed to phone me between the time I got home from work and the time Mike got back and he said he had to see me, it was urgent.

Immediately frightened, I asked what was wrong.

'Nothing's wrong. I just want to see you. I haven't seen you for ten days, so it's urgent. Isn't that reasonable?'

The only possible arrangement was the four of us meeting in the Legion on Saturday night. Mike wouldn't have gone if I'd told him Jane was going to be there and I don't suppose Jane would have if she'd known she'd encounter the whole clan of us: Mum and Len, Janis and Steve, Nick and Tanya and, of course, Mike and me. Jane was wearing the same clothes she'd worn to meet Ned at Stansted, a narrow trouser suit of navy blue silk with a white shirt. Her red hair was up in a neat French braid. It's easy for me not to think of Jane when I don't see her, but now I look at her and wonder if he ever touches her, if like Mike and me they still share one of those married people's double beds and sleep each on an extreme edge of it, or if, because he is obliged to stay with her, he acts the same loving husband she has always known. We never speak of it and I would rather not know. Mum says men always tell their girlfriends they've stopped sleeping with their wives and get caught with egg on their faces (her words) when the wives fall pregnant. Rex Newland was that sort of man by the sound of it and probably told Stella all sorts of lies.

You could see Jane didn't want to be with us. One of the teachers from UEA was there with her husband, sitting at a table in the corner, and Jane kept looking over in their direction, hoping to catch their eye. But when he'd bought our drinks Ned sat down next to me, between me and Steve, and reached for my hand and held it in my lap, between my thighs in fact, until I couldn't stand it and pushed his hand away. No one saw and no one saw our legs pressed close together—except Mum. She's blind to all sorts of things but when it comes to sex there's no escaping her eye.

She beckoned me over. On the face of it her motive was to give me a bowlful of crisps for our table. 'You thought of having them rods inserted, have you?' she said.

I hadn't the faintest idea what she meant.

'They're the latest contraceptive, guaranteed a hundred per cent. They stick them in your arm, like planting bulbs. Because if you've got two fellows on the go you want to watch it. The Green girl that's Jill Baleham's niece, she was on the pill and she still fell. You've only got to have diarrhoea the once and that pill can go right through you.'

'Mother,' I said. It's not often I call her that but she knows that when I do she's said enough.

I felt like throwing the bowl of crisps at her. I took them back to our table. Mike was talking about the building site in Regent's Park and the work soon coming to an end. Ned didn't look at me but the very fact that he didn't spoke what was running through his mind. I was sick with nerves. The dry white wine Mum's been serving lately takes the roof off your mouth, you could clean sinks with it. Janis said, right out in front of him, that she wished Peter'd get a job that took him away four evenings out of seven. She wouldn't be lonely, she'd like it, at which Peter said two could play at that game, and Jane, with a look of deep boredom on her face, got up and walked over to the UEA teachers' table. They said something to her, she answered and they all got up and left together.

Ned made excuses for her but you could see the others were offended. And Mike of course had all his worst fears confirmed. Five awkward minutes went by and then Ned said he'd better go home. The Norwich people were friends of Jane's and she'd obviously taken them back to Rowans for a drink.

We all stood up. He managed to whisper close to my ear, 'Please let me see you on Monday night, please,' and that told me the fern in his shoe had worked.

Then a strange thing happened. As the door closed behind him the other one swung open, the front door that's painted the colour of Stella's nails, and the woman who'd passed me twice in her car at Thelmarsh Cross came in. She's a bit older than me, blonde and good looking, and now there was more of her on show than her head and shoulders, I could see she was a bit overweight but in an attractive way. I recognized her at once and I could tell that she recognized me, but we didn't smile at each other and we didn't look for long. We both turned our heads away in the same moment.

'It was Gilda Brent,' I said.

Stella frowned. 'What are you talking about?'

'The mistress.'

She was quite irritable with me. 'I wish you wouldn't do that, Genevieve. I wish you wouldn't keep guessing at things. That's the second time you've done it. It most certainly was not Gilda. Gilda had quite another sort of part to play in my life but I hadn't even met her then. Rex's mistress was called Charmian Fry.'

She was a single woman who had never been married and who had never worked for her living either. She came of one of those county families, gentlefolk. Her father had been a High Sheriff and one of her brothers was Lord Lieutenant of the County. There was family money and she had a private income. Those families always own several houses and she lived alone in one of them, a big house near Stowupland. You wonder what people like that do with themselves all day long, don't you? Stella said Charmian hunted and shot, she gardened and she made pots out of clay for planting things like geraniums in. She went to sherry parties and she went out to dinner. It doesn't seem to account for a life, but she had Rex. No doubt he took up some of her time.

They'd known each other since he was twenty-one and she was eighteen. Much later, when she no longer cared, Stella asked him why he had never married her and he said it was because some women were for marrying and others were not. This didn't seem to depend on appearance or class or what Stella called reputation, it was just something he knew at a glance. Or so he told her. And it was true, she said, that she couldn't have imagined

Charmian as anyone's wife, still less as a mother.

How did she find out about Charmian? I forgot to say that, didn't I? Her father-in-law told her. He was in his eighties and dying and a bit mad too, I shouldn't wonder. He must have been mad or wicked to say a thing like that to a young woman who'd just had a child after an awful pregnancy, his own daughter-in-law too, just because she was ill and always pale and always weak.

'If you don't give him what a husband's got a right to expect,' he said, 'you'll drive him back into the arms of Charmian Fry and a little bird's told me he's there already.'

The rest came out. The old man wasn't at all unwilling to tell. It was a revelation to Stella and a terrible shock. Nothing in her life had taught her that men and women could behave like that. She had read about it in books, of course, but a husband's unfaithfulness could never happen to her or any woman she knew. It was impossible that a woman who sat down to dinner in her house, who kissed her cheek and called her by her christian name, could secretly do those things with her husband Stella thought of as sacred to marriage and a marital duty, even if not particularly delightful. It was impossible but, and she was obliged to face it, real and true.

Becoming used to it, bitterly accepting, she still could scarcely understand how a man, any man, could prefer a gaunt black crow of a woman with a face as dark as leather and long black hair going grey, to herself. Sometimes she would see Charmian in Bury, arrived in her old shooting brake to do her shopping, and across the street, unsmiling, she would raise one arm in a salute. Then Stella turned and stared at her own reflection in the glass of a shop window, her pretty face and figure, her carefully chosen or carefully made clothes, and at Charmian distantly behind her in dirty worn tweeds and a man's felt hat.

'Rex did come back to me,' Stella said. 'Whether he actually gave her up to come back to me is another matter. I had another miscarriage. It was a boy, it was far enough along to tell that, and of course he was dreadfully disappointed.'

She kept remembering, she said, she couldn't help it, those words of his when he'd asked her to marry him about wanting her so much it was killing him. It was beyond her understanding why he'd said that. Hadn't he meant it, even at the time? Or had he meant it *at the time* and only then? Had she been a disappointment to him? Was there something wanting in her appearance, her manners, her voice, her social graces? At that time she spent a lot of time in front of the mirror in her bedroom, studying her appearance, trying out ways of improving it, talking to herself as she stared, listening to the sound of her own voice.

'I thought it must be because I still hadn't given him a son. I didn't much like having babies, Genevieve. Of course it's worth it all for the child you get at the end, but suppose you get nothing at the end?'

Stella was looking penetratingly at me. Then she closed her eyes and let her head slip back against the cushion. I thought she had finished for the day, and I was about to get up and creep away, when she opened her eyes suddenly and stared at me. She put her hand out, reaching for mine, and I held her hand, giving it a little squeeze.

'I've just remembered the purpose of all this, Genevieve,' she said. 'It was to explain to you how I came to buy my house.'

'Was it?' I said.

'Certainly it was. Just that. I didn't mean to go into so much detail. I feel . . . I *fear*—oh, I mean, there are things I've told you I shouldn't want my children to know.'

'They don't know about their father and Charmian Fry?'

'I believe Marianne may have come near the truth. Richard was much too young. I'd much rather they knew nothing and of course Marianne can't *know*. It can only be conjecture on her part.'

I couldn't help thinking of my dad, who lived with one woman after another after he split up with Mum, got married again, got divorced, and now has a live-in girlfriend two years younger than me. No one's ever tried to keep all that from Janis and me and Nick, it wouldn't have crossed their minds. It must be a generation thing or maybe, more simply and what it more often is, a class thing.

'You see, Genevieve, Marianne was very well aware there was a mystery attached to her father's death. Well, not his actual death. He died of heart failure, cardiac arrest.'

'In a train,' I said, and wished I hadn't, for she sat bolt upright, all six and a half stone of her, her free hand fluttering. The other let mine go abruptly.

'How did you know that?'

I tried to speak in a casual sort of way, offhand. 'Richard told me. I don't remember why.'

She relaxed a little. These spasms of excitement she has wear her out, and the first sign is the pallor that creeps into her face.

'Well, of course he does know *that*. And it isn't quite true that Rex died in a train. He was taken ill in the train. He died in hospital in Bury.'

He'd been visiting Charmian Fry. This was years later, the end of the sixties, and she had moved from one family house to another rather smaller one, this time in Elmswell which has a station on the branch line that runs from Stowmarket to Bury. Perhaps she chose to live there for that reason. Rex had given up driving by then, he drank too much to drive and he ate too much for his health. He was sixty-seven and too old and too fat to have been doing what he had been with old Charmian. They found him collapsed and in pain, slumped in the corner of a first-class carriage when the train drew in to Bury. The return part of a ticket from Bury to Elmswell was in his pocket and the hospital people gave it to Stella with the rest of his effects after he was dead. So she knew where he'd been. He'd wanted Charmian so much it had killed him.

Marianne was fifteen. She knew Charmian lived in Elmswell and her father had been returning by train from there when he died. Stella was sure she made no connection between these two facts. She asked no questions. She had loved her father and she mourned him, ignorant of the life he had led. Stella's own attitude was that Rex could have kept a harem of women in Elmswell and visited them every night and she wouldn't have cared. She wouldn't have wished him dead but it was a relief when he died. All that was important to her as far as Rex was concerned at that time was to keep his doings a secret from her children, to have them believe a happy marriage had ended that night and left their mother a sorrowing widow. During those years between the boy she had miscarried and Rex's death, the most important thing of her whole life had happened to her. She hastened to tell me that she hadn't meant Richard being born, joyful though that was. She meant something quite different, she said, her eyes closing again, that ghost of a smile still there as she slipped into sleep.

I was still sitting with her and I'd taken her hand in mine again, when there was a tap on the door and Richard came in. I put my finger to my lips and he tiptoed across the room and sat down carefully so as not to disturb Stella. We sat there together for ten minutes or a bit longer, not speaking but smiling at each other sometimes, until at last I got up and whispered to him that it was time for me to go.

The cat that belongs to Sandra next door was torturing a greenfinch it had caught at my bird table. I managed to rescue it, it was a beautiful bird with bright yellow feathers in its khaki-brown wings, but it died in my hands.

If a bird dies when you're holding it your hands will shake for ever. I buried the poor bird in our rose bed and my hands shook so much while I was doing it that I was frightened. I thought I might be left with a palsy like my grandad, who had Parkinson's, but the shaking stopped after a few minutes. Mum doesn't know all the answers with her omens and her portents. But as I was getting ready to meet Ned I remembered that a dead bird also means a death in the family.

The sun had come out by the time I reached Molucca. It was going to be a fine evening. The sunshine was that gold colour you only see on autumn evenings, its rays long shafts of amber light. The trees in the fen were turning from green to yellow or brown and the dogwood to pink and crimson. Mountain ash berries, dropped by birds or half-eaten by birds, lay scattered over the doorstep. I was careful where I put my feet so as not to tread berries into the carpets, for they make stains like blood.

We're due to put the clocks back on the coming Saturday and that means that next week it'll be dark by this time. The candles would be needed, not for romance but for lighting our way up the stairs and keeping us from stumbling into furniture. Autumn is mild, the mildest for years, yet every week it gets colder, the oil heaters doing less and less to warm the air and burn away the damp.

I'd replaced those Christmassy candles with yellow ones and brought houseplants in pots instead of cut flowers. While I was waiting for Ned I had a look at the pictures that had been in the sideboard along with that photo Stella had wanted. They were much nicer than the insipid ones up on the walls, paintings of children with animals, or drawings rather, filled in with paint. There was one of a girl and a boy with kittens and one of the same boy with a tortoiseshell cat that had a coat like a Persian carpet. I wasn't feeling very kindly towards cats that evening but I could see how appealing these were. The interesting thing was that they seemed familiar. I'd seen those pictures somewhere before, though I couldn't think where. Each of them was signed in the corner with a name I couldn't read, an initial A, then a full stop and a T followed by a squiggle.

It wasn't for me to rearrange Stella's house for her but

I couldn't help thinking these pictures would look much nicer up on the walls than those blue-and-mauve washed-out things of moorlands and rivers. I was holding one of them up to cover one of the pale squares on the wallpaper when Ned's headlamps flooded into the room. The light poured across her portrait, her lively pretty face and the pink dress and the rose in her hand.

He was full of loving apology, so sorry, sorry, sorry for what had happened on Saturday night. Hannah had been taken ill and their sitter was about to phone the Legion just at the moment Jane walked into the house. It was as well he went home when he did. Hannah was wheezing and gasping and crying for her father and Jane had given her the drug she uses but in the end they had to take her to casualty. It frightens him when Hannah is like that, he can't think of anyone or anything else.

How can he tell me these things about Hannah and still believe he can persuade me to take him from her? He wants both worlds. I'm not educated like he is or sophisticated in his way, but I know better than that.

'Do you love me?' he said when I was in his arms. 'Say you love me, darling Jenny, say you love me.'

I can hardly speak when he says these things to me, I can only whisper, and my voice came out on a gasp, 'I do, you know I do.'

'But I need you to say it, I desperately need that.'

Other men aren't like him. They're frightened of that word. He needs it all the time. Like some need music playing or the spice of fear or a woman who'll dress like a whore, he needs to love and know he's loved.

It was eleven when I got home but the phone was ringing

in the dark house. I expected it to be Mike and he'd say he'd been trying to get me all evening, but it was Janis. Her voice was solemn and strange and she had to clear her throat before she could tell me.

Our dad had died.

He'd seemed so fit. I could hardly believe it. Janis said he'd been at home in Diss, cleaning this old Alvis he'd bought. A customer was coming round to take a look at it with a view to buying. Dad was polishing the chrome on the bonnet when he shouted out at the sudden pain in his arm and shoulder. Suzanne came running out but he was dead before she got to him, he'd fallen down dead of a heart attack.

That was at five, much about the time the bird died in my hands. I was more awe-struck than afraid, and that feeling, of the strangeness of it yet of the certainty of so clear an omen, distracted me from grief. It was in the small hours that I woke up, remembered at once and cried for the loss of my dad who had been loving and kind until he went away from us long ago. To my mind too there was something wrong in not being able to mourn him properly, to cry along with Mum, in a home I knew and had shared with him. Alive, he'd been parted from me since I was eight, and dead he was Suzanne's.

In the morning Stella had a visitor with her, not Richard or Marianne but a middle-aged woman accord- ing to Pauline, so it was the afternoon before I saw her. It's always so with Stella, when you think she's only inter- ested in her own affairs, that she's wrapped up in herself the way most of the residents are, she surprises you with her thoughtfulness. When I came up to her in the lounge, sitting by the french windows, she saw at once that something was wrong. She put out both hands to me.

'What is it, Genevieve?'

I told her. Most people don't really care, do they? They pretend to sympathize but they're not involved, they're embarrassed more than regretful. That's why I was so surprised by Stella's attitude, by her sudden pallor, the concern in her voice.

'But he must have been quite a young man.'

'He was fifty-five.'

'I'm so sorry,' she said, as if she'd known him. 'I'm so very sorry.'

We sat in silence for a while, looking out into the garden where there were still flowers on the buddle bush and still a few last butterflies, a tortoiseshell, a painted lady.

'I shall never see a swallowtail now, Genevieve,' Stella said at last. 'Will there be flowers at your father's funeral?'

I said I'd already phoned the florist and ordered a spray, but I didn't know when the funeral would be or who would arrange it. Janis had been seven and Nick only three when Mum and he separated. Ages had passed since any of us had been involved with our dad beyond seeing him maybe three times a year and sending a Christmas card. And there came into my head the thought of Hannah. If Ned left her things would be like that for her. Like me, she'd be a one-parent person and when he died someone else would decide whether or not he had flowers. Stella seemed to be pondering. Then she turned to me.

'My father's funeral was in January and it was very cold. Richard was nine months old and I left him with Rex's niece—well, his nephew Jeremy's wife. That was she who was here this morning, by the way, that was Priscilla. I thought I'd have to go alone to London for the funeral,

Rex wouldn't come, said he couldn't take a day off "for a mere father-in-law I only met once", but—' she hesitated, then brought the name out very self-consciously— 'Alan came with me.' She gave me a sideways glance. 'He met me on the platform at Bury and came up with me in the train.'

'The Alan who was your friend at school?' I said.

'The very same.'

'You'd met him again?'

Instead of answering, she said, 'You've never heard of him? Alan Tyzark?'

I shook my head. 'Should I have?'

'No, not after all these years. Perhaps not even then. He was an artist. A painter. When you were a child did you have any of those books called *Figaro and Velvet*?'

As soon as she said that I remembered. That was where I had seen those pictures before, in a book that someone, my Auntie Rita I think, gave me for my birthday when I was seven. A girl and a boy and their cats. Middle-class children, not like us, children who lived in a big detached house with both parents, a dad going to the office and a mum who stayed at home, and who had a pretty velvety tortoiseshell cat with magical powers. I liked the magical powers, that at any rate meant something to me.

'Alan Tyzark illustrated those books,' Stella said.

He'd come back into her story out of the blue, simply someone who had been at her father's funeral. 'He was a very funny man,' she said. 'He gave you the impression he was amusing without trying to be. These days they'd call it laid-back and they'd call some of his humour black humour. I was feeling very low in the train that day, not because of my father, I hardly knew my father any more, but for—well, other reasons, and Alan set himself out to entertain me, to amuse me. He turned a horrible day into a day out.

'He'd made a plan for the day. We would get the funeral over, then he'd take me out to lunch, there were things he wanted to show me in London, a house with an interesting history, a statue in the park, a monument, then tea at the Ritz. I'd never known anyone like him. I'd never known anyone who thought about these things. I must have known him for four years then because we—we renewed our acquaintance in 1959.'

I didn't know what to say. 'Was he good at art at school?'

'I suppose he was. He took art for his School Certificate, but so did most of us. He used to draw animals, I remember that.'

'And you just met him again?'

'He was Gilda Brent's husband, you see. He'd married Gilda.' She looked away from me, back at the sprays of purple flowers, now brown at the tips and drooping, a single red admiral with a ragged wing clinging to a stem. 'He did a terrible thing.' She seemed to be talking to herself. 'Well, *we* did a terrible thing together.' I tried not to stare. What did she mean? That she'd slept with him? When she turned back she had put on a face of sympathy. 'Genevieve, we shouldn't be talking about me, we should be talking about your father. Tell me about him.'

The important thing about my dad was his passion for cars. He loved cars the way some people love animals, dogs or horses. If it had been possible to breed cars he would have. It was sad really that he never had the money to drive the ones he wanted. He was doomed to selling them to people he knew would never value them the way he did. Even the Alvis he was polishing when he died was soon to be someone else's. I told Stella some of that but she's old and ill and what Ned calls her attention span wasn't very long any more. It wasn't her fault that she nodded off and was asleep before I'd finished. And she'd never told me how she came to buy her house.

Next day she was feeling better than she'd been for weeks. She said it was the sunshine, it was the little bit of summer we often get round the third week of October, but it's more likely to have been the radiotherapy. I'd already wheeled Arthur outside and Stella said she'd sit on the terrace for a while, outside the window where she watched the butterflies. It's rare for her to sit in the open air and without her book or her music.

'I'll tell you how I met Alan and Gilda, shall I?'

She doesn't realize I can't spend all the time with her that she'd like me to. Or, come to that, I'd like to. She's like most people who haven't worked for their livings, or haven't for a long time. They don't understand what a job means, that you can't just take hours off when you want to.

'Stella, I'd like to stay but I've got a lot to do.'

All the years when you're young and middle-aged and young-elderly you hide the way you feel. You smile and pretend you don't mind when people are late or won't stay or change the subject or show they're bored. But children aren't like that. They protest about these things and sulk and get angry. Maybe you know when a person's really old by the way childhood protesting and anger have come back.

Stella said quite sharply, 'Oh, all right, Genevieve. I don't suppose I'm very good company any more.'

'It's not that, you know that. I have to work. I'll come and sit with you at four, shall I?'

She said what I'd known she would. 'If I'm on my own. I may not be, I may have a visitor.'

But of course she was alone, as she mostly was. Radio Three was on and so was her recording machine. A woman's voice was singing, clear and very high, I suppose it was opera. I expected her to put a finger to her lips but instead she did something she'd never done before. As I came up to her chair and put out my hand she took it and, pulling me towards her with surprising strength, kissed my cheek. I kept silent, I didn't have to be told, and on an impulse put my arms round her, hugging her close. The music stopped and almost at the same time the tape clicked off. I stood up and looked at Stella. There were tears in her eyes.

'What is it?' I said.

'Nothing. Just the music. And I'm sorry I was so hateful to you this morning, Jenny.'

I said to forget it. 'You were going to tell me about Alan Tyzark.'

'You remembered his name!'

I sat down on the bed and took hold of her hand.

Her eyes were fixed on some distant point. When I'd spoken I fancied she flushed and the colour was still in her face. She had to make several efforts before she spoke, she seemed not to know how to begin. It was as if she had the same difficulty talking about this man in a normal way as I would have when speaking of Ned. Eventually she spoke boldly, but she had to clear her throat several times first.

'It was ages before I knew who it was that had come to consult Rex. Rex told me, of course, but he always said Gilda Brent and her husband. I suppose I thought he must be a Mr Brent. Even when Rex referred to him as Alan I didn't make the connection, I just thought of him as Alan Brent. I didn't know my Alan had become a painter, you see.'

Gilda Brent and Alan Tyzark had consulted Rex Newland about recovering money owed by a film company to Gilda. The company was no longer in existence in its old form, it had collapsed, and Gilda Brent had never been paid for the last two films she had made, *The Wife's Story* and *The End of Edith Thompson*. Or that was what she said.

It took a long time but eventually Rex was able to recover quite a lot of the money, about £2,000, which doesn't seem much, but remember this was 1959. Rex had had a good many meetings with the Tyzarks by then. They lived in Tivetshall St Michael, a village near Pulham Market, in a farmhouse called St Michael's Farm. Neither of them seems to have been doing any real work at this time. They were living on what came in from what they'd done in the past and on the occasional bit of money they inherited. Alan's father had died and left him a few hundreds. Gilda lost three aunts in quick succession and all of them left her money and some quite valuable objects, Stella didn't say what. But you wouldn't have guessed they were quite poor. They were a well-dressed, stylish and attractive couple.

Rex asked Stella to invite them to dinner. It was always the way with him. Anyone new he met and thought was

good-looking or amusing or from the right background
had to be asked to dinner. I wonder what I'd say if Mike
came home and told me he wanted me to cook a meal for
four fellows he'd met on the site and their wives too. It's
pointless speculating because he wouldn't. Rex seems to
have taken it for granted. He presented her with a guest
list, including Charmian Fry. I don't know why she didn't
throw it at him, let alone said yes. But of course Alan's
name was on the list, his full name, and that's how she
came to know who it was.

'I didn't say a word to Rex. I didn't give anyone a clue
Alan and I had known each other before. It was twenty
years, after all. But I don't really know why I didn't. And
when he came I didn't. I shook hands with him, I behaved
as if we'd never seen each other before. And he must have
taken his cue from me because it wasn't till we were at the
table, sitting next to each other, that he—well, he told me
he recognized me.'

Charmian came to the party, dressed in a floor-length
grey lace evening dress with holes that might have been in
the pattern of the lace or made by moths. She explained
that the dress had been her grandmother's, she had found
it in an old trunk. With a loud laugh, in her loud county
voice, she said it was a real find and that it would last her
out. Gilda Brent stared at her in astonishment but, when
Charmian came close, drew away from the smell of
camphor.

Gilda herself was very beautiful.

'She had the sort of appearance,' Stella said, 'you only
have when you've been taught how to dress and make up.
You only see it in actresses and mannequins—I mean
models. Gilda's make-up was terribly professional and she

had—don't laugh—the *cleanest* hair I'd ever seen. I don't think women washed their hair as much then as they do now, once a week was quite enough. Gilda's hair was golden and shoulder-length and—do they call it "squeaky" clean, Genevieve?'

There was a shampoo ad that used to, I said.

'She had a green dress on in the style they called "the sack", it was the latest fashion, falling straight from the shoulder to the knee. She was tall and thin and she had just the same legs as Marlene Dietrich. Her manner— well, what can I tell you? She seemed so self-confident, she called me darling the second sentence she spoke to me. I'd never met an actress before. Of course I got used to her, I came to accept her, but that first time I think I'd have gazed at her the way she gazed at Charmian if—if it hadn't been for Alan. Alan made everyone else fade, I suppose.'

At the table he sat between Stella and the niece by marriage who had been to see her the day before, Priscilla Newland, then a girl of twenty-six. He still had the face of a schoolboy, Stella said, young and cheeky. His hair was brown and not as short as most men wore it then and his eyes were a light clear brown. He grinned at her and said,

'We're making a conspiracy of this, aren't we?'

'Do you mind?' she said.

'No, I like it. Let's keep it that way. Don't you love secrets?'

She had never thought whether she did or not. He looked at Charmian in her dirty dress and with her long grey hair and said,

'Have much of a coven round here, do you?'

Stella said she'd never felt like laughing about Charmian before, she'd always seen her presence in their lives as a tragedy, but suddenly, because of what Alan said, Charmian became ridiculous to her, an ugly, elderly joke whose hold over Rex must be through some obscene secret rituals. She said what she had never before said to anyone, had scarcely admitted in actual words to herself,

'She's my husband's mistress.'

When she had said it she was frightened, although her voice had been a whisper, and she put her hand over her mouth. It was what a schoolgirl does, she said, the kind of behaviour Rex hated to see in her. Alan said, 'Double, double, toil and trouble,' and made a face, an eyebrow-raising, looking-down-the-nose face. Then he said, 'We won't mind them. Let's pretend they're not there, they've gone off to hell on her broomstick, your old man riding pillion,' and Stella found herself saying she wouldn't mind if she had someone like him to talk to about it. She was overcome by her own daring, she blushed, and then she laughed.

She had a marvellous evening. She couldn't talk to him all the time but it made her feel good just knowing he was there. It was like having a wonderful unexpected present, but better than that. Stella said that for the first time in her life she felt as if she was with the person she most wanted to be with in the whole world. At school it hadn't been like that, it had been simple friendship, and now that experience seemed shallow to her. The years had enriched what they had, though they had spent them apart. During the evening she several times caught his eye and he smiled at her, once he winked, and before he and Gilda left he came over to her alone and whispered that he was happy. That was all, he was happy.

'But you know, Jenny,' she said, 'the way we order society, he couldn't be my friend. That was what I thought I wanted but a married woman can't be friends with a married man.'

I knew it well.

'It was Gilda who became my friend. I often wonder how many women make a friend of a woman because it's her husband they really like. And that's the only way to get to see him. Even then you'll only see him when you see her or when all four of you are together. It's better than nothing, that's all.'

'Didn't you like her?'

She thought. After all these years she still had to think about it. 'I don't know. I suppose I did at first. The point was, she seemed to like me. She rang me up next day to thank me and asked if she could drop in and borrow some book I'd mentioned I'd read and said I'd lend her. That was the beginning of our friendship.'

'You often saw him?' I said.

'Alan? If I went to St Michael's Farm to see Gilda I'd see him. They were always coming to dinner and we were always going to them. I was never alone with him. For one thing, in the afternoons I'd have Marianne with me. I must have been very silly, Genevieve, because I didn't realize what was happening to me. You see, I'd never been in love before. Apart from my little girl, and that's different, I don't think I'd ever loved anyone before. The best I'd had was just finding someone quite nice to be with.

'When we became lovers at last, it was like a whole new world. You hear about born-again Christians, I was born again, I became a different person, I understood about being happy, that it was something positive, not just an absence of unhappiness. But that was quite a long way off in 1960. It was all still to come. It was long before I began to—make arrangements for us.'

She was tired now but there was a question I had to ask. I said,

'Did you ever think you might marry?'

Her look said I'd asked something no sensible person would have thought in doubt.

'Of course I did. *We* did. Especially after Rex was dead. I told you I always took an interest in the law. By the end of the sixties they were talking about new divorce laws. It looked as if divorce might be possible by mutual consent or even because just one party wanted it.'

Her eyes had closed. She spoke sleepily. 'We were going to be together. When I was a girl people were horrified by a couple living together without marriage, if a woman did she had to pretend to be married and wear a ring, but all that changed. It changed so fast, Genevieve, it was quite amazing. I would have lived with him and not worried at all.'

I couldn't follow the logic of it, if there was any logic. 'If Gilda was dead, you could have married, couldn't you?'

'Of course we could,' she said and she fell silent, closing her eyes.

11

Red and white flowers mixed together were the worst possible omen, Janis said, and she wanted the wreath of carnations and petunias our cousin's wife from Thetford had sent kept off Dad's coffin. Otherwise there'd be another death. She wasn't convinced that I'd made things better by picking a head of purple clary out of the hedge and poking it in among the carnations.

It was a good thing Mum wasn't at the crem to see it. Dad's second wife Kath wasn't there either. In fact it was a poor turnout, no relatives but Janis and me, not a single friend, and Suzanne in deepest black standing in the rain and crying. Dad's former partner in the garage business sent a wreath of yellow chrysanths and ivy in the shape of a bull-nosed Morris, but he didn't come himself.

It was because of the flowers that I wouldn't tempt providence further and meet Ned on Hallowe'en, the day he suggested. All Saints', the next evening, wasn't possible for him, so it had to be All Souls', November 2nd, which is a funny sort of night in my opinion. Philippa's Katie was born on All Souls' and she has always been a strange one, not needing much sleep, not afraid of the dark, a night bird. Some say it's when the dead come back and

walk, Nan swears she's seen old Mrs Thorn in the church-
yard on All Souls', picking the moss out of the letters on
her own gravestone, and I didn't feel too happy going
alone into Stella's dark house.

The clocks had gone back and it was light by six in the
morning but dark by six at night. I took a torch with me
and that got me into the hall where the first candles were.
Candlelight isn't a very reassuring sort of light, it quivers
and streams and leaves great spaces of dark, and it makes
you wonder if people in olden times were ever wholly free
from fear in the night. Candles were all they had. It's a
horrid thought, the wick burning down and consuming
the wax but having no other and no light switch, nothing
to alter the deep black darkness.

I lit one candle after another and went upstairs, carrying one in each hand. The light that is bluish and gold-
ish, shimmering and somehow cold, travelled a little
ahead of me but not very far. Walls of darkness turned
into rooms with little squares of grey where the windows
were. It was mild for November but still cold. For once
my longing for Ned and the happy excitement I usually
felt was overcast by the grimness of this place without
light or heating. I felt the isolation of it out in the fen and
I felt how easily a primitive kind of fear comes when electricity isn't there.

Stella had told me some more by then, but not yet
about how she came to buy the house, though I'd guessed
it was to have a place in which to meet Alan Tyzark. I was
thinking that night, in the dark, of what she'd said about
the terrible thing he'd done. The difficulty was she hadn't
said any more, I didn't know whether I wanted her to say
more, but I couldn't help thinking that maybe he'd done

whatever it was here in this house.

I started my heating going in the bedroom and set up
candles on the tables and the chest of drawers. To pass the
time I opened doors and drawers, but the cupboards were
all empty, and I wondered if they had always been so, for
this was a house kept for some other purpose than living
in. A house that was not a home but a refuge from the
world, a place to be secret from other people's eyes, a shel-
ter from the storm. I savoured a word I'd found in the
dictionary and used it for this house: a trysting place. A
trysting place for one pair of lovers and now for another.

Stella's wardrobe was a huge piece of furniture,
mahogany I suppose, on short curved legs with feet like
the paws of a lion. The little golden keys turned only with
difficulty, but I got the doors open and, instead of emptiness inside, the cavernous dark mustiness I expected, I
found summer clothes hanging up on a rail. They were so
like Stella, so *essentially* Stella, that they could have
belonged to no one else: a blue cotton dress and a pink
one, film clothes from the early sixties, a silvery-blue
shot-silk raincoat that would have been useless in the rain
but glamorous in a car on a wet day.

Pushed to the far end of the rail, on a hanger that jan-
gled like a bell when I moved it, was another dress. I
fetched my torch and shone it into the dimness and on to
the tight waist, the full skirt, the low neck. Cream-
coloured, with a pattern in blue and rose, it was a dress
that was absolutely Stella's except in one respect. It was
dirty. It made me realize that I had never seen her anything but immaculate, untouched by the frowsty shabbi-
ness of age. I was sure she had always been like that,
fastidious, dainty, the sort of woman whose clothes were

always at the cleaners or in the wash. But this dress was covered with black smuts. There was a grass stain on the back of the skirt and something that might have been blood on the front. I examined it curiously in the light of the torch and saw the brown smear of a burn mark on the hem, a singeing of the material, and then I stood back and looked at the whole. Dirty though it was, soiled and ruined by a careless iron perhaps, it was like a dress to wear to a wedding, a bridesmaid's or even a bride's. But the bride had dug a ditch or lit a bonfire.

Ned's car lights flooded the bedroom and died away. I closed the wardrobe doors and put out my torch. I watched him get out of the car and stand for a moment, looking up at the window. He could see nothing but the candle's faint glow, he couldn't see me, and I had the pleasure of watching him unseen, his face unguarded and full of longing and hope. I ran downstairs towards the candles in the hall and opened the door as he put his hand to the knocker.

Beyond the range of the heater, the air in the bedroom was damp and our hands were cold, in spite of the mildness of the night. The sheets were aired but they felt as cold sheets do, damp and stiff. Gooseflesh on gooseflesh and the turn-off of icy fingertips on anxious skin. We grew warm in time and our mouths were never cold but afterwards I thought, and I believe he thought, if it is like this now how will it be in the depths of winter?

It was ten-thirty when I got home and Mike was still working on the replacement of our dining-room window with french doors, before the building of the conservatory. This was his first week at home after the long months of work on the Regent's Park site. I had told him, with many misgivings, that I was doing overtime at Middleton Hall, and he had accepted this, he hardly seemed to hear what I'd said. He trusted me. On the other hand, if trust is a positive thing, an act of will, Mike hardly seemed to know it was called for, he hadn't thought about it.

He greeted me with, 'I haven't heard a word about the planning permission.'

While he was away I had scarcely realized how bemused I always was on coming back home after a meeting with Ned. It hadn't mattered then if I was in a daze, dreaming and remembering. I could sit down and close my eyes and give myself up to remembering our sexual pleasures and the happiness of love. With Mike there I had to talk. I had to respond.

Fortunately, he didn't want to know anything about Middleton Hall or what had happened there, he wasn't interested, and I was relieved of the necessity to lie. But I wondered, as he speculated about the time the planning committee might take to make up their minds, how much lying I could bear to do. Would the day come when self-disgust clamped down and made it impossible for me to invent excuses and produce alibis? Of course it would, and it wasn't far off, but I didn't know it.

But I was aware even then that I had begun thinking very differently about Mike and our marriage and our home. I looked at this man, thick-set, tallish, surely handsome still, and thought that I knew him utterly, I knew him inside-out, yet I didn't know him at all. I had no idea what went on inside his head, under that thick dark curly hair. It couldn't be nothing but house improvement and planning permissions, could it? Once, years before, when he had come home from work and I'd said he looked tired, he had turned to me and said,

'Building work is hard, it wears a man out. It makes you old before your time.'

And I had felt such a rush of love and pity. I took hold of his calloused hands and so many strange thoughts went through my mind, how he did this because it was all he'd been able to do, how he'd never been given the chance to get qualifications, it was all earn, earn, earn. Go out and earn at sixteen, start at eight in the morning and get overtime till dark if you can. I put my arms around him because he was afraid of hard labour wearing out his youth.

But that was the only thing I'd ever remembered him saying to me about his feelings. Not a word, ever, about love or need or being frightened or sad. Sometimes when I'd talked about having children he'd barely looked at me, he'd said without raising his eyes, 'That's up to you,' and another time, 'We've got a nice home together and you know what bringing kids into that would mean.' And now, in the evenings and at the weekends which might have been for leisure, he went on doing the work he'd said would wear him out and make an old man of him. He was beyond my understanding.

It was partly Mike and having to lie to Mike and partly knowing that whatever marriage was we didn't have it any more that started me on re-thinking my refusal of Ned. I mean my saying no to Ned when he talked of going off and living together. After all, Nick had been even younger than Hannah when my dad left. He hadn't gone to his funeral, he said he hardly knew him, but has that affected him for the worse? The truth was you can't tell how living with just one parent will hurt or not hurt a child. Lots of nasty people I know grew up with happily married parents living together.

Then there was Stella's house. Not just that it was cold and dark but that the day was coming when it wouldn't be available at all. I might so far transgress as to use it now without asking but I knew I wouldn't dare do that when, on Stella's death, it became the property of Richard or Marianne. We would have nowhere to go and my fears of losing him would come back.

It's a measure of how far the corruption process had gone that six months after I'd sworn I'd never take him away from his daughter I'd begun thinking of ways round that. Having said I'd never lie, I'd begun lying. I was trespassing on someone's property. I was acting out the words Ned had once told me and counting the world well lost for love. Or perhaps just decency well lost for it.

Had it been like that for Stella? I watched her while she slept and tried to see, when she couldn't see me looking, the young and beautiful woman who had fallen in love with Alan Tyzark. My eyes tried to put flesh on her fragile bones and peachy skin on that withered face, to make the white wool hair glossy brown, but I could only see an old woman wasting away, her closed eyelids walnut shells, the blue veins almost breaking through the papery skin. And when I took her hand, knowing she'd soon wake, I noticed something that gave me a shock. She'd stopped painting her nails. Her yellowish corrugated nails were the way nature made them for the first time since I'd known her.

Stella told me that Gilda Brent liked to be with her and wanted her for a friend because she saw her as an inferior. Ironically, as it turned out, Gilda never regarded Stella as a threat. Yet anything in the nature of a threat was what she most feared and what made her the neurotic person she was. Her failure as a film actress—she seemed to see her career not so much as having failed as been ruined from outside—was due as she saw it to the jealousy and envy and bitchiness of other women. Women had always 'had it in for' her. She thought of herself, or said she did, as exceptionally better-looking than any other woman, more striking, more stylish, more charming, and so as not to seem impossibly vain, she spoke of this as a burden she had to carry through life. In other words, beauty was a liability.

She saw Stella as a 'pretty little thing'. In fact, 'little thing' was a pet name she applied to her, though Stella wasn't particularly small and at the time she first met Gilda she was thirty-six. Gilda decided that Stella was a country girl without much education or experience. In Gilda's eyes, she had never worked for her living or seen anywhere beyond Bury, had never read a book or been to a theatre. But the point was, Stella said, that Gilda made a person for her to be, just as she made a person for herself to be.

Somewhere, underneath, the real Gilda must have existed, but what she was and where it was Stella never discovered. She didn't explain what she meant by 'the end'. Only twice before that did she have a glimpse of reality. The Gilda she saw, or who was presented to her, seemed always to be playing a part, striking an attitude, speaking in a false voice, expressing feelings she had decided were appropriate, not what she felt. A surface had been created, she said, like a mask or a veneer. Whether

Gilda had always been like that or whether she had learned it as an actress she couldn't tell. It was as if she had never really stepped off the set. Her life was a long-enduring film script.

She spent hours telling Stella of her experiences as an actress and in films, the celebrities she had known, the glamorous locations she had been to, the famous restaurants and clubs to which she'd been taken by distinguished or handsome men. She hinted at lovers with famous names. As their friendship developed, she did more than hint and told Stella scurrilous tales of adventures in hotel rooms, hiding from jealous wives in wardrobes, and of huge presents of jewellery and furs made to her. Of Alan she spoke in a way Stella, even then, wouldn't have dreamed of speaking about her husband.

'You know, little thing, everyone who was anyone said I must have married him because he made me laugh. But that was only half the reason. I don't know if I dare tell you the reason, you're such an innocent little thing. You always make me think of someone at an old-fashioned girls' boarding school.'

Stella was always willing to listen to anything about Alan. She must have been the way I am when I'm in the village shop or the Legion and I hear Ned's name mentioned. But she didn't reply. It was amazing, she said, how little she actually spoke when she was with Gilda, no more sometimes than a dozen words in two or three hours, and Gilda never seemed to notice. She was a monstrous egotist.

'Promise you won't be shocked, darling? So many of the sweet men who'd been in love with me were so much older—well, it's inevitable, isn't it? Young men haven't had time to achieve anything or make any money. And I wanted a young man, I wanted a *virile* young man. I happen to think bed's pretty important and Alan—well, if I say Alan is spectacular in bed, will you even know what I mean?'

She didn't know. It was a phrase she'd read in books, that was all. But Gilda didn't want an answer from Stella, or no more than a 'yes' and a smile. She never did. In her eyes Stella was a mouse who was lucky that one man, even a man who everyone knew was sleeping with that old witch Charmian Fry, had liked her enough to marry her. More than that, Stella said, in the on-going movie that was her life, she had cast herself as the heroine and Stella merely as the heroine's friend.

And Stella, though often wondering how she could bring herself to do it, suffered Gilda for the single benefit that came with her. She let her take her shopping in London, to the hairdresser's in Ipswich, to the cinema, to the occasional charity performance Gilda still got asked to, for the sake of seeing Alan before or after these visits. The Tyzarks had one car between them at that time, so if Gilda wanted to visit Stella and Alan also wanted the car, he would drop her off and collect her again. This was what Stella had begun to live for, seeing Alan in ten-minute snatches once or twice a week.

She thought she could exist on that for the rest of her life. She'd put up with the increasing horror of Gilda's company, of Gilda's unending talk of celebrities and feuds, clothes and jewels, adulteries and intrigues, if bearing it made seeing Alan possible. She'd endure Gilda's artificial manner, the pose that seemed more and more to be hiding a real person. And there were always bonuses when he went to see a film with them, there were the foursomes at dinner in one house or the other, drinks on the sunny lawn in Bury or tennis on the nearly derelict court at St Michael's Farm. In private, inside her own head, she conducted long conversations with him, she called them imaginary dialogues, in which she told him everything about herself and her life and he replied in that way he had, taking a light-hearted and optimistic attitude to even the saddest things, and eventually confessed to her, serious by then, that he loved her.

This went on for nearly two years.

In some ways, of course, Stella knew more about Alan than Gilda did. She knew about his childhood, for they had been inseparable friends from the age of eight to sixteen. She had known his parents and the family home, the things he liked to eat and the games he played. Gilda filled in the gaps for her, the twenty years of separation. After school he had been to the Slade School of Art. Then he was called up into the army. The commission to illustrate the *Figaro and Velvet* books came just after the war when he was twenty-six and struggling unsuccessfully to be a portrait painter. He and Gilda met when he was commissioned to paint her portrait for a film she was in. It was *Lora Cartwright* and the picture was supposed to hang on the drawing-room wall in her film-husband's film-house.

'The totally mad thing was,' Gilda said, 'that in the end the portrait wasn't used. They never shot a single scene in the drawing room.'

Stella asked why not.

'Need you ask?' Gilda said. 'The star didn't like it. She was madly jealous of me from the start and she couldn't bear it that my portrait was being painted and not hers. But Alan and I had met and fallen in love. It was love at first sight.'

'What happened to the portrait?'

'They weren't going to waste that, were they? Not when they'd paid for it. So far as I know it's still hanging in their offices in Wardour Street.'

After that Alan had painted Gilda many times, head and shoulders, full-length in the grey gown she'd worn in *The Fiancée*, even a nude. That nude hung in the living-room at St Michael's Farm. There are nudes and nudes, Stella said, and I know what she meant, something like the difference between a shot for a body-lotion commercial and a photo in *Playboy*. The picture of Gilda naked showed her pubic hair. She wasn't absolutely unclothed but wore high-heeled shoes and, hanging between her breasts, a long string of pearls. Gilda was always drawing people's attention to this picture. It embarrassed Stella when Marianne was there, she wanted to tell her daughter not to look but of course she couldn't do that. Gilda would strike an attitude in front of the painting, asking Alan if he remembered her sitting for it, and implying they needed many sessions because the temptation of her naked body was too much for him.

They had been married for nine years and those years had seen a gradual decline in their lifestyle. At the beginning they had lived in the West End, Half Moon Street I think it was, and Gilda had made her last two films. *The Wife's Story* was about a husband's infidelity, and *The End of Edith Thompson* was a thriller about a real-life murderess or a woman they thought was a murderess who was hanged for killing her husband. Gilda played the wife in the first one and a prison wardress in the second. The character was a sympathetic wardress, and like Edith a married woman in love with a younger man. But this part made Gilda madder than anything in her career. She talked about it as if taking it had been the biggest mistake of her life and every opportunity she had had to make the most of it had been sabotaged by the actress playing Edith. The casting director had said—she told Stella this as an example of the incredibly ignorant things people said to her—that he had picked her because she had an unmemorable face. They insisted she wore glasses and flat shoes.

No more parts came after that, not in films that is. Gilda said she wasn't surprised after what had been done to her appearance by the actress and the director, who she knew for a fact were having an affair. Not much radio work had ever come her way and when she was offered a part in a serial she turned it down. Gilda never said much about this. She implied that she'd had to say no because she and Alan were going to the north of England where he'd been commissioned to paint some murals in an old chapel. Alan told Stella what really happened.

'The part was a woman who was supposed to have been injured in an accident that left her with one leg shorter than the other. You couldn't *see* that, of course. This is radio we're talking about. That only made it worse for Gilda. She said it would damage her reputation because people would imagine her as a freak with one of her legs only half there. If you're waiting for the pay-off here it is. The serial was *Mrs Dale's Diary*. We'd have been set up for life.'

As it was, they weren't set up at all. Alan had bought

St Michael's Farm and for some reason put it in his wife's name. Stella didn't know why and she felt she could never ask but she guessed it was a fear that he might have to go bankrupt. A woman, then as now, can't be held responsible for her husband's debts, though he can for hers.

'That was to make trouble for us,' Stella said. 'If it had been his house or even half his house, things would have been easier. You see, he had nothing except the royalties from *Figaro*. And the books went out of fashion. He always said they couldn't stand competition from *Orlando the Marmalade Cat*. I suppose there's a limit to how many children's books about cats the market can stand. He went on painting, of course he did, and he was reduced to doing some rather—well, humble jobs for money.'

That was later, though. Alan showed few signs of money worries in 1961. One day, having returned to the farm with Gilda, Stella witnessed a terrible row between them. She had no idea how they felt about children, to have them or not to have them, for Gilda had never mentioned it. But a few days before Marianne had been with them, Gilda talking to her as she often did about becoming an actress—she always said Marianne had the potential to be an actress, and Stella didn't much like this, the child was only eight—and that evening at the farm Gilda suddenly said to Alan in her presence that she wanted a child like Stella's daughter.

Alan said, 'Why should it be like Stella's daughter? Or are you planning to make up to old Rex?'

Gilda told him not to be so disgusting. 'It's your child I want.'

'This is a new departure. You've always been scared of

having a baby.'

'I never said that!'

In Stella's world married couples didn't talk about such things in public or even in front of one friend. She said she must leave, it was time she went home. Alan offered to drive her. This had never happened before. If she was without her own car it was always Gilda who took her home, and the thought of being alone with Alan for half an hour filled her with joy. She jumped up.

'No, sit down, Stella,' Gilda said. 'I want a witness to this. Did you or did you not say that we couldn't afford children and that they were enemies—to something or other?'

'Any great enterprise,' said Alan. 'Yes, and hostages to fortune and all that jazz. But only because you said you have a low pain threshold and having babies hurt. Come on, Stella, let's go. This is no fit subject for your ears.'

'I said no.' Gilda's voice was rising by octaves, Stella said. 'It's a crime to deny a woman a child. There are some religions in which a man can be divorced for that.'

'What religions? The Zoroastrians?'

'You make a joke of everything.' Gilda had begun to shout. 'Suppose I stop using my cap? What then? I can have a baby and you can't stop me.'

Alan shrugged. 'I can think of a way.'

The mention of the cap had started the blood rushing to Stella's face. Gilda began to act the part of a furious woman. It was *The Wife's Story*, even to the dialogue.

'Look at her blushing. You always upset my friends, that's why I never keep any friends. She won't come here again. I shall die friendless and childless. It's so unfair. Doesn't it ever occur to you how lucky you are to be married to someone like me? I mean, look at you, you're just an ordinary man with a baby face. People turn round in the street to look at me. Any man would want me. Stella, don't you think it's outrageous he won't give me a child?'

Stella didn't answer. Through all this she still felt that Gilda was acting. This was just another part she was playing. She didn't want a child, she was the last woman on earth to be a mother, she wanted to act a scene, that was all.

'Say something,' Gilda said in a ringing, stagey way. She went up to Stella and stood over her. 'Say something, little thing. Haven't you got an opinion? Have you lost your voice?'

It was this unprovoked attack which made Alan say what he did. 'Face it, Gilda, why don't you? You've missed the boat. Forty-one's too old to have a first child.'

He must have known what effect this would have on her. She never told her true age. She let it be thought she had made her first film at sixteen. Stella thought she was younger than herself, no more than thirty-five, she'd given no real thought to it and didn't care, but it broke through the veneer. It destroyed the pose and the real person came out. Gilda began to scream at Alan. She picked up an ashtray and threw it at him. He ducked and it struck a mirror, breaking the glass.

'About the unluckiest thing that could happen,' I said.

'What, breaking a mirror? Maybe. It made a fearful mess. She threw some more, the book they wrote phone numbers in and a vase. He was laughing by then. I thought Alan could laugh at anything, though I was wrong there. He threw a cushion back, it hit her in the face, of course it was soft and it didn't hurt, but she fell over and lay on her back kicking and screaming. I'd never seen anything like it. I didn't understand then that she could only sustain the acting and the façade by sometimes having an explosion like this one. She was like a volcano that's a quiet mountain but has to erupt every so often. Her eruptions were a safety valve that opened up when some sort of pressure of frustration and unhappiness got too much for her.'

'What had she got to be unhappy about?' I said.

'Oh, Genevieve, you must never ask that about anyone. A lot of people would say that to be in this world is to be unhappy.'

I didn't say anything. I thought I knew, you see, and my conclusions weren't Stella's.

'Everything was behind her,' Stella said. 'Her career was over and she couldn't do anything else. She'd no children. Every day made her a little less beautiful, it must have been so in the nature of things. I expect money would have been a compensation to someone like Gilda but she had no money. She was bored, she had no interests. She never cooked or did housework, the farm was filthy. Isn't it strange how a woman can emerge immaculate, exquisite, from a dirty hole like that? But she could. It's no wonder she was unhappy and oh, she was, she was.'

Alan picked Gilda up off the floor. He gave her some brandy. She didn't speak another word but buried her face in the sofa cushions. Then Alan drove Stella home.

It was about twenty miles. Neither of them spoke. Stella thought of how she had longed and longed to be alone with him for half an hour, just to be with him, and now she was she had nothing to say.

'But I had this awful thought, Genevieve. Of course it was impossible but I thought, why don't I just come out with it and tell him? Why don't I just say, "I love you. I just want you to know. Not to do anything about it, but just for you to know I love you."'

'Did you say it?' I said.

'No, I couldn't. But while I was thinking like that he *asked* me.'

'Asked you what?'

She looked down at the hands in her lap. 'Richard's coming in a minute, you know.' It was one of her abrupt changes of subject. She put up her hands and held them out to me.

'You've stopped using nail varnish, Stella,' I said. 'Would you like me to do your nails for you?'

'No, thank you. I don't like it on my old hands any more. Do you know what Rex once told me? He said wearing red nail varnish came from the harem. The women painted their nails red to show the sultan, their lord and master, you know, that they were having a period and weren't available. I don't know if it's true but it stopped me varnishing my nails for ages.' She reverted to Alan as if there had been no break in the story. 'Alan said, "Are you in love with me, Stella?" It was a funny way of putting it, wasn't it? I blushed, I was horrified. I started to ask him whatever gave him that idea and then I didn't see the point. It was too late for pretending. So I just said, "Yes, I am."'

Alan said, 'What a relief. I thought you must be.'

He didn't behave like anyone she had ever known, yet he was still the boy she'd known. The more she was with him the more she saw how little his nature had changed.

He said, 'I'm very much in love with you and have been for ages. I suppose I was when we were at school but people aren't supposed to be able to be in love at fourteen.'

'Juliet was,' Stella said.

'That proves it then,' he said. 'I thought it might go away but it won't. The time seemed to have come for a declaration.'

He hadn't stopped the car, he hadn't pulled into the side, he just kept on driving and, necessarily of course, not even looking at her.

'We have two alternatives,' he said. 'We can never see each other again and somehow fix that with Gilda and Rex, not too difficult probably, I don't think they like each other much, or we can be lovers. Personally, I'd much prefer the latter. How about you?'

'Yes,' said Stella.

'Yes to the second alternative?'

Stella said yes again, very much more firmly this time.

'Good,' he said. 'I'm sorry to sound so businesslike. It's because we've only got ten minutes left. As soon as I have more time I'll say to you some things from the fullness of my heart.'

Stella was silent for a moment or two. She was looking at the door and seemed to be listening. Then she said, 'I was very happy that evening. I was happy for a long time. I trusted Alan, you see, and I was right to trust him. We met soon after that and he did tell me those things. But we had nowhere to go where we could be alone. He sometimes managed to come to me in the afternoons, but very seldom. Still, I was happy. Of course I was guilty and ashamed about Gilda and because I arranged it that I saw her less and less, I saw Alan less and less too.'

Someone tried the door handle and Stella looked up. 'Is that Richard?' I went to the door but there was no one there, just Lena at the other end of the corridor. 'Rex had had some sort of disagreement with Charmian. I don't know what it was but if I had to guess I'd say she'd been pressing him to leave me now that Marianne was older and he'd refused. Anyway, he came back to me. It had happened before, those times when he'd come back to me. They never lasted.'

'But you let him come back?' I said.

She sighed. 'I was his wife, Genevieve. It's different for you. It's different these days. Rex kept me, he'd given me a home, I don't like talking about these things, but it was he who earned the money, everything was his. I couldn't say no to him, it wouldn't have been right. He came back to me and that was when he gave me this ring I wear, my eternity ring.'

She held out her right hand. I was a bit embarrassed. It sounded like a financial transaction to me: sleep with me again and here's two thousand quid's worth of jewellery.

'The following year,' she said, 'Richard was born.'

The door opened and Richard came in. 'My ears are burning,' he said. He went up to Stella and kissed her. 'You said I was born. What else have you been saying?'

He was smiling, he hadn't heard, but Stella had gone white. 'Oh, darling, nothing, nothing. Do you know you're exactly the same age as Genevieve?'

'Exactly?'

'Well, your birthday's April the 12th and Genevieve's is April the 24th.'

'I knew I must be older.'

Stella has this amazing memory for people's birthdays.

If she forgets everything else she remembers your birthday. I bet she knows Maud's and Arthur's and Lena's as
well as mine. I got up to go but Stella kept tight hold of
my hand for a moment.

'Rex had longed for a son,' she said. 'He was so proud
of Richard.'

'Mother,' said Richard, but a lot more kindly than
when I say 'Mother' to Mum.

Part Three

12

The whistling shocked me, the unknown tune, its clarity, but above all because darkness had come. I'd seen no lights, I'd been on the stairs. I opened the front door and Ned was there, a yard from me, suddenly in my arms. He'd been whistling, he said, because he was happy. Go three times clockwise round the house to undo the ill-luck, I said, but he only laughed and wouldn't do it.

The fear of what he'd done or what he might have brought about stayed with me. While we were in bed, the only warm place in the house, I forgot about the whistling, I forgot everything, but I remembered later. Sometimes I tell myself that all these precautions of Mum's and my nan's are nonsense and not for somebody like me, young and living at the end of the twentieth century. And then I see how death follows a ringing in the ears, and the dangers that come to a person who's broken a branch from an ash tree or helped another to salt. I haven't the courage to give up these things in this world that's such a hard place. Something can go wrong and I'd look back and think how it could have been avoided by touching wood or keeping a crooked coin under your pillow.

So I watched and waited for the ill effects of Ned's

whistling in the dark and I didn't have long to wait. The first thing was Philippa getting a flu bug. There was a lot of it about, Shirley Foster had had it and the whole Baleham family, and Philippa's Katie who brought it home from school. She went down with it on the Thursday evening and the Friday was my day off. The kids were on half-term, so I collected them and brought them back to my place. But first I carried the TV up to her bedroom and when I went back with Katie and Nicola at five Philippa was sitting up in bed watching *The End of Edith Thompson*, black and white, made in 1954, with Joyce Redman as Edith Thompson and Gilda Brent as the prison officer.

I gave the girls their tea downstairs, took a casserole out of the freezer for Steve and went back up to Philippa.

'Is it any good?' I said.

Philippa wouldn't look round. 'They're going to hang her in a minute.'

On the screen Gilda Brent and Joyce Redman were sitting in Edith Thompson's cell and Gilda was holding Joyce Redman's hand. Wearing glasses and with her hair screwed up under a cap, Gilda looked uncannily the way she was supposed to, an ordinary dull woman without much character. She could never be ugly, she could never be anything but good-looking with those regular features in that well-proportioned face, but she could easily be made forgettable. Basically, she was much better-looking than Joyce Redman but it was Redman's face that would stay with you and Gilda's that would fade once you switched the TV off. This was what Philippa did immediately Edith Thompson was taken off to be hanged and the credits started to roll. She put the remote under her pillow.

'I think it's made me feel worse. Would you get me another jug of water, Jenny? I'm supposed to keep drinking. They said Edith and her boyfriend planned to kill her husband but Edith didn't actually do anything. It was the boyfriend stabbed him. Edith wrote a lot of letters about putting powdered glass in her husband's food.'

'I'll just get your water,' I said.

When I came back with it she was lying down. 'They hanged her for that. They wouldn't now, would they? They'd put her on probation or give her a holiday in a theme park. Can you imagine plotting with a man to kill Mike?'

'No,' I said. 'No, I can't.'

'Do you think people do plot with lovers and whatever to kill their husbands or wives?'

I said I didn't know. It made me uncomfortable talking about it as if I was somehow guilty myself, as if I was being reminded of events I wanted to forget. I told her I'd be back in the morning and do her shopping if she wanted me to, but she said Steve would be at home as it was Saturday. Mike would be home too.

He worked on the conservatory all that Friday evening. The planning permission had come through and he was excited about that. It struck me that there wasn't much difference between the excitement he was feeling at being told he was allowed to build a glass room twelve by twelve on the back of his house, and the excitement I felt at meeting Ned. Perhaps it would be more to the point to say that he seemed to me happier at the prospect of building this conservatory than he had ever been on our honeymoon. He whistled while he worked. He sang. He ran out of things to sing and put on Radio One.

When he'd worked since six on Friday before until six on Saturday with six hours off for sleeping and half an hour for eating, I suggested we go down to the Legion for a drink. He didn't want to, he wanted to work through till eleven, but he agreed, though only to stop me going on my own. Mike is only thirty-three but he doesn't think women ought to go into pubs on their own, not even when their mothers run them. He says it's not ladylike, which is the word his father used and his grandfather before him.

The first person I saw when we got in there was Jane Saraman, or Beaumont, as I should say. It's one thing for your heart to miss a beat when you see your lover, but when you see his wife? I suppose I thought he must be there too. He wasn't.

'Ned's filming in Cambridge,' she said, as if I'd asked. 'I've come down with Hannah and my mother.'

It may not be ladylike but when I'm in a pub I offer to buy a round of drinks like anyone else. Why not? I earn too. I've got the use of my legs and strength in my arms. Besides, Mike wasn't going to offer her anything, I could see that in his face, the sullen look he'd put on as soon as he saw her.

'Thanks,' she said. 'I'll have a Perrier with ice and lemon.'

It beats me why people go into pubs to drink water. Len was behind the bar, telling everyone that Mum had gone down with the bug, and making a silly joke about how he'd opened the window and in-flew-Enza. I got a white wine for myself and a half of bitter for Mike and Jane's fizzy water. Mike looked at his drink as if it was a bottle of champagne I'd put in front of him, blinking his eyes and staggering back. He winked at Ken Foster and said the wife must be flush and to make the most of it for it wouldn't last. I asked Jane how Hannah was.

Her eyebrows went up. 'She's not so bad.'

I remembered, too late, that my sole knowledge of Hannah's condition was supposed to be based on snatches of overheard conversation. I tried to cover myself, but even then I was thinking that this is what deceit does, these are the humiliations in which it involves you and the innocent one.

'I hoped,' I said, 'she was getting better,' though I knew she wasn't.

She spoke in a hard voice. 'It's pollution that causes it.' My guilt I suppose it was that made me hear an undertone of accusation, even a double meaning. 'She's best in the country air.' Jane is one of those who can smile with her lips while her eyes stay dull as stones. 'I'd like us to get a place in France, where you can be sure of the weather, somewhere in the south maybe. In any case, we're giving up the cottage next month. The lease runs out and we're not renewing.'

Ned hadn't told me. I remembered, suddenly and quite vividly, his whistling in the dark, his refusal to perform the antidote. Were these the effects of it?

Weakness took hold of me, I wanted to sit down, but there was nowhere to sit. It was pathetic, but I needed her to comfort me, her reassurance. A look of deep boredom had taken over where that cool smile had been. Then suddenly I understood. He was tidying up, he was setting things in order, because he had sensed the change in me, the gradual coming round to his point of view, that we should leave and be together.

'I think I see the people I'm meeting,' she said, indicating the pair from the University Ned had said were her friends. She put her glass down on someone else's table. 'Thanks for the drink.'

When she'd gone I started wondering if he'd tell me. Perhaps he wouldn't. Perhaps he was waiting to see what I'd do next, and meanwhile he was ridding himself of encumbrances like the cottage, even buying somewhere in France for Jane to use with Hannah. And Hannah was getting better. She'd need her father but not the way an ill child would. Over my shoulder I kept glancing at Jane. She was talking and laughing with the UEA man the way I'd never seen her talk and laugh with anyone before. The woman sat by, silent and placid. It wasn't too far-fetched, was it, to think Jane might be having an affair with this man? After all, that wasn't necessarily his wife or partner with him. It could be his sister or just a friend.

Mum says a woman who's having an affair with a married man always does that, tries to convince herself his wife is unfaithful. It makes her feel less guilty, you see, if what's sauce for the gander is also sauce for the goose.

'Have I said too much to you, Genevieve?' Stella said.

It was the following week and we were sitting in the lounge. I looked up at her and asked why she said that. She could trust me. I wouldn't tell anyone. She shook her head and smiled faintly. The day was wild, the windows rattled as a west wind blew, and we watched it tear the yellow leaves from the chestnut trees. The lawns were ankle-deep in fallen leaves. The gardener Stella complained about because he called her by her christian name was cutting back plants in the flower beds that the first frost of the winter had turned black.

'I've had a few bad moments, thinking I'd told you too much. You must have been—well, not shocked but . . . Astounded, Genevieve?'

'I'm married,' I said. 'I'm having an affair with a married man. I thought I'd told *you* too much.'

It didn't interest her. Perhaps she had forgotten. 'If it's any consolation, telling you has been a relief to my mind. There's no one else I can tell, you see. You're a very good listener, did you know that?'

I told her I'd seen *The End of Edith Thompson* on television, or seen part of it, and she gave me an intense look. Then she reached for my hand and held it.

'I think it's quite common,' she said, 'a couple plotting together to kill the man's wife or the woman's husband. There are always cases in the newspapers.'

'Are there?' I said.

She sighed. 'Perhaps no more than any other—dreadful cases. We notice things that are close to what preys on our own minds, don't you think?'

I nodded. I could agree with that. Tales of love attracted my attention now I had a love affair of my own, just as engagement rings had when I got engaged, and estate agents' ads when we were moving into our house. But did that mean Edith Thompson preyed on Stella's mind?

She changed the subject swiftly.

'My father died when Richard was nine months old,' she said, 'and when you were nine months old too, Genevieve.' She smiled, proud of her memory. 'You've just lost your father and I'm sure it's gone deep with you. You used to see him even though he didn't live with you.

But once I'd left my parents' home I never saw my father—well, not more than once or twice. He'd never seen my baby. He hardly knew Rex. He'd only once been to our house, that was five years before and he didn't even stay the night. But he left me his house.

'I was married to a lawyer and I knew a bit about wills but do you know it never occurred to me that my father might have done that. A letter came from a solicitor in London. It was a piece of luck for me that it was a Saturday when it came and Rex was still in bed. Of course I was always up hours before the post came. Richard was such a bright lively baby, he never let me sleep after six in the morning. Oh, Genevieve, I don't know to this day what came over me, but I thought to myself, why should I ever tell Rex anything about this? He won't ask, it won't occur to him to ask, and I'll keep it to myself. And I did.'

'You didn't tell him?' I said. 'You didn't tell your husband your dad had left you his house?'

'I didn't. I never did.'

'But why?' I said. 'What was the point?'

She gave me a sidelong glance. For a moment she looked less old, less ill. 'It was a place of my own, wasn't it? I'd nothing of my own. It was my independence.'

I just nodded, though it seemed very strange to me.

'You couldn't do it nowadays,' she said, 'not with the amount people use phones. I mean, those solicitors and then the estate agents would have been bound to phone and if Rex was at home he'd have answered and it would have all come out. But phoning from London to Bury was a trunk call, it was something you might do in an emergency. Everyone wrote letters.'

'So you managed to keep it a secret?'

'I kept it from everyone but Alan,' she said, 'I told Alan. He loved secrets.'

Her love affair with Alan Tyzark had stopped while she was pregnant and for a long time after Richard was born. But he was always there, a presence in her life, and they often met for just an hour or two. He would call for her and take her for a drive with the children. They dared not even kiss for fear of Marianne's watchful eyes. Then, one day when Richard was about a year old and Stella was in secret negotiations to sell the house she'd been left, Rex said it was time she had some permanent help in the house. She should have an *au pair* and he had found her one. She was Danish, adored children, wanted to perfect her English. *Au pairs* were coming into fashion then, in Stella's world they were the answer to what you did when you couldn't get servants. But at first she was suspicious of the idea of Maret.

It must be a scheme of Rex's to get himself a young girl to sleep with. That was what she thought. That was how she thought of him, a man who lusted after women and was always hunting them. And the fact that Maret turned out to be the reverse of Stella's idea of a nineteen-year-old Danish girl, being squat and dark and not at all good-looking, for a while didn't alter that conviction.

'But it was his guilt over me that made him engage Maret, it was compensation for his infidelity. And then I realized something I'd never quite understood before, Genevieve. He wasn't a womanizer. He was quite monogamous, only his fidelity wasn't to his wife, it was to Charmian. There was no one else in the world for Rex but Charmian. He'd gone back to her and they'd started off

again before Maret even came. And somehow that hard-
ened my heart. Do you know what I mean? I could have
endured a succession of young girls who meant nothing,
but not this old woman who meant everything. I think I
lost all feeling for Rex then.'

'Why did you stay?'

She repeated what she'd said before. 'It wasn't like it is
nowadays. If I'd tried to divorce him I'd have had to prove
adultery and I don't think I could have done. I'd have had
to employ private detectives and even then a man of
sixty-two calling on a woman of fifty-eight, an old friend,
wouldn't have been evidence. Then there was my own
adultery. That wouldn't have helped me, that would have
made it worse. And I had the children. It wasn't like it is
nowadays. Rex might have turned on me, divorced me
and got custody of my children. I was afraid to try,
Genevieve. I just wanted a little independence and the
chance to be with Alan. Having Maret was a great help,
but we still had nowhere to be alone together.'

Her father's house was sold by the end of that summer
and the sum of money it realized was just under £5,000
after the legal fees and the estate agent had been paid. She
opened a bank account. She had her own cheque book
and it made her feel rich. At first she had no ideas of what
to do with the money. Why do anything with it? The
time would come when a purpose would suggest itself.

With Maret in the house and Richard too young even
for nursery school, Stella couldn't allow Alan to come
there. Once or twice he took her to a hotel. But this was
awkward and difficult, deeply embarrassing for Stella.
They had to pretend to be married, pretend to stay the
night yet pay in advance. And Alan couldn't afford hotels.

They were in love, they were as close as two lovers could be, but she wouldn't have dared offer to pay a hotel bill.

One day, driving back to Bury from a roadside motel, she saw a cottage with a For Sale sign outside. It was on a main road, ugly, exposed to the winds that swept the Breckland, but it gave her an idea.

She said to Alan, 'I shall buy us a house.'

'Just like that?' he said, and then he said, 'When?'

'Before winter comes. When we find one we like.'

'Whichever is the sooner,' he said.

The house must be halfway between Bury and Tivetshall St Michael, within easy reach of both, in rather a remote place, standing alone, oldish but not ancient, not too big and at the right price. They discussed endlessly their requirements: a garage to hide a car in from passers-by, a little garden, a tiled roof, not thatch, no neighbours, a big bedroom with a view.

By a small miracle, Gilda was off to spend two weeks with a friend in the south of France. Stella and Alan went house-hunting and before Gilda came back they had found the flint-walled house with the red roof called Molucca.

I walked Stella back to her room. It might have been easier to have carried her. I'm sure I could, she's so light. She sat in her chair and put her feet up on a stool.

'I was so happy at that time, Genevieve.' Her voice was soft and rather sleepy. 'For the first time in my life everything was going right for me. I'd been in love with Alan for four years but I seemed to fall in love with him again. This time it was deeper, it was more intense. I was forty, and it wasn't like it is nowadays, forty was middle-aged.

But Alan made me feel young. I'd never had any real plea-sure—I don't quite know how to say this . . .'

'From sex, d'you mean?'

'Yes, from sex.' Stella closed her eyes. She didn't want to meet my eyes. 'I'd never had pleasure with Rex and I couldn't even imagine what it would be like. I mean, if you don't like doing something you can't imagine doing the same thing but liking it, can you?'

'Like ironing with the latest thing in steam irons,' I said. I hate ironing.

She smiled a feeble smile. 'So you could say, why did I ever want to—to make love with Alan if I didn't like love-making? I don't know the answer to that, Genevieve. But I'm sure I'm not the first woman who didn't have any pleasure but thought she could have if she was with someone she really loved. And the first time—the first time with Alan—well, it was quite different.' She looked at me. 'I'm sorry, it's rather embarrassing talking about these things. I was just trying to make you see that I loved him, I loved him in every possible way. And when we had the house to go to, it was wonderful. It was romantic.

'I would go over there in the late afternoon. Maret was at home with the children. As for Rex, he and I were lead-ing quite separate lives by then. He never asked where I was if I wasn't at home and I knew where he was so I didn't have to ask. He probably knew about Alan, or he knew there was someone, but he didn't care any more.

'I was proud of my house. It was *mine,* you see. You saw the deeds, in *my* name. That meant a great deal to me. I had such fun furnishing it. Alan and I had very lit-tle money but you could find amazing bargains in the antique shops and at sales in those days. He had the originals of the drawings he'd done for his children's books and we had them framed and put up on the walls. I always kept the house full of flowers. I cleaned it myself, I had to. It was the only place I'd ever enjoyed cleaning.

'Waiting for Alan I'd dress up. I'd put on a beautiful dress and jewellery and do my hair carefully. I'd take an hour doing my face and my nails.' She looked away. 'All to be untidied and spoilt when he came and we—we kissed and embraced and made love.' A little light laugh and one of her changes of subject. 'People didn't drink wine the way they do nowadays, they only drank it at meals, but I kept gin and tonic and angostura and vermouth and sherry there. I often cooked us a meal. I used to watch for Alan's car from the bedroom window and long and long for him and be sick with fear if he was five minutes late. Oh, Genevieve, can you imagine?'

Only too well. Apart from the fact that it was warmer then and the drink was different, there didn't seem much to choose between us.

'It was wonderful having a place to go to and a—a bed of our own. I suppose you'd say we played house. We played at being a couple, at being husband and wife. One evening, when we were having a drink and I was in an evening gown and for some reason he'd put on a suit, we were sitting there with the table laid and food cooking, and it was just as if we were waiting for friends to come to dinner. He said, "This is our dress rehearsal for being married." '

'You meant to get married, then?' I asked her.

She didn't answer but only reached for my hand. Since that first time she put her arms up to me, we've been giving each other a kiss when I come in the morning and when I go in the afternoon. Every time, the body I hug seems more brittle and birdlike and the heart to flutter more rapidly. I used to wait for Stella to make the first move but now I kiss her as a matter of course and when she's in my arms give her a squeeze that I hope she knows is loving. I kissed her then and her cheek felt hot as if she was still blushing for what she'd said.

Ned phoned soon after I got home. He was very casual about the move from the cottage, it didn't seem important to him, they'd never meant to take the place on for more than a year. Did it matter? I said no, it didn't matter, in a way it was better for us not to run into each other in the pub or the shop.

He was impatient with all that. 'When shall I see you?'

'Tomorrow if you like.'

'Of course I like. It's the one thing I like in an unlikeable world.'

A lover can't say better than that.

That night, while Mike was putting in the glazing bars, his meal on a tray on the crate they'd come in, I sat down with a glass of red wine and the encyclopedia to try and learn something about modern art. But I didn't get very far. I had a talk with myself instead. It was like two people talking in my head, one arguing for and one against. I was so young when I married I'd never thought about marriage, I'd never considered whether marriage should be something permanent, something sacred if you like, or if you ought to dissolve it when you'd nothing more to say to each other. One of my voices told me I should try to keep the marriage going and the other said what was the point when we'd nothing in common and there were no children.

And then the two of us inside me discussed Ned and Jane and Hannah. One said a woman with a conscience would never forgive herself for splitting up a family and taking a man from his child but the other said that people did it all the time, it was commonplace. Even out here in a country village people did it all the time. My father had done it and my mother had done it twice. Times had changed since Rex Newland and Stella had to behave the way they did, keeping empty marriages going at all costs, sneaking off for secret meetings until love itself at last wore out. Philippa had told me that of all the kids in Katie's class at school less than half lived with their own mother and their own father who were married to each other. And then I thought of having Ned's child. It might be that by this time next year I could have a baby that was Ned's and mine.

The first voice said, Hannah is only five, she's too young to understand, she'll want her father and Jane won't be able to explain. But she'll come and visit us, the counter voice said, she'll spend weekends with us, and maybe she'll come to love me. Or maybe she'll hate me and turn her father against me. I poured myself a second glass of wine and thought of living with Ned, of sleeping all night with him, of waking up beside him.

All the time I was sitting there, thinking and arguing with myself, a steady hammering came from the back room. I'd closed the door because now the window had gone there was nothing between the dining room and the garden but a sort of skeleton of a conservatory. It was a mild, damp night, and there was something dismal about the misty, still darkness and that regular rhythmic banging. When he's finished, if there isn't any work in

Norwich or London, he'll start on something else. Maybe he'll re-fit the kitchen, it's only been done twice since we got married, or turn the two downstairs rooms into one big room or build a garage at the bottom of the garden. There's plenty for him to do for the next thirty years. And when he's sixty-five and gets his pension he'll turn to me (if I'm still here) and say we're moving to a bungalow at Cromer, preferably a dilapidated one, so that he can take it to bits and put it all together again.

I took my wine and went into what used to be the dining room. The man on the steps with the hammer in his hand seemed nothing to do with me, a workman who was building something, doing overtime long into the night. Thick white mist had come down and you couldn't see the end of the garden. A heap of old timber loomed through it, the french door frames and what had once been the shed and a length of fence. My watch said ten-fifteen.

'Are you going to be much longer?' I said.

He didn't stop hammering. He'd got half a dozen nails clamped between his teeth. 'Give me another half-hour. You go to bed.'

'Can we talk, Mike?'

The nails dropped into the palm of his hand. 'I know you're upset about your dad. That's only natural, time will heal that.'

'Not as upset as I should be,' I said. 'It's not that. Can we talk?'

'Isn't that what we're doing?'

'I mean, have a talk. I want to talk seriously.'

The hammering stopped and he turned to me with an expression of acute irritation, his face reddening.

'You know something, Jenny. I've been working all day and when I get home I have to get started on this, I don't even have a break. I get tired. Can't you realize that?'

We'd never had a serious talk in the whole of our married life, but I'd never noticed before.

I went upstairs. We sleep in the front but the bathroom's at the back and I was cleaning my teeth when the frosted window was suddenly lit up with a yellow dazzle. I went into the back bedroom and looked out of the window. Mike had set light to the pile of timber. Because it was damp he had poured paraffin on to the wood and it was burning fiercely, sparks flying up into the damp dark air like rocket tails on Guy Fawkes Night.

It's sensible to think of the thatched roofs in the village when you light a fire, but there'd been too much rain to worry about that. The flames were leaping high and the fire already had a red heart where the hardwoods burned slowly.

I opened the window to feel the heat. On my face the blaze was like summer sun. The roaring was an intense, frightening sound that soon fetched Sandra Peachey out from next door with her husband Joe in his dressing-gown and the murderous cat in his arms. When they started shouting at Mike I closed the window and went to bed, into our double bed, on the left-hand side, right on the edge so that I wouldn't touch him when he got in.

13

No one will disturb me, thought Stella. They think I am too tired for anything. And so I am, too tired for anything but this. I no longer have the strength to carry that chair across the room and wedge it under the door. But no one will come in. After all, in a residential home they're glad if you're resting, if you're quiet, if you give no trouble . . .

I am going to say something I thought of telling Genevieve but I can't. I can't risk her telling him. No, not telling him. Unwittingly revealing it to him. If I were going to tell him myself I should have done so years ago. Perhaps I shall give him this tape but perhaps I shall not. After all, he can never find out. There is no evidence he can ever find that would point to his—well, his parentage.

I'll begin now.

When he was five, said Stella, Richard had to have a blood test. He was a very small, thin child and some sort of anaemia was suspected. As it turned out he didn't have it and he soon began to grow and fill out, there was nothing wrong with him, but this test was done.

I had never known whose child he was. I supposed,

and at one time hoped, he was Rex's. After all, Rex was my husband, he supported me, he kept the children, fed and clothed and educated them. That was how I looked at it at the time. That was the way married women who were not breadwinners did look at it. Still do, some of them, I expect. How strange this is, Genevieve knows this, that it's easier for me to talk about sex than money!

Richard was conceived at the time of one of Rex's returns to me. In the crucial month I must have had sexual relations five or six times with Rex and just once with Alan. That sounds very disgusting, uttered like that. I shall stop the tape and play it back.

It was even more disgusting to hear than to say. No one should behave like that, but some women do, some women don't have much choice. I told myself that the baby must be Rex's, I persuaded myself of that. The other possibility frightened me but I kept thinking of those figures, the five or six times and the one time. It haunted me. Instead of thinking with happiness about the coming baby I thought always of whose child it was. Every morning when I woke up it was my first thought. But the strange thing was that when Richard was born I stopped worrying, I almost ceased to think about it.

Babies are interesting the way they look and the way they change. Priscilla's Hugo looked a lot like my father-in-law when he was first born, at three months he was the image of his mother and when he was twelve he looked like a photograph of Jeremy taken when he was a child. Richard looked like me for the first five or six years of his life. His hair was fairer and his eyes were lighter than mine but they had the same features. At that time I hadn't realized that Alan and I were ourselves rather alike to look at, not twin-alike but as a brother and sister might be. If my child looked like me he must also look like Alan.

Then came the blood test. Richard's blood group was B, not rare but not all that common, about 6 per cent of the population. Rex and I had both at one time been blood donors and I knew we shared group A. It might not be DNA fingerprinting but it was sound enough. Richard couldn't be Rex's son.

Twenty years later, at least twenty years, I was reading an article in a newspaper about why women miscarry and came upon a theory, or perhaps something more than a theory. It suggested that families of children all of the same sex might not be that way as a matter of chance. Suppose the man carries some faulty gene that only affects boys and is so damaging that it kills the male foetus when it's, say, three months old. Then the mother would conceive girls and boys but carry only girls to term. I thought about that. All the babies I miscarried that were old enough for their sex to be known had been boys. Suppose that was a fault in Rex and not in me, in Rex's genes. He who had so much wanted a son could never have had one, no matter whom he had married. My boy, the boy to whom I had given birth, was Alan's son, not his.

I wish I'd read it when Richard was small. It would have made me feel less guilty. I had over a year of guilt and fear before Rex died, guilt that he had a cuckoo in his nest, fear that he would find out, that he would *see*. For Richard was beginning to look like Alan. He was changing and starting to look like Alan, or I thought he was. It may have been my knowledge of who his father really was that made me think like that, but I believed I could see a physical change and that everyone must soon see it too.

If I had been aware of the gene theory then I might not have felt so bad. After all, I had given Rex the son he could never have produced. He loved Richard and was proud of him. It might even be that he stayed with me instead of going off to Charmian because of Richard. At the time, though, that only made me the more afraid of what the effect on him would be if one day he looked at his son and saw Alan.

Rex died. The day I found Charmian's body in the barn and Alan took me back to the house and lay there holding me in his arms, on that day I told him. I had to get back, I couldn't leave Richard with Priscilla for the evening. I had to go back and fetch him and take him home. The conversation we had, I remember it word for word. I got off the bed and sat with my back to Alan and said,

'He's yours, Richard is your son.'

'Yes, I know,' he said.

I can't describe how casually he said it, how lightly. I might have told him it was ten past five or the sun had come out. 'You *know?*'

'Sure, I've known since he was a few months old. Same turned-up snout, or retroussé nose, as they say. He's got your eyes, I've always been glad about that.'

'Why didn't you tell me?'

'Why didn't you tell me, my dear? It was your secret.'

'Oh, Alan, are you glad?'

He got up and came round the bed. He put his arms round me and held me tight. 'It's the best thing in my life,' he said, 'after you.'

'Yet you were content never to mention it, have him accepted as Rex's? Would you ever have asked?'

'I've been waiting for you to tell me for nine months.' It was nine months since Rex's death. 'Come to think of it, we could have had another one in that time.'

You're terrible, I said. You're awful. It was what I always said when he made his bad-taste jokes. 'Shall we ever tell him?'

He thought about that one. My head was on his shoulder and he held it there lightly, his thumb moving against my cheek.

'Yes,' he said at last, 'but not yet. Not until we're all three living together or until Gilda sees, whichever is the sooner.'

It made me want to be with him more and I think it made him want to be with me more, now that we had said to each other what we both secretly knew, that Richard was our son. An illicit affair seemed—oh, I don't know, inappropriate. I needed some dignity in our relationship, and more than that, openness, propriety I suppose, a love and a bond that all the world could see. The three of us together, Richard and his parents.

I am feeling rather better today. A remission. Talking into this machine comes most easily first thing in the morning, when I am freshest. This the last tape I shall make and destroy. I regard it and its predecessors as practice, as rehearsals for the real thing. The next one will be the real thing.

It is true that driving a car has unpleasant associations for me. So does fire, though only in the sense of cremation. I have left instructions that I am to be buried. But it is the plough that troubles me most, or troubles me on some deep, barely conscious level. My lips, now, as I speak of it, grow stiff. Forming the word and uttering it is for me as it is for some people to speak the name of the creature they are phobic about: snake, spider, rat. Once or twice it has been the answer or part of the answer to a crossword puzzle clue and as I have written it in something has contracted inside me and a shiver has run up through my body.

When I have a bad dream that is what my dream is about. The strange thing is that it is never the modern machine that I see, the actual machine that gave rise to all this, but the hand-held or horse-drawn implement. I don't know why this should be. I can only recall once seeing such an object, and that was in a museum of bygones. I have seen pictures, of course.

Alan sometimes called me his star. 'My star'—because Stella means a star. Once he quoted someone and, telling me to look at the stars, said he wished he were the heavens so that he might look at me with many eyes. Last night, before I went to bed, I looked at the stars out of this window as I often do. I saw Charles's Wain up there, that some call the Big Dipper, and Ursa Major and—the Plough. The shape of it, the configuration of stars, is the shape of the thing in the museum. The effect on me was to dream of a man ploughing, an old man in medieval dress, pushing the plough through a stony field, only the earth he turned over was ashes and the flints that came to the surface were bones. And when he came close to me I saw that his face was Alan's face, grown old.

I have dreamed that a good many times before I sat at the window and looked at the stars. Dozens of times in the years that have passed. Twice since I have been in here. The ploughman usually has Alan's face but not always. It was another man that I saw trudging through a field of bones last time I dreamed it, a different face, one I've seen only once before but have never forgotten. That was the only time it printed itself on whatever screen of memory figures in our dreams.

I believe it performed this operation because I had been sitting with Genevieve talking for longer than usual that day.

The sooner I strip that from the tape the better.

14

Maud was to Lena what Stella is to me. I realized that when Maud was dead and I saw Lena's face swollen with crying. She'd sat up all night with her, being the daughter Maud never had, holding her hand to keep the life in till death got too strong and prised them apart. Even if you're running what Ned calls a granny farm, even if you're money hungry, you can still have your affections. I thought what a contradiction a person's character can be and for some reason it frightened me.

'You'd hardly credit it,' Sharon said, 'but she's got a waiting list of wrinklies queueing up to come here. Hope we get another old boy, the women piss me off.'

The undertakers' car was outside when Marianne arrived. She came on her own, driving a Volvo Estate. As she walked up to the front entrance the undertakers' men came down the steps with Maud's body on a stretcher covered up in black.

I was on the steps too and I thought she was going to drop. I went quickly up to her and took her arm.

'It's not. . . ?'

'It's old Mrs Vernon,' I said. 'She died in the night. Are you all right?'

'Oh, Jenny, I'm *fine*. You *are* kind.'

Marianne may be a bit neglectful and a bit scatter-brained but you can't help liking her. It's nice when people remember your name. It's nice when they talk to you as if you're old friends and don't have any side or give themselves airs.

'I haven't seen Mummy for a month,' she said. It was nearly two but I didn't say so. 'I've felt so guilty. I was doing this TV commercial in Ipswich and I said to myself, Marianne, you'll be an utter bitch if you don't take this chance to go and see Mummy, it's only a matter of whizzing up the A14. And then when I got here I thought I was *too late*. Of course it was my guilt distorting things, darling. I'm such a fool!'

Looking at her then I had some idea of what Stella had meant by saying she was like Rex. Of course I'd never seen even a photograph of Rex Newland but Marianne's large dark eyes and quite heavy dark eyebrows didn't come from Stella. They make an interesting contrast with her hair that isn't actually dyed even if it isn't naturally quite that red-gold. And her nose is a bit hooky, aquiline I think they call it, while Stella's is a neat little straight nose even now. She was wearing jeans and a white shirt and big silver earrings. It reminded me of what Stella had said about the way actresses look, their way of doing their make-up and their clean hair.

I walked her along to Stella's room but I didn't go in with her. The long package she was taking out of her bag I guessed was two hundred cigarettes. Marianne was the secret supplier Stella said she'd be tortured about before she'd confess.

Lena had asked me to sort out the few pitiful things

Maud had left behind her for the relatives if we could find any. She couldn't bring herself to do it, she said, and for once I didn't dislike her. I suppose I'd discovered she was human like everyone else. When I'd done that and taken Lois for a walk from one end of the house to the other and back—she's supposed to have a bit of daily exercise—I took Arthur his tea and carried a tray along for Stella.

The room smelt of smoke though they'd opened a fan-light. Seeing Stella almost every day, I suppose I haven't noticed the deterioration in her the way an occasional visitor would. Marianne caught my eye behind Stella's back and made a face of exaggerated distress. I asked her if she'd like a cup of tea but she shook her head and mouthed that she'd have it in a minute, she'd have it outside. She put her arms round Stella and started saying goodbye, she'd come back in a week's time, so I left them and walked slowly back down the passage.

Marianne came running after me.

'Oh, Jenny, isn't it dire! The change in Mummy! It was such a shock, I can't tell you.'

'I know,' I said. 'But she's not in pain. Her brain's very clear. And she's not muddled in her talk, she can talk as well as ever.'

'Can I speak to you for a moment?'

We went into the lounge. Carolyn was in there with tea on a trolley and no one to give it to but Gracie, who had fallen asleep in her armchair with one of Lena's cats in her lap. Marianne sat down by the french windows. I don't think she knew she'd picked Stella's favourite chair, the one where she always sat to watch the butterflies. I fetched her a cup of tea and one for myself.

'You said her brain's very clear,' Marianne began, 'but

do you think there's anything preying on her mind?'

All the things she tells me, I thought, and for some reason doesn't want you to know.

'What sort of thing?'

'I don't know how much you know about her, darling.' Marianne looked searchingly into my face. Her big dark eyes fix themselves on you and seem to see into your soul. 'Does she ever talk to you about my father?'

'She mentions him. Sometimes.'

'Does she talk about the way he died? I mean, where he'd been before he died?'

I don't know why I denied it, why I shook my head.

'She's never got over my father's death. Oh, yes, don't look like that, darling, I'm sure of it. She's never got over it. Let me tell you about it. It can't matter now, it's all so long ago, but you needn't tell her I told you. He had this long-standing relationship with another woman, you see. I was only fifteen but somehow I knew, I'd known for quite a little while. Terribly precocious of me, wasn't it? I was like Amanda in *Private Lives*, my heart was always jagged with sophistication.'

Perhaps you have the faintest idea what she meant. I haven't.

'I'm sure Mummy never knew about it. She's so trusting, Jenny, she's so *innocent*. He went on the train to see this woman—he'd given up driving by then—and coming back he had a heart attack. If he hadn't been alone in the carriage—well, it's no good talking about what might have been, is it? They found him when someone got into the carriage at Bury and they took him to hospital but he was dead when they got there.

'Mummy should never have been allowed to know

where he'd been. They should have had the sense to lie to her. It was this stupid doctor asking her if she knew where he'd been and telling her about the ticket in his pocket that did the damage.'

'You knew all that,' I said, 'at fifteen?'

'Not really. No, I didn't. I sort of pieced it together afterwards. I mean, when I was older. But I did know about Charmian—that was the girlfriend—and that she lived at Elmswell and he'd been there, and Mummy didn't know that. Not at first.'

'How can you be so sure?'

Marianne spoke almost triumphantly, 'Because of the result, darling, the effect on her. She was so absolutely devastated. She couldn't have been like that if she'd known all about the affair beforehand.'

'Look, Marianne,' I said, 'I'm not a psychiatrist. I mean, I'm not even a nurse. I'm just a carer. I don't know why these things affect people the way they do. I'm very ignorant really.'

'You've been kind to Mummy, darling, that's all I know. You've been more like a daughter than I have.'

It's awful, isn't it? The words that come into your head—and almost into your mouth—are the ones you're always hearing on TV or reading in magazines, 'I'm only doing my job.' Of course I wasn't such a fool as to say them.

Instead I said, 'You mean she was what you said, devastated, when your father died?'

'Not immediately. That was the strange thing. But perhaps it's not so strange, Jenny. Do you think shock delays things? It was months before it seemed to hit her. I mean, more than a year maybe, eighteen months, I don't know.'

I asked her what she meant. What convinced her Stella was in such a bad way? She didn't answer directly.

'Of course it was Mummy who found Charmian, but you know all about that.'

'I'm sorry?'

'Don't you know the story? I'm afraid I rather treat you like one of the family, Jenny. I take it for granted you know our family history as well as we do. Charmian shot herself. With a shotgun. I don't know the details, I've never known. It was quite a long time after Daddy died, months, but it was because of him. She couldn't bear life without him. Mummy found her.'

'Your mother *found* her? You mean found her dead?'

'She went to her house. She'd been jealous of her for years, she really disliked her, but I think she got to like her after Daddy died. I suppose she was sorry for her. Anyway, she went there and found Charmian dead in one of the barns. That was the beginning of it, I think. But I was so young, Jenny, and I had my own friends, and I was desperate to get to be an actor. There must have been so much I didn't *see*. But I know that before I went away to drama school when I was seventeen she'd gone into an awful depression—well, she'd just gone inside herself. I don't think she ever really came out, or not for years.'

'But that was two years after your father died,' I said.

'Yes, that's right, just before drama school. Mummy was depressed before I went away. It wasn't exactly depression, it was more as if she was—well, stricken. All sorts of things she used to do she just stopped doing. Driving the car, for instance. We had another *au pair* by then, Maret had left, we had a Norwegian called Aagot— amazing names they have—and Mummy just gave over the driving of the car to her. She drove Richard to school and did the shopping. Mummy wouldn't even go in the car. She had that friend, that actress, Gilda Brent, and Gilda's husband, whatever he was called . . .'

'Alan Tyzark.'

'That's right, Alan Tyzark. Mummy used to see a lot of them. I can remember him taking us out for drives, he liked kids, didn't have any of his own, and she used to go about with Gilda an awful lot, but after her depression started she never saw them. Just when she needed friends she dropped them. The only people she had anything to do with apart from us were the Brownings next door. I remember asking her why she never saw Alan and Gilda, if she wouldn't drive herself, why not let Aagot drive her over to see them, but she wouldn't.

'I was at drama school for three years and when I came home for holidays I used to try to get her interested in— well, things, people. I expect I interfered in things too much, but you know how you can be at that age, a right little do-gooder. I even rang the Tyzarks up, meaning to ask Gilda to come over and see Mummy but Alan answered and said Gilda was away. He'd always been tremendously nice to me but that time, it was the last time we ever spoke, I might have been a total stranger. Of course it was obvious there'd been a quarrel. Mummy seemed determined to quarrel with everyone. She didn't go anywhere, she didn't take on another *au pair* when Aagot left.

'She just devoted herself to Richard. Daddy had wanted him to go to prep school, boarding school that is, but Mummy wouldn't have that. I don't say she babied him, she didn't, but she wanted him with her. You could say she lived for him. And very gradually she got a bit better. We're talking about more than twenty years ago, and people didn't get treatment for depression. They were still caught up in that get-yourself-together thing. I can actually remember my cousin's wife Priscilla telling Mummy, "There's no one can help you but yourself, Stella." And the result of that was that Mummy quarrelled with her. They didn't speak for months.

'Mummy did get better and she never spoke of it, you know, I don't remember her ever mentioning my father. She absolutely never talked about him. But now . . . well, she mentioned him today. She just said, "I've been thinking about your father," and then she said, "I'm glad I married him because otherwise I wouldn't have had you." Sweet, wasn't it? But I think his death still haunts her. It's absolutely dire, you know, darling, to realize when your husband dies that your whole married life has been a lie.'

I couldn't tell her she'd got it wrong. I wasn't in the business of breaking up her illusions. She went back to have another word with Stella before leaving and as we came out of the lounge I tried to find a tactful way of telling her not to leave it too long before she came again.

'If you could manage it in a week or two?'

'Oh, darling, you mean she may not . . .'

'I don't know. No one knows. But to be on the safe side. She does love to see you. Could you come on her birthday?'

'I shall be seventy-one on December the 3rd, Genevieve,' Stella said to me when I took her breakfast in next morning. 'That's one year more than man's allotted span, quite a respectable age once upon a time. I shouldn't complain.'

'You don't complain,' I said.

'Have you a minute? I know I mustn't monopolize you but if you've just five minutes?'

I sat on the end of the bed.

'Poor Marianne has got it into her head I'm unhappy about Rex's death. Did she say anything to you?'

'She did a bit.'

'I like your discretion! Don't worry, I shan't ask you what she said.'

Stella was in good spirits. Skeletally thin she might be, and with a new wheeziness in her voice, but the light in her eyes was very nearly merry.

'I do love to see my daughter, Genevieve. And I must confess it amuses me to see her get hold of the wrong end of the stick, poor darling. Fancy her thinking I was sad because of Rex! Misunderstanding's an awful thing, yet I suppose it's inevitable if we're ever to have any privacy. The fact is I was so utterly indifferent to Rex by the time he died that his death was no more to me than the man next door's would have been. I'd probably have cared more about the man next door's, I always like John Browning.' She sighed. 'Charmian—well, yes, that was different.'

Her merriment had been short-lived. A cast of seriousness came across her face. She had been picking at a thin slice of brown bread and butter, but she pushed the rest of it away and made a little face of distaste. She eats practically nothing now. I think it's cups of tea and milky coffee that are keeping her alive. She looked at me, then away.

'Charmian,' she said. 'I pitied her so and she'd have hated that if she'd known. Imagine, Genevieve, she didn't know about Rex, she didn't know he had died. He used to phone her every day, he had done for years and years, even when . . .' a small almost cynical smile, her eyebrows pushing more wrinkles up into her forehead, 'he was supposed to be staging one of his come-backs to me. Every day, year in and year out, every single day but not, of course, the next day. He was dead and she didn't know. She must have waited for his call and it didn't come. She waited for three days before she phoned the firm. It was his nephew Jeremy who told her. But imagine her waiting like that, Genevieve, and growing more and more afraid and not daring to phone his home. Oh, the nightmare, it doesn't bear thinking of.'

Receiving the news, thinking what it might mean to her, Stella had forgotten all about Charmian. Or, rather, it had never occurred to her to let Charmian know. She even asked herself later if, unconsciously, she'd done it on purpose, if she'd tortured Charmian deliberately by keeping her in the dark. I don't see how you can do a cruel act unconsciously, if it isn't conscious it can't be cruel, but that's the way Stella is. None of it was her fault but she was filled with remorse. She said she was sorrier for Charmian than she'd ever been for anyone in all her life.

She wanted her to know that for years she hadn't minded about their affair. It was years since she had felt love for Rex. That only made Charmian worse, reproaching her for not loving Rex who 'needed love so much'. For some reason she thought Charmian would want to talk, but Charmian only attacked her for not suggesting divorce to Rex. If she didn't love him why had she wanted to stay married to him? Misunderstanding, Stella said, it was all misunderstanding.

But something happened that never had before. Out of the death of the man that had been the husband of one of them and the lover of the other grew a relationship. Given time, they might have become friends, but they weren't given time. They began seeing each other, they began meeting, and after a while they stopped talking about Rex and talked instead about the things countrywomen do discuss, the houses being built in the villages and the new road and how the hedges were being uprooted and the cost of the hunt.

Because Gilda insinuated herself into most things that Stella did, she too got to see Charmian sometimes. She would phone early in the morning to find how Stella meant to spend her day and if it included a morning visit to Charmian, would announce that she was coming too. Or she would invite them both in that overbearing way of hers that Stella at least found so difficult to defy. The three of them would talk and have coffee and sit chatting in each other's houses. It must have been an awkward situation, three women who didn't really like each other, Charmian still in love with Stella's dead husband, Stella in love with Gilda's living husband and Gilda always projecting the image she had made of herself as somehow superior to both of them, more sophisticated, cleverer, more beautiful and elegant.

And Stella, the 'little thing', was patronized by both of them. To Charmian she was the woman her lover had married but never loved, and, more than that, she came from the wrong background for Rex's wife. In her eyes Rex had married far beneath him. Gilda, of course, simply treated Stella as an ignorant 'greenhorn', on the way home speculating about what Rex could possibly have seen in Charmian and making guesses in raw sexual terms. Charmian looked 'such a fright', there must have been some other reason for her 'hold on him', some love-making technique or a even a—well, Stella called it a 'physiological peculiarity'. God knows what Gilda called it.

'Why did you put up with it?' I said.

'I suppose I was sorry for both of them. Have you ever heard of the mother of the Gracchi?'

Well, of *course* I hadn't.

'She was a Roman woman. A friend she was visiting spread out all her jewellery collection, boxes of it, for her to see and boasted of it. She called her two sons to her and said, "These are my jewels." I had my jewels, Genevieve, I had my children, and I had Alan too.'

Stella thought Charmian was 'getting over it' just as in a few years' time people thought she was beginning to get over her own trouble. One morning, having made a vague arrangement to call and see Charmian on her way to Ipswich, Stella got to Elmswell at about eleven. Charmian's car was on the drive that led, not to the garage, she had no garage, but to the various outbuildings behind the house.

There seemed to be no one at home, in spite of the car. Stella rang the doorbell a couple of times and when there wasn't any answer she thought Charmian must be in the garden. It was late summer and a fine day. Charmian grew dahlias, she was proud of her dahlias. Stella went round the side of the house.

'There was a great screen of cypresses,' Stella said. 'They were very ancient, far older than the house. Cypress wood is almost everlasting, did you know that?

The gates of Constantinople were made of cypress and they lasted a thousand years.'

A big paved courtyard with buildings that had once been stables were on one side of it, a dairy and cold room on the other, long disused, a coach house that other people would have converted into a garage with a flat over it but Charmian's family never had. The garden beyond was walled. Fan-trained fruit trees grew against walls of cut flints and underneath, in the borders, were the dahlias, giants and cactus and pom-poms, Bishop of Leandaff and King Albert's Mourning. There were heleniums too, mustard yellow, and pink chrysanths and silvery lad's love. Stella walked down the path, looking for Charmian, calling Charmian. She was expecting that witch-like figure to appear from among the flowers, to have been bending over, to stand up and raise an arm in that stiff salute. Coming back again between the giant cypresses that last for ever, she looked in the stables and the dairy and then she came to the coach house. She searched everywhere because by this time she was worried. She thought Charmian might have cut or otherwise injured herself while gardening and collapsed.

It was true that she had injured herself and true too about the collapse. Stella found her on the coach house floor. Although she was forty-five years old she had never before seen a dead person, so it was unfortunate that the first one she saw had half her head blown off. The blood, Stella said, oh, the blood, I shall never forget it, I shall never be rid of the sight of it.

Later on, at the inquest which she had to attend, it was told by the people who work out these things how Charmian had done it. She had taken a shotgun, a twelve bore, and standing up put the barrel not into her mouth, that would have been impossible, but pointing up under her chin, held it with her left hand and pressed down with her right thumb on the trigger. The result was so terrible that Stella screamed. There was no one near to hear her but she screamed and screamed.

No one had phones in cars then, Stella said. Anyway, she couldn't have held a receiver, she couldn't have driven her car, her hands, her whole body were shaking. She ran down the high street, calling out, screaming, crying that Charmian was dead, that Charmian had killed herself. She had lost all control, she barely knew what she was doing, it was too late for Charmian, she wanted help for herself.

The police, when they came, asked if there was anyone they could get in touch with to be with her. She said, Alan Tyzark. She said it without thinking. It was automatic, he was the first person in her thoughts, he always was. In her shock, she had forgotten Gilda, and by chance he was alone at home and Gilda was out. He came at once.

'He came in Gilda's car,' Stella said. 'I was at the police station, drinking a cup of tea. They were very kind to me, very considerate. I was watching for him from the window and when I saw this red car coming, this red Anglia, I thought, oh, no, it's not him, it's Gilda. That was her car you see, the Anglia, not his, she'd bought it secondhand a few months before.'

'A red Ford Anglia?' I said.

'He had a Rover, a grey one. They were both quite old cars, they couldn't afford anything newer. I thought it was Gilda in the red car but it wasn't, it was Alan on his own.

He put his arms round me, he didn't care about anyone seeing, and he said, "I'm going to take you to your house." I thought he meant my home in Bury, but he took me to our house where we always met, he took me to Molucca. We stayed there all day. We lay on the bed—not for love-making, I don't mean that—he just held me and we lay there side by side until the evening. He'd even arranged for Priscilla to look after Richard. I don't know how he explained it to Gilda, I don't know why he had her car and she had his, I don't know what he said to her. It was weeks before I spoke to her again.'

'Stella,' I said, 'that red car, is that Gilda's car in the garage at your house?'

She gave me one of her sidelong looks. It's the expression of a child who's accused of doing something naughty but not very bad and still doesn't quite want to admit it. Guilty but amused, slightly annoyed.

'What if it is?'

'I thought you said Gilda died in a car crash.'

'I was telling you about Charmian. She wrote to me, you know. She sent me a letter. Well, she sent it to my house, care of me, it was really to Rex. She wrote it to Rex who was dead. It was her version of a suicide note.'

Charmian must have gone out to post the letter that morning or perhaps the night before. The envelope was postmarked the date of her death and it arrived at Stella's on the following day. Her handwriting had always been unreadable and she typed everything on an antique typewriter that belonged with the house. She had typed simply, 'I cannot live without you. I have tried but the days are too long.' It was signed right at the bottom of the sheet with that scrawl of hers that was 'Charmian' but might have been anything.

Stella knew she should pass it to the coroner. But she wanted to show it to Alan first. He looked at it and then at her and said,

'My own sentiments. They're playing our tune.'

'You won't kill yourself though,' she said.

'How do you know what I'd do if you died?'

She said she shivered when he spoke those words. 'What shall I do with her letter?'

'Nothing,' he said. 'Let me take care of it.' And he asked her if she really wanted to see that in the papers, an admission that Charmian had been Rex's lover.

She didn't. She believed that was his reason for suppressing Charmian's letter. That was what she believed then.

'I don't want to break the law,' she said.

He laughed. 'Why not?' he said. 'Go on, be a devil. It's out of your hands now, anyway. I've got it. I'll put it in the archives.'

'You haven't got any archives,' she said.

'I have now.'

All that took a good deal more than five minutes in the telling. Stella's voice was hoarse and her skin had lost all its colour.

'You have to take it easy,' I said, and I took the tray from her and covered up her knees with the blanket.

'That was the beginning of it,' she said. 'The note that Charmian sent me, that was the start of it.'

'The start of what?' I said, but I got no answer.

When you're in my sort of love affair, unlike Stella's, you don't get much of a chance to talk to the person you're in love with. For one thing your meetings don't last long, it's all snatched moments, and for another the time is mostly taken up with making love. I tell myself that there'll be time enough to talk when I'm with Ned all the time. Every day I came a step nearer to deciding I *will* be with him all the time, though I'd said nothing to him then, at the end of November that is, I'd said nothing to Mike, I'd made no arrangements, it was still all in my head.

But we'd got to following a routine at our meetings in Stella's house and there was a little space for talking in it. It had been the mildest November since records began and would have been cold only if the month was, say, September. But it was cold enough. I'd get the place warmed up as best I could before he arrived, I'd take a bottle of wine with me and have it opened and breathing, the candles lit, the bed fresh and warm. And after we'd made love, necessarily under the heavy covers—that was when I began longing for the freedom of light, of naked-ness exposed and liberty of movement and hands and mouths—after that we'd lie with our arms round one another and talk a little. I never have much to tell him, only some small anecdotes of my day. After all, my life isn't exciting, or rather, he's the excitement in my life. But plenty happens to him, he's always meeting the clever and the famous, and he always has stories of what he's done and plans to do.

The next time we met after Stella had told me of the hidden letter, he would have been happy, I think, not to talk at all. When we finish and there's that high moment, that shared wonderful thing when my mind breaks open, I cry out into his mouth that's covering mine. And he holds me for a long time after we slide apart. He holds me and strokes my hair, he kisses my shoulders, he puts my head to rest upon him. He never moves away and turns his back. Sometimes we whisper to each other for a little while and he gets up and fetches the wine for us to drink. That's the time we talk, for we often make love again and we aren't like other lovers, we haven't all night at our disposal.

But that time it was me fetched the wine and poured some for him and some for me in Stella's crystal glasses that she and Alan Tyzark once used. And when I walked round the bed with the glass in my hand I saw that he was asleep. I love to watch him sleeping, for his face is lovely then. He looks very young and gentle. But I grudge him sleep because that's when he goes away from me. So I drank my wine and watched him and when he stirred I said his name and touched his face and kissed him. He woke very quickly, sat up and smiled at me.

I wanted him to tell me about his work, what he'd been doing, and he began to talk, telling me about the research for a programme he's making about some old Norfolk families. It was mere chance, I suppose, that I asked him how one could find out about birth and death dates, how did you do it and was it easy. I'd never thought about it before, that there must be some central place where everyone's birth, marriage and death is recorded, I imagined it was all in church registers. But Ned said no, they were kept in some place in London and that was where he would be checking the dates of these family members.

And then I thought I'd ask him to do something for me. Before that I'd never actually asked him for anything, I'd never said to him, would you get this for me, or would you do that? Yet it's what people do when they're together, isn't it? You could call it dependence on each other or you could call it support. It seemed to me the mark of our closeness, our absolute partnership, that I could say to him, would you do this for me?

'When you're doing that, would you find out something for me, the date of someone's death?'

'Of course I will,' he said, 'if I can.'

He looked so happy to have the chance to do it, I wondered why I'd never asked before. 'It's Gilda Brent,' I said.

'The actress? Didn't you tell me one of your old ladies knew her?' He's got a good memory. 'I'll do my best. When did she die?'

'About twenty-five years ago. Isn't that near enough? It's all I know.'

'Was Brent her real name?'

I remembered the cigarette card collection. I told him it had been Brent and her married name was Tyzark and she was around fifty when she died, if that would help. Now we'd begun on it I wanted to talk some more, to tell him something of what Stella had told me, of Charmian and her love for Rex Newland. Lovers always want to talk about love, don't they? And Charmian's plight, her hopeless suffering, had struck some chord in me, though I'd never experienced anything like it and hope I never will. But it wasn't what Ned wanted.

'Let's not talk any more about these old people and death and old, unhappy, far-off things,' he said, and he took me in his arms again, saying, 'Tell me you love me, Jenny, tell me you love me.'

15

On the Saturday that was Stella's birthday I was coming out of the Legion where I'd taken Mum's shopping when I saw the removal van outside Rowans. It wasn't a big one, it was about the size of a Land Rover, and they'd hired it themselves. The place was let furnished and I don't suppose they'd had much of their own stuff in it.

It gave me a shock to see Ned. It always does when I see him unexpectedly, and the shock isn't a pleasant one when he's doing something that's so definitely *with* Jane and Hannah. What he was doing, carrying out a cardboard box of books and putting it in the van, seemed utterly to exclude me. The books weren't mine or half mine, I didn't even know their titles, and for a little while he didn't know I was watching him. Jane came out and said something to him and he replied and I was suddenly filled with such a longing to speak to him and have him look at me that I almost cried out. I didn't but I called hallo and they both turned round.

He said, 'Hallo, Jenny, how are you?' as if I were Mum or the woman next door. He couldn't help it. What else could he do, but it stunned me and I seemed to see his face on the pillow, his eyes closed and his lips half-smiling in sleep.

I thought it would be impossible for me to speak but I spoke. I dare say my voice sounded normal. I asked them when they were moving and Jane said this was their last day here.

'We've found a place in Southwold. Hannah does so love the seaside.'

It didn't matter to me. It made no difference to me, I'd only twice been in that house and, whatever had happened, I'd never have gone there again. And they wouldn't be in Southwold, not all three of them, not together. Jane and Hannah might be but Ned would be with me. Muttering something about having to get on, she went back into the house, and Ned turned to me such a look of naked blazing love that even I, hungry as I am, was satisfied. I whispered, 'Phone me,' and he nodded.

Saturdays I was always off work but I was going in that day to see Stella. Instead of driving down the High Street I took the long way round, I didn't want to pass that emptying house again. I didn't want to see Ned again. If that sounds insane, it's explainable. When they were together, him and Jane, I always dreaded seeing some sign of love or companionship or even ordinary affection pass between them, some meeting of eyes, some intimate smile of special meaning. I never did, I never could have for it couldn't happen, I knew Ned too well for that, but still I feared it. I was afraid of an impossible sight that would spoil my day, my week, my life.

Love is a frightening thing. I realize that I'm frightened so much of the time, afraid of losing him, afraid of discovery, but more than that, I live in fear of not being his equal, of not matching up to what he wants, of him changing because he's disillusioned. And Stella has told me she felt fear every day, before their meetings, after their meetings, fear of Gilda and jealousy. Like me, she was afraid of seeing a hint of love between Alan and Gilda. One summer afternoon she had gone to their house and, hearing their voices, pushed open the front door and walked in without knocking. Gilda was picking out a tune on the piano and he was sitting on the stool beside her, singing words to it, they'd been trying to remember some old song. It was nothing; it shattered her. And how could it be nothing when she was alone and free but he was still with Gilda?

She was afraid too of that painting, that nude. Sometimes she would fancy the half-smile on the face was directed against her in mockery, that the painted Gilda was saying to her, 'Look at me, look at my beauty. Can you compete with that?' And when they were in that room Gilda would always position herself in front of the portrait. She had a settee so placed that the picture seemed to rise up behind it and she contrived to sit on this settee and put Stella in an armchair facing it. Whenever she lifted her eyes Stella was obliged to look at the naked Gilda in her high heels, one hand fingering the pearl string between her breasts.

She'd supposed Alan would ask Gilda for a divorce. They had no children. It wasn't a question of money, Gilda was much better off than he was. She would find another man, she was always telling Stella of all the men who were in love with her. As for the money side of it, Stella herself was well-off. The house in Bury was hers and Rex's shares in the company and his life assurance as well as investments of his. It didn't matter to her that

Alan had nothing but his royalties from *Figaro and Velvet* and a dodgy income from selling pictures in pubs.

'Didn't I tell you that, Genevieve?' she said. 'It was all he could do. He'd started painting landscapes and getting landlords to exhibit them for sale. Well, not only landscapes.' She looked ashamed. 'Pictures of dogs and cats and girls' faces and women in crinolines. And he did drawings of Norfolk villages for Christmas cards.

'I told him the money didn't matter, I had enough for both of us, but he hated the idea of me keeping him. And he said Gilda would never divorce him as the law stood. She'd have had to name me and he wouldn't have that.'

They'd heard, or Stella had heard through Jeremy Newland, that there'd be a major change in the divorce law in the future, it was already being talked about. Irretrievable breakdown would be grounds for divorce after you'd been separated for two years and you both consented, or after five years if only one consented. And it did come in. Mum and Dad were divorced like that, there wasn't any problem about them both consenting, and Mum got her divorce from number two like that as well. It's called the Matrimonial Causes Act 1973, though I should think Divorce Causes Act would be more appropriate. But for Alan Tyzark it was still a long way off in 1969. Stella said she didn't care about being married, she wanted him just to come and live with her.

Alan wouldn't do it. He said she didn't understand how Gilda would behave. Gilda would make their life hell. St Michael's Farm was hers, entirely hers, and if he went to live with Stella Gilda would start divorce proceedings, name Stella and take from him everything he had. Already, he said, Gilda suspected him. Once or twice when he'd gone to a hotel in Ipswich with some of the paintings he'd done, she'd followed him. He went out into Crown Street at nine one evening and saw her car parked on the other side of the road. She had cast herself in the role of her own private detective.

Richard's car was in the car park and so was Marianne's. That made me think I needn't have come, not when she'd got her own children, but I had a present for her and a card and I didn't have to stay long.

Sharon was in the hall, fiddling about with something behind reception. She always comes in on Saturdays. She beckoned me over and whispered in a dramatic way.

'Maud left Lena fifty grand, how about that?'

I didn't know what to say.

'Three times that to the cats and donkeys but fifty K's pretty brilliant if you ask me. Stella'll be next on her list, you see if I'm not right. She's in there now with the family, sucking up so's you could vomit.'

But Lena came out of Stella's room just as I turned the corner in the passage. She was flushed, she looked a bit bemused; I suppose she'd only got the news that morning, and instead of telling me off for being too friendly with a resident, coming in on a Saturday and so on, she gave me one of her toothy smiles and actually opened Stella's door for me.

I'd have knocked first but no one seemed to mind me just walking in. Stella had six birthday cards on her desk and two on a bedside cabinet. There was a marvellous new dressing-gown lying on the bed on top of its tissue and pink glazed paper wrappings, a quilted thing of patchwork in different sorts of gingham and rosebud patterns. But Richard had brought her a set of books, *A Dance to the Music of Time* by Anthony Powell. I looked at her and at those twelve books and thought, that'll be the last you'll ever read, and somehow I could tell from his expression, his smile and his sad eyes, that he was thinking the same.

I handed over my card and the two cassettes I'd been into Diss to buy. I don't know anything about music but I'd remembered that Richard said she liked chamber music, so I'd consulted Ned about that and he'd advised me, a Dvořák Serenade for Strings and a piece by Boccherini. Stella took the presents from me, caught my face in her hands in a surprisingly strong grip, and kissed me. Her wrinkled face is as soft as silk and as powdery as an iced cake.

My card was put on the desk with the others, the cassettes beside her player.

'They want to take me out to lunch, Genevieve,' Stella said. 'I've told them I hardly eat anything but Marianne says we can have *nouvelle cuisine.*'

Marianne put her eyebrows up at me. 'She's strong enough to go, isn't she, Genevieve?'

'If she wants to,' I said.

'You know I don't like cars, Marianne.'

'You do as long as I'm not driving,' Richard said. 'Marianne can drive at twenty-five miles an hour and I'll sit in the back with you and put a black bag over your head.'

They argued a bit more but I could tell, and perhaps they could too, that Stella really wanted to go. The car was the stumbling block but not such a great obstacle when Marianne assured her the restaurant they were going to was only three miles away and a new one, opened the previous spring. Stella put on her cream wool coat, picking a hair off the collar with an expression of distaste. One glove on and one off, she slipped the bare hand into the crook of Richard's arm, not so much possessively as with a kind of shy affection.

I followed them out, driving behind them for maybe a mile and then turning off down the Tharby road. My shoelace broke as I was getting out of the car. We wear trainers for work, white ones, and the laces don't last as long as the shoes. I'd noticed my left one fraying for the past week but I'd done nothing about it, mainly because Diss is the nearest place I can buy replacements. It's bad to break a shoelace, something to do with St Mark bursting the ratchets of his shoes when he was travelling to Alexandria, though why that should make it unlucky I don't know. But it left me with a sense of foreboding.

Mike was putting the glass in the conservatory windows. He had Radio One on very loud. When he saw me he said, 'Sorry, I'll turn it down. I won't stop for my lunch. Have to get the glazing done before the bad weather sets in.'

Bad weather never really does set in, does it? Not in this country. It's just as likely to be as nice or as nasty in December as it is in June. We hadn't had any rain for a week, which is what I suppose he meant, and it was unnaturally mild. He's doing this conservatory for me, or that's what he says, he says it to everybody.

'Come and see the conservatory I'm doing for Jenny.'

That means I'm his reason for building it and his excuse. It works with others and it works with me.

'No time for that,' he says, 'I've got Jenny's conservatory

to finish,' or, to me, 'I'm doing this for you, so have a bit of patience, will you?'

I've never asked for a conservatory. In fact, I don't want one. It will only make more work and I've got enough already. I can't grow house plants, our garden is full of the buried corpses of African Violets that have died on me. I shall never set foot in the place, I shall never clean it or polish those windows. So what am I waiting for? What word has to be spoken or trigger pulled? It's as if I'm waiting for the conservatory to be finished, to replace *me* in Mike's life.

It would be there but I would be gone.

Stella had been very tired after her drive and her lunch. She was brought back at three-thirty and had fallen asleep in her chair even before Marianne and Richard had gone. Carolyn said she was still asleep when she brought her dinner and of course she hadn't wanted anything to eat. On Sunday she'd have liked to stay in bed all day but Lena doesn't encourage that.

'This is a residential home, not a hospice,' she said to me. 'If they're bed-ridden and want nursing they're in the wrong place.'

Coming into a fortune only sweetened her nature for a couple of days. I found Stella up but still in her nightdress with the new dressing-gown over it. The cereal and bread and butter on her tray were untouched. She was drinking China tea.

'Marianne calls this a robe,' she said. 'I think dressing-gown may be an old-fashioned word. It's beautiful, isn't it? I'd like you to have it after I'm gone.'

The clothes of the dead don't wear long. They fret for

the person who owned them . . . Marianne may want it back, I thought, it must have cost a hundred pounds.

'Of course I will,' I said, 'if that's what you want.'

'I shan't go into the lounge again.'

'Not today, d'you mean?' I said.

'I mean, not ever. I'll stay in here. I'm best in here.' She added mysteriously, 'I have plenty to do in here.'

I asked her if she'd like me to help her dress. Would she like me to give her a bath? I always bath Gracie, though God knows what Lena would say if she knew. Stella shook her head, then she laughed. It was good to hear her laugh.

'I haven't come to that yet. I'm just tired. I shall sleep and I'll be better later.'

She was too. The human spirit is amazing. It's wonderful how people can rally if they fight. I realized that day that Stella had begun to fight.

Someone had moved her chair so that it was in a new place by the french window. From there she could look whenever she wanted to at the outside world, green lawns, leafless trees now, a low blue horizon. She turned round when I came in at four, beckoned me over and although she had already greeted me that morning, caught my face in her hands the way she does and kissed me on the left cheek and the right. That White Linen perfume she uses came off her warm skeleton body in waves. She felt almost feverish, and energy was coming from her like electricity.

Three months ago I remember thinking how reserved she was, how she kept all her past life to herself. And now she talks all the time. It's as if she'd picked up the two or three stones that dammed a stream and the water flooded through the gap. When she drew back and released my face from those electric hands she began to talk almost at once. She talked as if there were things she had to say before the time ran out through the hour-glass and there was no sand left in the top.

I kept hold of her left hand in mine. Her voice and command of words seem to grow stronger as her bodily strength fails. 'I said that was the beginning of it, do you remember, Genevieve? Charmian's letter was the beginning. And then the next beginning, the next step really, was when we all went to the cinema together to see *The End of Edith Thompson*, Gilda and Alan and I.'

As soon as one of her films was due to appear at a local cinema Gilda had to go and see it. She had seen it many times before, Alan had seen this one three times and even Stella had seen it once. But they had to go and see it again. It was on in Ipswich. All the way there in Alan's car they had to listen to Gilda talking about the making of the film, the way she was treated by the director, his ceaseless criticism of her performance, his insistence on her wardrobe being of the dowdiest kind, the star's malice towards her.

'You know the story. They called each other "darlint", not "darling", I don't know why. She put powdered glass in her husband's food, or she said she did. She wrote it in letters to Bywaters and they were used against her at her trial. It was Bywaters who stabbed Thompson in the street near where he and Edith lived, but Edith was hanged for it as well.'

'I've only seen the end of the film,' I said.

'Never mind the film. It isn't very good. I only mention it because it was the next day that Alan started what he—what we—called the Killing Gilda Tease.'

At five-fifteen on Thursday August 16th, 1969, Alan made his first Killing Gilda joke. Stella said the date was written on her memory more distinctly than her wedding or her children's birthdays or the date she first met Alan. There was only one date in her life more clearly recorded and that was yet to come.

'I don't understand,' I said.

'No, I don't suppose you do. I don't understand it myself now, why it seemed funny at the time, but it did. He just said in that casual way of his, in one of those throwaway lines of his, he said, "Let's do it, let's kill Gilda." '

'It was a joke, wasn't it?' I said. I truly didn't understand. 'He wasn't serious. It sounds like a game.'

'Of course it was a game.' She was suddenly quite heated. She was almost cross. 'We did play games, he and I. I told you we played house, we played at being married. We even dressed up once to look like the parents in the *Figaro and Velvet* books. Once we made ourselves look like Mr and Mrs Darling in *Peter Pan*.'

I'd almost lost her. I tried not to stare.

'Mr and Mrs Darling,' she said and she gave her throaty laugh. 'The Killing Gilda Tease was just another game we played.'

'You played?'

'I did it because he did,' she said, and she had begun to sound very weary. 'I'm ashamed of it now. It was silly and childish.'

'*Childish?*'

'All right, worse than that. Perhaps children wouldn't play that game. Do you know what *folie à deux* means?'

I shook my head. French wasn't very successfully taught at Newall Upper School. I did just about know it was French.

'It means madness for two, double madness. It's when two people who are close encourage each other to do something terrible, each one eggs the other on. A couple committing murder, for instance.'

'Bonnie and Clyde,' I said. 'The Moors Murderers.'

She gave the dry little laugh that ends in coughing. Once that was over she performed one of her sharp shifts of subject. She closes one drawer in her mind and opens another. It's usually accompanied by a bright smile.

'He wanted to paint my portrait,' she said.

'Wanted to? He did paint it. It's hanging up at Molucca.'

'He said it in front of Gilda. We had all been to the pictures to see *Seven for a Secret* and—what do you think?—the character Gilda was playing actually called another woman "little thing". She had even got that from a film script. Alan was sitting between us and I turned to look at him and he turned to look at me and we both burst out laughing. We shouldn't have, should we? It was unkind and Gilda wasn't pleased.

'And when we got home to my house and they came in with me, Alan suddenly said he'd like to paint my portrait. She turned viciously on me. Marianne was there, all eyes and ears, of course. Gilda said some awful things. Perhaps I deserved them—what do you think, Genevieve?'

'Perhaps all women in our situation deserve those things,' I said.

She hadn't expected that answer. Did she think I was

going to make excuses for her and me? She pursed her lips and was quiet for a moment. Then she said,

'Gilda said to him, "Isn't she a bit old?" as if I weren't there, and, "You once told me you only wanted to paint beauties." She was being revenged for my laughter in the cinema and revenged on him for his. He wasn't much of a painter, she said, he could manage puppy dogs and pussy cats and women with beautiful faces but he hadn't the talent to catch an ordinary middle-aged woman's likeness. Marianne, bless her, piped up and said, "I think my mother's beautiful," and Alan said he could paint *her*, for if what Gilda said was true, to catch her likeness would take no talent at all. Marianne loved that but Gilda didn't. She said that whoever Alan had in mind to paint, he wasn't doing it in her house, and just to remind him it was *her* house.

'They went home after that, he and she, that was the pattern, that was what always happened. Of course it did, she was his wife. When he did paint me at last it was the following June, at Molucca, when the roses were out. That's how I came to be holding a pink rose in my hand. Painters these days don't expect a sitter to pose for them more than once or twice. They use photographs. But Alan wanted a perfect likeness. Besides, he never worked on the picture except when I was there.' Stella lifted up her hand and looked thoughtfully at it as if she held a flower.

'It was while I was sitting for him that the photograph you found was taken. A couple came to the door to ask the way. They were lost. That had never happened before, I don't think we'd ever had any callers before. Alan told them how to get to Breckenhall and then he asked them if they'd take our picture. I expect they thought we were quite mad. The man stared at me in my pink silk dress and my pearls, but he took our picture, the two of us out in the front garden, looking into each other's eyes.'

She sighed. Closing her eyes for a moment or two is sometimes the way she indicates the subject is to change. 'How old were you when your mother and father separated, Genevieve?'

That took me by surprise. 'I was eight.'

'He left her?'

'She chucked him out,' I said. 'He'd got someone else, a woman called Kath. He'd promised to give her up but one night when he was late home again and he'd been seeing her, Mum said it was the last straw and to go and not come back.'

'She gave him the keys to the street,' said Stella, and when I looked mystified, 'It's what they used to say a long time ago. We'd say, show him the door, or give him his marching orders. Was it late August? Early September?'

'I believe it was,' I said.

Ned's researcher had found no record of Gilda Brent's death. I must be a fool, I thought Ned would search through the records himself, but of course he wouldn't, of course there must be other people to do that.

'You didn't tell me the time of year,' Ned said, 'so she looked through the whole of 1970. She wasn't there. I thought we should do a proper job for you and I got her to go through *The Times* obituaries too.'

'Her obituary would have been in the paper?' I said.

'Yes, why not? She was a well-known actress in her day. On the strength of *The Fiancée* alone they'd do some sort of write-up. Only they didn't, so she didn't.'

'Didn't what?'

'Didn't die in 1970. After all, I spoke to her agent in 1979. I don't think she's dead at all. I've a feeling I'd know. I would have read about it and it's not something I'd have forgotten. Maybe it's worth investigating. It could make one of those unsolved mystery features. You know the kind of thing—what became of Gilda Brent? *The Lady Vanishes*, something like that.'

In the bedroom the air was a cold mist. Our mouths were warm but not our hands. Our fingers felt each other like ice cubes run over the skin. It wasn't the love-making of summer, the languor and the long slow all-the-time-in-the-world, holding each other loosely because sweat broke too easily. In a few minutes it was over, it had to be, so that we could hug each other for warmth and watch our breath making white streams of fog over one another's shoulders.

December, it was only December. I thought, I have to make up my mind before Christmas and before Stella dies. Before the weather gets unbearably cold. Before I lose this house. No one could make it up for me. Asking him was useless, he would only tell me not to think, that thinking was fatal, but just to leave and come to him.

16

The tapes Stella had made she wiped clean. She told herself they were useless for her purposes, mere self-indulgence, an excuse for saying things she thought she would never say aloud. So much had been suppressed. Over the years so much had been battened down. Telling it at last was therapeutic. The effect was similar to talking to Genevieve but with greater freedom and therefore greater relief.

At least it has helped, she said to the recorder, it has emptied those things out of my mind, but the tapes are clean now and my words lost.

Or can they ever quite be lost? If you write something down and destroy what you've written, cut it to pieces or burn it, and if you have no copy, those words you wrote are gone for ever. But it isn't the same with the spoken word, or so I have read. Sound is never lost, it isn't absorbed by the ears which hear it, but flies on into space, perhaps beyond the earth's atmosphere and out among the spheres. Once a word is uttered it becomes inde-structible and everlasting. My words are out there, flying on and up, even maybe heard by mysterious beings on other planets.

But all that is fantasy, something I have no time for now. I shall make three more tapes. I shall shut myself up in here, making believe I'm more feeble than I am, so that I have the chance to speak in peace. The first one I shall play back to myself to test my voice as much as anything, for in making the rest I shall need all the strength I have remaining. I want to sound *sane*, a good witness, not an old woman sinking into senility and derangement. I want my hearer to be convinced of the truth that I tell, whatever she may decide to do with it.

It is Lady Macbeth who asks the powers or the spirits—Genevieve would know about that!—asks the 'murdering ministers' to unsex her, to come to her woman's breasts and take her milk for gall. That made us giggle at school which is very likely why I remember it. But it's what I want now that I am near my death, to shed the meek, gentle womanliness that everyone has ascribed to me all my life. Alan said I was the most feminine creature he had ever known. Yet it was not a feminine thing I did or helped to do, not a sweet, womanly thing. If I can't be masculine I must be Lady Macbeth.

Here begins the first tape.

It was all a joke, wasn't it? Genevieve said. She wanted to believe that and I am not in the business of disillusioning her while I'm still alive. What happens later is another thing. I must take my chance on that. She wanted to believe the Killing Gilda Tease was a game, as I too wanted to believe it. I wanted to believe it very much and I did. When we made jokes about poisons and greasing the stairs and a little push over a clifftop, I made mental reservations. It was as if I thought, it doesn't matter what we say to each other, he and I, so long as I say to myself, it's all nonsense, he doesn't mean it, it's a game.

Yet, in spite of our illicit affair, we seemed to have kept a kind of innocence that *folie à deux* was spoiling. I was aware of this but unable to say so to him. Gilda and I went to the seaside together one day, only to Dunwich where the cliffs are hardly high, but high enough. We walked a little way on the cliffs, it was a beautiful day, and the thought came to me that I could push her over. It's hard to credit what I actually thought, that I'd be able to go home to him and tell him I'd killed his wife, he'd be so *pleased* with me, it would make him love me more.

I didn't touch her, of course I didn't, but I told him what I'd thought. I wanted to amuse him, to please him. He said,

'Why didn't you?'

He'd been telling me of some poison he'd read about in the paper, how well it would work. 'I might ask the same of you,' I said. 'Why didn't *you*?'

'The pale cast of thought,' he said. 'You know, that stuff that gets in the way of resolution.'

If you talk about something enough, if you get used to it, it can become real. And for him it *was* real, he was serious about it. It wasn't a joke to him. Or it was no longer a joke. When the overt joking had virtually stopped, the real possibility had been growing in his mind. I understood that, that was what frightened me, but it was still a shock when he showed me Charmian's letter. I had forgotten its existence. A psychologist would say I had suppressed the memory of it, I'd blocked it off. Seeing the letter again frightened me, knowing he had actually kept it as he had said he would. In the archives, as he had put it.

I'd forgotten what it said and I had to read those words again. The first time they hadn't meant much to me but now when I read them they seemed to me desperately pathetic and sad. Of course my memory has never let me forget them again. 'I cannot live without you. I have tried but the days are too long.'

'How about faking Gilda's suicide,' Alan said, 'and making it look as if she left this note for me?'

It was absurd, of course. It would never have worked. The words were typed. I suppose Charmian had typed them because her handwriting was unreadable. The signature certainly was, a scrawl which might just as well have been Gilda as Charmian. Except that Gilda didn't write like that, her signature was quite legible, and she didn't own a typewriter. Alan hadn't left her, she wasn't living without him. Oh, there were a host of other objections but I need not go on. For that was not the point to me, none of that was. All that mattered to me was that he had reached a stage in the tease where he was serious. The joke was over and this was the real thing.

Yet the temptation for me was to go on with the joke, to laugh it off. The possibility that a man would think of killing his wife for my sake, to be with me, was too much for me. It was too far removed from any world I had ever known. Films and books were part of that world but not the life I led in the place I lived in, a middle-aged widow living in a suburb of a country town.

I didn't want to talk about it. I didn't want to go on as we were. I don't know what I wanted—well, for Gilda to die I suppose, to die a natural, quick, painless death. Is there such a death?

I didn't want to talk but I had to, I made Alan talk

about it, and then I said it must never be discussed again, there must be no more jokes. More than that, there must be no more serious intent. I thought I'd convinced him. I thought I knew how I'd convinced him. It was by telling him that talk of killing Gilda was changing him, corrupting him, making him into a different man from the man I loved.

It was summer, the time of the portrait. The time those people came and asked us the way, the people we had asked to take our picture. After they had gone I went back to my chair and took up the pose again with the rose in my hand. Alan started laughing.

'He was rather sinister, didn't you think? The photographer from hell. Did you notice his pointed eye-teeth? He means to drive her into the fen and strangle her.'

'Don't,' I said.

'Oh, come on, darling. It's some strange woman I'm talking about, not Gilda. Luckily for justice and the triumph of the law he's left his fingerprints on your camera.'

I dropped the rose. I got up and came close to him.

'Will you like it,' I said, 'if it isn't Gilda this kills but my love for you? Because that's what will happen.' It wasn't true, I thought then that nothing could have done that, but I said it. I said it again. 'It will change you. It will change you into someone else, the kind of person who could kill his wife, who could really do that. And if that happens I won't love you.'

The look on his face was one I shall never forget. Better say at this stage of my life that I never have forgotten it. He went pale. He looked like a child who has lost something it dearly loves and is incapable of understanding the explanation given for that loss. Richard looked like that when his kitten was run over in the street outside our house. It is an expression of such bewilderment and helpless pain that it breaks your heart.

After I'd played this back I played Genevieve's present to me, the Boccherini—lovely and so civilized, just what I needed. The music came through on the tape, an exquisite contrast to what went before.

My own voice sounds surprisingly strong. The moments of hoarseness can't be helped. This, as I said at the beginning, is the test tape. I shall destroy what I have said in a minute but first, because the more I talk of these things the easier it is—psychologically easier, I mean, not physically—I have a few more things to say about that summer.

Something about the way the farmers were tearing out the hedges in those days, uprooting ancient hedges and burning them. Because I'm not a keen walker and I don't at all care for sitting in the open air, having a picnic for example, many people have thought I am not interested in nature. In fact, natural history has always been an interest of mine. It was one of the many I shared with Alan, for we had a lot of tastes in common, the same books, the same pictures, the same music, the same attitudes to life. We loved the wild flowers of the fen and of the Suffolk coast. Both of us hoped to see a swallowtail one day. We hated autumn and winter and loved the summer. Neither of us ever walked if we could go in a car. We even liked the same food and we hadn't known each other long when we found we both had a favourite drink that had already by then gone out of fashion. It was a pink gin, gin and angostura bitters. Does anyone drink that now? Could you go into an hotel, for instance, and ask for a pink gin? And would they know what you meant?

The games we played, that we both liked to play, they were innocent games. Even Mr and Mrs Darlint had a sort of simplicity about them and a sweetness. The dressing-up was really for a rehearsal, practising for an ideal, not to titillate tired appetites. We weren't tired, our love was fresh, and every love-making like a young couple's first excitement.

But I have wandered off the point and now I can't recall what the point was. Perhaps there was no point, perhaps I was only talking for practice. But I'm tired now, anyway, and have practised enough.

Tapes are better than life. You strip off the words and make them new and afterwards it's just as it was before you said those things. You don't have to live for twenty-four years with certain acts and words, for you've wiped them away. They have flown away to the planets on invisible waves.

17

Someone sent Gilda a card with 'Now you are Fifty' on it, an unsigned card. The picture on it was of an old-ish smiling woman with waved silver hair, holding a bunch of flowers. Stella, of course, had sent her a card, the kind that makes no reference to the number of the birthday, and she was surprised, almost shocked, when Gilda showed her the unsigned one. She had expected her to conceal this landmark in her age or to lie about it, to stay forty-nine for the next ten years. But Gilda showed off the card, just as she showed off the two anonymous letters that had come.

Printed words had been cut from a book, not a news-paper, and stuck on to cheap notepaper. One said, 'Your husband has another woman', and the other, 'Alan is in love with a woman who is well known to you'. Stella wondered why they were shown to her, why she and Priscilla and Jeremy and even Marianne were shown that birthday card and those crude letters, why they were flaunted.

Stella began to look suspiciously at those she thought she could trust, at her neighbours, at Aagot, the new *au pair*. Then, when interest in the letters seemed to have died down, Gilda confessed to Alan that she had sent them herself. She had bought the card, the ugliest and most vulgar she could find, and she had composed the letters herself, cutting the words from one of the *Figaro and Velvet* books Alan had illustrated. The book was taken down from the shelf and she showed him the mutilated pages.

Because it was a children's story, the range of words available to Gilda was limited. He told Stella that she boasted of her resourcefulness, she was very proud of finding 'husband' and 'woman', words that occur rarely in children's books. Why then had she chosen that particular book? Because 'Alan' was on one of the early pages where the illustrator was named. And perhaps too because he valued it and spoiling it would hurt him.

Of course he asked why had she done it. Why send letters to yourself? What was the point?

'It was a way of telling myself the truth,' she said.

'I remember now,' he said to Stella. 'It came in one of her films. It's the classic domestic-thriller situation. A woman she played was receiving anonymous letters, only they were sent by an enemy.' He laughed. 'I've always said Gilda's her own worst enemy.'

Stella couldn't laugh. Any hint of madness affected her, as it does most people, with fear. Alan, as always, joked about it.

'That book was a first edition,' he said. 'I told her to use *Country Life* next time.'

But Gilda's own cryptic reply stuck in Stella's mind. It was a way of telling herself the truth. And Stella began to understand. Gilda lived in a world of role-playing, of so much acting and pretence, that it was not enough for her to know the truth, the reality, she had to see it written down. But even the writing down, the black-and-white of it, had to be a fake, had to come out of second-rate cinema. Because that was the only truth she knew?

Gilda still dressed well in the old glamorous clothes, the dramatic film-star dresses. The blonde hair was dyed now but it was still long and thick. The figure remained slender, if by now more string-like than willowy. When she told Stella that Alan had become indifferent to her, that they no longer made love, she struck a pose under the painting, leaning backwards, her head flung back, her long hair streaming, her breasts thrust upwards and her arms hanging.

'He'll never leave me,' she said. 'He can't. The house is mine and so is most of our income. He really hasn't got a bean.'

She said it dramatically and, bouncing forwards, threw out her hands. She leaned towards Stella in the confiding way she had, her head on one side, her neck stretched out. Her large blue eyes bored holes in Stella's face.

'Any fool who took up with him would have to be rich. But no one like that would look at him, what do you think?'

Stella wanted to defend him, to say that any woman would want him, but she dared not. When her opinion was asked or she was directly questioned she always felt that Gilda already knew and that she was testing her, interrogating her, laying traps. The 'woman you know' of the letter was herself and Gilda was waiting for her to admit it. Sometimes, in frank detail, she would describe to Stella the methods she considered using to 'get Alan back'. What did Stella think? And then she would fling herself down on the battered settee opposite Stella and inquire of some invisible non-existent third person what was the point of asking advice of someone so sheltered and innocent.

Yet always Stella waited for the direct challenge and tried to prepare herself.

'It's you, isn't it?'

The greatest surprise was when Gilda revealed that it wasn't Stella but, of all women, Priscilla that she suspected.

'When he was coming to me or to Molucca, she thought he was visiting Priscilla. She and Jeremy lived near Ixworth. It couldn't be me because in her estimation I was too old. Priscilla was only in her late thirties.'

Gilda judged people like that. Men wanted women because they were young or beautiful or both. Women looked for husbands who were rich and lovers who were 'good in bed'. She wasn't young any more, though she admitted no loss of beauty, but she told Stella she was confident Alan would stay with her because she 'held the purse strings'.

'One day in the spring Gilda invited herself to lunch. She knew Priscilla and Jeremy were coming with their children and John and Madge Browning. I was happy because Alan would come too. I can't remember what the occasion was, perhaps just Easter Saturday, perhaps Richard's birthday, though I would have had a children's party for that. Aagot cooked the lunch, she was an excellent cook, and after that, much later when we were having tea, Gilda made a terrible scene.'

She had been staring at Priscilla throughout lunch and afterwards. In her innocence, Stella had seated Priscilla next to Alan with Gilda opposite and Gilda kept her eyes fixed on Priscilla, leaving her food untouched. She had some sort of anorexia, if you can be anorexic at fifty. Nobody knew about it then, it was just losing your appetite because you were worried or ill. Stella thought Gilda was starving herself to stay thin and in fact she had got thinner and thinner, you could see the lines of her ribcage through her clothes. She always wore very tight clothes and that Easter she was in a bright green silk dress, very short, with a wide black belt cinching in the waist. Her beautiful strained face was brightly painted and her gold hair was shoulder-length.

She hardly spoke. The terrible thing was, Stella said, that no one seemed to notice. *She* alone noticed, perhaps because she was so alive to everything Gilda said and did at this time, but the others were happy to talk among themselves and possibly they were glad of Gilda's silence. After all, Gilda had become a great bore, she could only talk of the world of film in the forties and fifties, what this actor said to that actor, and the famous people she'd known—most of them half-forgotten by then—and of her own triumphs and, worse, the way she had been misunderstood, passed over and victimized. Probably she had always talked like that but people put up with it, were even happy to listen to it, when Gilda was young.

It was about four in the afternoon when Gilda broke her silence and broke her staring. Marianne and Priscilla's daughter Sarah had made tea and brought it in with a simnel cake. Gilda shook her head at the cake as if it really did contain the poison Alan used to joke about giving her. She waited till Priscilla had put a small square of cake with marzipan into her mouth and then she said,

'Tell me where you and my husband have been meeting.'

The extraordinary thing was, Stella said, that she recognized the line. She and Gilda had been to Sudbury a few days before to see *The Skies Above Us*. Gilda was playing the wife of an Air Force bomber pilot who suspected her young sister-in-law—with justification—of being in love with her husband, and when she confronted her those were the very words she used. Because of that, for a moment, Stella thought it must be a game. She thought Gilda was quoting from the film in order to start talking about the film.

Priscilla knew nothing about film. She never went to the cinema. 'What?' she said.

Gilda said it again, just as she did in the film. Patricia Roc, who's the sister-in-law, breaks down and confesses everything, promises never to see the pilot again and in the end everyone is made happy by the wife, the Gilda character, getting killed in an air raid.

But Priscilla wasn't going to conform to any of that. She said very quietly to Gilda that she simply didn't understand. Gilda replied by more quotations from the film, a whole speech of accusations. Then she came back to reality, to real people or what she thought was real. She knew Alan and Priscilla were lovers and had been for years and she wanted it to end. But Jeremy should know the truth and Priscilla's children know what their mother was. It was time too that Stella's eyes were open to reality and she understood the kind of people she had invited to her house. Priscilla and Jeremy could do as they pleased, but for her part she would forgive Alan and take him back if the affair stopped now.

262 ᎣᏅ   *Barbara Vine*

Priscilla behaved with great dignity. She apologized to Stella, she was sorry this had happened to spoil the day, she would phone her next day. She said to Jeremy, 'We'll go now,' and to the children, 'Get your coats. Don't argue, please. We're leaving.'

Alan had said nothing throughout all this. Stella had said nothing. When they spoke of it afterwards to each other they agreed that there was nothing they could have said. Alan, of course, could have denied it. There was no truth in that particular accusation, but no denying that he was constantly and consistently unfaithful to Gilda. It was just that Gilda had got the wrong woman. And for that reason, because Stella was the right woman, she too had felt unable to speak in anyone's defence.

When Jeremy and Priscilla had gone Gilda began to scream. It was the scene at St Michael's Farm about the child she couldn't have all over again. She threw and smashed two ornaments of Stella's, she lay on the floor. You are supposed to slap people's faces in these circumstances but no one slapped Gilda's. Marianne stared, appalled, then went away upstairs. Only Richard seemed unaffected. He continued to read the book Madge Browning had brought him, sitting on the floor in a far corner of the room.

But all that came later, after months of Gilda constantly raising with Stella the possibility of Alan's infidelity. Stella tried—had been trying for years—to see less of her. For one thing she felt guilty about taking the role of friend while she was having a love affair with Gilda's husband. For another, she had begun deeply to dislike Gilda.

'You could leave her,' she said to Alan. 'We could sell this house and go and live with Richard in *my* house. We could live on my money. It would be ours, yours and mine.'

Oh, she hated talking about money but she did to Alan. She had to. She held out Richard as an inducement because she knew Alan loved him. He loved children. Wasn't he an illustrator of books for children?

'You should have let me kill her,' he said.

'It was said so—well, so laconically, Genevieve,' Stella said. 'Just as someone else might say, you should have let me—oh, I don't know, close the door, make a phone call. I couldn't be angry. I couldn't help laughing.'

'Did you ever think of just stopping seeing Gilda? Cutting yourself off from her?'

'I did try. Even if I'd stopped being friends with her I'd still have seen Alan. Our relationship no longer depended on chance meetings, they were just a bonus. But Genevieve, you're the person you are, aren't you, you can't change yourself radically no matter how you want to. It wasn't in me to tell someone who'd been my friend I didn't want to see her again, tell her to go, break off with her. I can't be rude—sometimes I've wished I could. And then I was the—well, the guilty party, wasn't I? Being rude to her, breaking with her, would have seemed like adding insult to injury. Can you understand that?'

They lived twenty miles apart but Gilda was always 'dropping in'. She often seemed to come at the time Richard arrived home from school. Stella wondered if she purposely came at that time. Sometimes she was terrified. She fancied she saw her staring at Richard. Gilda had long ago given up saying she wanted a child of her own. Now she said she didn't like children. She had always been subject to mood swings and her present mood or her pose was that she disliked children, children were a nuisance. 'A drag,' she called them. She often said she was in sympathy with Herod who killed all the little boys in Bethlehem. And then she would smile as if a smile and a pat on Richard's shoulder made things all right.

Going out to tea in some country hotel had become a favourite thing to do, or finding some cinema where one of her own films was showing. She'd go into the cinema very self-consciously, smiling and nodding to the woman selling tickets and the usherettes. She was like a celebrity at an airport, certain everyone would recognize her, and that embarrassed Stella because she was sure no one did.

Richard had of necessity to be left behind. 'You can leave him with the *au pair*,' Gilda said, as if he wasn't there. She always pretended not to be able to pronounce Aagot's name. 'You need a break from that child.'

And then she would stare at Richard, the way a child stares at another child before making a terrible face, curling up its nose and sticking out its tongue. Gilda didn't make the face, she just looked as if she was going to. Stella always hugged Richard when Gilda spoke about him unkindly. She'd take him out of the room to Aagot and then come back and ask Gilda not to talk in that way. It took the summoning up of courage to speak like that to Gilda and the suppression of all those guilt feelings. For what right had she to reproach Gilda for anything? She had taken Gilda's husband from her, and worse, had made a game with him of killing her, talking about her in the worst possible terms behind her back, furthering her husband's disloyalty.

Richard was such a mother's boy, Gilda said. He needed a father, someone to take him to cricket matches and show him how to kick a ball. It was always these cliché ways of being a father that Gilda seized on; mothers were for hugging and kissing, fathers were for outdoor sports. She smiled at Stella in a particular way she had. It was as if she'd learned at acting school that this was what you did when you wanted to seem rueful and pitying, put your head on one side, lifted your shoulders, raised your eyebrows and smiled. She'd done it several times in *Lora Cartwright*. It was a pity, she said, that Stella was unlikely to marry again. A pity for her and for Richard.

That was more than even Stella could stand and she asked Gilda what she meant.

'Oh, you know what I mean, little thing,' Gilda said. 'He may need a father but a man would only take on a teenage girl and a little boy if he were madly in love, and that's not likely, is it?'

'At my age, do you mean?'

'That among other things. I know you don't care how you look or I wouldn't say it, but you've never laid claims to much in the beauty department, have you?'

Short of telling her they were no longer friends, she didn't want to know her, there was nothing Stella could have done. I would have said those things, and Mum would have said a good deal more, but Stella couldn't. She took the coward's way, pretending illnesses, previous engagements that didn't exist. Once she even pretended to be out when Gilda called, ashamed of herself because she had to make Richard pretend too, hide with her upstairs in a bedroom. She said she crouched on the floor and covered up her ears so that she couldn't hear Aagot telling lies to Gilda at the front door.

'Were you still playing the game?' I said.

'The game?'

'Killing Gilda,' I said. 'Did you still talk about that, pretend about that?'

'Oh, that,' she said. It mystifies me that policemen and lawyers think they need a machine to find if a person is telling the truth. The face itself and the tone of voice are lie-detectors. 'That was all over. It was only a joke, Genevieve, and never a very funny one.'

She had never talked to me for so long. She wanted to go on but I wouldn't let her. I fetched her blanket and covered her up. Her hands were cold so I rubbed them between mine before tucking them under the cover.

Philippa and Steve had been out for a meal on their wedding anniversary so she had had to choose between recording *Seaforth* and *Postcards From the Edge*. I did the one she didn't, which was how I came to take the video of the third episode of *Seaforth* round to her at eight.

Steve had gone down to the pub. She had the TV on, she always has the TV on, and was watching Peter O'Toole in *Stunt Man* while she wrote her Christmas cards. I hadn't even thought about Christmas cards, I hadn't done any Christmas shopping. Mike was doing a job in Yorkshire the following week, he'd be away for four nights, so he'd said he'd be giving any Christmas parties and family gatherings that might be going a miss and he'd work on the conservatory right through the holiday.

'Be thankful,' said Philippa, 'he's got something to keep him occupied.'

'Keep him out of mischief, you mean?'

'You said it, not me. Don't suppose he gets into

mischief, does he?'

'I don't know,' I said, 'and I don't care. I'm leaving him.'

She actually turned off the telly. I told her about Ned then. I told her how he'd wanted me to go away with him from the first and how for a long time I'd refused. She listened, she nodded, but I could read it in her look, her eyes: fancy a man like that wanting someone like you. Well, she could understand the wanting, but not the wanting *for ever*. I knew it, I'd wondered too, but I'd come to accept it as one of life's marvels, helped by the love philtre and the ferns in his shoe.

'When are you going to tell Mike?'

'Next week,' I said. 'When he gets back from Yorkshire. You can keep it dark till then.'

'You bet,' she said. 'There's one of your Gilda Brent's films on tomorrow, two p.m., you'll be at work, so d'you want me to video it for you? *The Skies Above Us*, 1945, black-and-white and dead boring, frankly.'

Mike was doing the glazing when I got back. He stopped for five minutes and gave me a lecture on thermostatic bars. They're window catches filled up with oil which make the windows open automatically when the sun shines and heats the oil so that it expands. The floor tiles would be coming next week, special ceramic jobs from Italy in écru and ivory and black. He won't be here so he'd like me to arrange to be at home and take the delivery in. I said all right, because it was easier than an argument, and I didn't want him to say that again, about him doing it all for me so the least I could do was open the door to the tile man.

Ladybirds are lucky creatures and this winter lots of

them have taken refuge indoors. Do they find places to sleep in till spring? I don't know but I'm careful not to harm them. Mum told me she only had Nick because of harming a ladybird. Of course she wouldn't be without him now and she was thrilled to have a boy after us girls but it was a blow to her at the time. She trod on this lady-bird by accident and instead of burying it, stamping on the grave three times and reciting *Ladybird, ladybird, fly away home*, she just sucked it up in the Hoover and that same night she fell for Nick.

I found twelve ladybirds in my bathroom that morning and another five in Stella's. The trouble is you don't know what to do for the best in the wintertime. Still, there was no frost on the ground, so I took the five lady-birds tenderly in my hands and put them out of Stella's window into a dry cosy spot under the scimmia bush. There's a poem my nan used to say that I've remembered all my life, more than I can say for the ones we did at school.

> 'This lady-fly I take from off the grass,
> Whose spotted back might scarlet-red surpass.
> Fly, Lady-bird, north, south, or east or west,
> Fly where the man is found that I love best.
> He leaves my hand, see to the west he's flown,
> To call my true love from the faithless town.'

That made Stella laugh. It was the laughter of pleasure, not at something funny. 'How clever you are, Genevieve! Where does that come from?'

My nan, I said. I didn't know more than that. I was thinking about the man I love and how he was my true love that I'd call from the faithless town, whatever that may mean. Maybe one of the ladybirds I'd saved would fly up to Norwich and find him.

Stella was still in bed and wanted to stay there, but Lena had said she had to get up. She could have a lie-in but staying in bed wasn't good for her and anyway Marianne had phoned to say she'd be along in the afternoon.

'No reason why you shouldn't stay there till just before your lunch,' I said.

'The pain is beginning,' she said. 'Do you know, I've not really had any pain till now.'

What could I say? I sat on the bed and took her hand. Her grip was still strong but she'd cut and filed down her once-sharp nails. She looked into my face the way she's begun to do, very searchingly, as if she's testing me, even as if she wonders about trusting me.

'Genevieve, have you still got the key to my house?'

It's funny how you feel yourself blush. When I was a kid and we used to have coal fires I'd put my face close to the flames and feel the heat on my skin. Blushing is just the same feeling, a flame heating the skin. She was look-ing at me, watching my face get red, I expect. I nodded. I thought she'd ask for the key back.

'That's all right,' she said. 'You hold on to it. As long as I know where it is.'

I knew then that I had to tell her. It was inside me, the guilt of it, swelling up and bursting to get out. For an instant I was a child again, back at school, owning up. I'm sorry, Miss, it was me, I did it. I took a breath.

'Stella, I've been going to your house. To Molucca. I mean, me and Ned have. We've been meeting there. I should have asked you, I know that, I honestly don't know now why I didn't. Well, I do know. I thought you'd say no.'

'You've been going to my house?'

'We had to have somewhere to meet. I'm sorry, Stella, I should have asked you.'

She smiled. Her hand gave mine a squeeze. 'I'm glad.'

'You're *glad*?'

'I like to think of happy lovers being there. We were very happy when we were there, Alan and I. There was only one occasion when we were there and we weren't— oh, tremendously happy.'

I felt a chill. That's always the way I react to an omen. 'But once you weren't?'

'Once we weren't. The last time. You must have been very cold there.'

I told her about the oil heaters. I told her how I'd cleaned the place and put flowers everywhere.

'I was going to have central heating put in. But it would have meant builders and a lot more people knowing the house was mine. It was still a secret place, you see. But I think I would have had it done that autumn.' She hung her head.

She does that more and more often now. 'The autumn after the summer I was telling you about. Only time stopped and we never got there.'

'You must have got there, you're here now.'

Stella gave her thin ghostly laugh. 'Barely. But I must hang on for a while longer.' She laid her head back on the pillow. She spoke softly. 'Do you believe you can fight death?'

'For a while, I reckon,' I said. 'Not for ever.'

'No, certainly not for ever. But you with your strange beliefs, I fancied you might have ideas about keeping death at bay.' She smiled at me. 'Never mind. Do you remember the day we saw the dalmatian and you said to make a wish?'

Of course I remembered. 'Mine's coming true now,' I said. 'How about yours?'

'Genevieve, you said we must have got to the autumn—well, we did, but not together. After Priscilla there was one woman after another that Gilda suspected, all their friends and neighbours—not that they had many. She talked to me incessantly about the evidence she had against Alan, all those absurd things like lipstick on his handkerchiefs and blonde hairs on his jackets. It was all made up or at any rate it was all in her head.'

'Why not you?' I said.

'I was too old, just as I was too old to have my portrait painted. She said as much. Oh, much later when she confronted us. "Why her? " she said. "Why not some young girl?" Men loved young girls, you see, men only loved beauties. That was the world she lived in, you see, the world of . . .'

'B movies?' I said.

She smiled. 'If you like. It went on all summer, Gilda talking about Alan's women. She turned him into a monster, much as I had turned Rex into one. Yet I've never known how much she really believed herself, if it wasn't just another scene in the dramatic scenario she had to make for herself. Instead of a life, Genevieve. Instead of a life. I sometimes thought she'd divided her existence into these phases, youth that was glamorous and exciting, marriage to the man who was madly in love with her, now middle age when he strayed and she fought to get him back. It was as if she was saying, this is woman's lot and I have to act it out.

'The part of the wronged wife—she'd played that in so many films, the words came naturally to her. I don't think she knew where it came from when she said she had given him the best years of her life and he'd cast her away like an old shoe. She just said it because that is what wronged wives say in bad films, so therefore it was what she *had* to say.

'When she followed him in her car, she was only doing what the woman did in *The Wife's Story*. She even told him about it, she boasted to him about it, how she'd followed him to Norwich and gone into a coffee bar to wait for him. She'd sat at a table by herself, she said, and everyone had been staring at her. Someone came up and asked for her autograph. She was distraught with grief, hardly knew what she was doing, and she told the autograph hunter she was going to kill herself. Alan asked her if she realized she'd just described the climax of *The Wife's Story* to him but that made her start screaming and over-turning the furniture. That was something she just couldn't take, having her acting exposed for what it was. Poor thing, poor Gilda.'

I think I must have been looking at Stella in amazement, or at any rate in a very bewildered way. At last I said, 'I don't really understand why he didn't leave her. What was there to stop him just leaving her?'

'But he did leave her,' Stella said. 'He did in the end.'

'He left her and came to you?'

'Oh, yes.'

'Why didn't you say so before?'

'I don't know. I meant to. He left her for me. But that's the end of the story, Genevieve. I mean, that's the end if you like.'

'A happy ending,' I said, though that wasn't the way it felt.

'Why not happy? You know what I wished when we saw the dalmatian? I wished for a happy ending.'

It's always clear when she intends to say no more. She cuts things off, terminates talk, calls a stop. She reached for her tape recorder and put in a cassette. She smiled, taking hold of my arm to stop me getting up.

Maybe I can get to like classical music the way she does. I educate myself with my dictionary and I try to learn new things all the time for Ned's sake. I'm trying to learn to read good books, appreciate art, so why not symphonies and operas too? A thin tinkly tune filled the air, unfamiliar, difficult stuff if you're used to country and western. I listened for a while, making an effort to understand. Then I gently removed Stella's hand, gave her a kiss and went off to see to Gracie.

When I next came along Stella's corridor a good many hours had passed and it was already dusk. No light showed under her door. Perhaps she was asleep. Then I heard her voice, low, conversational, yet a steady monologue. Unlike so many of them here, I'm not a listener at keyholes so I only paused momentarily. Something cautioned me not to open the door or even knock.

But when I asked Stanley, who was in the hall ready to take the dogs out, if Stella had a visitor he shook his head. A Mrs Browning had come in to see her but was gone by twelve.

Stella, alone, had been talking to herself.

∽

Philippa had dropped the video of *The Skies Above Us* through my letter box.

The bath was full of ladybirds. I wondered what it meant and phoned Mum to ask but Len answered and said she'd gone round to Nan's, so I picked all the lady-birds up in a silk scarf, put them in the flower bed and covered them with fallen yellow oak leaves.

Then I made myself a cup of tea and watched *The Skies Above Us*, another one of those dramas about the Royal Air Force, the Battle of Britain and women waiting at home for missing Spitfire pilots. Gilda Brent, who was one of the waiting wives, looked more like Joan Crawford than I'd ever seen her and her clothes were pure Hollywood, tailored suits and fox furs with little faces and tails, veiled hats and stilt heels for a bunch of women who were supposed to be dressing on clothing coupons.

It was uncanny hearing her say those things Stella told me the real woman had said: 'I've given him the best years of my life,' and, 'Why her? Why not some young girl?' About ten minutes before the end she asked the flight lieutenant's wife, who was played by Glynis Johns, 'Do you think you can take him away from me?'

But she had. Finally she had. And Gilda had run away and disappeared from their lives. All those ideas for killing her were over, they had never been real, anyway. Not really real. They had never meant them.

Stella and Alan had lived together in the house called Molucca and Richard had lived with them and learned to think of Alan as his father. They kept a bedroom for Marianne when she came home for the holidays. Gilda had left Alan her car when she went away and he and

Stella had kept it. They only needed one car, so they sold theirs and kept Gilda's. They were happy.

I expect you know about the theory of the parallel universe? Ned told me about it once. It's about what might have been or what might have happened if you'd taken a different road to the one you took. That alternative is going along at the same time but in different space from what's happening in your life. For instance, there's one universe with me in it living with Mike all our long lives and another, the real one, for me and Ned. That's how it must have been for Stella and Alan, and their real universe hadn't been the one I've imagined, but an ugly parallel of chaos and destruction and a living unhappily ever after.

18

All I know of making statements to the police is what I have read in detective stories, but I doubt if I could make a statement without someone there to question and prompt me. So I'm going to talk until I have said it all or until I'm too tired to go on. Whichever is the sooner, as Alan used to say.

There is a purpose in all this. Its purpose is to tell what happened to Gilda Brent, who was also Gwendoline Brant and then Gwendoline Tyzark. I shall soon die but I don't want to die and leave her alive, or at least officially alive, which as far as others are concerned amounts to the same thing. For no one is really dead unless death is recorded, registered, rubber-stamped as we used to say— computer data'd now, I suppose. So Gilda is not dead and will never die, will have eternal life, unless I or Alan speak, and Alan is dead.

I rehearsed those last few sentences. Well, as a matter of fact, I wrote them down and read them aloud. I shall not do that any more but just talk as the words come.

In the summer following their father's death, both my children spent a fortnight's holiday with my next-door neighbours Madge and John Browning and their two sons in a cottage they took in south Cornwall. It was the first time Richard had ever been anywhere without me but he enjoyed himself with his friends from next door, who went to the same school as he did. He wanted to go again when the Brownings took the cottage in 1970 and was very happy to be invited. I was very happy too—no, I don't quite mean that. I wasn't happy to be separated from him, I'd have done nothing to encourage him to go if he hadn't wanted to, I wouldn't have thought twice about it. But he did want to go, he was longing to go, and this meant I'd have two weeks with Alan, something wonderful and unprecedented, for Gilda was also going away at almost exactly the same time. She was visiting her friend in the South of France as she did most years, though not usually in the height of summer. Marianne, at seventeen, no longer wanted to spend her holidays with me, that was only natural, and though she'd been invited wasn't much inclined for a holiday in Cornwall with two middle-aged people and three little boys for company.

It was August. Marianne went off with three girlfriends to the Costa Brava and Mallorca on August the 20th. They were to be away for three weeks and though this worried me a little, I thought I could trust Marianne to be sensible; she was quite mature for her age in some ways. And of course she came to no harm, she had a marvellous time, it was her mother who came to harm. On August the 25th, the Brownings came and fetched Richard to take him with them to Cornwall. You see how I remember these dates as if I had written them down and memorized them. But they were never written down.

Gilda went away, or said she was going away—perhaps

I shouldn't have said that, but still, why not? I'm not in the business of creating suspense, I'm only telling a story that is grim enough without suspense. She went away on August the 28th, she left St Michael's Farm in her car, a red Ford Anglia, the model that was made in the early sixties I think, with a bonnet like a wide downturned mouth full of teeth, a grin like a piranha's. I always saw it like that. Perhaps I saw it like that because it was her car, I don't know.

The next day Alan and I went to Molucca. We went there to be together for the rest of our lives, though I didn't know it then.

We had been planning it for weeks. It was our main topic of conversation, the thing to drive away talk of killing Gilda. It was our new game, what we would do, what we would eat, which days we would go to the seaside and which we'd stay up all night and stay in bed all next day. The Killing Gilda game was over, the complicated insane methods we thought of and in which we collaborated to dispose of her, all these stopped and instead we played house again. I suppose you could say we played at honeymoons.

Most pairs of lovers in those circumstances would go away to a hotel in a holiday resort somewhere or go to Paris. I couldn't have afforded that—I had my children's education to think of—I couldn't have afforded it for both of us and he couldn't pay his share. He'd reached a point when he only had the income he made from selling landscapes in pubs at ten pounds a time and drawing cat pictures for birthday cards. But apart from that we both wanted to go to Molucca. It was the place where we had always met, the only place for the past six years, it was the scene for our being married game. All the things the two of us had collected together were there, our books, our records, our pictures. We kept clothes there. The crockery and cutlery, the linen, were ours, bought together, bought specially for us for that house. We'd cooked our favourite food in the kitchen and the utensils we'd used were all there. Our favourite drink was in the sideboard, gin and angostura, and our favourite white burgundy in the wine rack. You see, when we were together we never made do with the second-rate. We ate and drank the things we liked best, we did only the things we liked best, we were complete hedonists.

The one thing we'd never done was spend a night together. Ridiculous, wasn't it? We'd been lovers for ten years and we'd never slept side by side for a whole night in the same bed. I longed for that and so did he. The previous year, with my children both away, we'd often met at Molucca, but Gilda was at home, watchful, checking on his movements, already suspicious. There was no question of his staying away overnight.

When you're in love you want to see the person you love in every possible circumstance, in all possible situations, performing every action it's possible for a human being to perform, to see him when he's aware of you and when he's unaware. I'd seen Alan asleep but never by night, never in the darkness of the night, never seen a dream make him smile or an anxiety make his eyelids tremble. I'd never seen him wake up in the morning. I didn't know if he was a hard or an easy waker, if he lay there slowly surfacing or if he jumped out of bed, as alert first thing in the morning as at midday.

We meant to spend all those nights together, ten of

them if we were lucky. Part of the game was talking about those nights, how we would start the early evening with the right sort of dinner and the right sort of drinks. We planned what I'd wear and even the things we'd say. We knew that Gilda wouldn't be back till the end of the second week of September, nor would Marianne, and Richard wasn't expected till September the 8th, two days before his school term began. How I remember those dates! I could have made a statement to the police after all. Even Aagot had gone away. Not home to Norway but to be with her boyfriend who was at Durham University and had a holiday job in Newcastle. I even lent her my car to go in. It wasn't entirely altruism. She couldn't have gone without free transport and free petrol.

As it happened Alan and I never did have our ten nights together, not one night together. For we didn't even have one. We never did. We never came to sleep side by side in the same bed for a whole night. That's not to say we didn't pass a night together, we did, two long nights together, the longest I've ever known. Well, that is what I am going to talk about.

Whichever is the sooner turns out to be my voice. You can hear how hoarse I've become. I will do some more tomorrow.

Alan came down from Tivetshall St Michael to fetch me in his car, the old grey Rover that he'd had ever since I'd first known him. It was eleven in the morning, August the 29th, and very hot. We'd planned to go straight to Molucca and have our lunch there, then out for a drive to the coast perhaps. We were going to have dinner out, in some nice hotel, a romantic dinner in a lovely place, because after that was going to be our first night together. I believe he'd done a lot of work he didn't care to do to be able to afford that dinner.

You'll think it absurd the way I was dressed. But people's clothes were more formal in those days, and I—well, I think I was a lot more formal than some others. I suppose I still dressed in much the same way as I had in the fifties. Those were the styles that suited me, dresses with tight bodices and tiny waists with wide belts and full skirts, stockings, high-heeled shoes. I didn't possess a pair of trousers. I never wore sweaters or cardigans. When Alan came to fetch me I was wearing a cream-coloured cotton dress printed with pink and blue flowers, high-heeled cream patent shoes, a diamond watch, pearl earrings. The dress was very low-cut and off-the-shoulder and I wore a double-strand pearl necklace. My hair was turned under in a short pageboy, back-combed and lacquered. A woman wouldn't dress up as much as that to go to a dinner party these days, would she? Marianne goes out to dinner in jeans and an Indian shirt.

I don't know why I've talked about the clothes I was wearing, it seems irrelevant, but it wasn't, not really. If it were possible to make things worse, the way I was dressed made things worse. I didn't have any more—well, suitable, I suppose that's the word—suitable clothes at Molucca, just more dresses and more court shoes and the kind of raincoat that's more for show than it's waterproof, a shot-silk thing, silver and blue, you may even have found it there in the wardrobe. Are you surprised that I remember all these details, that I remember everything?

It was very hot. We had all the car windows open but there was no wind, not the least breeze. The farmers were taking advantage of the stillness to burn off the fields. There was always a risk unless you were very careful of setting hedges alight but that risk was much increased in windy weather. A day like this one was a godsend to them. A pall of smoke hung over the horizon, a thick pale grey that quite obscured the blue of the sky, and into this greyness spires of darker smoke rose as from chimneys on winter nights.

The idea was to kill weeds, I believe, rather than plough them in. Ploughing took place after the burning. I suppose there must have been fields where the farmer or one of his men remained behind to watch the progress of their fire, but I never saw any. I only saw the flames running through the lanes between the stubble, the whole field alight and the smoke pouring off it in black clouds, untended, unwatched, filling the air with a stifling, choking darkness. Scraps of charred stalk danced in it like swarms of flies. We closed all the windows. I already had black on my hands, powdery yet greasy fragments that smelt like dead matches.

We stopped once to buy food and he bought a bottle of champagne. I don't think we saw a soul apart from the shopman on that drive up over the Waveney to Curton. We followed one car for a while and met two. The countryside up here was very remote twenty-five years ago. Unspoilt, they called it. Suffolk was the second least spoilt county of England, and that must have gone for the borders of Norfolk too. But you'll know that, you'll have heard it from your mother and grandmother. There were places where you could drive for twenty miles, look across empty fields and woods, see perhaps three farmhouses and half a dozen cottages in all that distance. The

Breckland was still a wild, strange place and the fens still lonely and silent.

The rolling smoke was behind us when we reached Molucca. The sky was blue over the fen behind the house and we could breathe the air without inhaling charred remains of barley. It was utterly quiet. Birds only sing at dawn and before they go to roost, not at midday. We could be in that house for hours without a single car passing along the road beyond the long grassy space.

Once inside, would you have expected us to go straight to bed? We were past that stage, though we might have done if, like the previous August, we had only the daytime. But we thought we had ten nights. No, by then we thought we had a lifetime, because as we entered the house Alan said to me, 'This isn't a holiday, sweetheart. This is for ever. I'm never going back. I've left her.'

He took me in his arms and kissed me. I kissed him and hugged him and we danced.

The years between then and now began on September the 1st.

There was August the 29th and the next day and the night that followed and the next day, and then twenty-four years. I don't suppose I saw it like that at the time but that's how I see it now. At the end of those years.

These days they would call what I had a clinical depression, a term I've learned from Richard. I would have treatment, drugs, therapy, counselling. Then, I had nothing. I drifted through grey days, from which all the light had gone.

I am not asking for pity. Whom anyway could I ask it of? No one will listen to this. And I deserve no pity, though Alan does. I had my children. He had no one. His predicament was terrible but I could do nothing to relieve it. The thought of him, his name, memories of him, paralysed me. Even if I'd wanted to—and of course I wanted to—I could not physically have lifted the phone or dialled his number. I did write to him. The letters were never sent. How do I know that the same was true of him? That he too wanted to phone and tried to write? I know it, that's all.

Because this wasn't one of Gilda's films, we hadn't broken off immediately and dramatically. Gilda said I knew nothing of life but I know it isn't like that. We met the day before Richard came back, not at Molucca but at an hotel, a place where we had sometimes been to eat. We sat in the bar, not drinking our familiar favourite but he whisky and I some vermouth mixture. It was as if we each set out to do things differently from the past.

Events hung between us but they could not be talked of, we had each silently acknowledged that. How strange that there should be nothing else to say. We who had had so much to say, so much in common that we talked all the time we were together, had nothing to say. There are couples who can be together in 'companionable silence' but we had never been among them. The silence that descended on us was not companionable. It was nothing, a blank, that as it lasted filled with a kind of panic. Because we scorned small talk, or rather had kept it for others, knowing it was not for us, we rejected it now.

It was not that we wanted to talk of her or what had happened, but that what had happened had driven away everything else. Some people boast of living in the present, but if you try it you will find it's not possible. We were trying it, blotting out the past because it was too outrageous, unable to imagine a future, living in the here and now. And we discovered there was no present, only an emptiness that if you tumbled and fell into it would drive you mad.

I wanted him not to touch me, not even touch my hand, and if he felt differently he gave no sign. We drank our drinks and said we had better be getting back. To what? To two empty houses. Before we parted he said, in a tone made artificially light and casual,

'I'll pop over on Saturday, shall I? I'd like to see my son.'

The way he talked to Richard when he came to our house I recognized as a farewell. To me his words, though to the child only friendly and interested, were loaded with the sadness of last times. And when Richard had gone out into the garden on his own he said to me,

'It isn't going to work, is it?'

'No,' I said.

'It was lovely knowing you,' he said. 'It was the best thing I ever had. I don't suppose you want to kiss me and the funny thing is I don't much want to kiss you. That's the way it goes, I suppose. I won't hang about here any longer. Say goodbye to Richard for me, will you?'

Once Richard was back at school I drove over to Molucca. I was very nervous about driving, I was terrified. The house was in a mess. I cleared up, I emptied ashtrays and washed glasses. There were some flowers in a vase but they were still fresh and I couldn't bring myself to throw them away. They were love-in-a-mist, there's an irony for you. For some reason—did I think I would go back there again?—I took Alan's drawings off the walls and put them into the sideboard. The photograph of us that the man who came to ask the way had taken I took out of its frame and put with the drawings.

I switched off the refrigerator and opened the door but I didn't look inside. There was ham in there and a piece of cheese as well as the champagne. It seemed unlikely to me that I would ever drink champagne again. I went upstairs to find the dress I had worn that day and the next night, I intended to fetch it and take it to the cleaners, but the sooty sulphurous smell of it when I opened the wardrobe door made me nauseous. I pushed it along the rail to the far end and shut the door.

Before I left I went into the garage and looked at Gilda's car. No one would come looking for it. I knew that as well as I knew that this house was mine and my name was Stella Newland. No one would need or wish to look for it. Of course if I had it moved away or otherwise tried to dispose of it, that would be another thing. If, for instance, I tried to sell the house. But I wouldn't sell the house.

I drove home. That night I was ill, that was the start of an illness that was like a protracted flu. When I recovered I told Aagot I would never drive again.

Other people should have made things easier. They made them worse. It seems to me that everybody I knew asked me if I still saw Alan and Gilda. Where were they? Why did they never come? Why did I never go to them? By 'everybody' I suppose I mean Marianne—well, mainly Marianne. Since the scene at Easter Priscilla had behaved as if Gilda didn't exist, as if she had never existed. Jeremy took a slightly different attitude. He congratulated me on 'getting rid of' Alan and Gilda, those 'rackety people'.

One day Madge Browning told me she had encountered Alan in Diss. He was waiting at the bus stop. She hadn't asked him why he had no car and she hadn't asked after Gilda, but he told her all the same. Gilda had left him and gone to live in France. It upset me terribly when she told me that. Not about Gilda going to France, not that, he had to say that, but just that she had seen him and talked to him and—oh, I don't know. That was when Marianne interfered. She phoned him, asked why he had dropped me, what sort of a friend was he? I was ill and I needed him. Please to come as soon as he could. It's ironical really. I think, I really think, she hoped to marry us to each other, she was matchmaking.

I have hardly ever been angry with my children. She was terribly taken aback at my anger. Poor little one, she meant well, she was only eighteen. Of course he didn't come, he knew better than that, he no more wanted to come than I wanted to see him.

I never saw him again. I haven't seen him since September twenty-four years ago. It would be nice if I could say I've thought of him every day and never ceased to love him but I can't say that because when I have thought of him and tried to recapture my love for him I can only remember the burning fields and a green scarf and blood on the grass. And these things blot out the good memories the way smoke blots out the sun.

The next two tapes I make will be—what is it Marianne says?—for real. Yes, the next two will be for real. I shall label them and ask Richard to see that Genevieve gets them after I am dead. Perhaps they will be lost and she will never hear them or perhaps she will use them to record something without knowing the words they contain. So be it. I am not inclined to write cryptic messages on them. She will listen or she will not.

I only feel that for reasons which will become clear, of all people on this earth it is she who should be told. This is a dramatic and fatalistic way of looking at things, I know that. It is my way of giving some meaning to life, a pattern prescribed by destiny, that is all.

And what is she supposed to do then?

I paused, I stopped. Footsteps hesitated outside the door and then passed on. I asked what she was supposed to do. What she likes. Something or nothing. Whatever she likes.

19

I was moving into the country of last times. It's a strange place and being in it gives weight to everything you do. Mike had gone off to Leeds and I'd given him the last kiss I'd ever give him. For the last time I'd said I'd be seeing him on Friday, I'd walked down to the bottom of our garden for the last time, thrown out the last dead flowers from the wall vase. As for Stella, she'd eaten her dinner in the dining room for the last time, maybe done her last crossword puzzle, smoked her last cigarette.

But I felt no nostalgia for the home I was soon to leave, I'd lost all interest in it, I never wanted to be there. It was just a house Mike and I had bought on a mortgage, not because we liked it but because it was all we could afford, not in a place we chose but the only place we knew. Most of the people I know lived like that, not in the way they wanted to live but in the best and most prudent way they could manage. I wondered if that *expedient* way of living, that economical, obligatory way, was going to change now. To change for good.

My house, mine and Mike's, had been due, soon, to feel like a small and cosy prison, with two inmates and two prison officers, so I was going before that could happen. I was going while I still could and when I had a reason. Work was where I wanted to be, not in that house, so I'd told Lena I wouldn't take my day off, I'd swap with Carolyn.

Again, as I came up to Stella's door, I heard the murmur of her voice from inside. There was no one with her, she was talking to herself. It was rather eerie, like one of the women of my family speaking an incantation. Only in Stella's case there were no pauses for a candle to be lit or sulphur cast into the ring. My fingernail scraping the wood before I knocked was enough to alert her. Her silence was as sudden as an explosion. I could almost hear her jump. She must have expected to see Lena or Pauline—when had I last knocked?—for I found her sitting in her chair clutching the new patchwork dressing-gown about her, her expression quite guilty.

The old, lovely smile stretched her wizened face. She put up her arms. I kissed her and she managed a feeble hug. That, too, was a last time. She hated to complain, she said, but the pain was bad now. Lena had agreed to call the doctor. That's who she thought it was when I knocked. Did she want me to stay and talk? She shook her head, her eyes half-closed. I left her. I don't know why I broke my rule and, coming past her door an hour later with Gracie's tray, put my ear to one of the top panels of the door. Stella wasn't asleep, she was talking again, and although I couldn't make out the words they sounded far from a description of her symptoms to a doctor.

Next morning, when I went to her room, she was in bed and something about her colour and the way she was lying told me she wouldn't get up that day.

Her face was beginning to change. The dying get a

certain look a few days before they die. The eyes stare, the flesh falls. I sponged her face and hands and combed her hair. She wanted me to sit with her and for once Lena didn't object. Her right hand crept out from under the sheet and clasped mine. It was no longer a strong grip that she had. The fingers were weak and not quite steady. But after a while she was able to sit up against the pillows and talk. She asked me about her house, if I'd liked it, if I with what she called my superstitiousness had sensed unpleasant things there, forces, elements. I was able to tell her I had nothing but good feelings, a sense of happiness, comfort and peace.

'Not a faithless place, Genevieve?'

That reminded me of the ladybird poem and calling my true love. After she was gone, would anyone ever again call me Genevieve? I held her hand but she said no more. That was the last time Stella talked coherently to me, for the pain started to get bad and in the afternoon the doctor gave her morphine. Her voice altered, gravelly and thin, she said, relying on my understanding,

'He left her and came to me. My children don't know that.'

'I won't tell them,' I said.

'I wish I could have got over . . .' She tried again. 'I wish I could have—reconciled—yes, reconciled—myself . . .' There were tears on her eyelids or perhaps it was just her eyes watering.

Next morning there was no question of breakfast. Sharon felt she'd been very successful in getting her to have a sip of tea.

'She's starting to let go,' she said to me. 'It won't be long now.'

Richard was with the other doctor in the lounge. I felt what I'd never felt before, a kind of awe about Stella, that maybe I shouldn't just go in there the way I always had. Stupidly, I thought I ought to ask permission. The approach of death changes your attitude to all sorts of things. I listened outside the door, breathed in the silence, I knocked and getting no answer, not even a whisper, went in.

She was sitting up in bed, her eyes open, staring at the door. 'Marianne,' she said, 'is your father coming?'

That gave me a shock though it shouldn't have. I should have been used to wandering minds and mistaken identities at Middleton Hall, not to say faulty memories. But Stella was different. Stella had been so clear-headed and so precise in her speech.

Her skull showed under the parchment-like skin. I went up to the bed and kissed her. She said, 'Thank you, darling, that was nice,' and then, 'You're off tomorrow, aren't you? I hope you'll have a wonderful time.'

It's no use arguing with them when they're like that and it's no use being embarrassed. You have to play along. I said I was sure I'd have a wonderful time, and that at any rate was true. Every moment I've ever been with Ned has been bliss.

'Your father and I went to Iona on our honeymoon.'

She'd never said that when she told me about marrying Rex and maybe it wasn't true. The morphine discovers all kinds of dreams and false memories buried in the mind. I wondered what she'd call the real Marianne, the actress, the woman with the long reddish hair. The door opened and Richard came in. As soon as I saw him I thought, she'll take him for Alan, she'll think it's Alan come back. But if she did she gave no sign. She gave him her glorious smile, she was still capable of that. I got up to go and she said,

'You won't be able to move your car, Gilda. The garage will have to do that.'

Richard looked at me. 'That's all right,' I said. 'I won't try.'

I met Marianne in the passage. She clutched my arm, said, 'I'm not too late, am I?'

Mum has second sight, of course, she really can foretell the future, not to be wondered at when you remember she was my nan's seventh child and Nan was the seventh child too, or at least the seventh to grow up. People don't have seven children any more and maybe that's why Janis and I don't have Mum's gift, so it was strange how in that moment, when Marianne said that to me, I knew exactly when Stella would die.

'Friday,' I said. 'It won't be till Friday.'

'How do you *know*, Jenny?'

'I just know,' I said.

Marianne was wearing green, a dark green coat over her black pants and sweater. It made me shiver to see it. Of course I don't believe what they used to say, that it's because the fairies wear green that it's unlucky, that they don't like mere mortals to be seen in it. But I've known too many instances of ill-luck following the wearing of green to doubt. Whoever bought a green dress, my nan says, that didn't have to buy a black one afterwards? When Mum married Dennis she wouldn't even have green vegetables at the wedding reception, not a lettuce leaf on the table. If green is worn, love is down, they say.

Marianne made me go back with her. She put her arm

in mine. We stood there and watched Stella's hands plucking at the bedclothes. That was something I'd seen often enough before but no one has ever given me an explanation. Why do the hands of the dying hop and creep like crabs going sideways along the edge of a blanket and the hem of a sheet? Her eyes were shut but her hands worked, a pianist playing on a cloth piano. Marianne asked me why but I had to whisper back that I didn't know, only the dead know. She and Richard stayed all day with Stella and they were still there when I left for home.

The phone was ringing as I let myself into the house. I wonder if the time will ever come when the sound of Ned's voice doesn't send a thrill through me and raise the hairs on the back of my neck. I want that time to come, I want that to happen, an ordinariness, an acceptance, I want to take him for granted, because that will mean I've had a lifetime of getting used to him.

He said, 'Tomorrow evening, Jenny?'

'I've got something to tell you,' I said. 'We can talk about it tomorrow.'

'You've found somewhere warmer for us.'

'You could put it that way,' I said. 'We won't be going to Stella's after Thursday, that's for sure.'

'You're very mysterious.'

'No,' I said. 'No, I'm not. There's no mystery. It can all come out in the open now. Listen, Ned, I'm going to do what you asked me, I'm going to leave Mike and come to you and we can be together. I'm sorry I wouldn't do it before, it was stupid of me, I shouldn't have kept you waiting like that, you asked me so often. I've been such a fool.'

It was a lovely sound, his sigh of relief. 'Have you told him?'

'Not yet. I want to be with you first.'

He began saying something, his voice very tender and sweet, but the doorbell was ringing. I could see the shape of Janis through the frosted glass, her piled-up hair-do and her huge earrings.

'I love you,' I said, 'I have to go now. I'll see you tomorrow.'

Janis had run out of teabags, she was down to her last one, and the shop shuts at four-thirty. I gave her twenty out of my packet of PG Tips and she started telling me a long tale about how her friend Verna had been combing her hair by the open window, had twisted the combings round her finger and put them outside and a magpie had flown off with them in its beak.

'What, in December?' I said.

'That makes it worse,' she said. 'It's been so mild. I mean, you don't expect it. Not for them to be making nests. She got this really bad headache straightaway. What d'you reckon? Mum says she'll die within the year, but not to tell her, there's nothing she can do.'

She wanted to see the conservatory, so I took her into the dining room and showed her Mike's work.

'You are lucky,' she said. 'Steve can't open a tin without getting tetanus.'

I wandered round the house while I was waiting for the tile man, wondering what to take with me and what to leave behind. None of our wedding presents, I didn't want any of them, Mike could keep the lot. I'd take my books and my *Chambers Dictionary* but not the music centre or the CD player and the telly was too big to carry. Thirteen years. Mum would say it's *because* it's thirteen years, because we've just passed the unluckiest anniversary, the one she has a special name for. The first is your Cotton Wedding, the second your Paper Wedding, five years is a Wooden Wedding, twelve years Silk and Fine Linen, everyone knows twenty-five is a Silver and fifty a Gold— well, thirteen years is a Brimstone Wedding.

Maybe because it's explosive or because it's hard and dark like a burning stone, which is what brimstone means. I'd never asked Mum and I was thinking of ringing her up to find out when the man came with the tiles. And when he'd gone, though I'd only left there a bit more than an hour before, instead of ringing Mum it was Middleton Hall I phoned. Pauline answered. No, Stella was just the same, very feeble, weak as water, sleeping a good deal of the time, but that was from the doctor's morphine. Marianne had gone but Richard was still there. They were both staying at the hotel in Thelmarsh.

Mike phoned just as I'd put the receiver down. He wanted to know if the tiles had come. I was glad he didn't say what he would have done once, that he missed me and he'd be glad to be home again, because if he had I'd have felt guilty. I just thought of telling him on Friday evening and I did wonder a bit how he'd react. By asking me if that was the gratitude he got for building 'my' conservatory, I suppose. When he'd said goodbye and not even that he'd see me on Friday, I started speculating about various women in the village who'd be after him once I'd gone and wondering which one he'd take up with. It wouldn't be long, I was sure of that.

The first thing I heard when I got in on Thursday morning was that Lena had caught Stanley's flu bug.

She'd had the sense to go to bed and not spread her germs about. Stella was alone. As I kissed her I felt her cheek turn to me, but that was the only sign of consciousness she gave for a long while. For the first time of being with her in that room, perhaps because it was also the first time of silence and rest, I thought of the secrets locked up inside her head, moving in there, whispering unheard.

I'd been there half an hour and was thinking I couldn't stay much longer, I had Gracie and Arthur to see to, when she opened her eyes and said, 'Darling?'

'Yes, Stella?'

'What did you do to her?'

She said it, not strongly, not loudly, but so clearly it surprised me. Was it Alan Tyzark that she thought she was talking to? And did she need some sort of denial from him in order to rest?

'Nothing,' I said. 'I didn't do anything.'

She turned her face away. It wasn't exactly a snoring that she made, more a heavy strangled breathing. She had passed into a deep sleep. But there was a chance she would wake just as quickly. I sat there watching her, hoping she would wake but not daring to be cruel enough to will it, glad in a way I hadn't inherited Mum's powers to fetch the words out of her.

Richard arrived in the late morning, then, after about an hour, Marianne came with her children. The older one must be seventeen because when they'd been five minutes with their grandmother he drove the pair of them off in the Volvo. I went in once. Stella was conscious. At any rate, her tired eyes were open and there were traces of tears on her cheeks. Marianne wiped her face very gently with a tissue. I thought I'd never see Stella again, though

I was wrong there, and in saying goodbye to her, just the usual words I always spoke when I was leaving for home, I tried to speak in a more solemn and final tone.

'Goodbye, Stella.'

I kissed her and her cheek quivered. Marianne laid her hand briefly on my arm, the green sleeve on my blue. The room was darkening by then and before Richard got up to switch on the bedlamp I fancied I saw the figure of a woman standing silent and waiting between the window and the wall. My nan would have named her as Death, come to keep her appointment with Stella, but when the light came on I saw it was only the way the curtain had been carelessly pulled, catching at the corner of a picture frame.

Perhaps I shouldn't have gone. Someone I loved and had grown close to was about to leave this life, she was on her deathbed, and I was off to enjoy myself. Is that a strange way of putting it? Not really, not when you understand being with Ned was the greatest true enjoyment I've ever known.

I could say that Stella had her son and daughter with her, that she was slipping out of consciousness, anyway. Her room was no place for me while they were there. Yet I could have stayed in the building, sat in the lounge, waited in case I was needed. Come to that, I could have swapped with someone on the night shift. Once I would have, if it had all happened a year ago, before I met Ned, before I loved him.

For it's love that was responsible, love that overcomes your better nature and casts all those fine feelings of friendship and duty and the other kind of love, loving-kindness, to the winds. It's so urgent, it's so demanding, a force like a gale that blows you over or a wave of the sea that throws you on to the shingle, you can't resist and you don't want to. I wouldn't have resisted the pull of love for Stella's sake and I wondered if I would have for my own nan or even for my mother, or, if I'd had one, for my child.

That's not to say I wasn't guilty about leaving. I was ashamed of going and I fancied Lena looked at me strangely and Carolyn gave me a sidelong glance. But I left and closed the front door and went down the steps where the cold of night was closing in. Abandoning Stella bothered my conscience but to give up seeing Ned, that was unthinkable, there was no future on the other side of it.

Frost turned my windscreen into a bathroom window patterned all over with fern leaves. They made me think of the ferns in Ned's shoe that would draw him quickly to me. Our meeting would be another last time, the last time we would meet in a cold borrowed house and make love in someone else's bed.

Ned was due at seven. By that time I'd lit twenty candles and the two oil stoves and the house was full of that familiar but never exactly acceptable smell of wax and paraffin. Some people associate certain perfumes with their love affairs, or the scent of wood smoke or the bouquet of a wine. Perhaps it's because I'm not one of their sort, because I'm ordinary and working class, that my love will always be remembered when I smell burning oil, the poorest, cheapest fuel of all.

I wasn't thinking like that while I waited for Ned to come. I wasn't afraid of anything. They call it a low self-image, what I used to have and what in her different way

Stella had, but in my case he had done wonders for that. By loving me he had made me love myself. He had made me think something of myself, know that I look good and I have more brains than people give me credit for, that I'm as worthwhile a person as anyone else.

I waited for him, sitting close to one of the oil stoves, holding my hands spread over the grid on the top of it, only my hands and face warm, a chill seeping through the rest of me. But even that didn't matter much because it was the last time, because the coldness of this house and my struggles to warm it would soon be things for us to look back on and laugh about.

The curtains are never drawn till he gets there. When he comes I draw them to enclose us from the outside world. I'd wrapped myself up, blue jeans, thick blue sweater, blue shawl round me, all blue to counteract Marianne's green, I suppose, though what I was saving from harm I don't know. It was too late to save Stella. Protecting him, I reckon, from the hazards of the road, the ice and the freezing fog, twenty-ton trucks coming in the other direction. From his own mistakes, like whistling in the dark. As for me, for once I thought I needed no protection, I was safe, home at last.

I got up once or twice to look for him from the window. It was dark out there but the darkness was clear and glittering and when a car passed its lights showed the frost on the hedge and a line of it like white paint on tree branches. I suppose I watched ten cars pass. I know I did, for I counted. I watched for headlights to flare and swing blindingly towards me as he turned his car off the road and up the path to the house.

໑

It didn't happen. He didn't come. He'd been late before, he had much farther to come than I did, and it wasn't always easy for him to get away on time. I think the latest he'd ever been was twenty-five minutes. No, am I still deceiving myself that I didn't count? Twenty-seven minutes it was, not twenty-five. After twenty-eight minutes I started getting frightened.

Time passes so slowly when you're waiting. It goes so fast when you're with the man you love that it seems as if you're not talking about the same thing, as if there are two kinds of time, one for happiness and one for fear. The time passed more slowly than I'd ever known it while I waited at that window. Each second was like a single drop of water that you watch fall from a tap.

And outside there was nothing. There was no movement of any kind, only the empty road and the wide fields running away into darkness. In the stillness I seemed to see the frost itself descend on to the grass and the hedge, first a wetness, then a glitter. An owl called into the silence and at the sound shivers ran down my body, for its cry is an omen of the approach of some dire calamity. I could hear my nan saying those words as I waited there, just as she had spoken them to Janis and me as children when we heard the owl's shriek at night.

There were so many things that could have happened to him, there *are* so many, for I still don't know. A car crash, some accident at work, some action on Jane's part, something that she had done or said or he had that I don't know, that no one has told me. But my worst fear was for his safety, his life. You see, nothing would have stopped him coming to me, nothing ever did, and what but some terrible thing could have stopped him coming to me on this special evening when we had our future to talk about?

When you're in a situation like that you think of the awful things that have happened to other people you know or you've heard of. I thought of Charmian Fry saying goodbye to Rex Newland, then waiting and waiting for him to phone her. He never phoned and he never came to her again because he'd died in the train. Suppose Ned had died at the wheel of his car? I looked back over the day that was past and tried to think what I'd done that was changing fate. Gracie had spilt salt and I hadn't taken a pinch and thrown it over my left shoulder. I'd dropped a glove and picked it up myself.

I stayed there at Molucca till nine. It was ridiculous staying so long, for they were long those hours, they were the longest two hours of my life. I paced the house, I walked up and down the stairs more times than I know, I went out into the cold and walked to the road, looking this way and that in the blackness, as if I could bring him by my will and my peering into the dark. I wrung my hands, I'd never done that before or seen it done, but it's what you do when you're worried out of your mind, it's what you do in despair when you say, God, God, God help me!

When I'd blown out all the candles and turned out the wicks and the smell came stronger than ever the way it always does, I stood in the darkness with candle grease on my fingers. I wanted to howl aloud but I was ashamed to do that even though I was alone and the house stood there alone. The owl cried for me, screeching from a tree in the fen. When I opened the front door the cold air swept in and it was as if it mocked me. It made my eyes water or else I was crying. I stumbled out to the car.

It was crusted all over with frost and I scrubbed at the windscreen with newspaper till my hands were numb with cold. I shouldn't have been driving really, not in the state I was in. I just wanted to get somewhere, anywhere, as fast as possible. It was lucky for me—that's one way of putting it—that because it hadn't rained for so long there was no ice on the roads, only the thick white glitter of frost. As I put my key into the front-door lock the phone started ringing. It made my hand shake, it made me fumble with the key and I was terrified it would stop before I got there. I knew it was Ned.

It wasn't. The voice was Richard's.

'I'm so sorry, Genevieve, I know it's an imposition to phone you at this hour. But my mother has asked for you. She's talked to us a little; she's perfectly clear in her mind but she's very weak.' I remembered something I often forget, that he's a doctor. 'She may have to have more morphia quite soon. It's as if she summoned up all the strength she has left to ask for you.'

'I'll come now,' I said.

It was strange how that phone call brought me back to earth, to reality, and a realization that it's mad to pace a dark icy house at night, waiting for someone who obviously isn't coming because he can't come. It's crazy to work oneself up to howling point. I did what I should have done hours before, dialled his home number in Norwich. Phoning him at home is the last thing to worry me now. Isn't he already more mine than hers?

I got his voice on the answerphone. It's the first time I've ever heard his voice giving that message and I don't like it. I put the receiver back before the beep sounded, I got back in the car and drove to Middleton Hall.

The big heavy man who is Marianne's boyfriend was sitting in the lounge, smoking a cigar. Lena would have killed him if she'd known. I've read enough magazine psychology to wonder if Marianne picks the type her father belonged to.

Stella's room was insufferably hot, about as great a contrast as you could get to the temperature of the house where I'd been. It smelt as if someone had dropped and broken the flask of White Linen so that the perfume vaporized into the air. Richard and Marianne were sitting one on either side of the bed. Stella was unconscious. She was breathing harshly, her mouth open, she'd reached the stage when you begin to count breaths, for each one may be the last.

Marianne put out her hand, took mine and squeezed it. She got up and took me into the far corner of the room. 'Oh, darling, I don't think she'll speak again. She asked me to tell you this. I wrote it down, I don't know what it means.'

Nor do I. Marianne had written on a leaf torn from a block, *There is nothing in the house or the garden.*

'Did you try to get hold of me earlier?' I said.

'Richard tried at seven and again at eight. But, darling, you've a right to go out, you couldn't be expected to stay in for this. Don't, please, feel you have to . . .'

'No, I know.'

There is nothing in the house or the garden. Why tell me? Why not one of her children?

'I shouldn't stay,' I said. 'You'll want to be alone with her.'

The sweat was streaming off me. Marianne had got hold of my hand again. In spite of being halfway to a witch, my nan reads the Bible a lot. The days of our age are threescore years and ten, she says, and then adds a bit of her own, think yourself lucky if you get a bonus. The days of Stella's age were threescore years and eleven. It doesn't seem very old these days. I said that aloud but as I spoke a sound came from the bed that's unmistakable if you've ever been at a deathbed. The rattle that's the body expelling its last breath. It's awesome, that sound. No matter how many times you've heard it, it still sends a shiver through you. The last breath rattled out of Stella's poor, fallen, shrunken mouth and she was still.

Richard sighed. He looked at his mother, he nodded at me, and I nodded. Marianne put her head down on her arms and began weeping. I went up to Stella and touched her, felt the lifeless pulse, the waxen skin and under my breath I whispered goodbye. More than ever I wanted to kiss her then, but that was for the family to do first.

I went out of the room to fetch someone. Stanley was at the desk in the hall. I told him and walked away, ignoring his questions. My own terror had come back, filling my head with frightful images, turning me cold in that hot stuffy place. I met Pauline going off duty, told her Stella was dead, and then I went into Lena's office to try and phone Ned again.

Part Four

20

Being here is still strange, yet it's more like home than anywhere I've ever lived. Another thing is that I'm more alone than I've ever been. But that has to be, that is the only way I could bear what has happened and what it has done to me. It's only when you're alone that you can cry in the night without someone asking why.

The drive to Middleton Hall takes fifteen minutes instead of five and it's further to the shops. I wonder sometimes what I'd have done without this place, how I'd have coped. Rented a room, I suppose, got myself some-where in Diss, a bed-sit with breakfast and find your own evening meal. Because, after it was over and I knew there was no hope left, I couldn't have stayed with Mike. I couldn't have made the best of a bad job in that way. Philippa didn't see it like that.

'It's just as well you never said a word to Mike,' she said. 'You can go on now just as if nothing had happened.'

She meant well.

Even as she spoke I was thinking of how that would be, living with a man I'd no feeling left for and hiding from him all the feelings I had still for the man I'd loved. I went to Mum first of all. That's what you do, isn't it, when your marriage breaks up? You go home to mother. She didn't want me, she said as much, but she said something else too, that I had to come to her, she understood that, because a daughter's home is always her home even when she's nearly reached her third of a century.

I didn't know then where I'd go. I couldn't think of things, I couldn't make plans or do anything beyond going mechanically about my work. I'd been blasted, you see, shot to pieces. My young body felt old and broken and my mind floated free but full of him, nothing but him.

The day after Stella died was a Friday. So I was wrong about that too, with my clairvoyance and my wise-woman ways. Perhaps I made that forecast because it's well-known Fridays are unlucky, most accidents happen on Fridays, and it's not a day for starting any new enterprise. Old Mr Thorn that my late grandad worked for would never begin the harvest on Friday and the men went along with that. I used to feel that way myself though I've changed now, but that Friday when I woke up it was to an awful sense of dread and foreboding.

Before I left for work I phoned Ned's home and the answerphone was still on. I'd never phoned him at work and the thought of doing it frightened me. I suppose I'd read too many books and too many pieces in magazines about the unhappy consequences of phoning one's married lover at his work-place. Besides, the way those people talk unnerves me. But fears of this sort matter less and less after a time, everything like that is overcome by the terrible anxiety and the need to know. I think then, that

morning, I'd have forced my way into a private hospital
and past security guards and pushed his family aside to
get to his bedside. For that's what I thought it was by that
time. I thought he was lying injured somewhere in hospital.

I phoned the studios on Lena's office phone as soon as
I got in. It was too early and they had their answerphone
operating too. There was no point in leaving a message.
What could I say and who would bother to call me back?
As I passed across the hall on my way to the stairs the
undertakers came down the passage with fat Stanley trot-
ting after them. They had a body covered up in black on
a stretcher, Stella's body. I stood and watched them carry
her away. If she'd still been alive I thought I'd have asked
her what to do, I'd have asked her for help.

By the time I'd got Gracie up and taken Lois down to
the lounge in the wheelchair she's got now and read the
business part of the paper to Arthur, it was after ten. The
dogs were padding about but there was no sign of Lena.
Sharon was in the office. She went away quite meekly
when I said I wanted to make a private phone call. I'd lost
the number and I was looking it up in the directory when
I saw Richard go past the window on his way to his mother's room. I dialled the studios and asked for Ned.

They wanted to know who it was. I hadn't thought
they would or I'd have made up some important name.
'Charmian Fry,' I could have said, it would have been
appropriate, for I was in her shoes, not knowing and
afraid to know, but needing to know above all else.

It was ages I waited while music played, that
'Greensleeves' tune we'd sung at school. 'Alas, my love,
you do me wrong To cast me off discourteously, For I
have loved you, oh so long, Delighting in your company.'

Funny that I remembered the words after fifteen years. Another voice came on and said Ned Saraman wasn't in today. It was so cold and crisp, that female voice, that it paralysed me, it stopped me asserting myself. Could it take a message, it said, would I leave my name? I left my name but I didn't ask any more. I couldn't. At least I knew he wasn't lying injured somewhere—or did I know that?

I tried his home again and again got the answerphone. I told myself I had to be strong, however hard that was, I had to think of a way of finding where he was. You must keep calm, I kept telling myself, sit down and take deep breaths and *think*. Think it through. Find somewhere to sit quietly for five minutes. I went down the passage to Stella's room. Richard was in there. He was standing by the window holding up a copy of *The Times*. I apologized, I said I'd go away.

'No, don't. Please stay. I came to collect my mother's things.'

All bedding had been stripped from the bed. A big suitcase lay open on the mattress.

'Look, this is last Saturday's,' Richard said. 'She didn't finish the crossword.'

'That was a sign,' I said. 'She always finished it. Would you like me to pack her clothes?'

'That would be a great help.'

The blue dress with the coin spots, the flowered dress and jacket, the cream wool coat . . . I folded them the way my nan folds things, laid face down, the left side turned in, then the right, the sleeves parallel and flat. I took a deep breath. I said,

'May I ask you something?'

As soon as I'd said it I knew he thought I was going to ask for something of hers to wear. As if I would. The clothes of the dead don't wear well, they rot as their owner rots . . .

'Yes, of course. Anything. After all you did for my mother.'

'It's nothing like that. If you wanted to find out where someone was, I mean how to get hold of him . . .' I explained. I was discreet. I spoke, or I think I did, as if Ned was someone I slightly knew, someone who'd once rented a cottage in our village. It was important to speak to him. I made it sound as if for business reasons.

'I'll do it for you,' he said. He didn't ask if I'd like him to or if that would be all right. He just said he would, and he picked up the receiver on Stella's bedside phone.

I didn't want to be there. I wanted to hide myself so that I couldn't hear and then come back and find all was well, Ned was on the other end of the line, Ned wanted to talk to me. I couldn't hide myself, I had to be there. But I could touch wood. I stood there while he dialled, holding on with both hands to the edge of Stella's walnut desk, feeling the wholesome grain of wood, the healer.

Richard has a voice like Ned's. It's the kind that comes out of a public school and Oxbridge and say what you like it does impress people, it speaks to them of authority and know-how and control. Hearing him say Ned's name was the strangest thing, like being in a dream where people do things they'd never do in life and speak confidently to those they've never met.

He asked for Ned and I could hear the music playing, not 'Greensleeves' this time but 'The Lincolnshire Poacher'. They can't know much about music, the people who arrange these things, if they only put on tunes that I recognize. I started to hold my breath, waiting for Ned's voice to take over from the music. But I couldn't hear any more. I could only hear Richard.

'This is Richard Newland. Yes, Dr Newland.'

Silence. Murmurings.

'I'm not getting any response from his home.' Murmurings. 'Well, get me someone who does know, will you?'

It was strange how my mind went empty then. I seemed to be suspended in nothingness, hanging on to the wood of the desk as if it supported me in space. I could see nothing but the white walls, the open case, and Richard's back, thin like a boy's, the shoulder blades standing out under his jacket. In the suitcase the blue dress was on top and the coin spots began to dance, waving and jumping before my eyes.

Richard said, 'Yes,' and, 'I see,' and, 'When will he be back?'

The coin spots rushed and tumbled. I pulled away from the desk and leant on the bed, looking down into the red whorls on the pink mattress cover. The whorls shifted and twisted as if it was them doing the pounding in my head. Richard put the phone down and turned round. I made myself stand up.

'Are you all right?' he said.

'Yes, of course.'

'He's gone away on holiday,' he said. 'Skiing somewhere, they said. Innsbruck. No, Interlaken. Back on January the 3rd. Was it important to get hold of him?'

I couldn't speak. I couldn't even shake my head more than an inch each way. I made myself walk round the bed—I walked stiffly, like a robot—and took another dress off the hanger. My heart felt as if it wasn't beating at all, just as I wasn't breathing.

'Everything stops for Christmas for so long in this country,' Richard said. 'It's usually two weeks when in other places they have a couple of days. People here take it for granted the whole system shuts down for Christmas and no one's going to need them or try to contact them.'

'Thank you,' I said. 'Thank you for phoning.'

I wrapped Stella's shoes up in the pages of *The Times* and put them in on top. The jewel box I tucked into a corner.

Richard said, 'She wanted you to have the dressing-gown Marianne gave her for her birthday. Please take it.'

'She'd only worn it once,' I said.

He misunderstood me. 'It's as good as new.'

I must have had a wild look about me. Or my eyes were blazing. Anyway, he took a step back.

'Are you sure you're all right, Jenny?'

'I'm fine,' I said and I closed the lid of the suitcase.

He picked up the tape player and the half-dozen tapes in the little plastic box Stella kept them in and thrust them into my arms. 'She wanted you to have these. It was her wish. You mustn't say no. You did so much for her, you were much more than a carer, you were her friend. She loved you.'

'I know,' I said, and I went away, hugging the tape player and the patchwork dressing-gown because I couldn't talk any more.

Hearing it like that was a shock. It stunned me. But you're never in that state for long, you have to start thinking again, and very soon I was thinking of reasons. By the afternoon I'd come to see what must have happened. He'd told Jane what he intended, that he was leaving her for me, and Jane had made a terrific scene. She'd insisted he come away with her and Hannah, probably that holiday for her and her daughter had been arranged for months, and she'd made such terrible threats that he'd no choice. For instance, if he didn't come she'd see to it he never saw Hannah again.

There are a lot of holes in that theory but I didn't see them at the time. I didn't want to see them. I didn't want to ask myself how any of that could have stopped him phoning me. My theory depended on Jane being a monster, someone like Gilda Brent, though I'd no grounds for believing she was.

Mike came back in the evening and went straight to work on the conservatory. I phoned Ned's home number again but I'd have been surprised if I'd got anything but a recorded voice. I wasn't surprised. Drinking has never been the answer for me, or I thought it hadn't, but I've never been in a state like that before, as bad as that, so much in need of an answer. Once I'd have asked Mike to stop work and take me down the Legion but that was long ago, or seemed it. I went by myself.

It was bitterly cold and a little snow was falling. It must have been falling all day, for there were drifts of it underfoot, only I hadn't noticed. If the flakes are sharp and there's a wind blowing, the snow stings your skin like needles. The Legion always looks cheerful on a winter's night, the lights orange behind the diamond panes and a big lamp up on the wall shining on the swinging sign of the Roman soldier.

Mum was behind the bar and Janis with her, helping out. Mum was telling a man I'd never seen before how to get rid of mice. 'Have you got a bit of paper? OK, now write this: *I adjure all you mice to leave this place in a trice . . .*

He started writing on the inside of his cheque book.

'*Go hence over the river and betake yourselves to the mill and there eat your fill. Now begone and let my house alone.* Have you got that? You copy that out and pin it up on the wall and you'll never see another mouse.'

Rhyming mice away wasn't new to me. It was what Mum always advised and the same for rats. It doesn't work, I don't know why I hadn't seen that before. Well, I had but it hadn't registered. I think that was the beginning of giving up on charms and omens for me, that evening, an end to superstition. Perhaps that was the real beginning of the end, that I could call it superstition, which was the word other people used.

The man who wanted to be rid of mice seemed satisfied. He wandered off, presumably to spread the news of this amazing vermin repellent. I went up to the bar and asked Mum for a gin and tonic.

'What brings you here?' she said.

There are a lot of people's mothers you couldn't say this to but mine isn't one of them. I looked her straight in the eye.

'Despair,' I said.

'It's like that, is it? Where's your ever-loving husband?'

'Making that smashing extension to their house,' said Janis. 'I should be so lucky.'

Mum wouldn't say a word about Ned in front of her, but I could see she guessed. She 'twigged' is the way she'd put it. Len came in and she rounded on him. 'I told you not to put them red things on the bar—what d'you call them? Poinsettias—I told you not to put red flowers about. Just because it's Christmas, so what? Everybody on this earth but you knows red flowers are an evil omen.'

Maybe it was that which made me ask for only pink and white flowers when I phoned the florist in the morning. I was ordering a sheaf for Stella's funeral and I didn't know what to put on the card so in the end I settled for 'Love from Genevieve'. Mike was laying the floor tiles with Radio Norfolk full on playing Patsy Cline hits, 'I Fall to Pieces' and 'After Midnight', highly appropriate. I kept thinking, Ned will write to me, he'll write to me from this Interlaken, wherever it is, or he'll phone me when he can get to a phone alone. And then I thought, suppose he doesn't, suppose I have to wait till January the 3rd, I can't wait that long, I'll go mad.

By six I was back in the Legion. They'd put up the Christmas decorations a week in advance. Paper chains and the gilt chains I swear Mum wears for a necklace the rest of the year. No red flowers of course but a lot of holly, the thornless kind. It would be—if the holly that comes in at Christmas is smooth-leaved the woman of the house will be master for the year. Mum wasn't there, only Len. I asked him where she was and he said she'd be in later, which was a comfort as I'd decided to ask her advice. If I could get her alone I was going to ask her what to do.

I took my gin and tonic back to my table. Sooner or later someone was bound to come in that I knew. There were just four people in the bar besides Len and me. I didn't know whether I wanted to talk or not. What I wanted was for the drink to work and make me forget what I was going through. I wanted oblivion, then a stumbling home and a deep sleep.

It was then that she came in. The blonde woman whose car had twice passed along the Curton road when I'd been meeting Ned, who'd been in the Legion that evening when we'd all been there and Ned and Jane too. She came in alone, stopped for a moment and looked around her.

She's called Linda, but I didn't know that at first, Linda Owen. I still hadn't shed my superstitiousness, though I'd started calling it that, and I noted with a kind of dismay that under her fake-fur coat she was wearing a bright green trouser suit. A bright green and russet coloured scarf was round her head and the snowflakes glittered on it. The snow had started since I got there.

She looked at me and said, 'Hallo,' though we'd never really met. Len served her a glass of medium white wine and she took it to a table in the farthest corner from mine. For some reason I couldn't take my eyes off her, and with that urge to look at her came a feeling of the deepest foreboding. The green she was wearing seemed to be an act of malice against me, of course it couldn't be, it wasn't, but it felt that way. It was as bright as a traffic light or day-glo on a roadman's coat. Len turned on the telly behind the bar and I nearly cried out. The screen was filled by brightly coloured figures skiing, red and blue and orange against the white dazzling snow. Linda Owen picked her glass up off the table and walked over to me.

I watched her approach. Our eyes met. She'd taken off the scarf but hadn't combed her hair. It was untidy, a lock of it drooping over one eyebrow. She put her hand on the back of the chair opposite me and said, 'You don't know me though we've seen each other a few times.'

'Yes,' I said.

'My name's Linda Owen.'

'Jenny,' I said. 'Jenny Warner.'

'You may think I'm speaking out of turn but there's something I want to say to you. Can I sit down?'

I nodded.

'Are you still seeing Ned Saraman?'

A split second before she said that I expected her to say it. I don't know why unless it's Mum's gift coming out in me. A funny way to put it, isn't it? 'Seeing', seeing someone. Funnier than 'going out with' really. It means sleeping with, making love to, loving, being in love with, adoring, but it doesn't mean 'seeing' at all. That's the last thing it means, if 'seeing' is seeing into someone's heart and knowing his thoughts.

Another funny thing was that suddenly I didn't know the answer to that question. But I nodded and said yes and why did she ask. I wasn't angry with her, I wasn't offended, I didn't feel any of that.

'I saw you meet him,' she said. 'I saw you twice. And then I saw you in here with him. Look, you mustn't take this the wrong way, but I could see it in your face, how you felt about him. I should have said something to you then but I didn't have the nerve. I've only got the nerve now because—well, you're here on your own and I'm half an hour early for my date.'

'Said something about what?' I said. My lips were stiff.

'You know where you met him, at Thelmarsh Cross? That's where I used to meet him.'

'What do you mean?' I said.

'A woman called Rosie Ferrell was before me,' she said,

'and they couldn't meet in Thelmarsh because she lived up in Sheringham and the one before her, I don't know where she was or where they met.'

'It isn't true,' I said. He'd never been unfaithful to Jane before me, he'd told me that again and again. 'And if it is true—' oh, I was pathetic! '—if it is true, it's me now, it'll always be me. He loves me.'

It wasn't exactly pity in the look she gave me. Sympathy perhaps. At any rate, it was a kind look and it wasn't contemptuous. 'You'd better have another drink,' she said. 'Come on, I'll get us both another drink.'

Mum had just come in. She was got up in her fiercest gear, the way she is on a Saturday night, especially the Saturday before Christmas, a black miniskirt, tight as a bandage, a royal blue T-shirt, sleeveless, with The Thundering Legion printed on it in gold and under that a Gossard Wonderbra which is the last thing she needs. She gave me a look and put up her eyebrows. I don't know what was going on in her head but she served Linda and said,

'That's on the house, love.'

'Oh, really? Thanks a lot.'

'She's my mother,' I said. 'Look, you're wrong about Ned. I shouldn't talk about it, not yet, but we're going to move in together. He's leaving his wife. After they come back from wherever they've gone. It's private till then, but since you asked . . .'

'Jenny,' she said, 'he isn't going to leave Jane, he'll never leave her. He'll never leave his daughter. Oh, that asthma isn't as bad as he makes out but he won't leave her. He doesn't want to leave them. Jane suits him.'

I was tired of saying she was wrong. I said, 'I told you

it was private, I shouldn't talk about it.' I'd said that before too. I said something new. 'I know you mean to be kind.' She didn't say anything. 'Ned said he'd leave Jane for me any time I said the word. I couldn't imagine I'd ever repeat that to anyone but it's the truth. I wouldn't do it, not for a long time, I thought it was wrong, but in the end—well, I gave in.' A thought came to me that I liked—the first for quite a while. She was jealous. He'd left her for me. I couldn't quite say that. 'It may be a bit hard for you to take,' I said, 'but he really loves me. It's the real thing with me. It's different.'

She didn't laugh. I think that's to her eternal credit. She's a nice woman is Linda Owen. Believe it or not, we've got to be friends and we see quite a lot of each other. After all, we've a lot in common. She didn't laugh, rather the reverse, she looked miserable.

'Listen to me, Jenny. He does this all the time, it's his thing. She knows and she puts up with it because she knows he'll always stay with her. They take a cottage somewhere for a year, it's usually about a year. Two years ago they took one in Breckenhall. I'm in the Post Office there, that's what I do, the Post Office counter in the village shop. Before that was when they rented a place in Weybourne, up on the coast. I don't say she likes the way he goes on but at least she always has some idea where he is.'

'I don't see what this has to do with me,' I said.

'He asked me to go away with him, Jenny. He always asks the ones who won't. He knows they won't before he asks, they're the ones with a sense of duty, the ones who're set on not breaking up their marriages or upsetting their kids. I've got a daughter that my mum takes care of in the day. He knew I wouldn't uproot my daughter, take her away from Mum and her pre-school. He was safe with me till I changed my mind.'

'What do you mean,' I said, 'changed your mind?'

'My daughter got to be five. I said I'd be able to take her away now she was changing schools. I'd go with him. He'd said he'd get a flat in Dereham—mind you, he'd said that a good while before. Just as a matter of interest, when did he last ask you to go away with him?'

I couldn't remember. It was a long time and that was what made me suddenly turn cold. I drank some of my gin, but it tasted like disinfectant. When had Ned last asked me? Months ago, just about the time we first met in Stella's house. I hadn't noticed, I was so in love I hadn't noticed.

Instead of answering, 'He asked you that too?' I said.

'I'm sorry, Jenny. I'm over it now but it's going to take you a while, I can see that.'

There was a wildness starting up in me, in my head. It was like when you say you don't believe something you know you do believe. It was something that couldn't be happening, an outrage. Later, a lot later, I looked up 'outrage' in the dictionary and it said: 'a gross or violent injury; an act of wanton mischief'. It said a lot of other things too but those will do to be going on with. A gross and violent injury was inside my head, pushing to get out and scream aloud.

'But he *asked* me,' I said. I sounded like a child. 'He *asked* me. Suppose I'd said yes?'

'You did,' she said. 'You did in the end.'

And look what happened.

She didn't say that. I did, to myself, in my head, while

I was staring at her, trying to hate her but not able to. I thought then of something I hadn't faced at the time, that phone conversation last week when I told him I'd do as he asked, that we'd be together. He hadn't answered. Not really answered. He'd sighed and I'd taken it for a sigh of relief. I'd said meet and talk about it at Stella's house. And he hadn't come. He hadn't phoned, he hadn't come to Stella's house, he'd put his answerphone on and gone away skiing with his wife and child. Because that was what he always did, or something like it, when 'they' agreed to leave and be with him.

She spoke gently. 'To do him justice, if that's the word, he's like some women who can only do it if they think they're loved. And if they think they're *in* love. He can't get it up unless he's saying, I love you, I love you. It's sick. *He's* sick, poor thing. He's a pervert with a fetish and his fetish is love. But that doesn't make you care any the less, does it?

'He picks the sort he thinks won't make scenes. And if they do, Jane can handle it. She's had plenty of practice. I went to Norwich and told her about him and me and much good that did me. She knew already. If you come to think of it, a man's got a big advantage if his wife knows and loves him enough to put up with it. What can he lose?'

I jumped up then.

'I don't believe it,' I said. 'It's not true.'

'It's true.'

It still wasn't credible. Not a real thing like the conservatory was or Stella dying or Richard giving me that tape player. It was the dream of the kind you don't know is a dream and when you wake up it takes a while to realize it didn't happen.

Saying 'He *loved* me' was stupid and humiliating. I still said it, over and over. Pride's the last thing to go but it goes. 'He kept asking me to say I loved him,' I said, and I knew I was describing the kind of man she'd described.

'Did he find a place for you to meet?' she said. 'I mean, a hotel or anything? Or was it all done under a hedge? I'm sorry, but it was the same for me.'

'I borrowed someone's house,' I said.

'*You* did, yes. Sure. It has a familiar ring. Did he ever take you out for a meal? Did he ever buy you a present? I bet he offered to take you abroad with him, that's easy, all done on expenses, and he'd have a double room anyway. But did he bring you any duty-frees?'

I stood up. I wanted to overturn the table the way they do in films. Mum was reading my mind. She lifted up the flap at the end of the bar counter and took a step through. I felt my head drop forward and a gagging in my throat.

'I'll get you a drink,' Linda said. 'I didn't really get the last one.'

'No,' I said. 'It doesn't help.'

'Oh, yes, it does.'

My knees felt weak and I sat down again. 'I don't want a drink.'

'I didn't think you'd take it so hard,' she said.

She turned round and waved to the man who'd just come in. He was just a man, youngish, fair and heavy-set, her date, the kind who goes straight up to the bar wherever he is.

'I don't want to leave you,' she said. 'Will you be all right? I can tell him it's off for this evening. I'm not that

326 ⌒   *Barbara Vine*

keen on him. I could take you home.'

'It's all right,' I said. 'I'd quite like to be alone. I have to be alone to take it all in.'

'I'm sorry, Jenny,' she said. 'I'm very sorry.'

21

If I'd cast myself in roles like Gilda did I'd have been the village maiden betrayed by a seducer. But roles take no account of true misery, of living humanity. I was dazed and numb. I was silent. Pain made me clumsy, I dropped a cup and broke it, I tripped over a rug. When I picked myself up a grazed shin made me start crying and break the silence.

Mike didn't notice. He was still doing the tiles. I cooked the lunch because I've always made a roast on Sundays and we ate it, facing each other across the table. Or he ate it. I picked at the food and pushed it about but he didn't notice. He wasn't even reading the paper or reading the instructions on the tile pack, he was silent and preoccupied with his conservatory, his head full of it. To him it was a thing of dreams, a crystal palace, and if he'd been able to talk to me about it in those terms, as of a vision and a creation, perhaps it wouldn't even then have been too late.

Before he went back there he did speak. My face was wet with tears and he asked me if I'd got a cold. When it got to three-thirty I went round to Philippa's.

People talk about the country as if it's always beautiful.

The ones who don't live in it, that is. There's something awful about an East Anglian village on a Sunday afternoon in winter, something grim. The surrounding land is grey and shrouded in mist. The village street is long and straight, the houses are low and the trees are low while the sky is a huge lid, dull and dimpled like pewter. At four-ish the lights will come on but that's not for half an hour and meanwhile the low houses are dark and all sealed up, the windows dull and blind except for the eye of a TV screen glowing behind them in a corner. There's never anyone about but all the cars are there. They line both sides of the street nose-to-tail, some shiny and new but most the other kind. You can't live in Tharby without a car but that's not to say you can afford anything better than an old beat-up banger.

When a person speaks of car world you think of somewhere like Los Angeles, of tangled freeways and spaghetti junctions and gleaming limos slipping over suspension bridges. But this is the real car world, the English countryside, where you can't move without a car, where the bus runs once a week and the trains have disappeared. My dad knew what he was doing when he collected cars and lost his soul to the internal-combustion engine. Not long ago I read a letter to a newspaper from someone who said we all ought to give up cars. To save the world, the environment, the ozone layer. But he lived in the middle of a city and could walk to work or take a bus, it was easy for him to talk. In Tharby you're a prisoner without a car, it's the first thing you think of when you're seventeen, learning to drive and somehow acquiring a car.

There was a Christmas tree in Philippa's front window but its lights weren't on. She came to the window when I rang the bell and I think one look at my face told her. The telly had been on, she'd been watching a video of *It Happened One Night*, but she turned it off without asking. We never kiss and we didn't then but she put out her arms and I went into them and we held each other. We hugged each other for a long time, just quite still and close, and she didn't pat my back like people mostly do when they hug someone.

Katie and Nicola came in and stared at me. I told Philippa all about Ned and how I loved him and what he'd done, though I could still only half believe it. Or I couldn't face it. Confronting it hurt so much I couldn't attempt it without crying aloud. But I told her the best I could bear to. Seeing my tears, Nicola started to cry, and for some reason that made me think of Janis and me when we were small.

Philippa put an arm round her and an arm round me. It was then that she said that about it being just as well I'd never said anything to Mike because now I could go on as if nothing had happened. She didn't understand. How could she? You mustn't expect people to understand, I know that now. If they listen and they're kind that's the best you'll get and that's a lot.

'I'm going back now to tell him,' I said.

'But where will you go?' she said. 'Why do it now?'

'Because I want to be free to cry in the night,' I said, 'and I can't do that with him beside me.'

As soon as I'd said it I thought it was funny and I started to laugh. Philippa looked shattered. She didn't know what to make of me and who can blame her? I didn't know what to make of myself. By this time it was pitch dark outside and lights were on. The Legion was a fine sight, the old fir tree outside hung with fairy lights and a big holly wreath on the front door. Luckily Mum's red phobia doesn't extend to lights and she had 'A Merry Christmas to All Our Patrons' up in scarlet neon on the half-timbering.

I walked home and told Mike I was leaving him.

He wouldn't take it in. For one thing he wouldn't stop working. I tried to get him to stop by saying I wanted to talk to him, I had something very important to say. It was no use. He said he'd made up his mind to get the conservatory done by Christmas and this was his last chance till Friday.

He went on trowelling on the mortar between those tiles and while he did it he kept saying there must be something wrong with me, always trying to get him to talk, to stop working, to do something else, anything else but what he was set on doing. Why had I said I wanted a conservatory if I wasn't willing to let him get on with it?

I'd had enough. I said I'd never asked him, it was all in his head. He didn't answer. He said marriage was give and take, had I forgotten that? And was it something called PMT I'd got? The fellows on the site said their girlfriends got it and a real pain in the tit it was. Of course that made me laugh too. No wonder he thought I was going mad.

I didn't think I could just walk out without explanation, so I went upstairs and packed all my clothes, everything I had, into three suitcases. I brought them downstairs and put them in the car. He was still working, whistling happily. I said,

'I'm leaving you, Mike. I'm going now. I've tried to tell you but you won't listen.'

'Don't be silly,' he said.

'I'm going to the Legion,' I said. 'For the present. I don't want anything from you. You can keep the house. I don't want any money.'

He thought I was joking, though I must have sounded grim.

'Take the washing machine,' he said, 'but leave me the car.'

'It's my car,' I said.

It was. And in car world I needed it almost more than a house. Mum was about to open, putting out nuts on the bar top and mince pies because it was nearly Christmas. She wasn't pleased to see me, she didn't exactly make me welcome but there wasn't any question of her saying no. I'd never lived there, I was married before she took the Legion on, so I put my cases in one of the spare bedrooms, the one at the back with its windows looking across the fields. Sitting on the bed I thought, what a lot I'll have to tell Stella. I could tell Stella about Ned and somehow I knew she'd understand where Philippa hadn't understood. And then I remembered Stella was dead. I started to cry and I couldn't stop, though I wasn't crying for me but for Stella that I was never going to see again and never talk to.

Her funeral was on the Wednesday. We all went, Lena and Stanley, Sharon and Pauline and me. The florist had got my order wrong on two counts. She'd made the wreath with red and pink flowers and put 'In loving memory' on the card. I minded about the words being changed but red carnations among the pink chrysanths didn't worry me. What could happen to me worse than had already happened?

It was the first burial I'd ever been to. People nearly

always choose to be cremated, don't they? Stella had specially asked to be buried, and her children, unlike so
many, respected their mother's wishes. We sang 'When
the day of toil is done, When the race of life is run', and
trooped out through the rain to the graveyard. Marianne
broke away from the boyfriend, came up to me and took
my arm, which pleased me, I don't know why, because I
could sense she did it more for her own support than
mine.

The grave was a deep pit lined with synthetic green
stuff on to which the rain pattered. In the distance I
could hear winter thunder rumbling. The vicar said all
those things about ashes to ashes and dust to dust and a
woman that I think was Priscilla Newland threw a hand-
ful of earth on to the coffin. Marianne didn't throw earth
and nor did Richard. They asked us back to the hotel for
a glass of sherry but Lena said with a bright smile, No,
thank you very much, duty calls, and that went for all of
us.

Carolyn had been holding the fort, as Lena put it,
back at Middleton Hall and she'd received our new resident. That was worse than the funeral, nearly as bad as
seeing Stella die, finding a newcomer in her room. It was
a man, which no doubt pleased Sharon. He's eighty-one,
an ex-Brigadier, former Master of Foxhounds and reader
of books on World War II. I think he's brought his whole
library with him. What kind of a family must he come
from that he's moved into a residential home just before
Christmas? One thing I could be sure of, he doesn't care
for Lena calling him Tommy.

I was late leaving and didn't get back to the Legion till
six. Mike was in the bar with an Abbot in front of him.

As soon as he saw me he began haranguing me. When was I coming back? OK, I'd made my point but the joke was over now and it was time I came home. He'd meant to finish the conservatory by Christmas but how could he when I had him down at the Legion arguing every night?

If I'd ever thought in the past how it would be if I left my husband, the last thing to come to mind would have been that he'd fail to take my departure seriously. To this minute I don't know if it was cunning on his part that made him adopt that line, or if he just didn't understand; if he couldn't take it in because the idea that I could actually contemplate leaving him was incredible.

It's difficult to handle, that attitude. I didn't know what to do. I went upstairs to my room, but he came after me and stood outside banging on the door and telling me to stop my nonsense, to put my coat on and give him the car keys and he'd drive me home. It had been the same the night before and the night before that, only he'd varied it on the Monday by saying he was sick of waiting to get his tea cooked and on the Tuesday by asking me if I didn't want to see what the floor looked like now he'd got the tiles down.

There's nowhere to hide in a pub. I'd tried going round to Janis the evening before but he'd followed me and banged on *her* door. So I went out in the car. It was the only thing I could do and not be followed. I drove around for half an hour, not knowing where to go, sitting in a lay-by for a while until a man passing me in a van hooted and flashed up his lights. You can drive forty miles in this countryside and use up a lot of petrol and still only waste an hour. There was only one place to go and I went there. I drove up the wet and muddy track, parked the car and sat there in the dark for ten minutes before I went in.

Stella was dead and I had no business to be at her house
any more. Once I was inside I realized that what I was
feeling was surprise—surprise that the lights weren't blazing and Richard and Marianne in here discovering the
place for the first time, marvelling, wondering why their
mother kept her secret for so long. But not on the day of
her funeral. No, I could understand that. They would
come tomorrow.

I lit the candles and took one upstairs with me to light
my way while I fetched the oil stove. This would be my
last visit to Molucca. Down in the living room I had no
sense of waiting for Ned to come. I had only once waited here for him, I had always been up in the bedroom,
watching from the window, and we'd seldom if ever set
foot in this room together. The cold was just the same,
though, the cold that had been the most memorable
thing about those last days of my love affair and could
serve as its symbol. I sat on the floor up against the
heater, holding my hands half an inch from its black-
painted cylinder. Why can't I be angry with him, I
thought, why can't I hate him? Why is it I can only ask
over and over, why, why, why?

The house began to fill with the smell of oil. Pink
paraffin isn't supposed to smell but the truth is it smells
just a bit less than the blue kind. Another thing to remind
me of my love. One day, I thought, when I have a house
of my own, I'll have any kind of heating but oil, I won't
even have an oil tank in my garden.

'There's nothing in the house or the garden,' Stella had
said, she'd made them write it down for me. Sitting on

the floor, warming my hands, I tried to think what it meant, but I got nowhere. The truth was I could think of nothing and no one but Ned, though imagining him in that holiday place skiing, laughing with Jane and Hannah, the sharp snowflakes glittering on his hair, was the bitterest pain. I thought of him unwillingly, because I couldn't help it.

When it was nearly ten I wound down the heater wick and blew out the candles. I had to drive back the way I'd always driven when I was happy, when we'd made love and my mouth felt soft from Ned's kisses and my skin warm. I drove past the house he'd rented, its windows deeply dark. Inside the Legion it was very noisy and the air unbreathable with smoke. Mum said Mike had given up on me at nine-fifteen and taken himself back to Chandler Gardens.

'Dennis was the same,' she said, speaking of her second husband. 'Round here night after night, couldn't let things be, I'd find him in the bar regular as clockwork and I was married to Ron before it stopped.'

'That wasn't you, Diane,' said Len, 'that was the beer he come for.'

But, as it happened, I didn't see Mike again till Christmas Eve. He walked in the minute Mum opened at ten-thirty, said he was going to his parents for Christmas unless I'd changed my mind and was seeing sense at last, and this letter had come for me. He held it out at arm's length as if it smelt.

You won't believe anyone can be such a fool but I thought it was from Ned. I don't get many letters. Who is there to write to me? All my friends and relations live round here. Junk mail comes and bills come, but not letters and hardly any postcards. So I thought it must be from Ned. The blood went into my face and my heart jumped and I thought, he wouldn't do to me what he did to Linda Owen, he loves me, how could I doubt him, he can explain it all, oh, forgive me, Ned . . .

How can you think all those things in the instant it takes to receive an envelope into your hand from another hand? You can. You can dream too of everything being made well again, of love strengthened, mistakes set right, misunderstandings explained, all in a tiny flashing moment.

The postmark was Diss. The address was typed and so was the name, Mrs G. Warner. I felt the sun go in. That was just what it was like, the light put out and the dull grey weather coming back.

'Have a good Christmas,' I said to Mike. 'Tell your parents we've split up.'

'Tell them I'm getting a psychiatrist to see to you,' he said.

I went upstairs. I took the letter over to the window to open it and catch some of the gloomy light. It was from a firm of solicitors in Diss and started 'Dear Mrs Warner.' I couldn't take it in at first, it didn't seem to make sense. What was that sentence doing in there, those old-fashioned words I'd first read aloud to Stella back in August? 'The freehold property known as Molucca and situate in Thelmarsh in the County of Norfolk.' I'd repeated that line as we stood upstairs at Middleton Hall, looking across the fields, corn-green and goose-white and blonde like cropped hair. I read it again and at once all was clear.

Stella had left me her house.

22

Marianne and Richard might have been expected to mind but it was Lena who minded. How she found out I don't know. I didn't tell her. I was going to say that you can't keep secrets in a place like this and then I remember how successfully Stella had kept hers.

It was on the 2nd of January, a Monday, the day everyone has off but not carers in residential homes. The minute I got in Lena sent Carolyn to fetch me to the office.

She was wearing a new track suit, a Christmas present from Stanley I guessed, purple velour with a yellow cardigan over it. There was a dog sitting on either side of her, each of them brainwashed to be as fierce as a labrador can. Dobermanns or Rottweilers would have been more her kind of dog. Unfortunately for Lena the one called Ben started thumping his tail the moment I came in.

'Congratulations,' she said. 'Not that it took much effort, did it? Like taking a Yorkie bar from a retard, that must have been. A little kiss here, a little bit of hand-holding there, and lo and behold you're a woman of property.'

I didn't say anything. I didn't mention Edith and Maud, the latter-day saint and the Bible readings. Jobs are hard to come by and I need mine.

'It's the son and daughter I pity,' said Lena. 'Their nest egg they must have been counting on snatched away by a . . . by a . . .'

Cuckoo, I wanted to say but didn't.

'A predator,' said Lena. I don't think she knows what it means. 'That charming Dr Newland. I expect he and his sister will bring a lawsuit to upset the will.' She gets these expressions from American cop shows. 'It's only what anyone would do in their place. I shall be happy to testify old lady Newland went wobbly months ago.'

'You must do as you think best,' I said.

One of the first things I'd done after I'd got that letter was contact Richard and tell him I couldn't take the house. I phoned Marianne and told her I couldn't take it. They both insisted. They said no one would live in it if I wouldn't. They didn't want it. What could it mean to them when they hadn't even known their mother owned it?

'I don't suppose I'll ever see the place,' Richard said, 'unless you invite me round for a cup of tea.'

It was to the solicitors he and Stella had been that day when she dressed up and forced herself to go in his car. She'd told him she wanted to make provision for me in her will but not what she'd be leaving me. They were surprised about the house, he and Marianne, probably a lot more surprised than they let me see. Innocent people who have led blameless lives don't own secret houses. They must have wondered, they must have been afraid to find out.

I stood in front of Lena, waiting for her to sack me. One of the dogs got up, came over and started licking my hand.

'Sam,' she said, 'stop that!' Her eyes lighted on me and then were cast up to the ceiling. 'Well, don't stand there,' she said. 'Tommy's waiting for his breakfast. Call him sir, why don't you, and maybe he'll put you down in his will for all his war memoirs.'

That was that. Not another word. It was my day off on Wednesday and I moved in. Marianne and Richard knew I'd nowhere to go, you see, and if the family approved the solicitors had no objection. Mum promised not to tell Mike where I was. Of course there isn't a chance of keeping my new address dark for long, not with Len knowing it and Janis knowing it, neither of them being much renowned for discretion. Philippa would let herself be tortured, like Dustin Hoffman in *Marathon Man* she said, before she'd say a word.

The strangest thing was having the electricity turned on. I lit the boiler and real hot water came out of the taps. I ordered coal and lit fires in the fireplaces. But I couldn't sleep in that bedroom, though I did try. The dream I had was of Ned lying beside me and holding me in his arms, saying it was warm at last, why was it warm? I woke up to the empty bed and in the morning I dragged it and the rest of the furniture into one of the back bedrooms.

That magic day, the 3rd of January, when he'd be back from Interlaken, was past and gone. I didn't fool myself he'd tried to phone me at home and given up because I wasn't there. If you want someone you find her. You phone her at work, you go to the house where you used to meet, you inquire at the pub her mother keeps. You don't just give up. You aren't indifferent. Unless that's what you want, to get rid of her, as easily and as straightforwardly as he'd got rid of me.

Under Stella's will I'd inherited not just the house but all
its contents. Everything in it became mine. Did that
include the red Ford Anglia in the garage? The idea of
consulting solicitors unnerved me, I'd heard their charges
could be astronomical, but Richard's advice was free. I
told him that according to his mother the car had once
belonged to Gilda Brent. He traced it through the car tax
office and found the owner—or 'keeper' I believe they
call it—registered as Mrs Gwendoline Tyzark.

'I can just remember her,' he said. 'Marianne liked her
but I didn't. She frightened me. For some reason I confused her with Cruella de Ville in *A Hundred and One
Dalmatians*. I even thought she'd want to make me into a
fur coat.'

'So whose car is it now?' I said.

'Hers, I suppose.'

'Your mother said she was dead. Perhaps the car had
better just stay there for the time being.'

He suggested I advertise for her in the papers and I did
phone one of them to ask what it would cost. Forty or
fifty pounds, they said. I didn't have that kind of money,
money was very tight for me, and the chances are no one
would answer the advertisement anyway. But I thought
about Gilda a lot. It was a kind of game for me too, not
a Killing Gilda but a Keeping Gilda Alive, the purpose
being to distract my mind.

That of course wasn't really possible. When you've
loved someone and lost him the way I'd loved and lost
Ned it's not just love and sorrow that fill your mind but
a terrible bitterness and resentment. A sort of

indignation, maybe outrage is the better word, that anyone could deceive you so and delude you so, tell you such
lies, debase you so. For if I once said that Ned made me a
good self-image with his love, what did that do to me
when I knew he'd never loved me? He'd just used me to
feed a sort of sickness he has that makes him want women
to love him, any women, so long as they're nice to look at
and young, so long as they'll keep telling him they love
him and listen when he says the same to them. All the
things Mum said and Philippa implied about him wanting me for my looks and my body were true. And if they
hadn't said anything about him being a love fetishist that
was because they didn't know someone could be.

So if I wasn't to go mad or have a breakdown I had to
have something else to turn my mind to. It was as if I had
developed a switch in my brain that I pushed down when
my thoughts went to Ned. It switched off Ned and
switched on Gilda. Or that was the idea. It didn't always
work, it often didn't work, or it worked for a while and
then Ned and what he'd done by-passed the switch, came
back and drove everything else away.

But when I was in Gilda mode, as people who know
about technology might say, I thought about her leaving
Alan for another man, which is what some people said
she'd done, and the more I thought of it the more pecu-
liar it seemed. For Stella had never mentioned any other
man in Gilda's life apart from general admirers. Had some
man suddenly come along and swept her away? Stranger
things have happened but I found it hard to believe. And
if she had gone away with a lover to France, surely that
would have been just what Stella and Alan had wished for.
In that case there would have been no problem about

divorce and no threat from Gilda if they lived together. They would have married eventually.

Not only had that not happened, but Stella and Alan had stopped seeing each other. Marianne said her mother's depression, her reluctance to drive a car, her handing over of everything in the household to Aagot, had already been going on for some time by the autumn of 1970. That sounded as if she'd broken things off with Alan in the summer, even in the August which was the date she'd originally told me Gilda had died. It was obvious to me that her unhappiness dated not from anything to do with Rex but from her break with Alan.

But where was Gilda? Dead, Stella said. There was no record of her death. Can anyone die and there exist no record of her death? I could think of one way that could happen. It came to me in the night. I was in bed in the bigger of the back bedrooms at Molucca, asleep but suddenly awake for no apparent reason, my first conscious thought for Ned, as it always is, though I pray it won't always be. I operated my switch into Gilda mode and immediately those last words of Stella's came into my head: *There is nothing in the house or the garden.* They had been meaningless, those words, but they weren't now. Their significance leapt at me, crystal-clear.

It was spring by then and getting light early. I got up and looked out of the window across the fen. The trees and the underbrush weren't yet green but golden-brown with new buds, the dogwood stems crimson, the willows pale yellow. An unearthly pre-sunrise light lay on the fen, the blue pearl light of dawn. The first birds had started, the sounds they make more like a conversation than a song. I drew my gaze back and back until I was looking down into the garden, for garden it was by then, no longer a wilderness indistinguishable from the fen which over the years had crept in and embraced it. From the first weekend of living there I'd worked in the garden, clearing, digging, planting. That too had been a way of taking my mind from Ned.

By March it was a garden again, with a proper lawn and flower beds and a path. I understood what Stella's words meant: that Gilda was dead but her body was not buried in the garden here nor concealed somewhere in the house, under a floor, in the back of a cupboard. If that is what the message meant, it could only have meant one thing. Why had Stella thought I'd anticipate anything so monstrous? Because of the Killing Gilda Tease I might have thought it more than just a game? Dying, she recalled of course that she had left Molucca to me, and her first need was to reassure me that I could live there without fear. And it was possible I'd have come to think that way if not told otherwise, would have fancied bones beneath the soil that I worked on with my hands or some charnel thing packaged and bundled, poked into a cellar hole.

Knowing me then, Stella would have expected an even more horrid effect on me, that I'd see her house as haunted and sense Gilda's ghostly presence. She was not to foretell the future and understand how my superstitions were to desert me and along with them all those old beliefs in the supernatural that I'd grown up with, ghosts and spells, omens and magic. For they've gone, or I've lost them just as some churchgoers lose their faith. Instead of protecting me as they promised they'd let me down and I lacked the Christian's consolation of saying my god knew best, he moved in a mysterious way, for my god was no more than blue clothes and ladybirds and four-leaved clovers.

But later that day, or maybe that week, I did go all over Molucca inside and out, searching for signs and clues, for evidence of Gilda's fate. Some clothes still remained in the wardrobe. That was the single piece of furniture not removed from the bedroom Ned and I had used. For one thing it was too heavy and for another I didn't know what to do with Stella's clothes, the two dressing-gowns, the summer dresses, the beautiful bridal dress with the smut marks and the stains and the burnt hem, that silvery-blue over-feminine raincoat. I tried the pockets but Stella wasn't a woman to put things in pockets. She was not a woman to write things down either. If they exchanged love letters, those two, they burned them once read.

I looked through all the books but found only one piece of paper inserted among pages. Tucked between the flyleaf and the cover of *Figaro's Great Adventure* was a shopping list and the writing might have been Stella's or it might have been Alan's. I had no way of knowing. *Envelopes, matches, gin*, one of them had written, *tomatoes, lettuce, lamb chops, Weetabix*. That didn't interest me but the children's book did. I'd forgotten how lovely Alan Tyzark's drawings were. I know nothing about art and I can't describe anything from a technical point of view, but they looked to me like the nicest photographs you could imagine yet with that small something more, a grace or spirit that the camera can't give, a colour and a texture prettier than life. And I thought to myself that the man who could make those drawings, so tender and so delightful, and my Stella who was gentleness itself, could never have done the terrible thing I sometimes suspected, were incapable of any terrible thing at all.

I began to think I was keeping Gilda's memory alive solely for my own distraction and the time had come to bury her as perhaps she had never actually been buried. Then, some time after my thirty-third birthday in April, and Richard's thirty-third birthday ten days earlier—he took me out to dinner to celebrate both—I was looking through the TV listings in the paper and saw Ned's name and Gilda's side by side.

It frightened me, that conjunction. There seemed to me, for all my renouncing of occult things, something almost devilish in it. And I couldn't make out what it could be, this programme advertised as an exploration of a film star's vanishing into thin air. How could he know? If, as it seemed to be, this was Ned's own brainchild, where had the idea come from and what had attracted him to it? Then I remembered. *I* had. It had come from me. Once, in this house, on a shivery evening of love and icy hands and gooseflesh, he had told me of the research he had done for me and used the phrase which is the name of a film and perhaps a book too for all I know, the phrase that had become the title of his production, *The Lady Vanishes*.

I watched it. As I've said, I'd left our TV to Mike. When I wanted to watch something I went to Philippa or Janis. That evening I saw not having a TV as my excuse for not watching Ned's programme but I couldn't hold out, I couldn't think of anything else all day, all the time I was giving Arthur his bath and cutting Tommy's nails and reading to Gracie I was thinking of that programme. Not because of Gilda, or only a little because of her. The reason for my preoccupation was pretty pathetic. I thought there was a chance of seeing Ned. I thought he might have done one of the interviews himself or be there to introduce it or speak the commentary. Even Ned doing a voice-over would be something, just to hear his voice again.

Stupid, wasn't it? Stupid and pathetic to want to see him and hear him after what he'd done to me. I kept telling myself that and I held out all day, I wouldn't watch it, I'd banish it from my mind, I'd press the Gilda switch. The trouble was, when I did that, it brought me back to the programme because it was as much hers as his. So in the end I gave in, phoned Philippa and said could I come round and watch it with her. I picked her rather than Janis not only because she's my friend but because if I'd gone to Janis's it might have got back to Mum, which I didn't want. Mum's been frightening in her anger against Ned, like a lioness whose cub's been hurt wantonly, and she's been tough with me too, tearing me apart for being such a fool when she'd warned me over and over. She wanted to put a spell on him and his family, something done with a five-pointed star drawn inside a chalk circle. It wasn't my anger but my laughter that stopped her, my laughter that turned suddenly to a storm of tears.

I'd rather have watched the programme alone than in Philippa's company, than in anyone's company, but you can't ask someone whose house you're in if they'd mind leaving you on your own. And in the event Ned didn't appear, he was only there in the credit titles, just a name that used to make magic and now made misery and a kind of painful embarrassment. But at the start I didn't know whether he'd appear or not and I suffered, fidgeting and nervous, wondering what Philippa must think of me, hoping I'd be able to stop myself gasping or crying out if his face were suddenly to fill the screen.

It was only later, long after it was all over and I was back at Molucca, that I was able to think about what I'd seen and assess it. Ned, or Ned's team, had started from the standpoint that film stars who were icons, I think that's what he called them, icons, could fade from the public consciousness more easily than other famous people. Unless a star was a Garbo or a Hepburn, or unless her films had become cult movies, she could disappear without trace. That was what had happened to Gilda Brent, born Gwendoline Brant.

The name Brant sounded foreign, maybe German, which wouldn't have been a good idea in those days, so Brent she became. She had called herself Gilda not after the Rita Hayworth film as many thought—that wasn't made till 1946—but after a character in an opera.

I knew some of that. The first surprise was when the commentator said that Gilda's husband Alan Tyzark was dead. He had died two summers before at his home in Tivetshall St Michael, Norfolk. It made me shiver to think he'd still been living there after all those years, yet he and Stella had never met. Had she known he was dead? I asked myself if she'd begun to tell me her story *because* she knew he was dead, someone had told her or she'd read a death announcement. Another discovery, another surprise if you like, was that St Michael's Farm stood empty, couldn't pass to anyone else, even supposing there was anyone, couldn't be sold or even let, for Gilda Brent appeared to be still alive. At any rate no record of her death existed in this country or in France, where rumour said she'd gone.

Her agent had tried in vain to get in touch with her in 1972 and again in 1976. A cousin in India and the friend in France had written to her over the years but received no replies to their letters. St Michael's Farm was an isolated place, its nearest neighbour a cottage half a mile down the road. An interviewer had talked to the people from the cottage, a couple who'd lived there for thirty years. They used to see Gilda Brent driving her red Ford car along the lanes, the woman spoke to her once when she went to St Michael's Farm collecting for the Red Cross, but they hadn't seen her since, they hadn't seen her for twenty years, maybe more than that. The people in the village said she'd gone off with another man, and the postmistress claimed to have that from the horse's mouth, Gilda's own husband. Whatever the truth of it, Gilda had vanished, as if absorbed into the desolate countryside where she had lived.

They'd been very thorough in their researches, even finding the portrait Alan had painted for *The Wife's Story* that was the occasion of him meeting Gilda. It was still hanging on a wall in a room in Soho, though the offices were now owned by a company that made television commercials. They showed it on the screen, Gilda in a green evening gown, looking very young. No one said what had happened to the nude, it wasn't mentioned.

'I didn't think much of that,' Philippa said when the programme was over. 'I reckon I could have made a better job of it if I'd had his education, the bastard.'

It's funny how people think it helps, calling someone you love names, insulting them, just because they've hurt you. Still, it's loyal. It's well-meant. I value my friends more now that I have no lover.

No doubt it was a silly thing to do but I drove over to Tivetshall St Michael on my day off, just to have a look at the empty house. On the way there I had this feeling that perhaps a lot of other people would have had the same idea from watching *The Lady Vanishes* and I'd find a dozen cars parked in the lane and crowds with cameras scrambling to get a look through the windows. But there was no one.

If you look on a map you'll see great empty spaces in this part of Norfolk. The countryside is very deep there and the road between the cottage and the farm thickly wooded. A long avenue runs up to the house, a straight sandy road with lime trees on either side. I drove through the open gateway, planning excuses to give to anyone who stopped me, but no one did. The house was just as it was in Ned's film but shabbier and more dilapidated and wretched-looking. I remembered what he'd once told me, that everything looks better in photographs, everything looks better on television than in life, except maybe people.

No one had weeded the garden for years. The lawn had been cut, but by someone who didn't care, you could tell that, someone who sat on the mower and drove it round and round while smoking a cigarette and listening to a Walkman. It was years and years since the house had been painted. The roof needed re-tiling. A drain pipe was hanging half off the side wall. I looked through a window but what I saw inside made me so sad I had to turn away. It was squalid in there, like the interior of one of those junk shops that abound in the little towns round here, dull brown furniture, mostly broken or scarred, rucked-up carpets, pictures and mirrors stacked against the walls, ugly ornaments, their colours grimed by an accumulation of dust.

The effect was depressing, yet it was a beautiful day, the sun shining, the sky a soft blue and the hedges green with new leaves on the quickthorn. Whatever time and neglect had done to St Michael's Farm they hadn't been able to destroy the narcissi that nodded in the long grass or stop the cherry trees breaking into white blossom. From the woods I could hear the mechanical thrumming a woodpecker makes when he bores his beak into the bark of a pine tree, drilling for insects. It came back to me then, the fanciful theory that it was this countryside which had absorbed Gilda and hidden her away for ever.

It was soon after the film and my visit to St Michael's Farm that Mike wrote to me, asking for a divorce. I was relieved, I never thought he would, he'd said so many times and so determinedly that he'd never want a divorce, and I feared I'd have to wait five years before being free. But now he wants to be divorced on grounds of irretrievable breakdown, as soon as we've been apart for two years. He's met a woman he knows can make him happy as I never could. Mum had told me all about that, though I could scarcely believe it, because it was no one new or exciting but only Jill Baleham's niece, Angie Green, the one who got pregnant though she was on the pill. She's moved in with him, Janis said, her and the baby, and they have all their meals on an Ikea table in the conservatory. Well, I hope they'll be happy, I don't wish him any harm.

The worst pain of losing Ned, and the way of losing him, is beginning to go away now. Sadness is still there and loneliness but the knife whose point used to go in and make me gasp at the pain, that's withheld and just grazes the surface. I still think of him all the time but I no longer cry in the night the way I told Philippa I must be alone to do.

Some of the things Linda Owen told me about have helped. If I know he has this need to be loved and a need of his own at least to pretend love, my own humiliation is less bad. He may have deceived me but he deceived himself too. He was never one of those who tell lies to ensnare a woman. Perhaps he told no lies at all, for when he said those things he thought they were true. I try to think of him as someone with a sickness, an invisible illness, that I was able to heal for a little while. And though he lives in my mind, his face imprinted there and his words recorded, I know it won't always be so. I can imagine a time coming when minutes will pass by and then hours when I don't think of him, when the words he said to me, such as wanting me for a lifetime and loving me whatever I said or did, won't come back to me. Maybe the time will even come when I'll be able to say, I haven't thought of him at all since yesterday.

Meanwhile I have to make myself a life. Middleton Hall is a dead end, there's no future in being a care assistant, and the pay is worse than an agricultural worker's. It hardly mattered when I thought I'd give up work to have children, but that isn't going to happen now, or not as far as I can see or imagine, so I've decided to take a nurse's training and become a real State Registered Nurse, not one of those half-measures. In fact, I've applied and been accepted. I'm starting in September.

It was a wonderful thing Stella did in leaving me this house. Finding accommodation, that worries so many people, is one problem I don't have. And it's through her that I know Richard, who has been and is being a true friend to me. Philippa visits, though she finds it hard being deprived of the telly, so mostly I go to her. Mum has been good to me and so have Nan and Janis, treating me like a poor wounded thing who can be nursed back to health with kindness and white magic.

Linda Owen drops in sometimes to take me to the pub, the Swan at Breckenhall, not the Legion, and we go out drinking like a couple of the boys. We talk about cars like men do and shopping and running expenses when you own your own house but we never talk about Ned, that subject is taboo. My year with him has taught me a valuable thing though, that it's no use trying to make yourself into something for other people. If you do that it has to be for yourself. I'm ashamed of myself when I remember studying the encyclopedia and looking up words in *Chambers Dictionary*, not to mention learning about classical music, all to impress Ned, and maybe that's why I haven't played a single one of those tapes Stella made and passed on to me along with the player.

She was insistent I take her player, as if she hadn't already done enough to provide for me. If I'd known beforehand I'd have explained to her that I didn't need it, I've got a Walkman that I've had for years, though never used much. But when you're alone a lot, as I am, you need to hear voices or music, you need something to break the silence or you start wondering if your ears still work.

These summer evenings I walk in the fen a lot, taking the path that starts at my garden gate and winds among the

willows and the alders and meadowsweet, passes into
clearings where water lies and reeds grow, and back again
into the quiet woodland. I never see a soul, no one goes
there, it is all so silent, so still, that you could hear a water
beetle skim the surface of a pool. It was there, one evening
last week, that I saw a swallowtail.

Another item in my inheritance was Stella's butterfly
book. I looked it up and found that it's the only one of
that species in Britain with tails suspended from its lower
wings. Wonderful wings they were, yellow and black and
red in patterns on a wide span. It alighted on a flower of
the fumitory and stayed there, basking in the evening sun,
its wings spread, then fluttering a little before they fanned
out again.

I'm a fool, I know, but I thought of Stella who so
longed to see a swallowtail and never would now and it
made me start to cry. That was when the silence of the fen
began to trouble me and as I made my way home I
remembered people I'd seen walking about in Bury or
Diss with headsets on and a Walkman in their pocket,
and I decided to try it.

So next day, and that was the day before yesterday, I
bought myself a pack of batteries on the way home from
work, put two in the Walkman, and for the first time
since she died had a proper look at Stella's tapes. For some
reason I thought she'd recorded a lot, but she hadn't.
Eight out of the ten tapes are blank. The other two aren't
labelled with the titles of pieces of music, but wouldn't be
much use to me if they were, as the only pieces I know by
name are 'Nessun Dorma' and the Water Music. Stella
had simply printed 'Tape 1' and 'Tape 2' on their labels,
otherwise giving no clue to their content.

Barbara Vine

May as well start at the beginning, I thought, putting
'Tape I' in the Walkman, though by then I was wishing
I'd stretched my budget and bought the Emmylou Harris
Luxury Liner I'd seen in the battery shop. But Stella's
music would at least break the silence as I wandered
through the fen.

It was a very warm evening, utterly windless, and all
about me was the staleness of late summer, seed heads
instead of flowers, tired leaves hanging from unmoving
branches, nettles worn out and stretched to six feet in
height but still capable of stinging. I suppose I was nervous about starting the music, afraid of the sudden
assault of something I might not understand or appreciate breaking on my ears. I put my thumb on the start
button but I didn't press it until I was in the heart of the
fen. There, in a clearing, where drought had dried up the
pools but the grass was still green, cropped short by rab-
bits, I sat down on a fallen log and pressed the Walkman
button.

There was whirring and a sound like the waves of the
sea and then Stella's voice, sweet and very clear. It gave me
such a shock that coldness passed right through me and
broke on my skin in gooseflesh. Stella's voice said, 'This is
the first tape. The second follows. They are both labelled.'

I stopped it. I turned it off. After I'd taken a deep
breath and another, counted to ten, told myself to be sensible, I started it again.

23

This is the first tape. The second follows. They are both labelled.

Dear Genevieve, I am inclined to begin this as I would begin a letter, but I am speaking, not writing. I have had plenty of practice in speaking into this device. Does that surprise you? I think I have given you a lot of surprises one way and another. Once you thought nothing had ever happened to me, I could see it in your face, but now I feel that maybe you will think too much has happened to me.

When we last talked, the very last time, you told me your wish was coming true. Of course you meant you were going to be with the man you love. You meant he was going to leave his home and join you. I'm glad for you and I hope you're very happy now. I told you that in the end Alan left Gilda to be with me. What I didn't say—among so many other things—was that he didn't tell me this until we were together at Molucca. We had come for a ten-day holiday while my children were away and Gilda was, or was supposed to be, in France. Driving us to the house, he decided. We had talked and talked of it, on and on, for months—well, for years. He decided quite spontaneously, he said. One minute, inside his head, he was going on holiday with me, the next he was committed to me for life, never to be separated.

He told me so as we closed the front door behind us. 'This is for ever. I'm never going back. I've left her.'

I'd been going to prepare lunch for us, something light, sandwiches probably, but suddenly neither of us felt we could eat. He put the champagne in the fridge. That was the champagne you found, for we never opened it. We should have drunk it warm, as it came from the car.

We kept falling into each other's arms, we were drunk on nothing. Then he made us pink gins to celebrate while the champagne was cooling. We danced—ballroom dancing, Genevieve, do you know about that?—we danced with the glasses in our hands. We waltzed without music.

He said, 'Just before we went into that shop, I thought, what the hell am I playing at? I'm not on holiday, I'm on life. I'm never going back. So I bought the champagne. Mean of me, wasn't it? Not to discuss it with you, not to ask, just to decide. Do you mind?'

'You knew me,' I said. 'You know me. Why would I mind? It's what I've always wanted.'

So we waltzed some more. We tangoed from one end of the room to the other and Alan sang 'When They Begin the Beguine'. He had given me another drink, a glass of wine this time, when I heard the car.

It was a rare event, a car passing. A car coming up the drive was almost unknown. By then we were sitting on the sofa with our arms round each other. I stood up to see. I saw the piranha face before I saw Gilda. It seemed to be charging me, that red body, that snarling mouth with bared teeth in a scarlet face. But it didn't charge me. It stopped precisely next to and parallel with Alan's grey Rover. We are a couple, it seemed to say to me, we belong together, we shall always be side by side. I made a little sound and put out my hand, feeling blindly behind me to touch him.

One's first thought is to hide. There is no hiding, of course. If we had thought of that, anticipated this, we would not have left the car there, opened the windows, sat in this room together for anyone passing to see. Hadn't we picked a house with a garage to conceal a car if we needed to? But we wanted to hide. I even said to him, 'Hide!'

Alan didn't panic. I might have known he never would. He said, 'You mean, hide you or hide the car, whichever is the easier,' and he laughed. He actually laughed. He said later that there was nothing else to do.

Gilda got out of the car and slammed the door as hard as she could. It's strange what you notice. I noticed for the first time her unnatural thinness, that she was bones and a hank of hair. She had green trousers on and a black sleeveless blouse with a green chiffon scarf knotted round her neck, black sunglasses that hid any expression, green sandals with stacked heels. She stood there a moment, looking at the house. I don't think she could see us.

Alan said, 'We may as well open the door. She'll only break in if we don't.'

We both went to the door, but he went first. He opened it. She walked in. She didn't say a word. She pushed past us and went upstairs. We could hear her in the bedroom overhead, checking on our cases, I suppose, looking for our night things. Alan got hold of my hand, squeezed it and dropped it again. We didn't speak.

Gilda came downstairs and walked into the living room. We followed her. She looked round her and round again, like someone who had come to buy the place. She said to me,

'I suppose this house is yours?'

I nodded.

'It wouldn't be his, would it? He never had two half-pennies to rub together.'

I found a voice. 'It's my house. I bought it six years ago.'

'You mean that poor devil your late husband did. What did you do, save the money up out of the housekeeping?'

That line came straight out of *Lora Cartwright*. Hearing it repeated now, word for word, made me shiver.

Alan said, 'Why aren't you in France?'

'Good question,' she said. 'I never intended to go to France.' She looked at me. 'I followed him here last week. I didn't know it was you. I mean, why you, for God's sake? I thought he'd at least find someone presentable. The *coup de grâce* was planned for today.' She sat down, looked at our glasses. 'Give me a drink, please.'

Alan went to the dining room and brought back gin and sherry and the white burgundy and a bottle of tonic and more glasses on a tray. She didn't say any more until she'd had a drink, quite a hefty drink. Alan gave me a stiff gin and poured one for himself.

Gilda said to me, 'I thought you were my friend.'

That too came from *The Wife's Story*, but was none the

less true. What could I say? Not that I was sorry, I wasn't sorry. But that statement of hers, remark, *reproach*, whatever you like to call it, cut me to the bone in spite of having been written by a scriptwriter long ago. I shrugged, I shook my head. She turned to Alan.

'Why her? Why not a young girl? She's nearly as old as me and God knows she looks more.'

It didn't require an answer. It was said to cause pain. Probably it too was from a film, but one I hadn't seen. She began to talk then. I can remember much of it, though not all, but I shan't repeat it. What would be the point? She held out her glass for more gin and Alan re-filled it and poured more for both of us. We were all drinking while we talked, drinking as I at least had never drunk before.

But, you know, the absurd thing was that there wasn't much she could say, there was very little with which to threaten us. She tried. She told Alan she would never divorce him, that would make things too easy for both of us. She would tell Marianne and Richard what I was and what we had done, and tell our friends and neighbours, Priscilla and Jeremy and other relatives. More than that, she would bring an action against me for enticement. I always wondered how she even knew such a thing was possible, or had once been possible.

'I wish you'd take off those glasses,' Alan said.

She took off her sunglasses. Her eyes were red, and I mean not just the eyelids, her eyes were bloodshot, the whites scarlet round those blue irises. She looked like one of those photographs where the flash has turned the subject's eyes red and staring. Alan lined up three wineglasses on the tray and filled them with the white burgundy. I couldn't have drunk any more gin but I could drink that.

And yet the worst of it was over. At first it had been a shock, stunning, appalling. Now that she was there and talking, uttering threats that seemed to me empty enough, wasn't it even for the best that she had found out? I didn't put this into words, not even in my mind, but that was the general impression I had, the way I tended to feel. I felt hope. Yes, I did. Of course it was partly due to the drink, it was euphoria, but when Gilda began to insult me, calling me stupid and naïve and ignorant, an underhand schemer like a schoolgirl who is also a sneak, when she asked Alan what on earth he saw in me, I didn't mind, I knew it would make him despise her and love me more. I had absolute faith in his loyalty and his love. And I was right to have. That wasn't misplaced.

Alan said, 'She was a schoolgirl.' And then, 'She was at school with me.'

She put her hand up to her face. 'I don't understand,' she said and she went a dark red colour.

It came out then. She had never known and it made her angrier than anything else. The obvious things are not the worst betrayals. Perhaps that was how she saw it, his knowing me before he knew her, my knowing things about him she could never know. As her anger mounted she began to shout, finally to scream and while she screamed to grab and hurl everything within reach. She broke two glasses against the wall. She flung the empty wine bottle and it went sailing through the open window and hit the bonnet of Alan's car. Alan watched her, keeping out of the line of fire, but doing nothing to stop her. He knew her rages, that they burnt themselves out quite quickly, dissolving in tears.

A lot of our small ornaments got broken that afternoon. There's probably still a dent in the wall where Gilda threw a bowl at it. That was the last thing she threw before she started to weep and sob. I don't know what Alan felt. I felt the most terrible guilt. For the first time in my life I wanted to put my arms round Gilda and comfort her. It would have been—or have seemed—the height of cynical hypocrisy. But it didn't change my feelings towards him. I wanted him for myself, for ever, for my husband, to be a father to Richard, for everything.

I must stop now and rest before continuing. I may not be able to do any more until tomorrow.

We all remained sitting where we were. The gin bottle was empty. After a moment or two Alan got up and went to the dining room. He came back with whisky. There was no more gin. I had never told him what to do or what not to do, I had never said to him, don't do that, don't have any more to drink, and I didn't say it then. I trusted him. I thought he knew best in every situation. If he needed another drink, he needed it, he knew best. I put my hand over my own glass. He half-filled his. We had all been chain-smoking. The two ashtrays were piled high with butts.

Gilda stopped crying. It was always like that, as if she had cried all the tears she had. Alan had never said he was sorry or that he would do his best to make things easier for her and I understood that he was offering her no more to drink because she would have to drive home. I have said I felt hope and now I was feeling almost happy, I was pleased with the way things had gone. I won't say God forgive me for feeling like that because I have been punished for it, or for something, for everything. I have been punished for twenty-four years.

It was a tremendous relief that I felt when Gilda got up and said she was going. Then she said to Alan,

'I want you to come with me, please.'

It was as if she had forgotten all those threats, the separation, the enticement. She was taking him back with her, to forget, to start afresh.

'I shall never speak to you again,' she said to me, 'that goes without saying.'

I nodded, accepting.

'I'm not coming with you, Gilda,' Alan said. 'I've left you. I'm with Stella now. One day I'm going to marry Stella.'

She ignored that. 'You've drunk yourself into a stupor, haven't you?' she said. 'Just so that you couldn't drive.'

Perhaps he had. He persuaded her to leave. After a storm such as she had been through she was usually quite meek, he could make her do what he wanted. We had eighty cigarettes when we first arrived at the house, he and I, and eight or nine were left in the second packet. He lit one for her, gave her the rest. I could tell he had drunk too much but only by the faint slurring of his speech. He said,

'I'm not coming now, Gilda, but I will come. I'll come to you later but Stella must come with me. I will never again be separated from Stella. Do you understand that?'

She didn't answer. It sounds absurd but we both went outside with her. We were like a married couple in our own home seeing a guest off the premises. On the doorstep, where you say a mountain ash now grows, on the doorstep which was covered with broken glass and china, she turned to me, gathered saliva in her mouth and spat. Her spittle struck me on the cheek and ran down my face.

Who am I to make a fuss? Who am I to say I hadn't deserved that? At the time it horrified me. I cried out. I shrank away from her, gasping. A fool, wasn't I? I had led too sheltered a life. What had ever happened to me but finding Charmian Fry's body? Gilda had been right when she called me innocent, when she called me 'little thing'. Alan took his handkerchief out of his pocket and wiped my face. He did a strange thing, he did what my own mother used to do when I was a child, licked the handkerchief and wiped my cheek. I saw it as a symbol. How many people would you do such a thing as that for?

Gilda went to her car. I stayed where I was, my face feeling as if it had been splashed with poison, Alan's kind action no antidote. He took a few steps towards her car. She got into the driver's seat, put in the ignition key. And then, oh then, it happened, the beginning of the terror, the thing that opened the way to all the next events. Or, rather, did not happen, for Gilda's car wouldn't start. She turned the key and pressed down the accelerator, over and over, too many times, and it wouldn't start.

I don't know why. The heat? The age of the car? The battery was flat, though I didn't know that then. The car had brought her to Molucca and then, while she was inside, the battery had died.

Alan tried to start the car and failed as she had failed. I stood on the doorstep, watching. It was half past four in the afternoon. All that time we had been in the house, listening to Gilda, not defending ourselves, drinking. The hours had passed and in that time the blue sky had become overcast with smoke. Beyond the fields on the other side of the road I could see a black column of smoke streaming upwards. It was hotter than ever. Alan got out of the car.

'It's not going to start,' he said. 'I'll drive you home and we'll phone someone to see to your car.' He turned to look at me. 'Stella comes too.'

'No,' she said.

'Stella comes too. You can walk, if you prefer. It's only eight miles.'

'Put her in the back,' said Gilda. 'I'm your wife. I go in the front.'

I said that of course I would sit in the back. It made no difference to me. That wasn't true, it did make a difference, it always had when the three of us went anywhere together, Gilda beside Alan, I in the back, but I told myself it was the last time. In future I would always sit beside him.

My mouth was dry. I went out to the kitchen and I drank some water. Vanity remains, stays alive almost to the end, and I looked at my face in the mirror, patted my hair, put on more lipstick. That word she had used to me, 'presentable', that rankled. We would do our daughters a service if we brought them up not to care how they looked, if we broke all the mirrors, yet I brought my daughter up to be as vain as I.

We locked up the house. I got into the back of the car and Gilda into the front, into the passenger seat, the way it always was. There were no seat-belts in those days, or rather, there were, some cars had them, but their use was not compulsory. It was more than ten years later before you had to wear a seat-belt by law.

Drunk driving wasn't looked on the way it is now. I remember Jeremy going to Sweden on business and coming back with tales of people afraid to have a single glass of wine before driving, of someone he'd met whose brother-in-law had gone to prison, or a labour camp, for driving over the limit. As far as we were concerned, we thought we were safe to drink as much as we wanted so long as we didn't have an accident. John Browning boasted that he had once driven all the way to Peterborough with one eye shut because he'd drunk so much he had double vision. It didn't worry me that Alan would be driving after drinking half a bottle of gin and some whisky as well as wine, I didn't think about it.

I suppose I would have said I had more important things to think of.

Almost at once, within half a mile, we had driven into the kind of atmosphere there must have been in industrial towns on hot days in the last century. And this was the countryside in 1970. It was caused through stubble burning but for a while we couldn't see any smoke. We couldn't see the sky either, for the heavy overcast. A dense hot fog hung, still and brooding, over the fields and woods. The air smelt like a smoke-filled room.

There was no traffic. That's not quite true. Of course there was some, but I think we passed no more than one car before the accident happened. Alan was driving very fast. That is, he was probably driving at no more than fifty miles an hour but that's fast on narrow roads that run straight for a quarter of a mile and then inexplicably turn a right-angled bend. He wanted to get Gilda home fast, he wanted to be rid of Gilda. As we passed through Curton he had to slow down a little. In the heat and under the choking smoke its inhabitants seemed all asleep. I didn't notice the garage at the end of the village street, Curton Cars Ltd, the last building in the street. I noticed nothing but Alan and Gilda sitting side by side and the countryside travelling past, hazy, flat, still.

As soon as Curton was left behind he speeded up again. No one spoke—have I said that? We sat in silence. No one had spoken since Gilda said she was Alan's wife and I was to go in the back and I'd said I would. I remember her long blondish hair with the silver threads in it hanging over the back of the passenger seat, and the scarf she wore showing a harsh emerald green between the strands. I remember watching Alan's hands on the steering wheel. I wanted him to touch me, I ached for his touch. It was hours and hours, before Gilda came, since I had felt his hand on me, his mouth on my skin. We were never together without touching and the deprivation made me feel rejected and hungry.

He drove very fast round those bends and faster on those long straights. The car bounced over a humpbacked bridge that crossed a stream and Gilda gave a thin shriek. He must have been driving at more than fifty when the smoke rolled across the road in front of us. It came suddenly, a dense black cloud, almost horizontal, pouring over the hedge, engulfing the car.

Have you ever experienced that? Do you know what it's like? From inside a car you rely entirely on sight, on the visible world, and when it's taken away by a shattered windscreen or a sheet of cardboard blown against the glass you're as blind as if your corneas had gone.

That cloud blinded us. It blinded Alan. It blanked out the windscreen as surely as a coat of grey paint. I felt him flinch, I felt the seat in front of me jerk, and the reflex of his foot slamming the brake, the car leaping and buckling. But I don't remember the crash itself, only the bang, the huge explosion that wasn't in fact an explosion but the noise of violent impact. It was the loudest sound I have ever heard.

The car doors flew open. Do I remember that or did he tell me? I don't know. Somehow, from some instinct of protecting one's own and oneself, but also from that desire I had to touch him, a split instant before the impact, I had flung my arms round him from behind and held on. The seat was between us, a buffer between us, but still I held him as hard as I could and he said I saved him from the windscreen or the steering wheel piercing his chest, he said I was his seat-belt. I don't know. How do I know?

Perhaps I did in fact save him from being thrown out of the car when the doors were flung open. There was no one to hold on to Gilda. That was the first thing I saw when I opened my eyes, that Gilda wasn't there, that Gilda was gone, the passenger seat was empty. But I did nothing at first, I didn't ask him. I held on. I pushed my face into his neck like an animal nuzzling. There was some feeling in my mind of staying there for ever, of being there, clasped together, closing our eyes, sleeping even. I could feel a pulse beating in his neck and hear his harsh breathing.

He said my name in a voice that was a vibration without tone.

'Stella.'

I moved my face. My mouth was wet with his sweat. When I withdrew my hands I saw that they were covered with blood and that made me whimper. That is what you do when you've been in a car accident, you shake and make frightened sounds. You can't control your lips, they quiver and wobble. Your whole body trembles. My hands were covered with innumerable tiny scratches and my fingers were the same colour as my nails. The noise of the crash was still in my head, repeating itself and reverberating like the sound of big guns firing over and over.

He got out of the car, he staggered and then righted himself, and came round to the back and made me get out and then he put his arms round me. I was crying by then and uttering cries but I had to stop, I made myself stop. Alan wiped my hands with the handkerchief he'd used to wipe Gilda's saliva off my face. His were bleeding and blood was running down his face from a cut on his forehead.

I said, 'Where's Gilda?' My teeth were chattering.

'I don't know,' he said.

The smoke had passed. The air hung heavy with hot smoky fog. In front of us loomed through it a huge farm machine, a combine I suppose or a baler. It had been parked half on the road and half on the grass verge and Alan had gone into the back of it. The car was pushed into the yellow iron slab that was its rear end as if it had been welded there, its front wheels lifted off the surface of the road, its bonnet stove in like a crushed tin can.

Since that single car had passed, there had been no other. But one came then. If the driver saw us he didn't stop, though Alan tried to flag him down. He turned back to me with clenched fists and swore. I don't think I'd ever heard him swear before. When the van from the garage in Curton came it seemed like coincidence, an amazing stroke of fate, but it wasn't really. The garage man was on his way home, he always passed at that time, at five.

But it wasn't yet five when Alan stood there cursing, his fists clenched. I said,

'We must look for Gilda. We must find Gilda.'

The verge was wide, twenty feet wide, with trees growing on it and behind was a ditch and the hedge. We found her lying at the foot of a tree in the long grass. I say 'we' but it was Alan who found her. I gritted my teeth and clutched one hand in the other. He knelt down beside her, looking into her face. She opened her eyes and muttered something. I couldn't see a mark on her. We had all escaped injury by a miracle.

Or so I thought. It was absurd I suppose, what I said. 'Gilda, are you all right?'

Her eyes were fixed on Alan's face. She said something but I couldn't make it out.

'She'll be all right,' he said. 'She'll be fine. Let her rest there for a bit and she'll be fine.'

It was grotesque, only I didn't see it like that at the time. He knew her, he knew about these things, *he knew best.*

She had only been thrown a few yards out of a car. The green scarf was still round her neck. Then I saw the blood on her hair, seeping from the back of her head, brownish and wet on the blades of grass.

'Alan,' I said, 'I think she hit her head against that tree.'

He didn't look at Gilda, he looked at the tree. It was just a tree, I can't remember what sort, if I ever noticed. The bark was dark brown and rough. I couldn't see any special marks on it but it was all over marks, that was its texture, to be covered with scars as if a hundred people had been hurled against it.

All this time I was shaking, though it was subsiding a bit. I was coming back to reality, to practicalities. My hands had stopped bleeding. I sat down on the grass. I was wearing stockings and high-heeled shoes and there was a ladder in one of my stockings. It's strange how you notice these things. I was thinking about Charmian and how I'd behaved then, ridiculously, like a stupid child, I'd run down the street screaming. I said to Alan,

'One of us will have to walk back to Curton and phone for an ambulance.'

And then the van came. It was red and it had 'Curton Cars Ltd' printed in white on the side of it. There was no question of this driver not stopping. His window was open and he waved at us, made a thumbs-up sign. He pulled into the verge on the other side of the combine, got out of the van and came over to us.

He was in overalls, a tall, good-looking man, much younger than we were, perhaps thirty. He looked at the wreck of Alan's car, the bonnet crushed in, welded to the great steel bulwark of that combine, its front doors blown open, and then he looked at Alan. He asked the question that changed everything. Afterwards I thought of him as a messenger from fate, a not quite human character from a Greek play, someone come to give us a choice and offer us an answer. But he was an ordinary man, smiling and sympathetic at the same time. I was relieved to see him.

He asked the question.

'Just the two of you, was it?' he said.

A simple casual question. I nearly denied it. I nearly shouted, no, no, we were three, there was someone else, there was someone who's been hurt. I didn't. He wasn't talking to me but to Alan, to the man. I was the woman, taken for granted as the passenger, not the driver, someone who it was assumed, would know nothing. Besides, I was used to leaving things to men's decisions. What did I know? I could drive but I barely knew how the internal-combustion engine functioned. He repeated what he'd said, more gently this time. He must have thought we were in shock.

'Just you two, was it?'

Alan shut his eyes, opened them, said very quickly, 'Yes. Just the two of us.'

I don't know how I kept silent. I held my hand over my mouth. My fingers were all over scratches and I tasted the blood. The garage man was up by the wreck by then, walking round it, examining it.

'I ask because whoever was riding shotgun—' he looked at me—'must have been thrown out, taken quite a header.'

Alan said, 'My wife.'

For a moment I thought he was going to tell him about Gilda, *show* him Gilda, but it was me he meant. I was his wife.

'You were lucky.' He looked at the blood on Alan. 'Cut yourself shaving, did you?' And he winked.

Alan smiled. It amazed me, that he could smile. He said, 'I've got a lot of hair on my hands.'

They both laughed. They laughed knowingly the way men do, all boys together, the conspiracy of men is what Marianne calls it.

'No need to call the fuzz, then? Not if there's no one hurt.'

'No,' said Alan.

'Better not if there's no necessity.'

Alan said no again. He said it thoughtfully. It was as if he was learning, taking advice, catching on. He was like someone who knows a certain amount of a foreign language but needs to listen carefully when it is spoken to catch the hidden meaning. He was thinking, following the garage man's movements with his eyes. And then he had moved from where he was standing, he repositioned himself so that his body kept Gilda from view. No one in the road could have seen Gilda where she lay, deep in the long grass, but he was making doubly sure, screening the hidden woman.

It was then that it registered with me, how silent she was. Why didn't she cry out, moan, whisper something? A little breeze, the first of that day, ruffled the leaves of the tree above her. I looked away.

The garage man said he would go back to Curton and fetch his 'stuff', a pickup truck and a towing bar. He'd be ten minutes, if that. Alan remained standing where he was until the van had gone. There was something in his face I'd never seen there before, something calculating, assessing his chances maybe, I don't know. He said,

'I'm going to move Gilda out of the sun. She ought not to be in the sun.'

I was a grown woman, I was a *middle-aged* woman of forty-seven. Why didn't I insist on fetching an ambulance? Why didn't I point out the absolute imperative of telling the police? I don't know why. I didn't know then. Blame it on shock perhaps, on what had gone before the accident, the accident itself, on the amount I had drunk. I seemed to have no strength, no will. I was aware of more smoke billowing over us, of coughing and looking at my hands that were smeared with blood, blackened with burnt barley, of another car passing but not stopping, of Alan bending down and lifting Gilda up in his arms.

He carried her into the shade. But there never was much sun, was there? Was there really much difference between the smoky gloom under that tree and the shadow of the hedge? Now where he had laid her she couldn't have been seen except by someone specifically searching. He asked me if I would be happier sitting in the car. It would at any rate be more comfortable. I shook my head. I said to him,

'You said there were just the two of us?'

It was a strange reply he gave me. 'As far as I'm concerned there are just the two of us.' And then he said, 'You know, I'd never have thought of that if he hadn't suggested it.'

'What do you mean?' I said.

'I was about to start bleating about Gilda being injured and calling an ambulance and fetching the police and God knows what. And along he came and put that splendid idea into my head, that there were just the two of us.'

He gave me a cigarette and lit one for himself. I sat on the grass and hugged my knees. I sat there in my fussy dress and high heels and laid my head on my knees and shut my eyes. I had a raging thirst, the result of drinking, I suppose.

Alan had gone away from me. I lifted my head once and looked round for him but I couldn't see him anywhere. I could see only the road and the tall grass and that tree with the wounded bark. I closed my eyes again and saw the redness of light through the lids. And still the garage man didn't come. Water was what I wanted, a long long drink of water, and then sleep. A pulse was throbbing steadily inside my head.

Ages passed. I suppose it was about ten minutes. I opened my eyes and got to my feet. I looked up into the tree and saw Gilda's sunglasses caught on a branch. There was blood on my dress by then, but it didn't show among the flower pattern unless you knew. I reached up for the sunglasses. Alan was kneeling beside Gilda. I couldn't see Gilda, the grass was too long, more like hay, tall grass with tall plants in it, wormwood and thistles and tansy and willow herb. He got up and came to me and said,

'Don't scream. Cover your mouth. She's dead.'

24

I stopped for a while. I had to. Someone came in with my coffee while I was talking. The trouble is I no longer have the strength to prop a chair under the door handle. It was only Sharon and she thinks I'm an old madwoman, anyway. What could be more natural than for me to talk gibberish to myself?

She has gone and I can resume.

We were there at the roadside, waiting for the garage man to come back. Alan knelt down in the grass beside me. He took hold of my hands.

'She's dead,' he said again. And abruptly, 'Do you want to see?'

I shook my head. I couldn't speak.

He was very pale. His eyes were so bright I thought there must be tears in them. The enormity of what he had said was too much for me. I could only stare at him.

He said, 'I can hear the beating of your heart.'

'Oh, she can't be dead,' I said, 'she can't.'

'Darling, you must keep calm.' He was quite calm himself. 'Listen. Here's our *garagiste*,' he said. 'Trust the French to have a word for it.' Once again he took my bloodied blackened hands in his bloodied blackened hands. 'Don't speak, sweetheart. Be struck dumb by shock, will you? Leave it to me. It's best.'

The garage man was cheerful and reassuring. He kept saying what a lucky escape we'd had. I don't think he could understand the way I was behaving, as if I'd suffered more than shock in the accident, more than a few scratches to my hands. He eyed me the way men eye women who are 'making a fuss', indulgently, making allowances but with a level of contempt.

He told Alan, who I'm sure hadn't even thought about it, that he knew who the combine belonged to, he could give him the name. Then he fastened—but it's no use my trying to describe what he did, I don't know the names for these things, the tools, the techniques. What it amounted to was that he managed to pull the car off the combine and tow it behind his truck. While he was doing this he didn't speak to me at all. I don't mean he was rude. It was just that I was a woman, so could know nothing of these things, men's things.

We got into the truck with him. In the front, in the middle of the windscreen, a horseshoe was hanging, suspended on strings tied to its ends. He saw me looking at it and he winked.

'It's up that way to stop the luck running out.'

He didn't call Alan anything but he called me 'ma'am' and once he referred to me as 'your wife'. I let it pass. I didn't say, I'm not his wife, and Alan didn't say, she's not my wife.

'Cheer up, ma'am,' he said to me. 'It's not the end of the world. Let's see you smile.'

He didn't see me smile. I had begun to shiver. We left the wreck of Alan's car on the garage forecourt in Curton and went into the office and the man said did I want a cup of tea.

I have to call him 'the man' because I never heard his name. I don't think Alan did. What difference would it have made? There was a photograph on the desk. I sat there and looked at it while he made tea for us. It was of two little girls and a baby boy and when he came back I asked him if they were his children. He seemed pleased to be asked, he told me their names. I said his older girl must be about the same age as my boy. It was just small talk, something to avoid speaking of the accident.

Alan asked him if he had any jump leads. I didn't know what jump leads were then, I didn't know what he meant, but the man said of course he had, and when we'd drunk the tea he drove us home to Molucca. He'd get on to the farmer who owned the combine if we liked, he said, but Alan said no, he'd do that.

Gilda's car was outside the house. Of course it was, but I had forgotten about it, I had forgotten it wouldn't start. The garage man lifted up the bonnet, produced the wires they called jump leads and connected them to the Anglia's battery. I went into the house and started clearing up the mess, the litter of bottles and glasses and cigarette butts. It was something manual to do, a mechanical activity that needed no thought. When I went back Gilda's car engine was running and Alan was in the driver's seat with his foot touching the accelerator.

The man said, 'I've got the same model myself. It should be OK.' He held up his hands and said, 'Fingers crossed.'

I can see him now, on that hot dusty evening, holding up his crossed fingers. He was our fateful messenger but we were also his. He got into his van and drove away, home to those children, I supposed, till Alan set me right.

I got into Gilda's car next to him. Hundreds of times I'd sat there in the past, going out to tea with her, going to the cinema but I'd never been in it with him before. Alan started talking as if nothing had happened. The garage man had told him that thanks to us he'd be late home again. He had laughed and winked but he was serious. His wife had told him this was his last chance. If he was late again 'he'd had his chips', she was throwing him out, so since he'd be late anyway now he was going to keep a date he'd made with a woman called Kath and get home really late. Might as well be hanged for a sheep as a lamb, he'd said.

'Why are you telling me all this?' I said.

'I thought it might amuse you.'

I asked if he was going to phone the police or if he'd like me to do it. My voice sounded cold and hard. He looked into my eyes and shook his head slowly, as if by that shake of the head he was trying to make me understand many things. He lit two cigarettes in his mouth and gave me one.

'No one's phoning the police,' he said.

'We *must*,' I said.

'We can't. Think about it, sweetheart. We told the garage man no one was hurt. We let him think you were my wife and there had been just the two of us in the car.'

I said stupidly, shifting the blame, 'He *suggested* it.'

'So? We didn't have to do it, any more than he had to stop for us. You know, I actually thought of saying, "She's not my wife," but I couldn't. It made me think of that joke about the man who can't make love unless he keeps

saying to himself, "She's not my wife, she's not my wife."
I thought if I said it I'd start laughing.' One of the things
I loved him for was his light-heartedness. In that moment
I hated it. 'We didn't tell him Gilda was hurt,' he said.
'We didn't even tell him she was *there*.'

'But Gilda's not just hurt,' I said. 'She's *dead*.'

'All the more reason. What would you say to them?
That we had an accident and Gilda was thrown out but
we didn't mention it to the chap from the garage who
came to pick up the crash car. We didn't mention it
because she was dead by then and anyway, this lady is not
my wife and I was drunk. Is that what we'd say? And if
not what would we say?'

I said we should have got the police straightaway, we
should have got the police and an ambulance, before having the car moved. Why hadn't we?

Because the garage man came up with this idea, he
said. A godsend. A friend in need. A Good Samaritan,
one of those who hadn't passed by.

'I'd better keep the car going,' he said. I didn't know
what he meant. 'In case the battery goes down again.
When you're ready, we'll go.'

'Go where?' I said.

'To fetch Gilda.'

I nearly screamed. I would have done but I clapped
both hands across my mouth.

'That's why I had that chap fix the car,' he said.

We drove back. I was beginning to know that stretch
of road very well. The combine was still there. The only
mark Alan's car had made on it was to remove a few inches of yellow paint from its rear. Everything was the same,
the grass verge, the hay and the weeds that were six feet

tall, the hedge behind, the trees. Did I expect it to have changed? Only the sky and the air had altered, the smoke nearly departed, evening sunshine pouring through the haze.

This is the first side of the second tape.

Alan edged the car right up on to the verge. The ground was dry and hard. He turned the car so that the rear was to the hedge. A truck passed by, then a motor bike. A car came in the opposite direction. By chance we had come back there in Curton's rush hour, such as it was. Alan opened the boot and took out two deck chairs, that he must have fetched from the garage. He set them up on the verge with the picnic table between them and put a bottle on the table and a packet of cigarettes.

It's curious how, when something like this happens to you, you move very easily into the—well, scenario is Marianne's word—the scenario of a detective story. You become aware of things that up till then have belonged only in books. I said to him,

'If you do that anyone who sees us will remember we were here. They'll remember seeing picnickers.'

'There won't be anyone asking,' he said. 'It's for now not the future that I don't want to attract their attention.' He put out his hand and indicated the deck chair, 'Won't you sit down?' I did as he asked. 'Want a fag?' he said.

We each had a cigarette. We sat side by side admiring the view, yellow fields where the corn had been cut and black fields where the stubble had been burnt. A police car went by, and the driver raised one friendly hand in a salute.

I'd always been amazed by those people who drive out

into the country just to sit by the roadside. We were those people now. Lovers don't behave like that but married couples do. Who would have guessed we were guilty lovers? We were smoking and drinking wine at a picnic table on a warm evening, and in the ditch behind us was his wife's dead body.

When the traffic came to an end and the last car had gone home, we put one of the deck chairs back into the car and we put the table inside in the back. The other deck chair we used as a stretcher.

Alan took her head and I her feet. There were grass seeds in her hair. We laid her on the stretcher, carried her to the car and tipped her gently into the boot. She was very light, I doubt if she was more than seven stone. I looked just once at her dead face. The green scarf was no longer tied round her neck but lying across her chest. Even then I was sure that when she got into the car the green chiffon was at her throat.

We put the deck chair in on top of the body and closed the lid. I have described that in a very matter-of-fact way, but that was not at all how I felt. While I helped Alan move Gilda's body I felt unreal, as if in a dream. I would wake up and find myself on the sofa with my head on his shoulder, our dance over, the wine gone to our heads. But I believe this is the way all people feel when called upon to do some act that is utterly alien to their normal life, as if translated into nightmare.

Not a single car had passed while we did this. All was still and silent. We drove back to Molucca. Alan opened the garage doors and put Gilda's car inside, Gilda's body inside in Gilda's car. As we went into the house I noted that it was the exact time we had booked the table for our romantic dinner. He said,

'I'm going to have a bath and then a hair of the dog. How about you?'

'I don't know,' I said. 'I don't know what I'm going to do.'

He said conversationally, as if nothing had happened, 'They used to think eating a hair of the dog that had bitten you would cure the bite. Did you know that, my star?'

The last person you would have expected me to think about then was Richard. But I did think of him, down there in Cornwall, enjoying himself, on the beach all day most probably, and now having his supper, soon to go to bed. I thought how terrible it was for him to have a mother who could do what I was doing. When Alan came downstairs, bathed and his hair washed and in clean clothes, I was still where he'd left me and on my third cigarette.

He had never seen me look the way I must have looked then, dirty, my hair untidy and full of smuts, my hands bleeding, my bare legs scratched, my dress filthy with corn smuts and earth and blood. The sight of me made him laugh.

'Oh God, sweetheart, you should see yourself! The little match-girl. Mrs Guy Fawkes.'

He seemed quite restored. He was cheerful, his old self. I said to him,

'When I was sitting there, before the garage man came back, and you were kneeling beside her, what did you do to her? Did you do anything to her, Alan?'

He was laughing again. 'What do you mean?'

'She was only thrown a couple of yards out of a car.

Perhaps she hit her head against that tree and again perhaps she didn't. Would someone die of that?'

'She did.'

'Alan,' I said. 'Did you . . . ?' But I couldn't ask him.

The words I hadn't used are those you read in books or hear someone say on television. They have nothing to do with real life. You accept hearing them said, you even expect to hear them said in the course of a play or a film, but not in an ordinary day to day existence. In ordinary life they are grotesque. One would laugh at them, the scornful way one laughs at clichés.

I hadn't said them but he knew what I'd tried to say. He often knew what I was thinking, the precise words of my thoughts. But he was smiling, he was cheerful, he answered me cheerfully.

'Of course not. Of course I didn't.'

'You were alone with her,' I said, 'oh, for a long time.'

'I've often been alone with her for a long time,' he said. 'Too long. That's been the trouble.'

He picked up the phone and dialled the number the garage man had given him. I heard him start talking to the farmer who owned the combine. He was very polite, apologetic, hazarding a little joke about an irresistible force meeting an immovable object. I went upstairs and had a bath. Whatever happens, I thought, tomorrow I'll go out and buy myself a pair of flat sandals. I hung up my beautiful dirty dress in the wardrobe and put on another. I combed my hair and I thought about making up my face and asked myself, are you mad? But I did make up my face, as I'd have made it up if I'd been going to my own execution. When the man who worked the guillotine lifted up my head there would have been rouge on my cheeks and lipstick on my mouth.

So I went down again, dressed the way other women dress for a party or a wedding. Alan was sitting there, drinking tomato juice or, more probably, a Bloody Mary.

'Vitamin C is never wrong,' he said. And then, 'Nice chap, that farmer. He asked us over for a drink. I said I'd ask you and call him back.'

'You said *what?*'

'A joke. He said to forget about his machine and there was nothing a lick of paint, I quote, wouldn't cure.'

'What time is it?' I said.

'Two minutes past eight. We've missed our dinner. The problem would have been getting there. Of course we do have a car but, on the other hand, we don't exactly have a car. Remember the people whose grandmother died in Spain.'

'What people?' I said.

I must have been the only person in England who had never heard the story about the couple driving their grandmother over the border from France into Spain. The old woman dies and they put her body in the boot of the car to take her back into France. They leave the car for ten minutes in the town square while they have a drink and when they come back the body has gone, never to be found. But you've heard it, over and over probably, along with the other apocryphal stories about the cat eating the chihuahua and the human tooth in the hamburger.

It didn't seem funny to me. I said to Alan, 'How can you?'

He shrugged his shoulders. 'I'm hysterical. Ignore me,' he said. 'Is there anything to eat?'

'Only what we meant to have for lunch,' I said.

I remember every word of that conversation, trivial though it was. All the time I was wanting to ask that question again but I was afraid. After a little while he left the room and although he hadn't said I knew where he had gone. I watched him back Gilda's car out of the garage. He came in and said we were going out to eat, to the hotel in Thelmarsh, the White Hart. They did meals and they went on serving until late. I looked at the car, at the boot of the car, and he said not to worry about that, he'd seen to that, though on the whole what had happened to the grandmother in the story might be a blessing for us.

While we were out I tried to talk to him as if nothing had happened. I talked about Richard. I talked about my house in Bury and where we would live, there or at Molucca. After a while my voice tailed away, he hadn't said much anyway, we both fell silent. I couldn't eat but he could. He ate his way steadily through three courses and he drank a lot. It was a warm, sultry night. The sky had cleared and through the White Hart's window you could see a host of stars. I said—and it was very unlike me, 'I wish we could walk back.'

He still joked. He tapped his glass. 'We may have to.' When he'd paid the bill, he said to me, 'Why did you say that?'

'Say what?'

'Say "back" and not "home"?'

'I don't know,' I said, though I did know.

I drove us back, going slowly. I put the car into the garage. She was wrapped in a plaid car rug lying up against the left-hand wall. It was then that I thought, when this is all over I will never drive a car again. The time was nearly midnight as we entered the house. We went upstairs and lay down on our bed. I said to him,

'Did you do anything to her?'

His speech was thick. 'D'you mean, did I kill her?'

'Yes, that's what I mean.'

'Of course I didn't.'

'Alan, please tell me the truth.'

'I didn't kill her.'

I took off my clothes and put on a nightdress and a dressing-gown, washed my face and combed my hair. Not looking at him, I said, 'If you didn't do anything to her—' I couldn't say 'kill'—'why can't we tell the police? Why can't we have her taken away?'

He had fallen asleep. I lay down beside him for a while. I felt as if we were refugees, strangers fleeing from some disaster, and because neither of us had anywhere else to sleep we were obliged to lie on the same bed. I thought about what had happened and I understood the answers to my questions. If we were going to tell someone we should have done so at once, from the beginning, and we would have if the garage man had not presented us with a way out, had not advised us how to proceed.

He was not to blame, we weren't obliged to take his advice, but it had been given and we had taken it. From then on we had let him call me Alan's wife and the farmer do so too, for all I knew. We had sat on the grass verge in deck chairs having a picnic for the Curton rush-hour traffic to see. We had moved Gilda's body. We had gone out to dinner in Thelmarsh in her car. Her body lay some twenty feet from us now, on the garage floor. It was too late to tell anyone, too late for anything. I got up and went back downstairs and lay on the sofa where I finally did sleep. I slept till the birds began and the house was full of the sound of their singing in the fen.

It was strange, we met but we didn't speak. We went about the house, tidying up, making coffee, getting something to eat, but it was a long time before we said anything. Eventually he said, 'Do you really want to know why?'

'No,' I said, 'I know why.'

He smiled wanly. 'Good for you.' He had the most appalling hangover. 'I think I need to sleep some more.'

It was hot again and there was more smoke in the air, though not as much as the day before. I lay on the lawn at the back of the house, not sleeping, staring at the sky, wondering how normal ordinary people passed the time, what did they do all day, what was there to do? Somewhere about the middle of the day Alan came out to find me.

'You know what we're going to have to do, don't you?' he said.

'I think so.'

'Come into the house.'

We sat down opposite each other in the living room.

'I think I know how to do it,' he said. 'Have we plenty of oil?'

I stared at him. He might have been talking some obscure foreign language.

'Paraffin, I mean. Have we plenty?'

'Five gallons. It's in the garage.'

He said he'd go out and get some more. Then he told me what he planned to do, what *we* must do. I said nothing, I just sat there, shaking my head, but in wonder and horror, not saying no.

'Petrol too,' he said, 'or is that too dangerous?'

We had no phone at the house. There had never seemed the need for it. While Alan was away I walked down the road in my high heels to the nearest call box, it was nearly a mile, and used up all the change I had phoning Madge Browning to find out how Richard was. For some reason I had this premonition that while I was at the house, doing and contemplating these dreadful things, a more dreadful thing had happened to him and he was drowned or terribly injured in a fall. But he was fine and happy and, indoors for an hour for lunch, came to the phone and talked to me, telling me about the farm and the animals and the beach.

The day before I'd promised myself to buy a pair of sandals, but I didn't. It no longer seemed to matter if my high heels broke or my feet blistered. Alan had returned before I got back. His face lit up when he saw me and he seized me in his arms, he had been so worried, anything might have happened to me, his world collapsed without me. Where had I been? I told him. I let him hold me. Then we sat at the dining table and ate some of the food he had bought. We drank a bottle of red wine and we slept, but not together.

It was strange, the way this wasn't discussed but taken for granted, that I would lie on the bed upstairs and he on the sofa. I slept heavily. When I woke up the sun was setting. I went into one of the empty back rooms and watched it set behind the fen, an angry orange-red in a dusty sky. Alan wasn't downstairs. I went into the garage. He had the car boot open and Gilda's body back inside it.

The green scarf was nowhere to be seen. I remembered how it had been knotted round her neck when she came

to the house—yesterday, was it really only yesterday?—
but when we lifted her body to bring it here the scarf lay
loose on her chest. I shocked him, he didn't expect it of
me, that I would bend over the body, that I would touch
it, and examine the neck. She was cool and stiff. There
was no mark on the neck, the dark strangle line that you
read about in crime books, that wasn't there.

He knew what I was looking for. I saw it in his eyes,
but he said nothing. He put the paraffin in the boot and
the two cans of petrol he had bought and a pile of newspapers that had accumulated over the years.

'Put on your dirty dress,' he said.

'What?'

'You're going to get it dirtier.'

He closed the boot lid and got into the car and
reversed it out of the garage.

The tape ended there and I have turned it over.

I only remember one thing he said before we got into the
car and that was, 'I did my reconnaissance while I was
out. I think I know a place.'

It was nowhere, miles from anywhere, the end of the
world. Perhaps, by now, a few houses have gone up in the
area and perhaps more hedges have come down. Then it
was remote, distant, uninhabited. The fields went on and
on, with here and there green woodland to separate them
or the pale line of a winding lane. And some of the fields
were black where the stubble had burned and some were
already ploughed after the burning, brown and ribbed
and spotted with white and grey pebbles.

But now it was dusk and there were no lights from

houses or lamps. There was no moon or none yet risen. The countryside began to lose its colour, it was no longer green and earth-brown, it was all shades of grey and the black of the burnt fields. But why do I bother to describe it? What does it matter now?

Alan knew where to go, light or dark, dusk or day. He had found the place some hours before. He turned the car down a track that was an avenue of limes and backed it into the field he had chosen. The limes walked in pairs up the shallow hill and the track between them was a double rut of dry baked earth. There was no gate, just an opening, and boards laid over the ditch. Recently, the day before very likely, the field had been burned. And the farmer, perhaps because the time had seemed right, while he had his fire, had uprooted part of a hedge to enlarge his field. An ancient hedge it had been, of oak and hawthorn, maple and rose, elder and dogwood. A welter of half-burned logs lay still smouldering at the edge of the black stubble, limbs of trees and twisted roots. Smoke came out of their joints and gnarled growths in little thin trails. The fire, Alan said, had been raging when he came this way earlier in the day.

You told me once that farmers were supposed to leave six feet between the burning and the hedge, but he hadn't done that. He had meant to burn the hedge. A tree stood with its branches like burnt arms, the leaves still on them, shrunk and curled and black. A leaf fell as I stood there, spiralling down, stiff as a piece of rolled paper.

We began with the newspaper. I laid the fire among the ashes the way I used to in Auntie Sylvia's house, screwed up newspaper first, then wood, then a log or two. Logs were everywhere, and wood chips, too, on the grass, in the gouged-out pits where the hedge had stood for five hundred years. Some were burnt but most were raw wood, wounded and splintered by the axe. Alan poured on paraffin and then we laid Gilda's body on the pyre.

Not far away, down in south Suffolk, is a place where they burned a living man in the sixteenth century. There's a monument to him now. He was one of those martyrs condemned to death by Mary Tudor for refusing to be a Roman Catholic. I wonder how long it took to burn him. Of course there was no compulsion on those people to *destroy* the body. But what happened to it? No one ever says. No one tells you. Perhaps, like us, they kept the fire going for many hours. It took us hours, it took all night. To burn a body is easy. To destroy a body by burning is a long and laborious and terrible task.

I tried not to look until it no longer looked human. And that happened quite soon. I couldn't stop myself from smelling the smell. I tried. I held my nose, I turned away and retched into the ditch. When I came back I looked. I told myself this was another log lying there, an ordinary log that had been an oak branch, only a particularly cumbersome one. The smell changed and became sulphurous, the bitter, choking stench of brimstone, the burning stone.

Alan had brought a bottle of gin. We drank it, directly out of the bottle. I'd been sick but perhaps it was because of the gin that I was never afraid, that I never expected a car to appear suddenly behind us in the lane or see the blue lamp of a police van or a troop of angry men fanning out across the meadow. We took nips of gin. The raw fire of it running down our throats comforted us and gave us strength to work on feeding the fire, keeping the fire

going. Once, and once only, we turned to face each other
and closed together in a strange, mindless embrace.

We let the flames die, with a long branch we raked at
the cinders and the ashes, and, when it cooled, piled on
more fresh wood, surrounding that log that was no log
with more wood. Alan made a petrol bomb. He filled the
gin bottle with petrol and wadded the neck of it with his
handkerchief and told me to stand back.

'I've always wanted to make a Molotov cocktail,' he
said.

He lit the wad and threw the bottle. That was when
the rear of the car was burned. Petrol doesn't flame like
paraffin. It explodes. I should have known that. Everyone
who understands the principle of internal combustion
knows that, but there were many things I didn't understand before that night. Gilda's pyre went up with a roar,
the flames leaping into the sky and bringing a moment of
broad daylight. Neither of us was hurt, though Alan's eyebrows and the front of his hair were singed.

We knew, both of us knew, that we must never say,
that's enough, that will do, it's not good but it will do.
There was no discussion. We knew what the other was
thinking, for each of us had the same thought: there must
be absolute destruction, total reduction to an unidentifi-
able mass. A point had to be reached where we were satisfied, when what we had come there to burn was
changed into burnt wood and blackened stones.

It was daylight before that happened. It was the grey
dawn that comes before the sun rises. The place where we
had worked all night looked now much as it had when
first we came, charred logs from an uprooted hedge
smouldering on a dozen square yards of ash. We were

exhausted, we were drunk and filthy and sick and nearly mad. Alan drove us back, the car weaving all over the road. The awful thing, one of the awful things, was that we didn't speak but we weren't silent. He was groaning, making sounds like someone in intolerable pain, and I was crying without tears, a dry sobbing. But what does it matter how we were? It's self-indulgence to go on.

At my house we slept, he upstairs this time, I on the sofa. I gave up the bed to him, he had worked so hard. His hair was burnt and his hands were blistered. I watched him fall on to the bed face-downwards, but I don't think I could physically have brought myself to lie down beside him. Later in the day, when we had once more been through our bathing and changing-clothes rituals, we went out into the garden and sat on the grass. It was very warm and very dry. In the distance I could hear the sound of machinery, a farmer taking advantage of the weather to harvest or to plough. My head ached and I expect Alan's did.

He was nervous, in a way I had never seen him. We would have to go back, he kept saying, we would have to go back and check. He couldn't remember how we had left things. Had we really destroyed it all?

'I want you to tell me,' I said, 'what you did between the time that garage man went away and the time he came back again?'

'You mean, after he'd told us what to do, don't you?'

I made an impatient gesture. I'd never done that to Alan before. I'd never before put up my arms at him and shaken my hands from the wrists.

'After he'd told us there were just the two of us.' He looked at me as if I were a stranger. 'You mean, did I kill her?'

'Yes, that's what I mean.'

'I've told you I don't know how many times that I didn't. I did nothing. What matters now is how we left things last night. This morning, I mean. I mean this morning. I can't remember, I drank so much.'

'I can remember,' I said. 'Everything was destroyed. We knew we couldn't stop till everything was destroyed.'

'I still want us to go back.'

I went up to him. I crawled up to him on my hands and knees and squatted in front of him on the dry grass and said,

'Tell me the truth. Did you kill her?'

'For God's sake,' he said. 'She was going to die. That blow to the head, that was fatal. I untied that scarf she had on. I held it against her face, against her nose and mouth, just for a moment, a second, I don't know why. I said to myself, you can't do this, what the hell are you doing, and I took the scarf away, it was fifteen seconds at the most, it was no time, I took the scarf away and she was dead.'

25

Out in the garden I sat on the lawn in a deck chair and wondered if it was the one they'd used as a stretcher to bring Gilda's body home.

He hadn't killed her, had he? She'd have died anyway. I've got that green scarf here with me now, I've put it across my own face and pressed with my hands against my face, and it hasn't stopped me breathing. It's thin and transparent, you could tie it round your face to protect yourself against smog and still breathe normally.

On the other hand I'm not ill. I'm a lot younger than Gilda was and I haven't been injured in a car crash. No doubt, too, his hands were stronger than mine are, but I still think you couldn't smother anyone with that scarf.

Then why did he put it over her face and hold it there? Why did he? Because his intent was to kill her, it must have been. He was afraid she'd recover, so he put the scarf over her face to kill her and then he thought better of it, almost immediately—fifteen seconds is immediately, isn't it?—he took the scarf away. And she was dead. So did he kill her or did she just die? And if he meant to kill her . . . ? Oh, it's too deep for me, I can't untangle it, I don't know.

I listened to the second side. It's just half of the last side and then it stops.

I remember everything very clearly. I remember every word and gesture. Everything is clear-cut, precise, distinct, cut with a sharp knife.

When he had told me what he had done I asked him to repeat it, and he did repeat it, rather sulkily, like a child. And I listened, the stern parent, weighing up the pros and cons of punishment. But before he could say it, I said it.

'All right. I wanted it too. It wasn't just you.'

'She would have died anyway, Stella. I don't suppose I even hastened her dying.'

'From the moment that man asked us if we were just two we both hoped she'd die, we wanted her to die.'

'God knows, we'd played it often enough,' he said. 'It hasn't been much like the Killing Gilda Tease though, has it?'

As we were driving back to the place of the burning I knew it was all over between us. He knew too, but he wouldn't let himself believe it. He kept saying to me that we had to stay together, we must support each other. In case questions were asked. In case the work of destruction had not been complete. If fragments were found, bones, teeth. She had been his wife and he was talking about her bones and her teeth. In case the police came, he said. We must present a united front.

No one was burning stubble. The burning was ended and the air was clear. The sky was white, a roof of very high cloud, no sun, no wind. It was the 1st of September, the end of summer, the end of everything. And I saw it as an approach to absolute finality, termination, apocalypse.

The nearer we got to the place the more the dread I felt increased. It was as if something awaited us there. I don't mean the police or some sort of search party, I don't mean any officials or arm of the law. I mean retribution. I've never had any belief in the supernatural but I was afraid of unearthly agents, angels of vengeance, principalities and powers, of justice personified in unimaginable forms, waiting for us.

I even said to him, 'Let's go back.'

'We can't go back,' he said. 'We've come to see. We have to know. I want to sleep at nights.'

It was so quiet. All the way we had met no cars, followed or been followed by no cars. When a pheasant ran across the road in front of us with a shriek and a rattle of wings I cried out and clenched my hands.

As we approached the place we heard the tractor, the steady mechanical throb that is as much a part of the countryside in autumn as the neighing of horses must once have been and the clatter of their hoofs. The noise deterred us and Alan slowed the car. We crawled the last bit along the narrow road.

No avenging angels, of course. No one waiting at the gate to summon us before some bar of justice. Alan parked the car up on the grass verge. He put out his hand to take mine but my hands were clasped together against my chest. We looked into the field and he was silent but I made a little moaning sound. I whimpered like a puppy. Alan stared.

The field which had been black was brown, the signs of burning gone, for all fifty acres of it were going under the plough. He had wasted no time, that farmer. His stubble was burnt, his hedge uprooted and burnt, and now the plough was turning and grinding and burying the burnt cornstalks and the ash and the cinders.

He was nearly finished. The tractor was turning for the last time at the top of the field where the hedge had gone. He came slowly down the slope close to the lime avenue, lumbering like a heavy animal or a tank. He seemed to be coming straight for us, inexorably, our retribution. But I could see him in the cab, smoking a cigarette, an ordinary middle-aged man with a red face and receding fair hair. His smoke drifted from the cab, a wispy ghost of what had been.

Alan drove on a little to avoid being seen. We parked a hundred yards up the road. In the rear mirror we watched the tractor and the plough come out of the gate and turn laboriously on to the road. We watched. He was going home. To a waiting wife and a great farmhouse tea and his children perhaps, to his family and his friends and peace and good things. He passed our car and raised a hand to salute us.

Alan turned the car and drove it up the lime avenue as we had done the night before. He backed the car into the field over the boards across the ditch. We got out. There was nothing black any more, not a trace, no coal-like roots and branches. The earth here was a rich chestnut brown, soft as breadcrumbs, not many stones to ring against the plough-shares. It was ploughed in parallel lines, expert and even, like knitting, like the ribbing on a garment. There might have been no burning, all signs of fire were gone, absorbed by that soft brown crumbly soil, drawn under and hidden for ever.

Alan said in a conversational way, 'When they'd burnt

Carthage they ploughed over the site so that no one would ever find the remains.'

I stared at him, I asked him what he meant.

'Gilda's our Carthage.'

We put the car away into the garage. Gilda's green scarf was in the boot but I left it there, I didn't know what else to do with it. I had had enough of burning. Alan tried to take me in his arms, and when that failed he tried to take my hands. But it was no use. It was not that I didn't love him, but that I was no longer fit for him and he was no longer fit for me. That was all.

I seem to remember that we ate something, standing up in the kitchen. We drank some gin, not pink gins but the neat spirit in water glasses. I told him nothing about my feelings, I didn't explain. He said,

'I can never be a widower now. Because Gilda's not dead, is she?'

I asked him what he meant.

'How can I tell anyone she's dead? How could I, if I wished to, prove she was dead?'

'But why would you?'

'The house I live in is her house. Any money is hers. My car is a wreck but I can't use hers. Hers is in France with her.' He looked at me. 'I can never re-marry.'

Of course I understood then. It made me shiver.

'She's gone,' he said, 'but she'll never be gone. She's more dead than I ever wanted her to be, but she's more alive too.'

There was silence then, a long heavy silence.

'We'd better go home,' I said at last.

'Where's home?'

It should have been Molucca but it wasn't, not any more. Gilda had been there, Gilda had lain there dead. To me the place smelt of ashes. I spoke to him politely, as if he were John Browning or one of Marianne's friends.

'Will you drive me to Bury, please, before you go back to the farm?'

He shook his head. His glass was empty and he re-filled it.

'I told you, I can't use her car. I can't risk anyone see-ing me in it. It's supposed to be in France. I can't risk it ever being seen.' He drank the glassful and for a moment shut his eyes. 'There's a bus from Thelmarsh. God knows when it runs. I'll walk to the stop and wait for it.'

So he did. He went into a call box on the way and phoned for a taxi for me, the Thelmarsh station taxi. He hadn't told me he would, he simply did it. Anticipating my wants was something he was good at, he was a thoughtful man. The taxi came and I locked up the house and had the driver take me back to Bury. It still wasn't dark, it was only about eight. I cried on the way home, thinking of how kind he was to me, getting a car for me as a matter of course.

There isn't much more to say. I am tired and my chest hurts. You mustn't think we never met again, that we parted then and there for ever. I suppose we saw each other twice more, once at my house and once in a restau-rant. We had dinner, we thought we could manage some-thing, some reconciliation. But we couldn't. The fire was between us and the ploughing over of the site, that and the fifteen seconds he had held the scarf over Gilda's face. I dreamed about it a lot, and the dream went on for years, not about the scarf or the fire but the ploughing, everything drawn under and churned into the depths by the turning plough-shares.

Oh, well. It was a long time ago. I have wondered sometimes about *folie à deux*, those couples who conspire to kill someone, a wife or a husband. They seem to face each other afterwards, to live together, to go on loving. How do they do it? How do they forget and adjust? How do they lie beside each other at night and eat their meals opposite each other and laugh and talk and have a social life?

I abandoned him, but he abandoned me too. He looked at me as we were leaving the restaurant and said,

'Why did we do it? I can't remember, can you?'

And when I didn't answer, he said, 'Blame it on the *garagiste*.'

I saw him once more and then never again.

Richard is coming in a minute. We're going out for a drink to the White Hart at Thelmarsh and I'm going to tell him about my nurse's training. I think he'll be pleased. The tapes in their ordinary black cases are on the table in front of me and the woman in the portrait seems to be looking at them, her eyes cast down. What am I going to do with them?

Not tell Richard, not tell Marianne. God forbid. Not give them to Richard.

They were left to me with a purpose. Or at least for a reason. Because it was my father who made it happen, wasn't it? The man who said to them, 'Just the two of you, was it?' was my dad. It was my dad who advised them, put the idea into their heads, put them off telling the police, showed them a picture of his children, of his daughter with the unusual name. And if he made things happen to them, so they made things happen to him. It was reciprocal fate (I haven't pored over my *Chambers Dictionary* for nothing). If he hadn't come along just then things would have been quite different. He'd have got home early as he'd promised and Mum wouldn't have chucked him out and he'd never have married Kath but have stayed with us and I'd have been with him when he died. Maybe. And maybe not.

For I don't believe in fate. I don't believe in destiny or patterns in life but in chance and that what happens is what you do yourself. I shall pull out the tapes, unravel them and burn them. Somehow it seems my right.

This evening I was going to give Richard the clothes Stella left in this house, but I've changed my mind. He won't want them and I do. It's spitting with rain and when we go out I'm going to wear Stella's silvery coat. It's very pretty, it's come back into fashion.

The clothes of the dead wear as well as any others. Why didn't I see that long ago?

Ruth Rendell writing as
BARBARA VINE

A Dark-Adapted Eye

"Ruth Rendell... at the height of her powers... a rich, complex and beautifully crafted novel.
— *P. D. James*

LIKE MOST FAMILIES
THEY HAD THEIR SECRETS

And hid them under a genteelly respectable veneer. No onlooker would guess that Vera Hillyard and her beautiful sister, Eden, were locked in a dark and bitter combat over one of those secrets. England in the fifties was not kind to women who erred... so they had to fight it out behind closed curtains using every weapon they had.

In this case, murder.

A PENGUIN BOOK

Ruth Rendell writing as
BARBARA VINE

A FATAL INVERSION

"DAZZLING... Vine at her formidable best."
— *New York Times Book Review*

"No one gets inside psychological states like
Rendell/Vine, and no one writes books that are
more continually surprising and exciting."
— *Los Angeles Times Book Review*

They were five young people who turned the Victorian manor
of Wyvis Hall into a commune one strangely hot summer long
ago. But that idyll has long been shattered, and that five have
gone their separate ways, vowing never to speak of what
happened there — until Wyvis Hall's quaint pet cemetery yields
its buried secret. A tiny human skeleton and the bones of a
woman set off an explosive chain of events that leads back to
the end of that long, hot summer. But what had been done
there? To whom? By whom? And why? The web of tension and
deceit spun by master spellbinder Barbara Vine takes readers
across the fine line between freedom and anarchy, disillusion
and vengeance, sensuality and passion, and into the darkest
recesses of the human mind.

A PENGUIN BOOK

Ruth Rendell writing as
BARBARA VINE

The House of Stairs

"This is the third psychological thriller by Ruth
Rendell writing as Barbara Vine and when I say it
surpasses the first two that's really saying
something... Vine has not only produced a quietly
smoldering suspense novel but also presents an
accurately atmospheric portrayal of London in the
heady '60s. Literally unputdownable."
— *Time Out*

"Revealed in baleful flashbacks, a chilly obsession
takes shape, a convicted murderess and a cruel
design sidle out of the shadows. Writing again as
Barbara Vine, Ruth Rendell brings artistry and full
enchantment to the dark places of the psyche."
— *Observer*

A PENGUIN BOOK

Ruth Rendell writing as
BARBARA VINE

GALLOWGLASS

When Sandor snatched little Joe from the path of a London tube train, he was quick to make clear the terms of the rescue. 'I saved your life,' he told the homeless youngster, 'so your life belongs to me now.'

Sandor began to tell him a fairy-tale: an ageing prince, a kidnapped princess chained by one ankle, a missed rendezvous. But what did this mysterious story have to do with Sandor's preparations? Joe had only understood his own role. Sandor had taught him the new word. He was a gallowglass, the servant of a Chief....

"Of all living writers, she can enter most convincingly into the criminal, or even pathological, mind."
— John Mortimer in the *Sunday Times*

A PENGUIN BOOK

Ruth Rendell writing as
BARBARA VINE

King Solomon's Carpet

Winner of the 1991 Gold Dagger Award

"Vine, quite audaciously, deliberately, makes the
London Underground the central character of the
book... Wonderful, weird and compelling...
her finest work."
— *The Times*

"Vine charts the violent horrors of social disarray to
spine-shuddering effect. The pathological world she
creates is intensely powerful because she arouses a
genuine fear that all that is normal is
in danger of being lost."
— *Sunday Times*

A PENGUIN BOOK

Ruth Rendell writing as

BARBARA VINE

Asta's Book

"The best yet from the Vine/Rendell bureau.
An absolutely enthralling novel... Seductive and
fathomless, it sets its puzzles and keeps its secrets
up to and beyond the final page.
Essential reading."
The Literary Review

It is 1905. Asta and her husband Rasmus have come
to East London from Denmark with their two little
boys. With Rasmus constantly away on business,
Asta keeps loneliness and isolation at bay by writing
a diary. These diaries, published over seventy years
later, reveal themselves to be more than a mere
journal. For they seem to hold the key to an
unsolved murder and to the mystery of a missing
child. It falls to Asta's granddaughter Ann to
unearth the buried secrets of nearly a century before.

A PENGUIN BOOK

Ruth Rendell writing as
BARBARA VINE

No Night is Too Long

"A dark, watery masterpiece from Vine/Rendell,
suffused with sexuality... and an ingenious
twist at the end."
The Times (London)

"*No Night is Too Long* is a story in which good and
right triumph over evil and in which love, after
huddling a long while on a dark, wave-battered
shore, finally finds a safe harbour."
— *Calgary Herald*

In a silent, ghostly house overlooking the sea, a
young man writes his confession: a confession he
will never be able to complete. Tim Cornish waits
for his crime to be discovered. And he knows that
redemption will never be his...

A PENGUIN BOOK